Simon Kernick lives near London and has two young children. His previous novel, *Relentless*, was selected as a Richard & Judy Summer Read.

The research for Simon Kernick's novels is what makes them so authentic. His extensive list of contacts in the police force has been built up over more than a decade. It includes long serving officers in Special Branch, the National Crime Squad (now SOCA), and the Anti-Terrorist Branch, all of whom have plenty of tales to tell.

For more information on Simon Kernick and his books, see his website at www.simonkernick.com

Also by SIMON KERNICK

THE BUSINESS OF DYING
Featuring DS Dennis Milne, full-time cop,
part-time assassin.

'Taut, gripping, disturbing – a most assured
and original début'
Daily Mail

THE MURDER EXCHANGE
Ex-soldier Max Iversson is hired to provide security
for a meeting that goes disastrously wrong.

'From hardboiled cops to ruthless women on the
make, Kernick generates a potent cocktail of thrills'
Guardian

THE CRIME TRADE
DI John Gallan and DS Tina Boyd uncover a
murderous conspiracy that will take them to the
heart of London's most notorious criminal gang.

'A taut gritty novel in which Kernick uses every trick
in the book to keep the narrative breakneck'
Time Out

A GOOD DAY TO DIE
Exiled cop Dennis Milne returns to London to hunt
down the murderers of a close friend.

'Great plots, great characters, great action'
Lee Child

RELENTLESS
Tom Meron finds himself on the run, pursued by
enemies he never knew he had . . .

'This is the sort of book that forces you to read so fast
you stumble over the words. Phenomenal!'
Evening Standard

SEVERED
You wake up in a strange room on a bed covered in
blood. And you have no idea how you got there . . .

'If you like lots of non-stop action, this is for you'
Guardian

Deadline

Simon Kernick

CORGI BOOKS

TRANSWORLD PUBLISHERS
61–63 Uxbridge Road, London W5 5SA
A Random House Group Company
www.rbooks.co.uk

DEADLINE
A CORGI BOOK: 9780552156608

First published in Great Britain
in 2008 by Bantam Press
a division of Transworld Publishers
Corgi edition published 2008

Addresses for Random House Group Ltd companies outside
the UK can be found at: www.randomhouse.co.uk
The Random House Group Ltd Reg. No. 954009

The Random House Group Limited supports The Forest
Stewardship Council (FSC), the leading international forest
certification organisation. All our titles that are printed on
Greenpeace approved FSC certified paper carry the FSC logo.
Our paper procurement policy can be found at
www.rbooks.co.uk/environment

Typeset in 10.25/13.5pt Palatino
by Falcon Oast Graphic Art Ltd.

Printed in the UK by CPI Cox & Wyman, Reading, RG1 8EX.

2 4 6 8 10 9 7 5 3 1

For Anna Bridges.
May your spirit never stop soaring.

Prologue

When his girlfriend greeted him at the door dressed only in a T-shirt and thong, then kissed him hard on the mouth without a word before pulling him into her ground-floor bedroom, she was so worked up she didn't even notice that he was wearing gloves. They'd talked on the phone five minutes earlier and in that conversation he'd explained in intimate detail what he planned to do with her when he got to her place. So it was with a hint of regret that, as her hands headed southwards, he kicked shut the bedroom door, slipped the knife from the concealed sheath beneath his cheap suit jacket, and drove it silently between her ribs and directly into her heart. In the short time he'd known her, the girl had proved to be adept and enthusiastic in bed, and it would have been a pleasant distraction to have had sex with her one last time. But that would have meant leaving behind incriminating evidence, and he was a professional who didn't let the desire for cheap gratification get in the way of business.

He clasped her close to him while she died. The single blow had been enough, as he knew it would be, having used this method of killing on several occasions in the past. The girl made barely a sound. There was the surprised, pained gasp as the blade went in, of course, which was accompanied by a single juddering spasm, not unlike an orgasm, as her muscles tensed for a final time and her fingernails dug into the material of his suit jacket, but it didn't last long and was quickly followed by the long, slow release of breath as she relaxed in his arms.

He counted to ten in his head, then, still holding on to her, reached into the inside pocket of his jacket with his knife hand and produced a handkerchief. The blade made a strange hissing sound as it was slowly withdrawn, and he used a well-practised combination of both hands to wipe it clean, before replacing it in its sheath. When this was done, he placed the body on the carpet next to the unmade bed and briefly admired his handiwork. Because she'd died so quickly, there was very little blood, and she looked remarkably peaceful lying there with her eyes closed. It was the quietest he'd seen her. In life, she'd been quite a talker.

Leaning down, he tried to push her under the

bed, but there wasn't enough of a gap between the bottom of the frame and the floor, so he squeezed her in as far as she would go, then covered the rest of the body with one end of the duvet cover. It was only a tidying-up gesture. Concealing the body would do nothing to mask the smell that would soon be coming from it, but he wasn't overly concerned about that. He doubted if she'd be discovered for a while. She lived alone in her tiny ground-floor flat, and had few friends in the city, which had always been one of her complaints about it. He knew she spoke to her mother back home once a week but that was always on a Sunday, so it would be another six days before the mother had a reason to worry about her daughter, and several days more, at least, before anyone did anything about it.

No one had ever seen him with her. Their few clandestine meetings had always been in this flat. As far as he knew, she hadn't told anyone about him either, although even if she had it would make no difference. He'd given her a false name and background, one of four different identities he periodically used in order always to keep one step ahead of the authorities. His DNA would be in this room, of course, but then so would the DNA of those few friends the girl had, and since they were mainly illegals, it would be difficult to trace them.

He saw the girl's pink Nokia mobile phone on the bedside table. He picked it up and put it in his pocket to be disposed of later, then took a last look round. Seeing nothing else that might incriminate him, he left the bedroom, shutting the door behind him, leaving the girl in her makeshift tomb.

As he stepped out of the front door and into the bright sunlight, he looked at his watch.

It was time.

Part One

One

The first thing Andrea Devern noticed when she stepped out of her Mercedes C-Class Cabriolet was that there were no lights on in the house. It was 8.45 p.m. on a breezy Tuesday night in mid-September, and she had only a minute of normality left in her life.

Clicking on the Mercedes' central locking, she walked the five yards to her front gate, glancing both ways along the quiet residential street because as a Londoner born and bred Andrea was never complacent about the potential for street crime, even in an area as upmarket as Hampstead. Criminals moved around these days. They no longer kept to their own patches. They gravitated towards the money, and on Andrea's tree-lined avenue of grand three-storey townhouses, barely spitting distance from the Heath, there was plenty of that.

But there was nothing out of place tonight, unless you counted the fact that her house was in darkness. Andrea tried to remember if Pat had told her that he had arrangements, or whether he'd taken Emma off somewhere. She'd had a stressful day dealing with the management team of one of the five health spas she and her business partner owned. They'd taken it over a year ago and it had underperformed ever since. Now they were going to have to make redundancies, something that Andrea never liked doing, and it was up to her to decide who was for the push. She'd been mulling over who was going to have to go all the way back from Bedfordshire, and still she couldn't decide. By rights, it should be the manager. He was paid well over the odds, and since he was the one who'd presided over the mess the spa was now in, it appealed to Andrea's sense of justice to give him the boot; but with no one to replace him, that was looking less and less viable. Better the devil you know, and all that.

Andrea decided to worry about it tomorrow. For now, she needed a long, slow glass of Sancerre and a relaxing cigarette. Not the healthiest of options, but a woman needs some pleasures in life, especially when she worked as hard as she did.

She pressed the card key against the pressure

pad on the security system and stepped through the gap as the gate slid open smoothly. As always when she entered her front garden and left the outside world behind her, she experienced a familiar sense of relief and pleasure. Sheltered by a high brick wall, the garden was a riot of colour, courtesy of the eight hundred quid a month she paid to the gardening company responsible for making it look like something from the front cover of a magazine.

She breathed in the thick, heady smell of jasmine and honeysuckle, relaxing already as she opened the front door and deactivated the alarm.

Then the phone rang.

It was her mobile. She reached into her limited-edition Fendi Spy Bag and fished it out. The ringtone was 'I Will Survive', Gloria Gaynor's classic anthem of feminine defiance. It was only later that she realized how much grim irony there was in this.

The screen said 'Anonymous Call', and though she never liked answering her phone to anyone she couldn't identify, she also knew that it was possible it was business, even at this hour, and Andrea never said no to business, particularly when the market was as tough as it was at the moment. As she stepped into her empty hallway she put the phone to her ear and said, 'Hello, Andrea Devern.'

'We have your daughter.'

The words were delivered in a high-pitched, artificial voice which sounded vaguely like a man impersonating a woman.

At first she thought she'd misheard, but in the slow, heavy silence that followed, the realization came upon her like an approaching wave.

'What? What do you mean?'

'We have your daughter,' repeated the caller, and now Andrea could tell that he was using something to disguise his voice. 'She's not there, is she? Look around. Can you see her?' His tone was vaguely mocking.

Andrea looked around. The hallway was bathed in gloom, the rooms leading off it silent. There was no one there. She felt a rising sense of helpless panic, and fought to keep herself calm.

'You can't see her, can you? That's because we have her, Andrea. And if you ever want to see her again, you'll do exactly as you're told.'

Andrea felt faint. Needing some kind of support, she leaned back against the front door, her movement clicking it shut. Keep calm, she told herself. For God's sake, keep calm. If they're phoning you, then it's got to be a good sign. Surely?

'What do you want?' she whispered, her whole body tensing as she waited for the answer.

'Half a million pounds in cash.'

'I haven't got that sort of money.'

'Yes, you have. And you're going to get hold of it for us as well. You've got exactly forty-eight hours.'

'Please, I'm going to need longer than that.'

'There's no compromise. You have to get us that money.'

Andrea began to shake. She couldn't believe this was happening. One minute she'd been thinking about winding down after her meeting, the next she was plunged into a crisis involving the most precious person in the world to her: Emma, her only daughter. She exhaled slowly. It was still possible this was some kind of hoax.

'How do I know you're not lying?' she asked.

'Do you want to hear your daughter scream?' replied the caller matter-of-factly.

Oh, Jesus, no.

'Please, for God's sake, don't do anything to her. Please.'

'Then do exactly as we say, and don't ask stupid questions.'

'She's fourteen years old, for Christ's sake! What sort of animal are you?'

'One who doesn't care,' he snapped. 'Do you understand that? I don't give a toss.' His tone became more businesslike. 'So listen closely. It's ten to nine now. At nine o'clock on Thursday, in forty-eight hours' time, you're going to receive a phone call on your landline. At that point you'll have the half a million ready in used notes, denominations of fifties and twenties. Do you understand that?'

Andrea cleared her throat. 'Yes,' she said.

'You'll be told where and when to deliver it. As soon as we've received it, you get her back.'

'I want you to let me speak to her now. Please.'

'You'll speak to her when we're ready.'

'No.'

'No? I'm afraid you're not in any position to argue with us. We have your child, remember?'

She took a deep breath. 'Please. Let me speak to her. I need to know she's OK.'

'You can speak to her next time we call. When you have the money.'

'How do I know she's even alive?' Andrea shouted, determined not to cry even though she felt the tears stinging her eyes.

'Because,' said the caller calmly, 'she's no use to us dead. Now go and get that money, Andrea. Then you can speak to her. And don't even think about going to the police. Because if you do, we'll know about it. We're watching you. The whole time. The first sign of the police and Emma dies. Slowly and painfully.' There was a pause. 'Nine o'clock Thursday night. Be ready.' The line went dead.

For several seconds Andrea remained frozen to the spot, the shock of what was happening still seeping through her system. Someone had taken her daughter. Her lively, pretty fourteen-year-old girl who did well at school and who'd never hurt anyone. A complete innocent. Her poor baby must be absolutely terrified. 'Please don't hurt her,' Andrea whispered aloud, her words sounding hollow in the empty hallway.

Andrea Devern was a tough woman, and her life hadn't been easy. A successful, financially independent entrepreneur, she'd had to fight hard to get to the position she was in now. She'd taken one hell of a lot of knocks on the way, knocks that would have finished a lot of other, more privileged people, and she'd always held firm. But nothing could have prepared her for this. Emma was Andrea's world, no question, and to think of her now, trapped and frightened with no understanding of what was going on, filled her with a helpless dread. And that was the worst part, the sheer helplessness. Her daughter was missing, and there was absolutely nothing she could do.

Except satisfy the demands of the anonymous caller and find him half a million pounds.

My only child . . . If anything happens to her . . .

She flicked shut the phone and walked into the kitchen, the heels of her court shoes clicking loudly on the mahogany floorboards. She grabbed a glass from one of the cupboards and filled it with water from the tap, then drained it in one go.

She had to keep calm, but it was hard when you were alone. And that was when her thoughts turned to Pat.

Pat Phelan. Andrea's husband of two years, and Emma's stepfather. Charming, good-looking and five years younger than her, she'd been infatuated with him when they met. A whirlwind romance had been followed by a marriage barely four months later. Her mother had described her as a 'fool' and Pat as a 'ne'er do well'. At the time Andrea had thought her mother was being short-sighted, and maybe even a little jealous, but in recent months she'd begun to get the first hints that maybe the old woman, spiteful as she'd always been, had a point. After all, it takes one to know one.

She needed Pat now, more than she ever had.

So where the hell was he?

She refilled her glass with water and swallowed another couple of large gulps, then walked over to the landline and punched in the number of his mobile. Pat didn't work. He was between jobs. It seemed he'd been between jobs pretty much ever since they'd met. His trade, if you could call it that, was bar work. He'd been working in a bar in

Holborn when she'd first seen him. A month later he'd had an argument with the owner, and the job was history. He tended to be something of a house husband now. He ferried Emma to and from school most days, and picked her up from friends' houses when Andrea was at work, but more and more in the evenings he liked to go out for a couple of drinks at the local pub, or to one of his old haunts down the road in Finchley, which was where he'd been brought up. Sometimes he didn't come home until well after she was in bed.

But the thing was, Pat didn't leave Emma alone in the house. He'd only ever go out when Andrea got back from work. It was a situation that suited her well, although occasionally she wished he'd show a bit of get up and go, and maybe secure some gainful employment.

The phone rang and rang, but Pat wasn't answering. It went to message and, keeping her voice even, Andrea left one, asking – no, telling – him to call her back as soon as possible.

She slammed the receiver back in its cradle, cursing the fact that he hadn't picked up, then stood by the sink, her eyes closed, taking slow, deep breaths, trying to make sense of the situation she found herself in. Emma had been kidnapped by a ruthless individual who, from the way he spoke, clearly had an accomplice, or accomplices.

She forced herself to look at things logically. The motive for abducting Emma was money. Which meant there was a good chance of getting her back. There had to be. Andrea knew she could raise half a million in the time given. It wouldn't be easy, but she had access to ready cash in a way that other people didn't. There were numbered accounts, and cash that had been squirrelled away, far from the prying eyes of the taxman, in a safety deposit box in Knightsbridge. Probably just enough to cover this amount. If she did what she was told and delivered the money to where they wanted it, she'd have her daughter back.

The thought filled her with relief, but it was an emotion that lasted barely seconds, because it relied on trusting Emma's kidnappers. What if they didn't release her? What if, God forbid, she was already dead? A spasm of sheer terror shot up her spine. If anything happened to Emma, she was finished. The thought of life without her was simply too much to bear.

Andrea reached into her handbag and pulled out a cigarette, lighting it with shaking hands. She took a long drag and tried Pat's number again, but there was still no answer. She left a second, curt message: 'Call me now. It's urgent.'

She leaned back against one of the kitchen's spotless worktops. This house had been Andrea's dream home when she bought it five years earlier for close to a million cash, which was most of the proceeds of the 40 per cent stake she'd sold to her current business partner. It had character, space, land, everything that had been missing in the tiny flat in which she'd grown up with her two sisters and mother. It was her and Emma's safe and private haven, where they could relax and spend time together. Yet tonight it felt alien, like a place she'd just stepped into for the very first time. Normally at this time there'd be noise: music playing in Emma's room; the tinny blare of the TV; the sounds of life. Tonight her home was dead, and she wondered whether it would ever feel the same again.

She went into the lounge and over to the drinks cabinet, avoiding turning on the lights. There were photos in here, of her and Emma – Emma as a toddler; her first day at school; at the beach. She didn't want to see them. Not now. She averted her eyes and poured herself a large brandy in the gloom, taking a big hit of it. It didn't make her feel any better, but at the moment nothing was going to.

With the drink in one hand and a succession of cigarettes in the other, she paced the darkening house, upstairs and down, walking fast but heading nowhere, eyes straight ahead so she didn't have to see any reminder of Emma.

Thinking, worrying, trying to keep a lid on the terror and frustration that infected every ounce of her being. She wondered where they'd snatched Emma, and how. There were no signs of a struggle anywhere in the house, and besides, the alarm had been on when she came in.

But they have her, Andrea, said a voice in her head. *That's the only thing that matters. They have her.*

Half an hour passed. In that time she stopped walking only once, to refill her brandy tumbler, and to look out of the French windows and into the darkness beyond, wondering if even now there was someone out there watching her, checking her reactions. She drew the curtains and resumed her pacing. She knew now she wouldn't be able to sleep until Emma was safe, and in her arms. In the meantime, all she could do was pace the prison of her house alone.

Where was Pat?

An hour passed. She called him again. Still no answer. This time she didn't bother leaving a message.

She was getting a bad feeling about this. It wasn't like him not to answer his mobile. He carried it with him everywhere. It finally occurred to her that he might be at the Eagle, a pub he often liked to drink in on his evenings out. She didn't know the number, so she looked it up in the Yellow Pages and gave them a call.

A young woman with a foreign accent answered. In the background Andrea could hear the buzz of conversation, and immediately felt a pang of jealousy. Sounding as casual as possible, she asked if Pat Phelan was in tonight.

'I'll ask,' the girl replied. 'Hold on, please.'

Andrea waited, the phone clutched tight to her ear.

Thirty seconds later the girl came back on the line. 'I'm afraid no one has seen him for a long time,' she said politely.

Andrea's jaw tightened. Tonight was Tuesday. Pat had told her he'd been at the Eagle the previous Friday night, and last Wednesday.

'Is that everything?' asked the girl.

'Yes,' said Andrea quickly. 'Thank you.'

She hung up and stared at the phone. So Pat had been lying about his whereabouts. But why?

An unpleasant thought began to form in her mind. Could he possibly be involved in this? It was difficult to believe. After all, they'd been together nearly two and a half years, and although, if she was honest, she didn't entirely trust him, particularly where other women were concerned, he'd always got on all right with Emma. They hadn't been the best of friends, and Emma had certainly not welcomed his arrival into their close family unit, but she'd come round in the end. If anything, their relations had been improving in recent months. It was too much of a step to imagine him hurting her like this.

And yet . . . Pat was one of the only people in the world who knew she had cash reserves she could call upon without attracting too much attention. Near enough half a million pounds of cash reserves, in fact. Nor was he whiter than white. He'd admitted to her that years earlier, as a young man, he'd had a few scrapes with the law, and had even served a few months for receiving stolen goods. Receiving stolen goods was a long, long way from abduction, but even so, in her weakened state the thought preyed on Andrea's mind that the man who, for all his faults, she still loved might have betrayed her dramatically.

'Please don't let it be you,' she whispered, staring at the phone. Because she knew if that was the case, she'd be totally on her own.

Another hour passed, and as the clock ticked towards midnight with still no word from him, her doubts grew stronger. It crossed her mind more than once to call the police, but the people she was dealing with were ruthless, and clearly well organized, and they'd already told her what would happen to Emma if she did. Andrea didn't have much faith in the forces of law and order anyway. She'd had too much experience of them for that.

No, she needed someone she could trust. Someone who'd know what to do.

There was one person who could help. She might not have spoken to him for more than a decade but she was sure he would respond in this, her hour of need. The problem was, if she brought him back, she might also be unleashing forces outside her control.

But what choice did she really have? She couldn't do this alone.

There was a grandfather clock in the hallway, bought from an Islington antique dealer at an exorbitant price several years earlier, which had always looked out of place. Something about its relentless ticking tended to soothe her, though, and when it chimed midnight she stubbed out her latest cigarette in the ashtray and made her decision.

She retrieved a small black address book from her handbag on the kitchen top and found the number she wanted in the back, with no name next to it. She turned on the overhead light to dial, stopping at the last second. Thinking. They might have bugged the landline, and if they heard her . . . She couldn't risk it. Instead, she fed the digits into her mobile and stepped out into the back garden.

The night was silent as she walked to the pear trees at the end, thirty yards from the house, and stopped. She looked round, listening, remembering what the kidnapper had said: *We're watching you.* But they couldn't see her in the back of the garden, she was sure of it.

So, taking a deep breath, she pressed the call button on the mobile.

And took her situation to a whole new level.

Two

Jimmy Galante answered on the third ring. 'Hello,' he said quietly, his accent still firmly east London.

There was no background noise that Andrea could make out, which surprised her. Jimmy had always been something of a nightbird. Maybe he'd changed.

'It's me,' she said, keeping her voice low, knowing the risk she was taking.

'Who's me?' he asked.

'Andrea. Andrea Devern.'

He gave a raucous laugh down the phone. 'Jesus, now there's a ghost from the past. How you doing?'

'Bad. Very bad.'

'Shit, I'm sorry to hear that,' he said, but she could almost hear the smirk in his voice. Jimmy Galante was not the kind of man who wasted time or effort on sympathy. 'How did you get my number? You been keeping tabs on me, Andrea?'

She had, but she wasn't going to tell him that. At least not yet. 'Someone gave it to me.'

'Oh yeah? Who?'

'That doesn't matter. What matters is I need your help.'

'To do what?'

Andrea took a deep breath, looked round in the gloom. 'My daughter's been kidnapped. I need you to help me get her back.'

Jimmy's husky trademark chuckle rumbled down the line again. There was something inherently cruel in it. It made Andrea think of a child pulling the wings off a butterfly, or cutting a worm into quarters, and it still made her nervous, even now, years afterwards.

'Sure, Andrea, whatever you say. You don't speak to me for God knows how many years—'

'You haven't been here. You've been in Spain.'

'You could have called,' he snapped. 'In all that time, you could have fucking called. But you didn't bother, did you? Because you didn't want nothing then, but now you do, so it's' – and here he did a nasty, high-pitched imitation of Andrea – 'please, Jimmy, help me find my daughter, some nasty man's kidnapped her.' He chuckled again. 'It don't work like that, babe. I've got business interests over here now. What do I want to come back to a shithole like England for? Fuck that for a game of soldiers.'

Andrea sighed. She'd been expecting this, but it still hurt to hear his complete lack of interest, either in her or in Emma. But his reaction told her something else too. Jimmy Galante, for all his faults, wasn't involved in this. If he had been, he'd have asked more questions.

'I want you to help me, Jimmy,' said Andrea, knowing that the sudden firmness in her tone was born of desperation.

'Sorry, babe, forget it. You still ain't given me a good reason why I should.'

'Because,' she answered, 'Emma isn't just my daughter. She's yours too.'

There was a long silence at the other end, and then Jimmy started to say something, but Andrea cut him off, pressing her advantage. 'Emma's fourteen years old. Her birthday's April the second. Think of the timing, Jimmy.'

'I can't think that far back. It's been too long.'

'Try. Fifteen years ago, the summer of 1992. We were together, weren't we? That's when I got pregnant. Just before you left.'

'How the fuck do I know she's mine?' he barked. 'You was married, Andrea. Remember? You was the one shagging around behind your old man's back. Or has that conveniently slipped your mind now as well?'

'Billy was impotent,' she said, not wanting to speak ill of her dead husband, but knowing that she had no choice. 'And you were the only man I was sleeping with then. She's yours, Jimmy. Face it. Your child. And now some bastard's taken her.'

She could almost hear the cogs whirring as he thought things over down the other end of the phone. This time she left him to it.

'What's happened then?' he asked eventually, a tone of resignation in his voice.

For the first time since the phone call more than three hours earlier, Andrea experienced a tiny, barely perceptible twinge of optimism. It seemed like she might be getting Jimmy Galante onside, which meant there was a chance she was no longer facing this nightmare alone.

Constantly mentioning Emma by name, and keeping her voice as quiet as possible, she detailed the evening's events, trying not to leave anything out. When she was finished, Jimmy asked her if she could raise the money in the time she'd been given, and she told him that she reckoned she could. 'It's not going to be easy, but I can manage it,' she said.

'And your new old man . . . he's missing?'

'Yes,' she said slowly. 'He is.'

'You certainly know how to pick 'em, don't you, babe?'

'Don't, Jimmy.'

'Think he might be involved?'

'To be honest, I can't see it, but . . .' She paused a moment. 'But I can't say for sure.'

'All right. What's his name?'

'Pat Phelan.'

'Don't know the name.'

'He's from Finchley.'

'I know a couple of people up that end of town. I'll ask around. You haven't gone to the cops, then?'

'No. And I don't intend to either.'

'Good, no point involving those bastards. So, what do you need me to do?'

'I just need you here with me, OK? I'd feel better. After all, you are her dad.'

'I'd better be, Andrea,' he said ominously, his voice barely more than a whisper. 'Because if I'm not, and you've dragged me back under false pretences, then I really ain't going to be very happy at all. You understand what I mean?'

There was no doubt at all what he meant. There never was when Jimmy talked like that. 'Yeah, I understand,' she answered. 'But you are. I promise you that. You are.'

There was another pause.

'I'll be on the first available flight into Heathrow tomorrow,' he said at last. 'I'll call you.'

'Thanks.'

'Don't thank me,' he said blankly. 'I ain't doing it for you.' And he hung up.

Andrea exhaled loudly as she flicked the phone shut. Now there really was no going back. Part of her was afraid of what involving Jimmy was going to mean for Emma's safe release. Jimmy was a violent man. He was capable of inflicting serious injury, even killing someone, but perhaps, in the end, that was what she wanted. Revenge on the people who'd abducted her daughter and put her through such pain. And Jimmy was no fool. He wouldn't rush in guns blazing and put Emma and everyone else in danger. He possessed an animal cunning, an ability to sniff out danger, something that had served him well in the past and something, she knew, he wouldn't have lost, even during his years in Spain. You didn't lose cunning like that. It was instinctive. And she needed someone with it in her corner.

She went back inside and locked the door behind her, feeling a little better. At least she'd actually done something now, and the paralysis born of utter helplessness which had affected her all evening seemed to dissipate a little. She drank another glass of water, smoked a last cigarette, and thought about having another brandy, but decided against it. Andrea had a strong tolerance of alcohol, having consumed it regularly throughout her adult life, but she'd had more than enough tonight. She needed to keep her wits about her. It would have been all too easy simply to lose herself in the oblivion of the bottle, and behaviour like that wouldn't help Emma.

Emma. Her baby. A fourteen-year-old girl enduring her first night as the prisoner of those animals.

If she's still alive . . .

Andrea stopped the thought, took a deep breath and told herself not to weaken.

'Think positive. They won't hurt her. They want money.'

She repeated it to herself three times, praying to God that it was true. Then, with slow, listless movements, she got herself ready for bed knowing that, for better or for worse, Jimmy would be here tomorrow. Jimmy Galante. Armed robber, violent thug, and possibly her only hope.

As she lay under the silk sheets in the master bedroom, staring at the ceiling, with a gap beside her where Pat usually lay, it wasn't her husband she was thinking about. It was Emma.

And Jimmy.

Three

Jimmy Galante had always been a smooth bastard. Now forty, two years older than Andrea, he still looked damn good as he walked out of the arrivals gate at Heathrow's Terminal One, dressed in a tailored suit and open-neck shirt, and Andrea noticed more than one pair of female eyes glancing at him as he walked across the concourse with a casual confidence that bordered on arrogance. Tall, broad-shouldered and tanned, his thick wavy black hair was longer than she remembered, but still as lustrous as it had been all those years ago. Even under the current circumstances, even after all these years, Andrea still felt a twinge of excitement. She wondered what it was about her, why she always seemed to go for the smooth bastards. It was something her business partner, Isobel, had once asked her, with more than a hint of disapproval in her voice, and it was a question she hadn't attempted to answer. Some women just go for the wrong sort of men, Andrea told herself, and maybe she was one of them.

As Jimmy approached her, he smiled, and there was something so knowing and cocky about his expression that it made her realize immediately why their relationship had ended. Up close the lines on his face were more pronounced, and the scar that ran down in a jagged line from just below his earlobe to his chin seemed deeper than before. But the eyes, so dark they were almost black, still commanded attention.

'Hello, babe,' he said, looking her up and down. 'You look good.'

She knew he was just saying that. She felt awful, and she was pretty sure she looked awful as well. She'd hardly slept the previous night, tossing and turning in the silence, knowing that Emma was out there somewhere, desperate for her mother's help. Emma was a tough young thing – she took after her mother in that respect – but there was no way she could have been prepared for what she had to be going through now. Andrea had always protected her from the darker things the world had to offer. She wanted for nothing materially (although she wasn't spoiled); she was being well educated at a decent private school (girls only); and her mother had always been there for her, never failing to make time in her busy schedule for her daughter and providing her with the nurturing hand any child needs. They'd always been a team, the two of them, with Andrea the senior partner.

Today had been easier than the previous night because she'd been able to keep busy. Having called Isobel to tell her that she wasn't feeling too good and was going to take the day off, she'd then phoned the dentist's and found out that Emma had kept her 4.45 appointment. She didn't know how this helped her, but for some reason the knowledge that Emma had been alive and well the previous afternoon, only a few hours before the kidnapper had called her, made it feel more likely that she was alive now.

Andrea had then spent the remainder of the morning and much of the first half of the afternoon raising the half a million she needed. This had involved emptying the two private deposit boxes she rented in separate banks in Knightsbridge, which gave her the grand total of £439,000. It was money that had been built up over a number of years as a result of various cash deals, and she'd viewed it as her retirement fund, her nest egg should things ever go badly wrong. And now they had. She'd then called the three banks where she had personal accounts, and organized the transfer of cleared funds between accounts to secure the remaining £61,000, which had proved a lot less easy than she'd anticipated, since no one these days seemed to want to hand over large sums of cash. When this had been done, she was left with a total of £11,561 in liquid assets – a pretty poor return for fourteen years of hard graft.

There'd still been aspects of the business to attend to as well. She'd received a number of calls from the company accountants regarding the Bedfordshire Spa, and even a couple of semi-apologetic ones from Isobel on the same subject. She'd dealt with them as best she could but it was hard to concentrate on anything other than Emma. Andrea had built up her company, Feminine Touch Health and Beauty Spas, from absolutely nothing into a thriving business which generated turnover in excess of five million cash. Yet ultimately, when it came down to it, this huge achievement and all the hard work that had brought it about would count for absolutely nothing if her daughter didn't come home.

Which was why Jimmy was here. To make sure she did.

'Any news?' he asked as they stood there looking at each other.

'No, nothing yet.'

'You got the money?'

She thought she saw a glint in his dark eyes when he said this, and felt a twinge of unease. The expression on his face remained irritatingly casual, and his lips formed the vague, knowing half-smile of someone who always has the answers. It concerned her that he didn't seem to be too worried about his daughter.

'I'll have it by tomorrow night,' she told him. 'Come on, let's go. I want to beat the rush-hour traffic.'

They walked in silence through the arrivals hall and into short-term parking.

'My, my, you are doing well,' said Jimmy when he saw the Mercedes.

'I've worked hard for it,' she answered curtly.

'You didn't tell me what you did for a living.'

'I know,' she said, getting inside.

They didn't speak again until they were through the slip road and on to the M4, heading back into London. Even though it was still before five, the traffic both ways was heavy, and the atmosphere in the car was tense.

'Why didn't you tell me about my daughter, Andrea?'

Andrea sighed. 'Because I thought we'd be better off without you.'

'*You're* certainly better off. That's for sure.'

'You know something, Jimmy? You haven't even asked her name. Your own daughter.'

Now it was Jimmy's turn to sigh. 'You already told me, Andrea. Her name's Emma. And cut me a bit of slack here, please. Number one, I didn't even know I had a daughter until last night. I still ain't seen a photo of her so I don't even know what she looks like. And number two, and much more important, I'm here, aren't I? I didn't have to come.'

'OK, OK, point taken.'

Andrea wiped sweat from her brow. The car's interior was cold with the air con blasting out on full, but she felt hot and vaguely nauseous.

'Are you all right, love?' he asked, leaning over towards her.

She could smell his cologne. It was strong but pleasant.

'Yeah, I'm fine. I think I need to eat something. I haven't had anything since a sandwich yesterday night.'

'We'll get something for you. What about your old man? Mr Phelan. Any sign of him yet?'

She shook her head. 'Nothing.'

She remembered how strange it had seemed waking up this morning without him there. He never stayed away from home. She did occasionally, for business, but not Pat. He always made it back to their bed, even if sometimes it was in the early hours. She still prayed that he had nothing to do with this, but with each hour that passed without any word from him it became more and more difficult to believe otherwise. But she didn't want to say that to Jimmy. It was bad enough that he was probably thinking it, without her admitting that once again she'd ended up with the wrong kind of man.

'I found out a little bit about him,' said Jimmy. 'He's a bit of a crook, ain't he?'

Although his tone was remarkably free of any gloating, she couldn't let it go.

'That's rich, Jimmy.'

'I was never a small-time little peasant like him, peddling dope and knock-off electrical goods.'

'He's not like that any more.'

'He doesn't need to be any more, does he? He's got you.'

Andrea fell silent. Conceded the point.

'Listen,' he said, putting a hand on her shoulder, 'I'm not trying to score points. I'm just trying to work out whether he's involved or not.'

'And do you think he is?'

Jimmy shrugged. 'Hard to tell. He's still missing, ain't he? That doesn't look too good. But it's a big step from flogging hookey gear to kidnapping.'

'Oh God, Jimmy. I don't know what to think, I really don't.'

'It'll be all right, babe. Don't worry. I'm here now.'

But it wouldn't be all right, Andrea knew that. Whatever happened, the life she'd worked so hard to build up, and the life of her precious daughter, had changed irreversibly. Even in the best-case scenario, with Emma returned to her physically unharmed, she would be a different person, permanently scarred by the trauma of this situation. And Pat ... well, Pat wasn't coming back. There was no doubt about that. And the thing was, she thought they'd been pretty happy. She would miss him, too – unless, of course, he was involved. But her instincts told her he wasn't; that he wasn't capable of putting Emma through such an ordeal. Because the thing was, as Jimmy had pointed out, he really didn't need to. He had access to money, he drove a nice car, he didn't need to work for a living, he enjoyed two or three foreign holidays a year, and he had freedom, too. Andrea cut Pat a lot of slack, so why put it all at risk for a share in half a million pounds, and the possibility that he'd end up in jail for the next ten years? She didn't buy it.

But she still couldn't explain his absence.

Jimmy's hand massaged her shoulder, slowly and deliberately. The sensation filled her with conflicting feelings. She still loved Pat, or at least she thought she did, but Jimmy had always done something to her, and even now she felt the first stirrings of arousal, accompanied by sharp pangs of guilt that she could even think about sex when her daughter was in the position she was in. Yet she couldn't help feeling much more secure with Jimmy here with her. He was strong, stronger than Pat could ever be, and she needed that now. But he was also trouble, and there was no part for him in her life now. Once this was over, she'd say goodbye to him for ever.

Although something told her it wasn't necessarily going to be as easy as that.

Four

'Half a million quid. It looks beautiful.'

Jimmy Galante had always loved money. He just hadn't liked the part where you had to work for it, which was why he'd chosen armed robbery and major drug dealing as his means of making a living.

The ransom was in a large Adidas holdall that Andrea had dug out from the loft, which was now sitting open on the coffee table in her living room. Jimmy was sitting on one of the leather armchairs with a large wad of fifties secured by a rubber band in his hand. His dark eyes moved from the wad to the contents of the holdall, then back again. The expression on his face was pure, unadulterated excitement.

'It's not all there yet,' she told him. 'I'm still sixty short. I need to pick up the rest at the bank tomorrow.'

'Where did all this lot come from, then?'

'Never you mind.'

He grinned. 'Been hiding it from the taxman, have you?'

'It's none of your business, Jimmy. The lucky thing is I've got it. It means our daughter can come home.'

The grin disappeared, and he nodded soberly, returning the wad of fifties to the holdall.

Initially, Andrea had been reluctant to bring Jimmy back here. She knew the kidnappers had been watching her and was afraid they might have bugged the house, so on Jimmy's advice they'd driven to a shop in Kensington which sold surveillance products and Andrea had bought a bug finder for a hundred pounds.

When they'd got back it was already dark, and after checking there was no one watching from the street, she and Jimmy had hurried inside, and he'd gone to work with the bug finder. It had taken him only seconds to locate a tiny electronic trip switch attached to the bottom of the skirting on the front door which would have alerted the kidnappers remotely as soon as the front door was opened, and was clearly how they'd known to phone her as soon as she'd got home the previous night.

Inside the house, though, the bug finder hadn't picked up anything, but this didn't stop Andrea feeling that the place had been violated by the kidnappers. It was now twenty-four hours since she'd found out about Emma's disappearance.

She watched Jimmy carefully as she sat smoking what was probably her fortieth cigarette of the day and drinking her third glass of red wine, and wondered if she could trust him. She'd hoped that telling him that Emma was his daughter would stir his parental instinct, but now she wasn't so sure it even existed. In the four hours since she'd picked him up from the airport, he'd hardly asked about Emma at all, seeming far more concerned about filling his stomach. He'd insisted on ordering an Indian takeaway, at the same time bemoaning the quality of them in his little corner of the Costa del Sol. Andrea had hardly been able to touch hers, but Jimmy had fallen upon his food ravenously. He'd eaten enough for two men, and washed it all down with four cans of Stella.

When Andrea had shown him a picture of Emma she'd brought with her to the airport, she'd said quietly, and with a sense of awe in her voice, 'This is your daughter, Jimmy. This is Emma.' His reaction had been a vague half-smile and a murmured, 'She's pretty.' Nothing else. Just those two words. She's pretty. For Andrea, this hadn't been enough. She'd wanted more. In truth, Emma didn't look much like Jimmy, but then again she didn't look much like either of them. Andrea was a natural brunette, with features that were sharp and well defined – a very attractive woman, but one with a hard edge to her. Emma, meanwhile, was a natural blonde, with small, delicate features, a round snub nose, and lively blue eyes. She was pretty in a sweet, cherubic way, and looked young for her age. The photo Andrea had shown Jimmy was a head-and-shoulders shot taken on Hampstead Heath the previous summer. Emma was grinning at the camera, showing a neat row of white teeth courtesy of the brace she'd been wearing for the previous six months, and which had been taken out the week before that shot. It was a celebration smile, and to Andrea the most beautiful smile in the world. It killed her to look at it. But not Jimmy. All he could manage was, 'She's pretty.'

She wondered if he genuinely believed he was the father or whether he'd concluded she was bullshitting in order to get his help. It was difficult to tell. That was the thing with Jimmy. He rarely let on what he was thinking, preferring to play mind games and keep people guessing.

As she sat there watching him, she realized she'd never really known him. On the one hand he was a ruthless bastard capable of terrible violence. On the other, he was also capable of great shows of affection. She remembered how once, not long after she'd first started seeing him, she arrived at his flat for a prearranged visit only to find that he wasn't there. Even though it was the early days of mobile phones, both of them had one, and she called him. He didn't answer so she took a walk round his neighbourhood before trying his number again. This time he answered, and he sounded breathless. Apologizing for the delay but not going into any detail as to what had caused it, he told her that he'd be back at the flat in fifteen minutes, although it was actually nearer half an hour before he finally pulled up in his Jaguar XJ6.

As he stepped out, Andrea could tell that something wasn't right. He was looking worn out, and his hair, usually so immaculately styled, was unkempt. His shirt was partly untucked, and as he jogged across the road towards her she saw a handkerchief tied tightly round his left hand.

'What happened to you?' she asked with a smile, looking towards the hand.

'Nothing for you to worry about,' he answered with a smile of his own, kissing her on the lips before ushering her inside the building. 'Sorry I'm late.'

Andrea knew better than to ask too many questions. She was aware that Jimmy operated outside the law. That much was obvious. He didn't appear to have a proper job but always had plenty of money. He'd told her he owned a construction business but was suitably vague, and tended to keep very odd hours for someone running his own company, often staying in bed with her until mid-afternoon on a weekday. Andrea was no fool. She knew. And the truth was that at the time it didn't bother her unduly. In fact, she found the whole thing very exciting. Jimmy was handsome and mysterious, a fantastic lover, and possessed the kind of wild streak a young woman like her couldn't help but find attractive.

Once they were inside the flat, Jimmy showed that wild streak by pulling her close and kissing her hard, then lifting her in his arms and taking her through to the bedroom, where he flung her on the bed and tore off her clothes. They made intense, passionate love, several times in quick succession, and when they were lying, sated, in each other's arms, his free hand – the one with the handkerchief wrapped round it – gently stroking her belly, he said he had something for her.

'What?' she asked, intrigued, trying to ignore the tiny flecks of blood on his fingers, just visible beneath the fabric.

He clambered off the bed and walked over to where his jeans lay on the floor. She watched as he leaned down to pick them up, admiring his naked body, thinking about the orgasm she'd just had, thinking about how happy Jimmy made her, wondering how she was ever going to tell her husband.

When he returned to the bed he had a small black box in the palm of his good hand.

'For you, my lady,' he said with a mock bow.

She smiled. 'What is it?'

'Open it and find out.'

So she did. And let out a little gasp. It was a gold necklace, eighteen carat at least, with a gold-lined emerald heart roughly the size of a five-pence piece on the end.

'Oh, Jimmy,' she whispered. 'It's beautiful.'

'I bought it this morning,' he told her.

She reached up and kissed him tenderly on the lips, feeling for that moment like the happiest woman in the world.

'I love it. Thank you.'

They spent the rest of the afternoon and much of the evening in bed. The lovemaking was some of the best Andrea had ever experienced. She could remember what they'd done together even now. The following morning, wearing that beautiful necklace and thinking that she'd really landed on her feet, she cooked Jimmy breakfast in bed, then went out to get the papers.

Glancing through the *Sun* on the way back to the flat, a photo caught her eye. It was of an ordinary-looking middle-aged man with a beard and a side-parting, and the headline beside him read 'Hundred K Robbery: Security Guard Fights for Life'. Even before she read the article, Andrea knew instinctively that Jimmy was involved. What followed simply confirmed her suspicions. It seemed that a gang of four robbers armed with a variety of firearms had held up a security van as it made a cash pick-up from a branch of Barclays Bank in Wembley. The security guard carrying the case containing the money, whom the paper identified as forty-seven-year-old father of two Alan Jones – the man in the photograph – had tried to resist when one of the gang had grabbed the case. In the ensuing mêlée he was punched savagely in the face several times and knocked unconscious, having struck his head on the concrete as he fell. An eyewitness was quoted as saying that the robber had then kicked him several times, even though it was obvious he was no longer any threat. He was now in intensive care where his condition was described as 'poorly but stable'.

Andrea saw that the time of the robbery was 2.10 the previous afternoon, barely an hour before Jimmy had turned up back at the flat looking dishevelled and wearing a makeshift bandage on his left hand. Jimmy had told her that at one time he'd been an amateur middleweight boxer and had won eleven of his twelve bouts, six by knockout. Not exactly overwhelming proof of guilt, but it didn't need to be. Andrea just knew.

Stupidly, she didn't say anything. Instead, trying to be as casual as possible, she watched him out of the corner of her eye as he lay in bed, casually perusing the paper, a cigarette in his mouth, as calm as you like. He went straight to the robbery story – she counted the pages – and read it twice before running through the sports pages at the back. Then, with a predatory half-smile, he chucked the paper aside and patted the sheets.

'Why don't you come back to bed, love? We've got some unfinished business to attend to.'

And she had, too, something which when she thought about it now made her cringe with shame. They'd made love again twice, and all the time she couldn't stop thinking about the security guard lying in a hospital bed connected to a load of tubes while his family sat round him, waiting for news. But Jimmy . . . Jimmy had forgotten him already. The whole thing was simply business to him, nothing more and nothing less.

After they'd finished, he got a call on his mobile and went out of the room, talking quietly. He returned a few minutes later, saying he had to go out. He was still acting casually, but she could tell he was tense.

And that's when she came out with it.

'You didn't have anything to do with yesterday, did you, Jimmy? You know, that robbery where the guard got hurt?'

'Course I didn't,' he answered, but she could tell that she'd rattled him. It was something in his eyes.

She looked at his hand. The handkerchief was gone now, but the knuckles were dark with bruises. He glanced down at them as well, then back at her. This time his expression had changed. There was a darkness in it.

'Why'd you think that?'

She immediately regretted asking. What, after all, was the point? He was always going to deny it.

'I don't know. I . . .' She stopped, not sure how to finish the sentence.

'I told you, I work in the building trade.'

She nodded. 'Sure, Jimmy.'

He came over to the side of the bed.

'Don't I treat you right or something?'

'Course you do,' she answered, feeling a little uneasy, not liking the way he was looking at her.

He crouched down so they were level, the smile he was giving her devoid of any warmth, his dark eyes boring into her.

'You know, I like you a lot, Andrea. I think we could do real well together. That's why I bought you the necklace.' He paused, touching the emerald heart. 'But don't go asking silly questions, all right? About stuff that doesn't concern you.' The fingers of his good hand stroked her

56

cheek tenderly but she felt herself tensing under the touch. The truth was, she was scared. 'Because otherwise . . .' He wrapped a lock of her hair round his middle finger. 'Otherwise we're going to fall out. Understand?'

She nodded.

'And I don't want that to happen. Because I like you. I really do.'

She felt a sharp pang of pain as he yanked the lock of hair, and she cried out. Immediately he let go, his lips parted in a pleasant, loving smile that almost made her think she'd imagined what had just happened. He leaned forward and kissed her gently on the lips, before pulling back.

'I've really got to go, luv. I'll call you later. Let yourself out, OK?'

And that was that. Chucking on some clothes, he'd left her there alone, wondering what on earth she'd got herself into.

She should have finished it there and then, of course. Someone who could beat and kick an innocent man to within an inch of his life and then, an hour later, come back home as if nothing had happened and make love to his girlfriend clearly had no conscience. And already he was exerting his dominance over her. If he could pull her hair like that, it wouldn't be much of a jump to hitting her. She didn't need this. She had a husband, a man who looked after and cared for her. It wasn't as if she was one of those women who put up with abusive partners because they had no self-esteem. Andrea knew she was a good-looking woman. She'd always been able to attract men.

But she hadn't finished it. To her eternal regret. And now, years later, Jimmy Galante was back, staring at money that she, Andrea, had worked so hard to earn. And she still feared him, although in her current situation she feared not having him around even more.

He drank from the tumbler of whisky she'd poured for him and looked over with one of his mocking smiles.

'Half a million quid, eh, Andrea? Who'd have thought you'd ever have that kind of money.'

'I always did,' she answered firmly.

'You know,' he said, watching her over the rim of the glass, 'I've been following your progress over the years. I'm impressed by how far you've come, living in a nice, big, flash pad like this.' He gestured vaguely with an arm.

'Money isn't everything, Jimmy.'

'It is when you ain't got none.'

'I'm sure you manage. You don't look like you're starving.'

'You think there's money out in Spain? There's fuck all. I get by, that's all.'

He sounded bitter, which was Jimmy all over.

Andrea had no sympathy. No one had ever given her anything. She'd had to go out and graft for it and had proved that you could be successful if you were willing to put in the sweat and the tears. No one had ever given Jimmy anything, either. He'd grown up in a Hackney council flat, with damp on the walls and cockroaches in the grime-encrusted spaces behind the cheap, flimsy kitchen units. The difference was that he hadn't wanted to work, and had taken what wasn't his, and by any means necessary. His fly-by-night lifestyle might have been exciting to her once, but she was young then. Now it simply depressed her that she'd ever fallen for his charms.

Andrea changed the subject. 'If you've been following my progress all these years, you must have known I had a daughter.'

He nodded. 'Yeah, I did.'

'And it never occurred to you that Emma might have been yours?'

He shrugged. 'No, it didn't. I mean, let's face it, babe, you weren't exactly whiter than white where men were concerned, were you?'

It was a cheap shot, but she let it go.

'I mean, she doesn't exactly look like me, does she?' he continued.

'She doesn't exactly look like me either, Jimmy, but I can tell you with total and utter certainty that she's mine.' She paused. 'And yours.'

He nodded, conceding the point, then once again his eyes drifted down towards the holdall of money. 'I'm looking forward to meeting her,' he said, but his tone was vague and it was clear his attention was focused elsewhere.

'You'll love her,' said Andrea quietly, feeling a sudden and terrible longing for her daughter. Tears stung at her eyes. She'd held it together so well today, but now, more than thirty-six hours since she'd last seen and touched Emma, the grim reality of her situation once again took her in its grip.

And there was something else, too. Could she really trust Jimmy?

The phone rang. The landline. It startled her. She and Jimmy exchanged glances. She got to her feet, walked out into the hallway and picked up the receiver.

'Hello?'

'Mum?'

Relief and shock soared through her. It was Emma. Her Emma!

'Darling, oh God, is that you?'

'Yeah, it's me.'

'Are you OK, baby? Is everything OK?' Tears were streaming down her face, but she didn't care. She was just ecstatic to be hearing her daughter's voice.

'I'm fine,' answered Emma, her voice small. She

sounded afraid. 'They say I should be home tomorrow, if you've got the money.'

'I've got the money, baby, don't worry. We're going to have you home by tomorrow night, I swear it. God, it's so good to hear you're all right. They haven't hurt you, have they?'

'No, but it's . . .'

Emma broke off, and there was a minor commotion at the other end. It sounded like she was being moved away from the phone, and Andrea felt a wave of panic, as if she was losing her all over again. Emma cried out, but the cry was cut short. It sounded as if it was being muffled.

'Emma?' she shouted as the panic shot through her. 'Emma, darling, are you OK?'

For a few seconds there was silence. Then came the sound of a door being shut and a new voice came on the line.

'You've spoken to her, and you know she's alive, so we've kept our side of the bargain.' Once again the voice was disguised but the tone was more aggressive. Andrea thought it might be a different person from the one who'd called the previous night. 'Now it's your turn to keep yours. Have you got the money?'

'Most of it,' she answered breathlessly. 'I'll have the rest by tomorrow.'

'Good. Then you'll be hearing from us

tomorrow night to make the final arrangements.'

'Don't hurt her, please,' begged Andrea, hating herself for showing her desperation, but unable to stop. The line, however, was already dead.

Slowly, she put down the phone. Jimmy had followed her out into the hallway and was staring at her with a look of concern. He didn't say anything for a couple of seconds, then he stepped forward and took her in his arms. She sank into them, burying her head against his chest.

'It's going to be all right,' he said quietly, the deep, gruff intonation of his voice suddenly making her feel safe.

That was the thing with Jimmy. Even now, he could inspire so many different and conflicting emotions. She breathed in his scent. He must have splashed on some more cologne after he'd had a shower earlier. It smelled strong, but somehow comforting.

'I spoke to her,' said Andrea, pulling away and looking at Jimmy. 'She's alive, Jimmy. She's alive.'

'See, I told you it was going to be all right, babe,' he said, continuing to hold her. 'These guys are professionals. They're not going to do anything to hurt her. She's their prime asset.'

Andrea didn't like his choice of words, nor the fact that he still hadn't referred to Emma by name, but she was too excited by the fact that she'd spoken to her to pay too much attention to that.

Finally, she had confirmation that Emma was OK. She was scared, but it didn't sound like they'd hurt her, which meant she was going to get her back. This time tomorrow, she'd be safe and sound.

Jimmy's hand ran down her back and moved across her buttocks. At the same time, he pulled her closer, and she could feel the hardness growing between his legs. 'It's going to be OK, babe. I'm here now. I'm back.' His grip on her tightened as he rubbed his cock against the material of her gypsy skirt.

She thought of Pat. Her husband. How their love life, once so vigorous, had slackened in recent months until, in the past few weeks, it had evaporated to almost nothing. Pat wasn't coming back. She was sure of that. One man leaves her life, another returns.

Jimmy lifted her chin so she was looking up into his dark eyes, seeing the lust in them.

'You still look beautiful, babe,' he whispered.

But she didn't want Jimmy. Not like that. She'd already betrayed one husband with him. Whatever Pat's faults, whatever he might have done, she wasn't going to betray a second. She pulled away from his kiss, trying to move backwards, but his hand grabbed her chin roughly and turned it back so she was facing him.

'Come on, I know you feel the same way.'

He was smiling now. As cocky as ever, forcing her towards him. She could smell the booze on his breath. Anger overtook her – anger that the bastard could be so cold to both her and Emma's plight – and she slapped his hand away, wrenching herself free from his grasp with more force than she'd intended.

'You fucking bitch,' he snarled, clenching his fists; but she stood her ground, glaring back at him.

'I'm not the little girl you used to know, Jimmy. So don't you dare try it. Think of someone else for a change. Like Emma . . . your daughter.'

'Still a tease, ain't you, babe?' he said quietly, and then with a snort of derision he walked past her back into the living room.

Five

The next day, Thursday, was excruciating. It was the waiting.

Jimmy apologized for his behaviour in the morning, which was typical of him. Always changing tack. She accepted the apology but she didn't believe it was genuine. Jimmy Galante was not the sort of person to feel remorse about anything he'd done. If he was, he'd never sleep at night, and she knew from experience that he slept like a log.

Their conversation over coffee in the kitchen was strained, and she was pleased to get out of the house and leave him behind. He'd wanted to come with her as she drove to the bank to pick up the remainder of the money, but she told him it would be easier if he didn't. 'It'll just arouse suspicions,' she explained, knowing that this was just an excuse. She took the holdall containing the money with her as well.

'Don't you trust me or something?' he asked her at the door.

And the truth, of course, was that she didn't. But she didn't say this. Instead she looked him right in the eye and said, 'This money represents our daughter's freedom. It's not going out of my sight today.'

Jimmy nodded and left it at that.

The bank were reluctant to part with the money, even though it was hers, and she had to go into the back and endure a lecture from the manager about the perils of being in possession of large sums of cash and sign a load of paperwork before they let her out with what was rightfully hers.

For lunch she grabbed a sandwich and took a walk on Hampstead Heath, leaving the money locked in the boot of the car. Usually it was a place of tranquillity where she could relax and enjoy the illusion of being somewhere in the country. Today, however, she paced relentlessly, counting down the minutes and hours, worrying about someone stealing the car and therefore the money, and when she encountered passers-by she felt bitterness and jealousy at the way they went about their easy lives while she suffered alone in hers. Waiting, always waiting.

She was home by mid-afternoon, and carried the holdall with difficulty up to the front door. Half a million pounds, she was discovering, weighed one hell of a lot. Jimmy was out, for which she was thankful, and she took the opportunity to sit on a lounger in the back garden, look out at the trees and listen to the sounds of early autumn. This was her refuge, her place of peace, and today it gave her hope. There was still that numb fear that it could all go wrong, and that these people, whoever they were, were simply stringing her along, but Andrea was a pragmatist, and the more she thought about it the more she shared Jimmy's view that their primary motive was money. If she did what she was told, they would release Emma. And then maybe, just maybe, things could start to get back to normal. Just the two of them together again.

Jimmy returned at seven o'clock, telling her not to worry because he'd been careful leaving and coming back. She didn't bother asking him where he'd been, assuming he'd been visiting associates. Frankly, she didn't care. She just wanted tonight sorted, and then she wanted rid of him for ever. It remained to be seen whether she'd made a mistake by involving him at all, but it was too late to worry about that now. Tonight she had to focus on the task ahead.

And so, for the next two hours, the waiting continued. They didn't speak much. There was little to say, and it was difficult to plan anything given that neither of them knew what procedures the kidnappers intended to set for them. Andrea kept looking at her watch. Sometimes she counted the seconds ticking on the clock in the hallway, and all the time the tension cranked up inside her little by little.

The clock struck nine.

She looked across at Jimmy. Her mouth was dry. He looked back, and for the first time she saw that he too was worried. He was frowning, his eyebrows almost touching, the lines on his forehead heavily pronounced and suddenly making him look his age. The room was thick with silence.

A minute passed. Andrea counted the seconds on the clock. Neither of them spoke, but Jimmy looked at his watch several times and sighed. It was a cheap thing with a black plastic strap, not like the Cartier he'd worn when she'd first known him. Times had obviously been hard for Jimmy. Maybe even hard enough for him to consider getting involved in a kidnap ... No, she didn't want to go down that route. She had to trust somebody, and right now there was no one else.

The phone rang. The receiver was next to her on the coffee table. She picked up immediately.

'Yes?'

'Have you got a pen and paper?' asked the disguised voice – the one that had first called her, she thought.

'Yes.'

'Good. Do exactly what I say and you'll have your daughter back before the end of the night.'

'That's all I want,' she told him.

'Fuck us about, though, and she dies. Painfully. Do you understand?'

She tensed, thinking of Jimmy. Was it a big mistake bringing him in? She said that she understood.

'Here are your instructions. Get in your car – the Mercedes – and drive up to the junction of the M1 and the M25, then proceed eastbound on the M25 to junction twenty-five. Turn left on to the A10, then turn left again at the next roundabout on to the B198 signposted to Rosedale.' He waited while she wrote all this down. His breathing was audible on Andrea's end of the phone. 'There's a turning on the left about two hundred metres down. Follow the road for approximately three quarters of a mile until you see a sign on the right for Gabriel's Saw Mill. Drive down there two hundred metres.' He paused again. 'At that point the track forks. Take the right-hand fork and follow it approximately fifty metres. A burnt-out single-storey building with no front door will appear on your right. You can't miss it. Stop the car but leave the engine running. Take the bag containing the money inside, and drop it against the front wall so that it can't be seen from outside.

There's a turning circle another twenty metres down the track. Drive down to that, turn round and leave.'

'What about Emma?'

'When you get back on to the road, turn right and keep going about half a mile and you'll come to a phone box on the left. Go inside and wait for our call. As soon as we've confirmed that all the money's there, and you haven't tried anything stupid, we'll make contact and give you instructions on where to collect your daughter.'

'I need to speak to her.'

'Not now. Do as you're instructed and you'll be seeing her soon enough. One other thing: turn off your mobile and don't bring it with you.'

'OK,' she said reluctantly. She didn't like the idea of being without it.

'Now get moving. You've got exactly forty-five minutes to get to the drop-off point. And remember, we're watching.'

The line went dead and Andrea put the receiver down.

'What's the plan?' asked Jimmy, looking at her closely.

Briefly, she went through the instructions she'd been given. 'I don't think you should come,' she added when she'd finished. 'They said they were going to be watching me. If they see you, it could jeopardize things. I can't afford that.'

'She's my daughter too,' he answered. 'I'm coming with you.'

'What's the point, Jimmy? I'm delivering the money, that's all.'

'Because I don't trust them. That's the point. What if they're bullshitting about letting her go?'

'But you were the one who told me they just wanted cash. That they didn't want to hurt her.'

'Well, maybe that is all they want, but there's still no guarantee they'll release her. They might hold out for more cash. But if you drop me off a couple of hundred yards from where you're making the drop, I'll make my own way down there and keep an eye on the place. I'll see who goes in, see if I recognize them. I might be able to get their registration number.'

'What good'll that do?'

'There's still a couple of coppers I know. They'll be able to trace who the car belongs to.'

Andrea didn't like the sound of this at all.

'But it's risky, isn't it? What happens if they see you? Then they're not going to let Emma go, are they? They might kill her.'

Jimmy shook his head. 'They ain't going to kill her. She's worth more to them alive. And they ain't going to see me, either. I'll be quiet. And I'll be careful. I don't want anything to happen to Emma either, you know.'

Andrea sighed, trying to think. Not following

the kidnappers' instructions to the letter was a huge risk, but what if Jimmy was right? What if they weren't going to let Emma go? Surely it was better to have an insurance policy in the form of Jimmy watching the place – someone cunning enough to spot a double-cross, and hard enough, if necessary, to do something about it. But, did she even trust him? She wiped sweat from her brow, wrestling with the alternatives, knowing she had only seconds to make up her mind. Knowing that even one wrong move could end the life of her only child.

She took several deep breaths, telling herself to keep calm, for Emma's sake.

'What if they're out there now watching the house?' she asked. 'If they see us leaving together . . .'

He shook his head. 'They're not watching the house. If they were, they'd already know I was here. Anyway, there won't be enough of them to do that.'

'How do you know?' she demanded.

'This ain't a big firm, babe. No way. There'll only be a couple of them. Any more and there'd be too much chance of a leak. Also, they'd stand out sitting in a car in a nice, quiet street like this for hours on end. They won't want to risk that. But we'll play it safe. You go out the front, and I'll come out nice and quiet behind you, and I'll stay down in the seat. It'll be dark, no one'll see.'

His words were filled with a quiet confidence that was proving seductive.

'What happens afterwards? Where will I pick you up from? They told me not to bring my mobile phone.'

He reached into his pocket and retrieved a cheap Nokia handset. 'Take this,' he said. 'It's a spare one of mine.'

'I told you, they don't want me to take one.'

'No, babe, they don't want you to bring *your* mobile phone. There's a difference.'

'What do you mean?'

'They're just covering themselves. If you have gone to the police then one of the ways they can track your movements would be using your mobile. That's why they don't want you to have it. They probably know your number so they can phone to check whether it's switched off.' He handed her the Nokia. 'But they don't know the number of this one.'

'OK,' she said uncertainly as he gave her the handset.

'Put it on vibrate, OK? I've got another phone. You drop me off just before we get to the ransom drop. Then an hour after we part company, I'll text you. If it's safe for you, you call my number and we can arrange to meet.'

She nodded, coming to a decision. 'All right, let's go.'

Six

At 9.47 p.m. Andrea's Mercedes was moving at a steady thirty miles an hour along a quiet country B road with a cornfield stretching into the darkness on one side and a bank of beech and oak trees rising up on the other. A car passed them going the other way and moving far too fast, but there was no traffic behind. Andrea slowed as she spotted the dilapidated sign for Gabriel's Saw Mill nailed to a tree up ahead.

'This is it,' she whispered, indicating right.

Jimmy was hunched down in the front passenger seat, a position he'd adopted ever since they'd left the motorway.

'All right, babe,' he whispered. 'I'm out as soon as you make the turning, unless I hear any different.'

'I don't like this, Jimmy, I really don't like this.' The doubts were savaging her now. *If he makes a mistake . . .*

'It's just an insurance policy. Better safe than sorry.'

She steered the Mercedes into the turning, little more than a dirt track which was only just wide enough for the car. Ahead, the trees loomed, blotting out the light of the moon.

'Wish me luck, babe.'

'Good luck,' she answered without looking at him as she peered through the windscreen into the darkness.

A second later the door opened – a foot, maybe a foot and a half – and Jimmy slid through the gap. Then he shut the door silently behind him and Andrea drove on, risking a brief glance in the rear-view mirror as he disappeared into the woods.

Suddenly she was on her own.

Up ahead the trees seemed to rise up to greet her, and the only sounds were the tyres crunching on the track's loose gravel and her own low, tense breathing. This was it, the moment of truth. Close to all of Andrea's life savings were in the holdall in the footwell of the front passenger seat. She would have given everything, down to the clothes on her back, to have Emma returned to her safely, but if this failed and her tormentors didn't keep their side of the bargain she didn't know what else she could do, or where she could get any more money from.

The track forked as the kidnapper had said it would, and she followed it to the right as instructed. The road surface became pitted and potholed and she was forced to slow right down as she manoeuvred the Mercedes round the worst of the holes. Nothing moved in the darkness up ahead and on either side of her the wall of trees looked impenetrable.

And then it appeared to her right, a concrete outbuilding with blackened walls set back a few yards from the track, its roof all but gone, a black hole where the front door was.

She stopped the car and jerked on the handbrake, slipping the gearstick into neutral. For a few seconds she just sat there, listening to the silence, wondering if the man on the phone was watching her now, the man who'd abducted her daughter. Wondering too whether he'd hear Jimmy's approach and call the whole thing off.

Nothing moved. Andrea could hear her heart beating.

Finally, she bent down and pulled up the holdall, leaning back against the weight, and manoeuvred it awkwardly out of the car. As she stood up, she took one last look around before walking slowly up to the building, carrying the holdall two-handed, stopping at the gap where the front door had been.

It suddenly occurred to her that it might well be

easier for the kidnappers simply to lie in wait, take the money and kill her, then go back and do exactly the same to Emma. Job done. *Right now, Andrea, there could be someone just inside this door, a crowbar in his hand, ready to smash your skull in.*

'Just do as he said,' she muttered to herself: drop the money, leave, go to the phone box and wait for the call that would reunite her with her daughter.

She stepped inside. Pale shards of moonlight shone through the huge hole in the roof, revealing an empty room with cement flooring, and a few tins of paint in one corner. To her right, a wooden door hanging off one of its hinges led into a poky little room which had probably once been a storage cupboard. The air smelled musty and vaguely of turps. There was no one there, no crowbar-wielding maniac. Taking a deep breath, she put the holdall on the floor next to the wall, then quickly turned and walked back outside.

And stopped.

She thought she saw movement in the trees ahead of her, something rustling. She stood still, staring, but as she watched, the movement stopped. But she knew she hadn't imagined it, and, feeling a new and very strong urge to get out of this place, she hurried over to where the car sat idling and jumped inside, reversing back the way she'd come in rather than going any further into the woods and using the turning circle she'd been told to use.

It was only when she was back on the road that she sighed with relief. She may have just parted with half a million pounds of her hard-earned money, with still no sign of her daughter, but at least she was out of that place. She wondered if it had been Jimmy she'd heard. She hoped it wasn't. If he could draw attention to himself like that then it might not just be her who'd noticed his presence. It wasn't something she wanted to think about.

A few minutes later the phone box she was after – a modern glass BT one – came into view at the edge of a village which was little more than a tiny collection of houses. It was up on a verge just beyond a bus stop, and partly concealed by the branches of a large oak tree. She pulled up twenty yards short of it, parking her car as close to the verge as possible, and banged on the hazard lights.

Once she was inside the phone box, she stood and waited for the last act, praying that this was finally it. The end of the nightmare.

The time was 9.56 p.m.

Seven

The phone didn't ring. Ten minutes passed, then twenty, and still Andrea stood in the bright light of the booth, staring at the receiver as the occasional car hissed past in the darkness outside, willing the call to come through. Hoping, praying . . .

A memory came back to her of a time years ago when she'd lost Emma on a crowded beach in Spain. They'd been on holiday with a new boyfriend of Andrea's, an Aussie bar manager called Bryan she'd met a few months earlier. Andrea had been besotted with Bryan, who was tall, blond and a lot younger, and for a very short time she'd even thought he was going to be the one. She was all over him on the beach that day, and for just a few moments – no more than that, because Emma was always the most important thing in the world to her – just for those few moments, she hadn't paid attention to her four-year-old daughter, and when she'd pulled away from Bryan and looked around, Emma wasn't there any more.

God, the terror she'd felt. It had almost been worse than when she'd got the call from the kidnapper. She'd jumped up, called out her daughter's name, looked round desperately, but all she could see was a sea of half-naked strangers stretching in both directions as far as the eye could see, like something out of the worst kind of nightmare. She'd panicked, really panicked. All she could think was that Emma had been taken. *My baby's been snatched by paedophiles, predators who'll abuse her and kill her. I'll never see her again, and it will all be my fault. Because I put myself before her.* She'd run round, not sure which way to go, knowing that the wrong decision would take her even further from Emma, ignoring the blank, uncaring stares of the other beachgoers as she called out, her voice an anguished howl.

In the end it was Bryan who found her, walking along the shore several hundred yards away, all alone, crying her eyes out. She was only missing five minutes, but Andrea could still recall the intense, almost physical joy she'd felt when she saw Bryan coming back with Emma in his arms. She'd never experienced anything like it, either before or since.

Within weeks she'd finished with Bryan – not because he was at fault, but because she would forever associate him with her own selfishness – and she'd sworn then never to let anyone get in the way of her and Emma. She'd kept to her vow, too. Until now.

There was a vibration in her jeans pocket. It was the mobile Jimmy had given her. She looked at her watch. It was 10.18. Pulling it from her pocket, she saw that he'd sent a text.

She read the words on the screen, then read them again.

GET BACK TO DROP-OFF POINT NOW.

It was half an hour since she'd dropped him off. He'd specifically told her he wouldn't contact her for an hour. Something had made him change his mind. Could it be good news? But if so, why hadn't he just called? She thought about calling him back, but stopped herself. Far better simply to wait here, as she'd been instructed, until the kidnappers called. But why hadn't they done so already? They must have counted the money by now.

The minutes passed. Outside, another car drove past, slowed down, then accelerated again. She suddenly felt very exposed out here in the middle of the country late at night, illuminated for all to see by the phone booth's light.

God, what the hell was Jimmy doing? Had he

done something stupid, like confront the kidnappers? Had he beaten a confession out of one of them? If he had, she'd kill him. All she wanted was her daughter back. Christ, they could have the money. It was totally and utterly irrelevant to her now without Emma. Everything was.

The phone vibrated again. It was another message from Jimmy.

GET BACK TO DROP-OFF POINT NOW. URGENT!

Andrea leaned against the glass panel of the phone booth, staring down at the screen, her stomach churning, wondering what the hell she should do. Then she made a decision and called Jimmy's number.

It rang and rang. She counted each ring, and when the number hit twelve she hung up. What the hell was he playing at?

She replaced the mobile in her pocket and stared at the phone unit on the booth's wall. The gunmetal-grey stand was covered in carved teenage graffiti, and the receiver was scratched and old. It was also not ringing.

What are you going to do, babe? They're not calling, are they? You could be here for hours.

But if I go . . . If I go and they call . . . What then?

Andrea agonized. She clenched her fists, and gritted her teeth, squeezed her eyes shut. Tried, tried, tried to make the right decision. Cursed herself for bringing in Jimmy. Cursed Jimmy for complicating things, and then not being there when she needed to talk to him. And still the fucking phone wasn't ringing, and it was now 10.35.

Flinging open the door in one angry movement, Andrea hurried out of the phone booth, jumped back in the car and executed a rapid three-point turn in the road before driving back the way she'd come, going fast and trying her best not to think about the fact that even now the phone might be ringing away as the kidnapper called to give her instructions about where to find Emma.

She was back at the turning to Gabriel's Saw Mill in under two minutes. Once again the track was empty and silent as she drove down it, taking the right-hand fork, looking for but not seeing any sign of Jimmy. She could only assume that he'd meant the abandoned outbuilding when he'd said in the message to get back to the drop-off point, but when she stopped the car outside, it looked just as deserted as it had done before.

This time she killed the lights and the engine, and put the keys in her pocket as she got out. It was a risk – she might need to make a quick getaway – but if she moved away from an idling car, she fancied the idea of someone driving it off and leaving her out here alone even less.

'Jimmy?' she called out, trying to keep her

voice down as she slid her gaze along the silent tree line.

No answer.

She turned in the direction of the outbuilding, and swallowed. She didn't want to go back in there, but nor did she want to stay out here, with just the slow, quiet rustling of the leaves in the breeze for company.

'Jimmy?' she called again, a little louder this time, but with exactly the same effect.

She walked up to the hole in the outbuilding where the door had once been, and slowly poked her head inside. The holdall containing the money was gone. Aside from that, everything was just like it was before. The smell of turps, the inner door hanging off its hinges . . .

Except, now there was the sound of dripping.

At first she thought she was imagining it, that it was the wind playing tricks. But it wasn't. It was definitely there.

Drip, drip, drip . . .

Coming from the room off to the right.

'Jimmy,' she hissed, 'are you there?'

Nothing.

Fear ran its fingers up Andrea's spine. She wanted to run. But where?

Get back to the phone box. Now. They might be calling. You could miss them!

But where's that dripping coming from?

Suddenly every drop seemed loud inside her head, and as her fear built, so too did her curiosity. She took three paces inside the room, turned her head and looked into the gloom beyond the hanging door.

'Oh Jesus,' she gasped. 'Oh no.'

Her hand shot to her mouth, covering her scream as she took a step backwards, unable to take her eyes off Jimmy Galante's corpse. They'd impaled him on a rusty butcher's hook, which had been rigged up on an exposed wooden beam running below the ceiling join. He hung there unsteady and sprawling, like a stringless marionette, head slumped forward, feet just about touching the grimy stone floor, arms dangling uselessly at his side. The sky blue polo shirt he'd been wearing earlier was stained black in the semi-darkness, and the dripping she could hear was the blood splattering steadily on to the floor from the gaping wound in his neck where his throat had been sliced wide open.

But there was worse. All his fingers were missing, on both hands. They'd been crudely hacked off, leaving nothing more than uneven, bloodied stumps.

She couldn't believe what she was seeing. Jimmy had been such a powerful presence, and to see him butchered like this was almost too much to bear.

'Oh Jimmy,' she whispered. 'What have they done to you?'

His right arm twitched. She was sure of it. She stared hard into the darkness, asking herself if she'd imagined it.

But then it twitched again.

Oh God, he was still alive.

She rushed forward, half-slipping in the pool of blood that was forming on the floor, and leant down in front of him.

'Jimmy, it's me,' she said urgently, putting one arm round his shoulders and using her free hand to lift up his chin. 'We're going to get you . . .'

She never finished the sentence, the shock of Jimmy's sightless, dead eyes staring back at her stopping her dead in her tracks. He was gone. The man she'd been relying on was gone. She let go of him and staggered backwards, wondering how this nightmare could get any worse, unable to believe what she'd just witnessed because to believe it was to admit to herself that the animals she was dealing with were capable of the worst kind of atrocity.

And as she leaned against the opposite wall, unable to move, she barely noticed the mobile phone in her pocket as it started to vibrate.

Eight

Andrea ran outside into the darkness, desperate to put some distance between her and Jimmy as the mobile continued to vibrate. This wasn't a message. It was a call.

She pulled it from her pocket and said 'Hello?' breathlessly into the mouthpiece.

'Hello, Andrea.' It was the artificial voice of the kidnapper, his tone neutral.

'You've got the money. Now where's my daughter?'

'She's safe.'

'But where is she? I've given you the money, every penny of it. I've kept my side of the bargain—'

'But you haven't though, Andrea, have you? I told you to come alone, didn't I?' He paused, taking his time. 'And you didn't. You decided it would be better to bring someone along to spy on us. That was very stupid. I told you we were watching your every move.'

Andrea felt her heart lurch. 'Please, I'm so sorry. I just wasn't sure what to do. You've got your money. Please let my daughter go.'

'It's going to cost you.'

'For Christ's sake, I've got no more money. You've had everything.'

'There's always more.'

'Listen, please—'

'No, you listen, and you listen very carefully. You fucked up. You didn't follow the simple instructions you were given. So now it's going to cost you another half a million if you want to see your daughter alive again.'

'But I told you, I haven't got that sort of money.'

'You've got another forty-eight hours to find it. That's the deadline. Use the time wisely. And remember, do not tell anyone this time. No one at all. Or Emma dies.'

'Let me speak to my daughter. You've got to let me speak to her.'

'You'll speak to her again, but when we're ready. Not now.'

The line went dead while Andrea was still talking desperately into the mouthpiece, the knowledge that she had indeed totally screwed up ringing round her head. It was all Jimmy's fault. Even after all these years he still had the capacity to cause her pain. But this was pain like she'd never felt before.

Hold together, Andrea. You owe it to Emma. Hold together.

But God it was hard. It was so damn hard. Tears stung her eyes and she wiped them away angrily as she ran over to the car and jumped inside, switching on the engine. She lit a cigarette and took urgent drags, then drove down to the end of the track and turned round.

As she got back on the main road and drove back in the direction of London, she stared wide-eyed out of the windscreen, silently repeating the mantra over again: *Stay strong, stay strong, stay strong.* She knew she couldn't collapse under the pressure, because if she did she would never get up again, and right now she couldn't afford that, not while Emma remained in the clutches of those animals.

She thought about them now, the people she was up against. Jimmy Galante was no pushover. He was a hard man, a street fighter with the kind of low cunning that only the truest criminals possess, and yet he'd been discovered by the man or men he was supposed to be watching, and butchered like a dog. These people were ruthless. And worse, they knew exactly what they were doing. She couldn't fight them alone, she knew that. Yet involving others had already backfired. Which left what?

There was, of course, only one alternative. The police. At least they might know what to do. It was a huge risk, given how brutally efficient Emma's kidnappers were. If they found out that the police were involved, they might panic and kill her, but then they might well kill her anyway, especially if Andrea couldn't raise the new money fast enough. Once again she was being forced into a corner, knowing that the wrong move would have terrifying ramifications.

So intensely was she concentrating that she didn't notice that her car was veering into the centre of the road until she saw headlights rushing towards her and heard the sound of the other car's horn. She swung the wheel hard left and slammed on the brakes, going into a wild skid that whirled the car round a hundred and eighty degrees in a screech of tyres before she finally came to a halt, facing the wrong way down the empty road.

Except it wasn't empty. The car that had been coming towards her had now stopped about thirty yards ahead. As she watched, her hands gripping the steering wheel as if it was the edge of a cliff she was hanging from, it did a three-point turn and started driving back towards her, the lights on its roof flashing a bright blue against the night sky.

Andrea cursed. Of all the bad luck, she had to

run into probably the only police patrol car in a ten-mile radius.

Act natural. For Christ's sake, act natural.

She glanced briefly in the rear-view mirror and was shocked by the face that stared back at her. Her expression was tight and haunted, making her look a good five years older than she was, her hair a tangled mess.

Stay calm. Act natural.

The police car came to a halt five feet in front of her bumper, and its two occupants slowly clambered out of each side, donning their caps.

She wound down her window as the driver stopped beside it and leaned down. He was middle-aged, heavy-set but running to fat, with a thick moustache and a gruff expression that suggested whatever she said wasn't going to be enough to stop her getting booked for careless driving. But she had to try.

'I'm sorry, officer,' she announced before he had a chance to speak. 'I think I must just have lost concentration. I've had a very busy day at work.'

'I'm afraid that's not an excuse, madam,' he told her sternly. 'You really shouldn't be driving if you're tired.'

Typical copper, she thought. *Always acting holier than thou. I bet he's driven knackered plenty of times.* But she knew she couldn't say anything to antagonize him. Instead, she apologized for a second time.

'Where have you been this evening?' he asked, his expression unchanged.

Belatedly, she realized her hands were still gripping the steering wheel. She removed them, saw that they were shaking, put them in her lap.

'Work,' she answered.

'Where do you work?'

Her mind went blank. Completely. For a moment, she couldn't even remember where she was. 'Erm . . .' Her hesitation sounded ridiculous, she knew it. But she just couldn't think. 'Er . . .'

'Would you mind stepping out of the car, madam?' he asked, reaching in with a gloved hand and removing her keys from the ignition. 'I have to tell you that I've got reason to believe you've been drinking, so we're going to ask you to take a breath test. Do you understand?'

She nodded weakly. 'Sure.'

Stay calm, Andrea, stay calm. You haven't been drinking. One shot of brandy two hours ago, nowhere near enough to make you over the limit. The worst that can happen is they book you for dangerous driving. They'll issue you with a ticket, let you go, and you can go home and try to think of a way of finding another half a million pounds in cash by Saturday to save your fourteen-year-old daughter's life.

She stepped out of the car, unsteady on her feet as all the knocks of the past forty-eight hours rose up and battered her like winter waves on a sea wall. She was finally crumbling, and she knew it.

'Are you all right, madam?' It was the driver's colleague. He was a taller, younger guy, with the air of the college graduate about him, and he was holding a breathalyser under his arm.

'Yeah, thanks. I'm fine.' She tried to smile but didn't quite make it.

The young cop was staring at her chest. 'What's that?'

'What's what?'

She looked down, saw what he was staring at. There was a thick patch of blood on her jacket where she'd grabbed hold of Jimmy. Jesus, how could she have missed that? There were further flecks of it lower down, as well as a single thumb-sized spot on her T-shirt, which suddenly seemed to stick out a mile in the flashing lights.

The older cop stepped forward, staring too.

'Have you been hurt?' he asked.

She turned round quickly. 'No, I'm fine. Honestly.'

'This is blood,' he said. 'You'd better take your jacket off. You might have cut yourself.'

'I haven't.'

The two cops were watching her closely. The older one seemed to come to a decision.

'Take your jacket off, madam.'

She felt like asking why, but knew she was going to have to cooperate eventually, so she slipped it off and gave it to the older cop, who lifted it to his nose and sniffed it suspiciously.

'This is definitely blood,' he said.

Andrea stood there, her heart pounding. Now that they could see she wasn't hurt, one of them was going to ask the obvious question. It was the younger one who did.

'Care to explain how it got on your shirt and jacket, madam?'

Andrea took a deep breath. The decision about what her next move would be had finally been made for her.

'Yes,' she said, looking at them both in turn. 'I think I'd better.'

Part Two

Part Two

Nine

When SG3 Mike Bolt of SOCA, the Serious and Organized Crime Agency, was woken at just after 5.30 a.m. on a Friday morning in mid-September by a call from his boss telling him to get down to their offices fast, he had no idea that one of the hardest days of his life had just begun.

His team had just come off a job tracking a gang of professional money-launderers who were now safely banged up awaiting trial, and he'd booked the day off as holiday. He had big plans for the coming weekend, his first off in close to a month, which involved driving down to Cornwall to spend a few relaxing days with a twenty-eight-year-old artist from St Ives with raven hair and a dirty laugh. He'd been introduced to Jenny Byfleet a couple of months earlier when she'd been up in London, and he was very keen to get to know her better. Jenny was the kind of girl a man could really fall for, and Bolt felt that he deserved a bit of romance in his life, even the long-distance kind. Things had been a bit sparse in that department for some time now.

But the romantic weekend was going to have to wait because this was an emergency: an ongoing kidnap situation, according to the boss.

Most of the public don't know it, but kidnapping is a comparatively common crime. On average, there's one every day in London alone, but the vast majority of these are drugs-related, involving squabbles over money between criminal gangs, particularly those from ethnic minorities. This case was totally different, and far, far rarer. A fourteen-year-old middle-class white girl abducted for ransom was a frightening development, and a senior cop's worst nightmare. Although none of the top brass would ever admit it, Bolt knew that the police service had no real problem tolerating kidnappings involving a few thugs snatching and torturing a crack addict over an unpaid couple of hundred quid, because frankly the press, and therefore the public, weren't really that interested. But if the media got hold of something like this, they'd have a field day. It had all the elements of a great story, particularly now that the kidnapper or kidnappers had murdered a friend of the victim's mother during an attempted ransom drop the previous evening.

The stakes, then, were extremely high, and the pressure for a successful result was going to be enormous.

And Mike Bolt was the one who was about to be chucked headfirst into the eye of the storm.

The details he'd been given were still sketchy. The victim's mother had been stopped at just before eleven o'clock the previous night, having been spotted driving erratically by a police traffic vehicle containing two officers from Hertfordshire Constabulary. As she'd got out of her car, she was seen to have bloodstains on her clothing, and when questioned about this, the woman, who'd been in a distressed state, had told them about the kidnapping and the subsequent murder of her friend.

The woman had refused to return to the spot where her friend's body was, claiming that the kidnappers might still be there, but a second patrol car had eventually been dispatched, only to discover that the body had been set on fire and was already badly burned. There was no sign of anyone else in the vicinity and so, despite her protestations of innocence, the woman had been arrested on suspicion of murder and transferred to Welwyn Garden City police station where she'd given a lengthy statement explaining what had happened to her over the previous two days.

It was a difficult and highly unusual situation

for Hertfordshire police. On the one hand they had an obvious murder suspect in custody, but one who nevertheless remained insistent that her daughter had been kidnapped, and was acting like someone telling the truth. In the end they'd decided to escalate the inquiry, and because she'd been picked up outside London's city limits, the senior investigating officer on the case had approached SOCA rather than the Met's over-stretched Kidnap Unit, hence the call to Bolt.

It had just turned seven a.m. when he arrived at the office where his team was based. The Glasshouse, as it was known, was a 1960s ten-storey office block with windows that were tinted with the grime of age rather than lavishness of design, set on the corner of a lacklustre shopping street a few hundred metres south of the river in Vauxhall. It was a fine sunny morning, the fifth such day in a warm spell that had followed one of the wettest, most disappointing summers on record – which for England was really saying something – and if it hadn't been for the fact that he was missing out on seeing Jenny, Bolt would have been in a good mood. He liked cases he could get his teeth into, and they didn't come much more meaty than this. More and more these days, his work took him and his team into long-drawn-out inquiries where the slow and usually laborious process of evidence-gathering took weeks, sometimes months, to complete. The money-laundering job they'd just finished was a case in point, having started right back in early June; and he'd once been part of a people-smuggling investigation that had lasted the best part of a year. During a career that had spanned two decades, Bolt had learned the art of patience, but even so, the idea of taking charge of a case whose resolution could be measured in hours was one he was never going to pass up.

Bolt's team was based in an open-plan office on the fourth floor of the Glasshouse, and when he arrived about half of its dozen members were already there, drinking coffee and generally looking pretty groggy. They'd all been rousted from their beds earlier than they'd been expecting, and Bolt knew he wasn't the only one whose day off had been interrupted before it had even got going. The team had had a major drink-up two nights earlier in the West End to celebrate the arrests of the money-launderers, and it looked like one or two of his people had continued the cele-bration the previous night as well.

At least Mo Khan looked fairly ship-shape. Mo was one of Bolt's team leaders and the guy he trusted most. They'd been colleagues for close to five years now, first in the National Crime Squad, then at SOCA, and though, with his big round face and friendly, twinkling eyes, he bore more than a passing resemblance to a short, squat cuddly bear, the appearance was deceptive. Mo Khan was tough, efficient and unflappable under pressure, and these were three traits Bolt knew were going to come in very useful today. There was no sign yet of Tina Boyd, his other team leader, or his overall boss, SG2 Barry Freud, although Bolt knew he would be around somewhere since he was the one phoning everyone up at half past five.

He'd only just managed to say his hellos to the team members when Mo came over and collared him.

'Our mystery lady got here twenty minutes ago,' he said as Bolt poured himself a cup of strong black coffee from the percolator. 'Big Barry wants us to start the interview straight away. She's been up all night and he thinks that if we leave it much longer she's going to be too exhausted to talk.'

'Fair enough. Where is she?'

'Over in Interview Room B. Everything's set up and we're ready to go.'

'Blimey, you're quick off the mark this morning,' said Bolt, following him out the door and down the corridor. 'What time did you get in?'

'Half an hour ago. I was moving fast.'

Bolt grinned and gave him a playful punch on

the arm. 'You never move fast, Mr Khan. How did you get here? Levitate?'

'I'm a man of many talents, boss.'

'So, have you seen her yet? This Mrs Devern?'

He nodded. 'I spoke to her briefly. She looks absolutely shattered, but she's very keen to talk to us.'

'I'll bet she is.'

Bolt slowed down to take a sip from his coffee, burning his lip in the process.

'Have the Hertfordshire cops checked her story out?'

'Parts of it. She's definitely got a fourteen-year-old daughter, but they haven't searched her house yet to check that she's actually missing. They're leaving that to us, in case the place is bugged.'

'So this whole thing could still be a load of bull-shit?'

Mo shrugged. 'I talked to the cops who brought her in. They think that if this is all an act, then she's one hell of a good actress – but, yeah, it's possible.' He stopped outside Interview Room B. 'Guess there's only one way to find out, isn't there?'

Mo entered first, and as Bolt followed him in he experienced a lurch of shock that almost knocked him backwards. It had been a long, long time, but even looking as drawn and exhausted as she was now, with all the life sucked out of her features by whatever ordeal she'd endured these past few days, there was definitely no mistake. He knew the woman sitting in front of him.

And at one time he'd known her far too well.

Ten

Andrea Devern stood up as they came in. Mo introduced Bolt to her and they shook hands formally. Knowing that he couldn't let on that he recognized her, Bolt sat down opposite Andrea. Pleased that she made no sign of recognition either, he explained that they were only talking in such formal surroundings because their conversation could be monitored and recorded. 'This way, it'll allow us to go back over your statement more easily. But don't worry. It's not an interview under caution. We just want you to go through everything from the beginning, trying not to leave anything out, so we've got a full picture of what's happened.'

This wasn't entirely true. Given that the truth of her story had yet to be confirmed, making her repeat it would give them an opportunity to check for discrepancies later, should the need arise.

Andrea yawned, putting a hand over her mouth, and Bolt noticed that one of her manicured nails had been broken. 'I've already told everything to the detectives in Welwyn Garden City. I just want you to find my daughter.' Her tone was weary, almost irritable.

'It's important for us to hear it from you. Just in case there's anything you've forgotten. That way it'll help us to get your daughter back safely.' He gave her a reassuring smile.

'OK,' she said, meeting his eyes. 'I understand. Can I smoke in here?'

'Well, this is a non-smoking building, and Mo here has just given up a forty-a-day habit, but . . . What do you think, Mo?' Bolt smiled. 'Will you be able to concentrate?'

Mo didn't look too happy about it but he nodded his assent. He'd only quit the dreaded weed six weeks earlier and by his own admission was still wobbling at the precipice, but Bolt was one of those people who still believed in a common-sense approach to how the law was enforced, and it seemed churlish to deny Andrea a small pleasure at a time like this. Big Barry would probably have something to say about it, given that he usually had something to say about everything, but Bolt would worry about that later.

Andrea thanked him, removed a pack of Benson and Hedges from an expensive-looking handbag on the desk in front of her, drew out a cigarette and lit it. She took a long drag, clearly enjoying it, before blowing a thin column of blue smoke skywards. And then she started talking. As she spoke, Bolt listened carefully, taking notes, only occasionally interrupting her narrative to question her about points that needed clarification.

It's possible to tell a great deal from a person's body language about whether or not he or she is telling the truth. Liars tend to limit their physical movements, and those they do make are towards their own body rather than outwards. They touch their face, throat and mouth a lot, and will often turn their head or body away from their questioner when they talk, so that they're not facing him or her directly. Andrea exhibited none of these tendencies. Hers might have been a highly unusual story, but from Bolt's point of view she was telling the truth.

There were three reasons for this. First, she came across as genuine. Second, there was, in the end, no real point in her lying, since it would take very little time for him to verify the truth of many of her claims. And third, and perhaps most importantly, he knew her, or at least had known her once, and didn't think she was capable of a charade like this. Underneath a hard, occasionally defensive exterior, she'd always been a good-hearted person.

It was why he'd once been in love with her.

Having no children of his own, Bolt couldn't begin to appreciate the extent of the ordeal Andrea was going through, but it was clearly taking a terrible toll. She was still a very attractive woman, with thick, shoulder-length auburn hair and well-defined, striking features that would make most people look twice, but today her face was haggard and puffy from lack of sleep, with dark bags under the eyes and a greyish, unhealthy tinge to the pale skin. The eyes themselves, a very light and unusual hazel that he remembered being so pretty, now appeared haunted and torn, and more than once when she looked at him as she spoke he felt an urge to reach across the table and touch her. It was an urge he fought down. There was no room for personal involvement in something like this.

'I made one mistake,' she said when she'd finished, looking at both men in turn. 'I trusted them.'

'No, Andrea,' Bolt told her, 'you made two mistakes. You trusted them, and you didn't come to us first.'

'I thought I was doing the right thing.' She sighed, stubbing out her third cigarette in the coffee cup in front of her. 'I guess I was wrong.'

Mo looked up from his notes and spoke for the first time. 'Do you have a picture of Emma we can copy, Andrea?'

She nodded and produced a small colour photo from her purse, handing it to him. 'This was taken last year. I'd like it back, please. It's very precious to me.'

'I'm sure it is,' he answered, his tone sympathetic. He gave it only the briefest of glances, not wanting to make the moment any more painful than it had to be, before slipping it inside a small clear wallet.

'Do either of you two gentlemen have children?'

'I'm afraid I don't,' answered Bolt.

'I have,' said Mo. 'Four of them.'

Andrea looked at him with new interest, as if he was a kindred spirit in a way that Bolt could never be. 'You're very lucky,' she told him. 'I hope what happens to me never happens to you. You can't imagine what it's like.' And in that moment, her features, tight with tension and pain, almost cracked. Almost, but not quite.

'I promise you we'll all do everything in our power to help you and bring your daughter back,' Mo told her. 'But you're going to need to help us as much as you can. Now, there are some points that need clarifying, and some questions that need answering. Can I speak frankly?'

She nodded. 'Of course.'

'Your husband's missing, and he has been since Tuesday, the same day that Emma was kidnapped. Do you think he could be involved?'

She paused for several seconds. 'I've thought about that a lot but I just can't see it. He's always got on well with Emma, and he's not the sort to do something like this to her.'

'Has he acted at all differently around you and your daughter in the last few weeks?' asked Bolt.

'Not that I've noticed.'

'So, where do you think he might be?'

She threw up her hands. 'I honestly don't know. Maybe they've taken him as well.'

Mo made a show of consulting his notes. 'According to what you've told us, you never asked the kidnapper who phoned you whether he was also holding your husband, or what might have happened to him?'

'It's about priorities, isn't it? I've only had a few very short conversations with the man holding my daughter, and in all of them that's who I've been focusing on: Emma.' She sighed. 'Look, the thing is, I don't know whether Pat was involved or not, but I'm pretty damn certain he wasn't. He's not that sort of bloke. Besides, why would he bother? He's got a pretty good life. He doesn't have to do a lot. He drives a nice car, gets decent holidays. Goes out when he wants. If he asks me for money, I give it to him. I probably shouldn't do, because I'm hardly motivating him to get off his arse and get a proper job, but I do. So, why would he put all that at risk? For a share in half a million quid? I don't think so.'

It was, thought Bolt, a good point.

'Kidnapping a child for this kind of ransom is highly unusual,' he said, 'and it's clear that you weren't chosen at random. Is there anyone you can think of, in either your personal or your business life, who might have a motive for putting you through this?'

Andrea was silent again, then shook her head firmly. 'I can't think of anyone, no.'

But there was just the briefest flickering of hesitation in her eyes when she spoke, and Bolt, who was trained in such things, noticed it.

He looked at Mo. 'I think that's everything for the moment, isn't it?'

Mo nodded. 'I haven't got anything else.'

'So what happens now?' Andrea asked, her voice shaking.

'The kidnapper gave you forty-eight hours,' said Bolt, leaning forward in his seat. 'There's still nearly forty left until he makes contact again. During that time we're going to be gathering what clues we can as discreetly as possible in an attempt to ID him.'

'If they find out about you, though . . . I mean, these guys know what they're doing.'

Bolt fixed her with a calm stare. 'So do we, Andrea, so do we. In the meantime, you'll be supplied with a team of trained liaison officers. They'll look after your day-to-day needs and provide support until the situation's resolved. We'll also house you in secure and comfortable accommodation. Any calls to your home landline will be automatically re-directed to you there, so when the kidnapper makes contact you'll still be able to speak to him and we'll be able to monitor the conversation.'

'No. I want to go home.'

'That's not going to be possible,' said Mo. 'The logistics would be too difficult.'

'I don't care. I want to go home.' Her voice was panicky now. 'These people have been watching the house. They must have been to know that Jimmy was there. If they're watching it now and they see that I'm not at home, they'll suspect that I've gone to you. I can't risk it. They said they'd kill Emma if I went to the police, and I believe them.'

'It's very unlikely that your kidnapper or any of his accomplices are watching your house,' Bolt explained, knowing that Mo was right: letting her back home would be a real problem. 'They won't want to risk drawing attention to themselves, and there won't be many people involved in this either. Two, possibly three at most, so they won't be able to spare the manpower to keep watch on all your movements.'

'That's what Jimmy said,' Andrea countered, 'and look what happened to him. I'm sorry, but I want to go home. That's all there is to it.'

Bolt sighed, knowing from the decisive expression on her face that she wasn't going to budge on this. 'All right, we'll see what we can do.' He stood up, and Mo followed suit. 'Someone'll be along shortly to take you to a more comfortable room. But don't worry, I'll be giving you regular updates.'

He turned to go.

'Mike?'

Bolt flinched at her sudden familiarity, and Mo looked at him. He turned back, avoiding his colleague's gaze. Andrea's hazel eyes were full of anguish.

'Promise me you'll get her back. Please.'

Bolt felt his mouth go dry. This was hard, far harder than he was used to. He wanted to promise her but knew that there was absolutely no way he could. It would be a dereliction of duty. Emma's kidnappers had already killed once; it was entirely possible they could kill again. If he said one thing, and then another happened . . . well, it wouldn't look good.

'I can't provide a cast-iron guarantee on anything. I'm sorry.'

She turned to Mo. 'You've got children. You must have some idea of the pain I'm feeling.'

'I do,' he said softly. 'I really do.'

'Please . . .'

'We'll do absolutely everything in our power to get Emma back,' Bolt told her firmly. 'Absolutely everything.'

She gave a slight nod and reached for her cigarettes with shaking hands, ignoring a single tear that ran down her cheek.

For the moment, there was nothing more to say.

Eleven

When he first started out as a nineteen-year-old probationary constable, having failed to secure the A Level results needed to get into the universities and polytechnics he'd applied for, Mike Bolt's first posting was Holborn Nick in the heart of central London, directly between the West End and the City. Having grown up on a diet of 1970s cop shows from *Z Cars* to *Starsky and Hutch*, he'd always quite fancied the idea of joining the police, but in an abstract way, like someone wanting to be an astronaut or a jockey. Had he made university, his life would probably have taken a completely different turn.

He'd spent five and a half years at Holborn, the first three in uniform, before joining the station's CID. One of his first cases as a detective was the death of Sir Marcus Dallarda, a fifty-eight-year-old City financier who'd made a fortune in the late 1980s developing rundown inner-city brownfield sites and turning them into blocks of luxury flats. Sir Marcus was one of the few people to foresee the end of the property boom and had sold virtually all his property holdings before the great crash, and as interest rates soared, he'd lent his profits to the money markets where the returns were suddenly enormous. To some people Sir Marcus was the worst kind of capitalist, a man who created nothing and simply sat on a growing pot of money that had been gained through other people's sweat. But the media loved him. He was a good-looking, flamboyant figure with a ready stream of amusing one-liners, and he exuded the kind of unashamed joie-de-vivre that made him difficult to dislike. With two divorces, more than one love child, and a string of mistresses under his belt, he was tabloid heaven, and he possessed that strange upper-class ability of creating an affinity with the masses that someone middle-class could never dream of achieving.

So when he was found, after an anonymous tip-off, naked and dead in the penthouse suite of a renowned five-star hotel in the Strand, with several thin lines of white powder on the table beside him and a condom hanging rather forlornly from his flaccid penis, it was always going to be big news. Although a DCI was made the senior investigating officer in charge of the case, it was Bolt and his boss at the time, DS Simon Grindy, a world-weary forty-year-old for whom the term 'half-empty' could have been invented, who'd been given most of the legwork.

'Dirty old bastard,' Grindy had mused, with a gruff mixture of admiration and jealousy, as he and Bolt stood in the opulent bedroom looking down at Sir Marcus's rather spindly body. 'If you've got to go, I could think of worse ways.'

Bolt wasn't so sure. He always felt sorry for those whose deaths had to be investigated by the police. There was a certain indignity about being inspected by various people while you lay helpless, and in Sir Marcus's case in a somewhat humiliating pose. Like most people at the time, Bolt had enjoyed reading about Sir Marcus's rakish antics, and he remembered thinking at the time how powerful death was that it could crush even the most larger-than-life characters. It was something that had remained with him ever since.

It hadn't taken long to determine what had happened in this particular case, though. The post-mortem concluded that he'd died of a massive and sudden heart attack, at least partly brought on by the cocaine in his bloodstream. If he'd been indulging in intense physical activity before his death this could also have been a contributory factor.

Since Sir Marcus's friends and colleagues

insisted he would never normally touch drugs, it was concluded by the media that whoever had been with him that night, and had made the anonymous call, had also supplied him with the illegal contraband. There was an appeal for witnesses and it turned out that two young women had been seen leaving the hotel in a hurry shortly before the call to the police, which had been made from a nearby phone box. At the same time, a search of the room and Sir Marcus's possessions turned up a business card in the name of a 'Fifi' who provided 'relief for all your tensions'. On it was an east London telephone number.

A call to BT had provided a name and address for the number in Plaistow, and so it was on a grey drizzling afternoon, three days after Sir Marcus had shuffled off his mortal coil, that Bolt and Grindy knocked on the door. The address itself was a small 1950s grey-brick terrace on a lonely back street in the shadow of a monolithic tower block. 'This girl ain't going to be pretty,' was Grindy's less than deductive take on things. 'If she was making money there's no way she'd be cooped up in a shithole like this.'

But Simon Grindy had not been the best of detectives, the accuracy of his predictions never likely to be giving Mystic Meg cause for concern, and this one was no exception. The girl who answered the door was a very attractive willowy brunette in her early twenties, wearing a pleasant smile, a black negligee and not a great deal else. The smile disappeared the moment she saw the two men in suits and raincoats standing on her doorstep.

'Whatever it is, I'm not buying,' she'd said dismissively in a strong east London accent.

'I can see that, Fifi,' Grindy had replied with a leer. 'If I was a betting man, I'd say you were selling.'

She'd pulled a face. 'Not to you, mate. Everyone's got to have minimum standards.'

Bolt had almost laughed but managed to stop himself. He hadn't been working with Grindy long and had no wish to fall out with him. But he liked this girl. She had balls.

'We're police officers,' he'd told her, pulling out his warrant card, 'and we want to speak to a Miss Andrea Bailey. Are you her?'

She seemed to notice him for the first time then, and gave him a quick appraising look that would have made him blush if he'd been five years younger before reluctantly opening the door and leading them into a cramped living room. She motioned for them to take a seat on a threadbare sofa while she put on a dressing gown and asked them what they wanted.

Andrea Bailey was a cool customer. When Grindy told her harshly that they knew she was the woman who'd been with Sir Marcus Dallarda and demanded that she tell them who her companion was, she'd sat in the chair opposite and flatly denied it, and for the next ten minutes batted off their questions with a quiet confidence that Bolt couldn't help but admire. When asked how her business card had got into Sir Marcus's wallet, she'd replied that she had no idea. 'I've got hundreds of business cards. I give them out. That's what they're for. I can't keep track of where they end up.'

'And what exactly is your business, Miss Bailey?' Grindy had growled menacingly.

'Read the card. Massage, of course.'

And so it had gone on, with Grindy's attempts at intimidation failing dismally.

'We can get a warrant to search this place,' he'd said at last.

'I'm sure you can,' she'd answered with just the hint of a smirk. 'You're a policeman.'

'In fact we've got it here,' he'd added, producing it from his raincoat pocket with a flourish, as if this would throw her off-balance.

It didn't. She remained casually impassive, even giving Bolt a cheeky wink.

Bolt knew she was trying to embarrass him, and didn't rise to the bait.

'Have you got something in your eye, Miss Bailey?' he'd asked her coolly.

'Just a twinkle,' came her answer, and he'd always remembered that. Cool and witty. It made Bolt wonder what she was doing in such a dump when there was a whole world out there she could have conquered.

They'd searched the house from top to bottom, supposedly looking for the same kind of drugs that had killed Sir Marcus, and Bolt had had to go through her underwear drawer while she watched.

'I don't enjoy doing this, you know,' he'd told her as he rummaged through the various lacy little numbers.

'Course you don't,' she'd said with a chuckle. 'But ask yourself this: how many other blokes get into a pretty girl's knickers as part of their job?'

They'd bantered on and off throughout the search. Andrea was a terrible flirt but there was something hugely engaging about the way nothing seemed to faze her, and Bolt was pleased she hadn't taken offence to them turning her house upside down.

There hadn't been any drugs – there hadn't been anything illegal anywhere – and Grindy was in a horrendous mood when they left. 'Cheeky bitch,' he'd complained bitterly. 'You want to keep away from women like her, Mike. They're trouble. Take it from me. I know.'

Grindy had never struck Bolt as an expert on

women, but in this case his boss was right. Andrea, however, had definitely got under his skin, and he'd thought about her often afterwards.

It was three years before he saw her again. He was still living in Holborn but had joined the Flying Squad, and was walking down the Strand one afternoon when he heard a woman's voice call out, 'Mr Bolt, are you ignoring me?' He'd turned round to see a woman with jet black hair, a good suntan and big sunglasses coming out of a designer clothes shop. She was dressed in a white sleeveless top, figure-hugging jeans and high-heeled black court shoes, and was carrying several bags. There was something familiar about her, the voice especially.

She smiled. 'Plaistow, 1989. My knickers drawer.' Then she removed the sunglasses and it came back to him in an instant.

'Andrea Bailey?'

She shook her head, coming forward. 'No, Andrea Bailey's dead. Meet Andrea Devern.' She put out a manicured hand, and they shook. 'I'm a married woman now,' she added, just in case he hadn't noticed the wedding band and diamond-encrusted engagement ring.

'Congratulations. You've dyed your hair.'

She shrugged. 'I fancied a change.'

'It's good to see you again,' he told her, and it was. 'You look well.'

'Thanks. You don't look so bad yourself. Still a copper?'

He nodded. 'Yeah, but not at Holborn any more. I'm in the Flying Squad these days.'

She raised her eyebrows. '*The Sweeney*? Very glamorous. So' – she looked around – 'you fancy buying me a drink, or are you too busy?'

Bolt was single at the time. It was a Saturday afternoon and he'd just been wondering about doing a bit of shopping without any real plans.

'Sure,' he answered, 'why not?'

So they'd found a wine bar round the corner, got themselves a nice quiet table and proceeded to demolish a bottle of Chablis.

It was one of those occasions when everything just clicked. They'd only met that one time years earlier, and hardly under ideal circumstances, but even so they talked like old friends. Andrea told him about her upbringing in a council flat, the middle of three daughters brought up by a single mother; how she'd left school at a young age with no qualifications and got herself a job in a local corner shop which she really enjoyed, before a friend turned her on to drugs. 'I got in far too deep, far too fast. Problem was, with my wages, I couldn't pay for them, so my mate told me a great way of earning big money.' She rolled her eyes. 'I was young, and I suppose it seemed like a good idea at the time. I didn't want to work for some pimp, though, so I set up on my own, got business cards printed, and worked through recommendations. I didn't enjoy it, but . . .' She shrugged. 'It got me money. My idea was to kick the coke, raise a couple of grand and put myself through college. I wanted to do a business course.'

'But you never made it?'

'Oh, I made it all right,' she told him with a smile. 'I kicked the gear, but I took a quicker route to the real money and married it.'

'Always a good move,' he said.

'He's a nice guy,' she told him, her expression suddenly serious. 'He looks after me.'

But on that day at least, Andrea hadn't been in a hurry to get back to him, and with one bottle consumed she'd asked Bolt if he fancied sharing another. He knew it wasn't right to fool around with married women, but he was twenty-four, and the sad truth of the matter was that he was never going to say no.

And so the afternoon drifted lazily on, the conversation veering here and there, covering both their lives. Andrea now lived in Cobham with her husband, a businessman twenty-five years her senior who was, she claimed, one of the nicest guys she'd ever met. 'Present company excepted, of course.'

'Of course,' said Bolt with a smile.

Eventually they got round to how they'd

originally met, and with the case of Sir Marcus Dallarda now firmly set in the past, Andrea admitted that she'd been with him that night. 'I'd never met him before but a girl I knew in the business had and she said he was a decent bloke and a good payer, so I went along with her. I never normally did threesomes – I'm not that kind of girl, believe it or not.'

Bolt wasn't sure that he did believe it, but as a trained detective he preferred to listen rather than pass immediate judgement.

'Well,' she continued, 'to cut a long story short, there we were, doing the business, and he conked out. Just like that. Grabbed his chest and keeled over.' Her eyes widened as she recalled the events, and although she was clearly trying to stop herself, a small smile appeared. 'It was comical really, the way it happened. Like something off the TV. I know I shouldn't say that, but it just didn't seem real.

'Anyway, we didn't know what to do. My friend was panicking. She thought we might get the blame for it, especially as he was a bit of a celebrity as well. So I said, let's just get the hell out of here. And that's what we did. But obviously we didn't want him to get found by the cleaner the next day, so we phoned the police and told them. I didn't want to bullshit you when you came round to interview me, but I didn't actually think

I was doing anything wrong, you know.' She paused, fixing him with an expression of mild amusement, her eyes twinkling. 'So, what do you think of me now?'

Bolt may have been mildly drunk, but what he thought was that Andrea was a liar. A funny, engaging, attractive and intelligent one, with beautiful twinkling eyes, and loyal too, because she'd never given up her friend, even when he and Grindy had turned her house upside down, but a liar nonetheless, and one who wasn't much good at remembering the details of the past either. Otherwise she would have recalled that the police had originally been led to her by the fact that it was her business card in Sir Marcus's wallet, and not her friend's, meaning that Sir Marcus had almost certainly known her before that night. It seemed a strange lie to tell, given that she'd already admitted that she'd been a prostitute. Why not simply admit that she was the one who'd approached her friend about the threesome, not the other way round?

Not that Bolt said any of this, of course. Instead, he put down his glass and returned her gaze.

'I think,' he said quietly, 'that if I stay here much longer I'll do something I regret.'

'Here's to regrets,' she said, and lifted her glass.

Don't get involved, he told himself. *You will regret it.*

'You're a married woman, Andrea,' he said, but it sounded lame, even to his own ears.

She sat back in her seat with a wide smile on her face. She was a little drunk too, but her eyes remained sharp and focused. 'Ah, I forgot, I'm talking to a policeman.' She raised her hands in mock surrender. 'All right, you've convinced me. I shouldn't even think about making love to you.'

But it was clear that neither of them was thinking about anything else. Andrea was in London on a weekend shopping trip, and she was staying at a hotel in Bloomsbury on her own. So once they'd finished their second bottle of Chablis Bolt had walked her back. She'd invited him in. This time he hadn't even bothered to resist, and they'd gone to her room and made love before ordering room service, making love again, and finally sinking into the slumber of the drunk and the contented.

The next morning they'd made love a final time before Andrea told him she had to get back to Surrey. 'I'm really glad we met up,' she'd whispered, touching his cheek and leaning over to kiss him on the lips before getting off the bed and walking naked into the bathroom to shower.

Bolt remembered what an effect she'd had on him: a potent mixture of lust, satisfaction, jealousy and anger. The anger was the worst part, because he wasn't used to getting so worked up over a woman. He'd had a great time with her, a fantastic time, but he couldn't get over the feeling that he'd been used and was now being discarded, which hurt his young man's pride. Even in those days he'd known that the best way to woo a woman was to play it cool, to pretend you didn't care that much, but it hadn't worked and he'd still left his card on top of her handbag, hating himself for it, before walking out and shutting the door behind him.

And here he was fifteen years later, and still she was having an effect on him. The shock of seeing her again that morning was wearing off as the operation to find Emma cranked rapidly into gear and the team focused on the hunt for the kidnapper, but Andrea still possessed that 'something' Bolt had always found so irresistible, even in her current state. He wanted to help her. He told himself it was because she and her daughter were both crime victims, but he knew it was more than that. A part of him still wanted to impress her, to prove that he was the tough guy who could rescue a damsel in distress.

As he walked down the corridor to his boss's office for a strategy meeting, he knew that, just like last time, Andrea's presence in his life spelled trouble.

Twelve

'What do you mean she wants to go home?' SG2 Barry Freud, the SOCA equivalent of a DCS, sat behind the huge slab of glass he called a desk, looking incredulous. 'That's not how we do things. There are procedures to follow in cases like this.'

Bolt, who was sitting on the other side of the slab, told him she was insistent. 'She says that otherwise she's not going to cooperate.'

'What choice does she have? She's got to co-operate if she wants her daughter back. It'll be far too much hassle allowing her to go home. I can tell you that for free, old mate. Far too much hassle.'

Big Barry Freud called every man he knew 'old mate'. It was supposed to be a term of endearment, but it never came across like that. As bosses went, Bolt scored Barry as decent enough. A big bluff Yorkshireman with a bald, egg-shaped head and a pair of peculiarly small ears, he made a hearty effort to come across as one of the lads, but never quite managed to make it look natural. Like a lot of senior officers, both in SOCA and the police services beyond, he always had one eye on the next rung of the ladder and did what he thought would go down well with his own bosses. He also had an inflated idea of his own importance. Word, probably put about by Barry himself, had it that he was a distant relation to the great psychoanalyst with the same last name, which gave him a natural insight into the minds of the people he was paid to catch. But Bolt couldn't see it himself. If you were part of such a distinguished family tree, you really weren't going to name your first-born son Barry. However, he was a decent enough organizer and he usually left Bolt alone to do his job, for which he was thankful.

That wasn't going to be the case today, though. Today, it was all hands on deck, and Big Barry was looking excited. He was the kind who tended to look at a crisis as a potential career opportunity.

'Can't you persuade her to see sense? The logistics of getting her home'll be a nightmare.'

'I've tried. I think it's going to be easier just to live with it.'

'That's your opinion, is it?'

Bolt nodded.

'She's still under suspicion of murder.'

'And we'll still be able to keep an eye on her there. I know it's unusual, but if we play it right, it won't compromise the op.'

Barry sighed. 'Well, if she absolutely insists, I suppose we can do it. I'm going to trust your judgement on this one, old mate. But make sure she knows that it means using resources that could be used helping to locate her daughter.'

'I will.'

Barry lifted a huge mug of coffee to his lips and took a loud slurp.

'What do you think of her story?' he asked.

Bolt hadn't mentioned the fact he knew Andrea because to do so would almost certainly mean him being removed from the case, but he answered honestly. 'I think it's true. You don't make something like that up. We know her daughter kept her dental appointment on Tuesday afternoon at a quarter to five, but that's the last confirmed sighting.'

'Have they got CCTV at the dentist's?'

'They have. It covers the car park and the front entrance, but it works on a loop and gets wiped every forty-eight hours, so it's already gone.'

Barry looked annoyed. 'Stupid woman. She should have come to us earlier. We could have had the daughter back by now if we'd been involved

131

from the start. We need to know where she was snatched from, Mike. If it was in a public place, someone might have seen it.'

'I've got Mo and his people on that,' said Bolt, 'but this is the interesting thing. So far there's been not a single reported abduction anywhere in Greater London on Tuesday between four forty-five, when we know Emma was at the dentist's, and eight forty-five, when Andrea received the first phone call from the kidnappers. Also, when Andrea arrived home that night, she specifically said in both her statements that the alarm was on. If anyone had snatched Emma from the house, there's no way they would have stopped to reset the alarm.'

'So it looks like it could be an inside job? What about the old man, Phelan? What have we got on him?'

Bolt consulted his notebook, even though he already knew Patrick Phelan's form. 'He's got old convictions for drug dealing and receiving,' he answered, wondering why a livewire like Andrea was so often attracted to deadbeats. 'Nothing major, but he served a year behind bars in the late nineties for receiving a load of hi-fis that had been lifted in a hijack a few weeks earlier. That was his last conviction. He's been straight since then. For what it's worth, Andrea doesn't think he was involved.'

Barry grunted. 'She wouldn't, would she? It wouldn't say much for her judgement if her old man was capable of kidnapping his stepdaughter and holding her to ransom. The fact is, he's missing. Which means he's either dead, or he's one of the kidnappers. Fact.'

'Phelan's car's missing too,' said Bolt. 'I've got Mo's people checking the ANPR to see if we can track it that way.'

The automatic number plate recognition system was the latest technological tool available to the police in the twenty-first-century fight against crime. It used a huge network of CCTV cameras which automatically read car number plates to log the movement of vehicles along virtually every main road in Britain. These images – some thirty-five million a day – were then sent to a vast central database housed alongside the Police National Computer at Hendon HQ where they were stored for up to two years. Not only was it possible to trace the movements of Phelan's car on the day, but also where it had been in the days and weeks leading up to the kidnap, although Bolt knew it would take time and effort to gather this information.

'What are Tina Boyd's people doing?' Barry asked, taking another noisy slurp of his coffee.

'Background checks on everyone involved in this. Looking for motives. Andrea told us she had a lot of cash stored in deposit boxes, which made up most of the half million she paid out to the kidnapper. I think someone knew she had those deposits, and we need to find out who.'

Barry nodded. 'If it is personal, then it's someone who really hates her, isn't it? To kidnap her only child, take the half million, and then renege on the deal. You've got to be a truly nasty piece of work to do that.'

'Well, these people are certainly nasty, and they took out Jimmy Galante, so they know what they're doing.'

'You knew him?'

'I knew the name from my days in the Flying Squad. He had a reputation as a hard bastard. We had him down as a suspect in a couple of armed robberies but we never pinned anything on him, and he ended up running a bar in Spain, like Andrea said.'

'But why are they asking for more money? That's what I can't understand. They've got what they wanted. Why not just release the girl and have done with it?'

Bolt shrugged. 'Because they're greedy, I suppose. Maybe they figure that if it only took Andrea forty-eight hours to come up with half a million, then maybe they were selling themselves short. I don't suppose the fact that she brought someone along to the ransom drop made any difference. I think that was just an excuse for them.'

'So they were always going to keep squeezing . . .' Barry shook his head slowly. 'We're going to have to catch these bastards, Mike.'

'All I'd say, sir, is, don't expect miracles. We haven't got a lot of time until the next deadline.' He looked at his watch and saw that it had just turned ten a.m. 'It's only about thirty-six hours until she's meant to come up with the next tranche of money.'

'All right, point taken.' Barry put down his mug. 'So, what are we going to do about this one, old mate? Negotiate, or take them out?'

It was the big question. Bolt knew only too well that the problem with kidnap cases, what made them so different from other equally serious crimes, was the fact that the investigators had far less control over events. It was the kidnapper who set the tempo, and since the circumstances of kidnappings varied so much, the police procedures for dealing with them had to be far more flexible than they would be in, say, a murder case where a set of very specific rules applied.

There was an uncomfortable silence.

'I think the girl's still alive,' Bolt said at last. 'And I think they'll keep her alive while they need her as a bargaining chip. They've already said that

Andrea can speak to her again before the next ransom drop, and there's no reason at the moment to believe that they'll renege on that.'

'But?'

'But, as we both know, they're ruthless. They've killed once. They may well have killed Phelan too for all we know. So if we spook them by trying to negotiate when they next make contact, my guess is they'll disappear back into the woodwork and that'll be the last we see of them. And there's no guarantee they'll let Emma go either. Especially if they think there's the remotest chance she can identify them. To them, she's just a loose end. We go the negotiation path, I think there's a good chance they'll kill her.'

Barry didn't look convinced. 'But there are a lot of things that can go wrong if we try to trap them, and if we mess it up it could be disastrous for SOCA. We're in need of some high-profile successes at the moment, so the public can see where all their tax money's going. A high-profile failure's going to set us back years.'

'You asked my opinion, sir. I think negotiation's the wrong move. If we can put trackers with the ransom money and play things right, we should be able to get our kidnappers to lead us right to Emma. It's risky, and there's a chance it might not work, but there's also a chance she's dead already. If we want to catch these guys, and we can't ID them before they make contact, then this is the best way.'

Barry massaged his head with pudgy hands, and tipped his chair back. 'Well, I'm going to send it upstairs. See what the head honchos have to say. I'll let you know their decision as soon as I've got it.'

As Bolt got to his feet, sensing that the meeting was over, there was a knock on the door and Tina Boyd entered the room, carrying several sheaves of paper in one hand.

Tina was a relatively new member of the team, whom Bolt had brought on board after he'd met her during a case a few years earlier. At the time she'd just resigned from the force, and it had taken a lot of persuading to get her to join the team. An attractive woman just short of thirty, with dark hair cut into a jaunty bob and smooth, delicate features that shaved five years off her easily, she had that look that was unmistakably educated and middle-class, and she could have passed as a primary school teacher just as much as a cop. But the look belied the tough time she'd had down the years. Bolt knew that Tina had seen and done it all. Shot during a hostage-taking drama four years earlier, she'd also lost two colleagues, both murdered. One of them had been her lover, earning her the unwelcome nickname of the Black Widow in some quarters.

When she'd finally joined the team a year or so back, Bolt had harboured the odd romantic aspiration where Tina was concerned, but any attempt at warmth or even flattery had come up against a brick wall, and he'd quickly realized that he was on a hiding to nothing. Tina was polite and she was pleasant, but it seemed you didn't get close to her. Even when she socialized with the team, she was always one of the first to leave, making her excuses before heading home alone.

'I've got some interesting news,' she said, approaching the giant glass desk.

'Tell us more, Tina,' said Barry with something approaching a leer.

She looked at them both in turn. 'Andrea Devern might be a high-flying businesswoman but her company's not doing that well. Turnover in the last financial year was £4.81 million but the overall operating profit was only forty-eight thousand pounds, which for a company that size is piss poor. It's also a seventy per cent drop on the year before on a higher turnover, and they've got serious debt to service with the banks. Andrea owns sixty per cent of the company. Her main business partner, and fellow director, is a woman called Isobel Wheeler.' Tina consulted one of the sheets of A4. 'She's a forty-two-year-old lawyer, divorced with no children, who bought into the company ten years ago and now owns the remaining forty per cent. Both women pay themselves generously. They draw salaries of one hundred and sixty grand each.'

'Nice work if you can get it,' grunted Barry.

'Very nice, but it's not going to last. With profits that feeble, the banks are going to be having serious words. And Andrea and her husband are big spenders. Their joint credit card bills mount up to a hundred and twenty K a year.'

'So, what's the interesting part, Tina?' asked Barry, cutting to the chase. 'They're big spenders. So are most other people in this country. It's why the economy keeps doing so well.'

Tina gave him a mildly dismissive look, but when she spoke her tone was even. 'Well, I Googled Andrea's name and her company, and it seems that there've been a couple of articles about her in trade publications, but nothing of any significance. She certainly hasn't got a public profile. She earns good money but nothing special, so the question is, why on earth target her?'

Bolt nodded. 'It's what I've been thinking. This isn't random. It's personal.'

'You need to talk to Andrea herself, old mate,' Barry told him, manoeuvring himself slowly to his feet, 'and find out who the hell knew she was sitting on that half million in cash.'

'I will, but I reckon we can count in Pat Phelan

straight away, and I reckon her business partner's a strong possibility too. Which means we need to turn up everything we can on the two of them.'

'We're on it already,' said Tina.

Bolt felt a rush of excitement. It was the knowledge that the clock was ticking; the realization that this case was going to be concluded in hours rather than months; and that he was in the centre of things.

It was a good feeling.

And one that wasn't going to last.

Thirteen

She had to be brave.

Emma Devern had said this to herself countless times since they'd brought her here. But as the hours dragged into days and still there remained no prospect of her being released back to her mum, it became harder and harder for her to manage it.

They were keeping her in a dank, carpetless cellar with one narrow window coated in grime, high up on one wall and well out of reach, which let in thin shafts of daylight. She had to wear a pair of handcuffs, and was chained to the wall by one ankle. The chain was long enough so she could move around, but she couldn't reach the steps at the end of the room or the far wall, and she knew in her heart that there was no way she was going to be able to escape.

She thought this was the third day she'd been

here, which meant it was Friday. It was difficult to know for sure because the days simply flowed into one another, but she was trying hard to keep track. At nights it was cold. She slept on a horrible little bed with filthy sheets and she was forced to wrap herself up in them to keep warm, even though they smelled awful.

On the first night she'd been too shocked about what had happened even to cry. She remembered very little about how it had all started. She was going back to the car after the dentist appointment. Her dentist was called Mr Vermont, after the American state. He always said what good teeth she had, and she did too, because she looked after them well and didn't stuff her face with sweets like a lot of her friends. It had just been a standard check-up. She liked Mr Vermont. He was good-looking with a nice tan, even though he was a bit old and his hair was beginning to go a bit thin on top. The check-up had gone well. For the third visit running nothing needed doing – which was just as well because she hated having her teeth messed about with – and she'd been in a good mood as she crossed the car park at the front of the building.

Pat had been in the driver's seat with the paper in front of him, checking the sports pages, like he always did, but as she opened the door and got inside, something immediately felt wrong. He didn't greet her like he usually did, with a big grin and an 'All right, baby, how'd everything go?' in his rough London accent. Instead, he turned and stared at her, and she saw that he looked really frightened. His eyes were wide and there was sweat running down his forehead.

Then she heard a noise behind her, a kind of shuffling, and before she could even take in what was happening she was grabbed round the neck and pulled back into the seat. The next second, a wet cloth that smelled of chemicals was pushed against her face, and suddenly she couldn't breathe any more and she was struggling and kicking, trying to attract attention, help, anything . . .

It was all over so quickly, even now it didn't feel quite real. Her last image was Pat turning away from her and starting the car's engine with a low rumble. Then everything went black, and she couldn't remember another thing until she'd woken up in this cold, featureless room with a terrible headache and feeling really sick.

She wondered what had happened to Pat. She'd always liked him. He was good fun. They liked to joke together, and he seemed to make her mum happy. At first she hadn't been sure about him. She was used to it being just her and her mum. That was the way it had always been, the way she'd always preferred it. She didn't know her real dad. She'd never met him and she didn't even know who he was. Whenever she asked her mum about him, she'd always said that it was just a man from a long time ago, that he'd gone away, and that it would be best just to forget about him. She wanted to find her dad, but she didn't push it with her mum, and anyway, Pat made quite a good dad. And her friends were jealous because he was nice-looking, and not too old either.

She hoped they hadn't done anything bad to him.

'They' were the two men who were keeping her prisoner. She was not allowed to see them, and had to put on a black hood like something an executioner in a medieval history book might wear whenever the cellar door opened. One of them wheezed when he walked, making a horrible sound like something out of a horror film. She might not have been able to see him, but she could always hear his approach. And she could smell him too. He absolutely stank, a really horrible combination of BO, old socks and toilets that was so bad she thought she might gag whenever he got too close to her. He was the one who usually came down twice a day to check up on her. He'd bring food – Marmite or jam sandwiches, and fruit – and change the bucket they made her use as a toilet.

When he'd come down on that first night,

telling her to put on the hood, she'd been absolutely terrified. But he'd told her not to worry, that no one would hurt her, and that she'd be going home soon, and even though he'd talked in a strange rasping voice as if he was trying to disguise it, and had stroked her arm with cold, gloved hands, his touch lingering that little bit too long, something told her that he meant what he said.

As time wore on she'd begun to lose hope of going home and being reunited with her mum and her friends, and everyone she cared about. But she had to be brave. She just had to be. It was just that she really didn't want to die. She was happy. She'd never done anything wrong, and she couldn't see why anyone would do this to her. It wasn't fair. And when she thought about what might happen to her, she got really scared. Although she trusted the smelly one, she definitely didn't trust the one he was working with.

He'd only been down once, on the second night. When he'd called out to her from the top of the stairs, telling her to put on the hood, his voice was harsh and cruel, with no kindness in it at all. She'd done what she was told to do and had then sat there waiting, but she hadn't heard his approach. He was that silent on his feet it was like he was a phantom. All that told her he was in the room was the faint smell of cigarettes, and a feeling that someone was watching her.

After a while she'd asked uncertainly whether there was anyone there.

'Yeah,' came the reply, like he was mocking her. 'I'm here.'

'What do you want?'

'You're going to talk to your mum. You're going to tell her that if she pays the money, then you'll be going home tomorrow.'

She felt a rush of excitement. 'And will I?'

'If she does what she's told, yeah,' he answered, but it didn't sound like he meant it. 'Now turn round on the bed so you're facing the wall.'

She did what she was told.

'Bet you're not used to being told what to do, are you? Little rich girl like you. Bet you usually tell the servants what to do, don't you?'

'I don't have servants,' she said quietly. 'I'm just normal.'

'You don't know what normal is, you little bitch.'

'Why are you doing this to me?' she asked, because she really didn't understand why he was being so cruel to her.

'You don't ask the questions,' he said, ripping the hood from her head in one movement. 'You obey orders. Keep staring at the wall, and remember what you've got to tell your mum. If she does what we say, you go home tomorrow.'

He'd pushed a phone roughly against her ear and a couple of seconds later her mum had come on the line. Emma felt a huge burst of emotion. She wanted to cry so much but she knew she had to hold it together for her mum's sake, so she'd said she was fine and that if the money was paid she'd be back tomorrow. She'd wanted to say more but the phone had been snatched away with a hissed 'Don't turn round', and then a few seconds later she'd heard the key turn in the lock of the cellar door.

After he'd gone, she'd sat there shaking for several minutes, part of her feeling hope now that she'd heard her mum's voice, but a much bigger part feeling fear. She'd never come across anyone truly evil before, and now that she had, it made her wonder whether she was ever going to get out of here alive. Because they hadn't let her go, like he'd said they would. She was still here, hoping that the smelly one would keep the cruel one from doing anything to her, which was why she'd been as nice as possible to him whenever he came down.

They were talking upstairs now, their voices muffled, and she wondered what time it was. They'd taken her watch, or at least she thought they had. When she'd woken up in this place for the first time, it was gone, as was her handbag, which had had her mobile phone in it. All she'd been left with were the clothes she was wearing when she'd been taken – a black T-shirt, denim skirt and her favourite wedge-heeled sandals – and she was still in them now.

The smelly one had already been in that morning to give her sandwiches – Marmite this time – and to change the bucket. That was a while back now. He'd seemed in a strange mood. Normally he was quite friendly, but today he'd been quiet, and it had worried her. She'd asked him if everything was all right, and when they were going to let her go like they'd said they would, and he'd come over, sat down and put his arm round her, telling her it was going to be fine and that she'd be home very soon. Even though she'd felt like throwing up with him so close to her, she'd told him once again that she just wanted to be back with her mum and her friends, because she thought that if she said it enough times he'd feel sorry for her and would help to make it happen. He'd told her not to worry, every-thing would be all right, like he always did, but this time it seemed as if he was making an effort to say it, and that maybe it wasn't true.

The voices were getting louder. They were arguing. She got up from the bed and walked as far as the chain would allow until she was almost at the bottom of the steps, then stopped and listened, straining hard to hear what they were saying.

The voices stopped before she could make out any words, and then suddenly the key turned in the lock and the door flew open, slamming hard against the wall.

Emma darted back, rushing for the bed, but not before she'd seen the man at the top of the stairs, partly silhouetted by the bright light behind him. She'd only got the barest of glimpses, just enough time to note that he was of normal height and build and had dark hair. For just half a second their eyes had met, but she knew straight away that she'd made a terrible mistake.

'Get your hood on. Now,' the cruel one called out from the top of the steps.

Shaking with fear, trying hard not to cry, Emma sat on the bed and pulled the hood over her head. She heard the door shutting, followed by a pause that lasted long enough that she began to hope he wasn't coming down at all, and then she heard the footfalls moving fast, louder than last time. She tensed as she heard him stop in front of her.

'Did you see me?' he hissed, venom in his voice.

'No,' she answered, shaking her head vigorously.

'Did you see me, bitch? Tell me the truth.'

'No, I promise.' She pushed herself back against the cold stone wall, her heart pounding.

He tore the hood off and she turned her head away from him, shutting her eyes, not wanting to see him, knowing only too well what seeing him would mean. He grabbed her roughly by the chin, squeezing the flesh, and pulled her towards him.

'Look me in the eye, bitch. Did you fucking see me?'

She opened her eyes and saw that he'd put on a black balaclava. His face was only inches away from hers.

'No, honestly, I didn't,' she said, finding it hard to get the words out. 'Please, you're hurting me.'

'This ain't hurt, bitch. You don't know the fucking meaning of the word. But you will if you're lying. I'll hurt you good. I'll hurt you until you're screaming with the pain. Do you understand?'

She nodded rapidly, feeling the tears well up, but determined not to cry in front of him. 'Yes, yes. I'm not lying, I promise.'

He released his grip on her chin. Behind the slits his eyes were dark and cold. 'Good.' He pushed the hood back over her head. 'Now, we're going to send your mummy a little message. So you can let her know how much fun you're having.'

His tone had changed again. He was mocking her, pleased that she seemed so terrified. He was enjoying this. It was difficult, almost impossible to believe, but he was actually enjoying this. Underneath the hood, away from his terrible gaze, the tears flowed freely down Emma's face.

And then she felt something touch the bare skin of her arm. Something cold and sharp.

Oh God, no. He's got a knife.

Fourteen

There were serious logistical issues to be addressed in order to get Andrea back home, and Bolt spent most of the remainder of Friday morning organizing them. He had to operate on the assumption that the kidnappers were watching the place, even though he thought it highly unlikely. It didn't take long to confirm that no properties with views on to Andrea's house had been rented out for more than eighteen months, so any observation point being used by the kidnappers would have to be on the street itself. With Big Barry's authorization, he managed to get a twelve-person surveillance team from another area of SOCA pulled off their current job, and they were sent to Andrea's neighbourhood. Having discreetly confirmed that there was no one suspicious hanging about, either on foot or in a car, they'd set up at various points and now had the street under continuous observation.

With the area secure, Bolt had given Andrea's card key, house keys and the burglar alarm code to one of his team, SG5 Matt Turner, who'd gone to check out the property. Although Jimmy Galante had searched the place for bugs, he'd bought a cheap device from a spy shop, so it was likely he'd only have been using a radio frequency detector, and not a very good one either, which would have been inadequate for the task at hand. Bolt knew that RF detectors were designed to pick up signals from active transmitters and radio telephone taps, but couldn't detect switched-off or remote control devices, nor could they find hard-wired microphones and telephone taps, or recorders. In other words, the place could have been bugged to the hilt and neither Jimmy nor Andrea would have known about it. Turner was armed with the latest cutting-edge counter-surveillance equipment, including a Time Domain Reflectometer used to detect breaks and splices in cables; a Harmonic Radar to find cables and mikes buried in walls, cavities and furniture; and a Multi-Meter to measure line voltages within the telephone line.

However, when he called Bolt just after midday, Turner hadn't found anything either. 'The place is clear, sir. I've given it a complete once-over, and there's nothing here.'

Bolt trusted Turner's judgement on this kind of thing.

'Any sign of a struggle in there, Matt? Something that might suggest Emma Devern was snatched at the house?'

'Nothing like that. The place is spotless. Also, I reckon it'd be too risky trying to abduct someone here. There's a security gate running round the property, with only one entrance from the front, and it's pedestrian access only. No room to get a car through it. So the kidnappers would have had to take her out on to the street, and I think that would have been too risky in broad daylight. That's my take on it, anyway.'

Bolt sighed. The kidnappers had managed to track Emma's movements on Tuesday, and find out about Jimmy Galante's involvement in the ransom drop, but for the moment, how they'd done so remained a mystery.

He thanked Turner and rang off, then went to tell Andrea that he would drive her home. She'd been kept in the only office in the building with a sofa all morning and, according to the female liaison officer assigned to her, had spent most of the time asleep on it. She was awake when he went in there, though, and seemed pleased by the news that she was going back to her house, even if it was without her daughter.

It felt strange for Bolt being so close to Andrea

again, and their conversation for much of the journey was stilted. He wanted to bring up the past, to talk about the old days, but Marie Cohen, the very short, very earnest liaison officer, was in the back seat of his car, which made any such conversation impossible. Eventually Andrea fell asleep again, leaning against the passenger side window. Occasionally Bolt glanced across at her, trying to look natural in front of Marie Cohen. Andrea was still a very attractive woman, but the lively spark in her eyes that had drawn him in all those years ago had long since gone.

Poor, rich Andrea. She'd never really had much luck with men, and Bolt wondered whether in Phelan she'd made the worst choice of all.

She woke up when they were stuck in traffic on Hampstead high street.

'How long have I been out for?' she asked, rubbing her eyes.

Bolt checked the clock on the dashboard: 12.49. 'A while. The traffic's been murder.' In his rear-view mirror, he saw that Marie had also gone to sleep in the back. Clearly his effect on women wasn't quite as electric as he would have liked.

Andrea yawned. 'Do you mind if I smoke?'

He smiled. 'Well, technically it's illegal as this is a work car, but I guess under the circumstances we can make an exception. I'd ask Marie, but she looks flat out.'

Andrea looked round, checked that she was, and opened her window halfway before lighting up.

'Thank God for that,' she whispered, looking at Bolt. 'She means well, but I wish she'd just leave me alone.'

'She's just trying to help.'

'Yeah, but sometimes you can try too hard.'

Bolt watched as she put the cigarette to her lips. Her hands were trembling and the drags she took were short and urgent. The tension was coming off her in waves.

'You know, Andrea,' he said, turning off the high street, 'we've checked out your house, and the area round it, and we can't work out how the kidnapper could have known Emma's movements so thoroughly.'

'So you still think it might be an inside job?'

'It's a strong possibility.'

Andrea sighed, taking another drag on the cigarette. 'I just can't see it being Pat, that's all. He's got faults – big ones, like the fact that he's a waster – and if I'd known about them when I first met him I'd never have married him, but he wouldn't have done something like this to Emma. He's not cold enough. And I've met some cold people in my time.'

Bolt thought of Jimmy Galante. She was right on that score.

They were almost there now, and Bolt used a

dual-band radio to call the surveillance team. He needed confirmation that the area round Andrea's house was still secure. When this had been given by the team leader, he slowed the car down and turned into Andrea's road.

It was a leafy avenue of grand semi-detached houses, lined with mature oak trees planted fifteen yards apart, with expensive-looking sports cars and 4×4s parked on both sides. Instinctively, Bolt checked for occupants, but they were all empty, although he spotted a white van with blacked-out windows and the name of a plumbing firm down the side, which he recognized as a SOCA surveillance vehicle. A pretty young woman with oversized sunglasses who was busy putting a toddler in the car seat of a brand-new Range Rover seemed to be the only person around.

Andrea's place, one half of an impressive-looking three-storey Edwardian redbrick building, was about halfway down on the right-hand side. It was fronted by a brick wall approximately head height, mounted with freshly painted black railings, which enclosed the entire property but wouldn't have put off a determined intruder. Bolt found a parking spot about thirty yards further down between a Mercedes and a BMW people carrier. In the back, Marie woke up with a start.

As Bolt got out of the car he saw a shadow move across one of the upstairs windows of the house opposite. It had been turned into an observation post by the surveillance team, giving them a perfect view of the portion of the street to the front of Andrea's house.

Bolt let Andrea lead the way, with Marie bringing up the rear. He thought about how much Andrea had moved on since the old days when he'd first known her. It was all down to her own efforts as well. He admired her for that, but then she'd never been short of spirit and drive. It was spirit she was going to need now.

'We've got something called a trace/intercept set up on your landline,' he told her as she pressed the buzzer on the security gate and waited for Turner to let them in. 'It means that if they make a call to your home, we'll be able to pinpoint the location of the caller very quickly.'

'I don't want you to do anything that risks hurting Emma, Mike.'

'We won't,' said Bolt, but it was a lie, and he knew it. Whatever they did, they risked hurting Emma.

Matt Turner buzzed them in, and as they stepped inside the gate Bolt was immediately struck by the strong scent of flowers. The garden was a riot of colour, well kept with neat flowerbeds bordering the house's exterior wall. It was also very well stocked, with thick walls of greenery rising all round the terraced lawn. His wife Mikaela would have loved this place. She'd always wanted to live in a big, rambling house with a couple of kids and a couple of dogs and plenty of space, somewhere that with his copper's salary and hers as a primary school teacher they were never going to be able to afford.

Turner met them both at the door, greeting Andrea with a formal 'Mrs Devern' and moving out of the way to let her pass.

The front door led into a rather grand tiled hallway with a flight of stairs disappearing up to the next floor. The decor was all very neutral, with off-white colours dominating, which in Bolt's opinion gave it a rather soulless feel – not that he was any kind of expert in interior design. Straight ahead of him, above a vase containing partially wilted orchids, was a large professional portrait photograph of Andrea and Emma. It was a good shot of both mother and daughter, who were smiling widely at the camera, their faces side by side and touching, and the twinkle was firmly in Andrea's eye. Emma was a pretty kid with dark blonde hair down to her shoulders and a cute button nose. She looked young in the picture, probably no more than ten.

Bolt looked away quickly, not wanting to draw

attention to the photo. Marie asked whether anyone would like a cup of tea.

Bolt smiled at her. 'I'll take coffee, thanks, if it's going.'

Turner said he'd have the same.

Andrea didn't appear to have heard her. She was staring at the picture.

'What do you think of her, Mike? Isn't she beautiful?'

'Yes,' he said, keen to keep Andrea's spirits up. 'She's beautiful. And we're going to bring her back.'

'You've got to.'

The hallway fell silent and Marie and Turner went into the kitchen, leaving Bolt and Andrea alone. She ran a hand through her hair, turning away from the photo.

'I don't know what to do, Mike. It's the waiting. It's killing me.'

'Why don't you lie down for a bit?' He felt uneasy standing so close to her. 'We'll let you know of any developments.'

She nodded, and started up the staircase.

Bolt watched her go, then went to get his coffee.

The kitchen was large and modern with a breakfast island in the middle, and gleaming pots and pans hanging from hooks all around. Again, he thought about how much Mikaela would have loved a place like this. She'd been a great cook, but had had to do all her cooking in a place about a quarter of this size.

Marie and Turner were at the far end of the room, talking while she poured boiling water into the cups. Turner was approaching thirty and still resolutely single, a situation he seemed increasingly desperate to remedy. He tended to get first dates – he was a proud member of at least a dozen internet agencies, so was always getting introductions – but second ones proved a lot more elusive, which Bolt thought was a pity. Prematurely balding with a long hangdog face designed for frowning, and an obsession with the technical, the guy was definitely the kind of acquired taste a lot of people never get round to acquiring, but Bolt liked him. Turner might have had a geeky exterior, but he also had a bone-dry sense of humour, he never moaned, and there was a certain vulnerability about him that Bolt found endearing. Lately, he'd been smiling a lot more, as if he'd been taking charm lessons.

When Bolt walked in, Marie was laughing at something Turner had said, and he almost felt as if he was interrupting something. They both stopped speaking and turned his way, and Marie looked a bit sheepish.

'Andrea's gone to lie down,' he told them with a smile to show he hadn't seen or heard anything untoward.

He took the coffee cup from Marie and added a couple of sugars to it. There was another photo of Emma attached to the cupboard above the kettle, this time just a snapshot. In it she was flanked by her mother on one side and a lean, good-looking guy with unkempt brown hair on the other. They looked like a typical family. It made Bolt feel slightly jealous, although he wasn't a hundred per cent sure why.

'Do you think the husband's involved, sir?' asked Turner, seeing Bolt looking at the photo.

'Part of me says definitely,' he answered quietly, aware that he had to be careful what he said in front of Marie, who wasn't officially part of this inquiry, 'because it would explain how the kidnappers knew Emma's movements. But the other part says that if he is, why on earth did he then disappear? Surely he'd have known it would only arouse suspicion. It'd be far better to let the kidnappers know when and where to make the snatch, then act completely innocent. Even if we suspected him, there'd be nothing we could do about it.'

'That's what I was thinking,' said Turner. 'It's all wrong somehow, isn't it?'

Bolt was about to tell him not to speculate too much out loud when he heard a rapid set of footfalls on the stairs, and Andrea came rushing into the room dressed in a full-length dressing gown, her mobile phone in her right hand.

'They've called.'

'When? Just now?'

'Yes. On the mobile.'

'What did they say?'

'He asked if I was getting the money together for tomorrow night. I said I was, and he told me to turn my computer on and check my emails.'

She took a deep breath, and Bolt could tell she was using all her strength to hold things together.

'They said they've sent me a warning.'

Fifteen

While Andrea fetched her laptop and turned it on, Matt Turner called in to HQ and asked them to run an urgent trace on the last number to call Andrea's mobile. 'They'll get back to us in five,' he said as he and Bolt followed Andrea through the hallway and into a large, spacious study at the back of the house.

Andrea set the laptop down on a desk at the far end of the room which faced out on to the back lawn, and sat down to wait while it booted up. Bolt and Turner stood behind her while Marie Cohen remained further back, in the doorway. The desk itself was expensive mahogany and scrupulously tidy. There were two framed photos on it: one of Emma as a toddler, dressed in a pink swimming costume and playing with a hosepipe, laughing at the camera; another more recent one of mother and daughter smiling.

'What do you think they mean by sending me a warning?' asked Andrea, turning round in her seat and looking up at Bolt.

'Let's just see,' he said calmly.

'That's easy for you to say, isn't it?' she snapped, turning back and double-clicking on her internet icon.

Bolt didn't answer. The problem was that he wasn't very good around victims of crime. He never had been. He much preferred the process of detective work, of breaking up criminal enterprises. Of identifying targets and hitting them. He might have suffered his own private tragedy but the fact remained that he wasn't trained for this, and being intimately acquainted with this particular victim wasn't helping either. He looked over at Marie Cohen, wondering if she was going to intervene with soothing words, but she remained silent, motioning him just to leave it.

Andrea's homepage appeared on the screen and she clicked on her emails. There were a dozen or so unread messages but it was the one at the top, sent from a numbered hotmail account, which was the one they wanted. The word WARNING was written in block capitals in the subject column, and there was an mpeg attachment.

Without speaking, Andrea opened it. The message said simply WATCH THE FILM.

'Oh God,' she whispered.

Bolt tensed. 'Maybe it's best if we watch it first, Andrea,' he told her, putting a reassuring hand on her shoulder. He didn't add 'just in case', but he knew he might as well have done.

She took another deep breath. 'No. She's my daughter. I've got to watch it.'

'It might not be a good idea, Andrea,' said Marie, moving into the study.

'I am going to watch it. End of story.' Her words were loud and decisive, cutting across the room.

She clicked on the mpeg file and waited the twenty seconds while it downloaded. The room was silent, with just the peaceful sound of birdsong coming from outside. With trembling fingers, Andrea pressed play.

Immediately the screen was filled with the top half of a person sitting against a wall in a darkened room lit by a bulb somewhere off camera. The quality of the recording was very good, and Bolt knew that he was looking at Emma even though she had a black hood over her head. The arms beneath the black T-shirt she was wearing were pale and skinny – kid's arms.

Andrea let out an audible gasp.

For two or three seconds Emma sat there, absolutely still, then very slowly she lifted a copy of *The Times* until it was in full view. The main headline was about the run on the Northern Rock bank. The camera panned forward until it was fixed on the date in the top right-hand corner. It was today's.

'See, Andrea, she's alive,' said Bolt, trying to sound positive. 'And it's in their interests to keep her that way.'

Andrea didn't reply, but her shoulders were shaking, and he realized she was crying silently as she stared at the screen.

The camera panned back so that Emma's upper body filled the screen again, and then the camera suddenly jerked as the cameraman reached forward with a gloved hand and roughly removed the hood, revealing the pretty teenage girl with the dark blonde hair and blue eyes whose photo was all over Andrea's house.

Her face was terrified and wet with tears as she stared uncertainly at the cameraman. He appeared to give her some sort of off-camera prompt because she started to speak slowly and carefully, her voice shaking with fear. 'Mum, they say that if you get the money, they'll let me go tomorrow night.' There was a pause again while she appeared to get a second prompt. 'But Mum . . . they said that if you don't pay, or you call the police . . . they said they'd hurt me really bad.' As she spoke these last words, the tears began streaming down her face again.

Then she gave a short, tight gasp. She was

staring at something they couldn't see, her eyes widening.

'Oh God, Emma,' whispered Andrea, her own voice cracking under the strain. 'My darling.'

And then they all saw it. The long, gleaming blade of a hunting knife, held in a black-gloved hand, moving slowly across the screen from right to left, mocking the viewers with its presence. It belonged to the cameraman. His camera shook very slightly as he moved it. The knife then changed direction as he leaned forward, pointing the tip of the blade at Emma's neck. His arm beyond the glove was covered by a black sweater. There was no flesh showing, nothing that might even hint at a possible ID.

A torturous wail came from Andrea. 'No, Jesus, no. Please. Don't hurt her.'

Bolt felt his mouth go parchment dry. This was total sadism, something that, thank God, was rare. In twenty years of law enforcement he'd only seen something similar once before when he'd been forced to watch an old amateur videotape showing the sexual abuse and torture of a three-year-old child by her father. That was a long time ago now, yet he could still remember every single moment of it. It was etched on his brain, like a hideous tattoo, for ever. This was similar, and in a way all the more painful in that the victim's mother was someone he'd once cared so much for.

'Let's turn it off, Andrea,' he said. 'We can watch it again in a minute.'

She shook her head angrily. 'No. I've got to see. I've got to.'

On the film, Emma pushed her body back into the wall, craning her head away from the blade, her pale blue eyes never leaving it.

Andrea's moaning grew louder. It stopped abruptly when the point touched Emma's neck. Ever so gently.

No one moved a millimetre. It was as if they'd been frozen to the spot, staring hypnotized at the screen. Waiting.

The blade traced a slow path up the contours of Emma's jawline and on to her cheek, brushing the pale skin but not breaking it, stopping at the fold of skin just below her left eye. Half a centimetre more and it would be caressing the eyeball.

Bolt steeled himself for what might be coming next. He prided himself on being a hard man, able to take some of the worst experiences the world had to offer, but this was tearing him up inside, and he wondered how many times this scene would be revisiting his dreams in the coming months.

The knife jerked suddenly to the side, moving like a flash. Disappeared from view.

Emma cried out. Andrea gasped. Bolt stopped breathing.

The camera panned inwards. Emma's face filled the screen. Terrified, but unmarked. Then it panned slowly outwards as Emma crumpled into a fetal position on the bed she'd been sitting on, dropping the newspaper to the floor. She was wearing handcuffs, and there was a chain attached to her ankle by a metal loop.

Something dark rose up from the bottom of the screen, blocking out everything else, and the camera took several seconds to focus on it. It was a piece of paper. Five words were written on it in bold capitals: NO POLICE OR SHE DIES. The camera stayed on it for a full three seconds. Then abruptly the film ended and the screen returned to Andrea's homepage.

For a long moment, no one spoke. Bolt was just about to open his mouth to tell Andrea to be strong, that this was just a method for the kidnappers to cow her into submission so that she'd get them the next tranche of the ransom money – even though he wasn't at all sure he still believed it – when in one ferocious movement Andrea swept the laptop off the table, sending it crashing to the floor, and jumped to her feet. She grabbed the photo of Emma as a toddler from the desk and hugged it to her chest. Pushing Turner out of her way, she swung round to face Bolt, her tear-stained face a twisting combination of torment and rage.

'They're going to kill her, aren't they? That's it. They're going to kill her.'

Bolt put a hand on her arm, trying to calm her. 'No, Andrea, they won't. They're far better off keeping her alive.'

'They told me not to involve the police, and now look at you all here.' She yanked herself free and swept an arm dismissively round the room. 'Standing around while my daughter's tortured by these bastards. Oh God. If they kill her . . . if they kill her, it's all going to be my fault!'

'You can't think like that, Andrea,' said Bolt, but she was no longer listening. She strode rapidly past them and out the door, leaving behind only grim silence.

Sixteen

Marie went after Andrea, and Bolt heard them both going up the stairs, Andrea shouting at Marie to leave her alone. He stood staring at the upended laptop, wondering how Andrea was ever going to recover from this. Finally he broke his reverie and turned away.

Turner was speaking into the phone. When he hung up a few seconds later, Bolt asked him if they'd got a trace.

'He called from a mobile on a back street in the N18 postcode. But he switched off straight away so we can't follow him.'

'So he knows what we can do with mobile phones.'

'Looks that way, doesn't it?'

'Any chance of getting anything from the email he sent?'

'We won't get much out of the email address

172

itself. Anyone can set up a hotmail account anonymously. But we should be able to locate the computer he sent it from. It might take some time.'

'Get the team on to it straight away. We've just got to hope this guy makes a mistake.'

'He hasn't made any so far.'

Bolt might have liked Turner, but his occasional habit of accentuating the negatives could grate at times. Especially times like this. 'Just do it,' he said, turning away and pulling out his own mobile. 'And get the local cops down the street where the call was made from, just in case he's still there.'

He unlocked the French windows in the living room and went out into the back garden, dialling his boss's number. When Big Barry answered, he explained to him what the kidnappers had done. 'These guys are good, sir. They know exactly which buttons to press. But there's something else too. The way they're tormenting her – this is personal. I'm sure of it. Someone really wants Andrea Devern to suffer.'

'Well, let's hope you're right, because that might help lead us to them. The woman can't have that many enemies. In the meantime, though, I've had authorization for us to set up a sting. Looks like the ladies and gents upstairs agreed with you about negotiation. It's pointless with people as ruthless as this.'

'It's definitely the right move. This way we'll be the ones in control.'

'We'll use bundles of counterfeit notes fitted with trackers.'

'These people are professionals, sir. They're going to spot something like that.'

'We'll be right on their tails. By the time they realize the notes are fake it'll be too late and they'll be in custody.'

Bolt wasn't convinced. 'But it also might be too late for Emma. If they pick up the money, then check the notes in the car, see that they're not real, they'll know we're involved. In that case, they might never lead us to her.'

'Come on, old mate, how am I going to get authorization to use half a million pounds of real money? And where am I going to get it from? The Christmas kitty? Think about it.'

'You said we're not going to lose them.'

'We're not.'

'So we can afford to use the real thing, surely?' Bolt thought of the photo of Emma as a toddler, playing with the hosepipe in her pink swimming costume. 'This is a young girl's life we're talking about.'

'Let's not get sentimental, Mike.'

'I'm not. But if we use fake money and it all goes wrong, it's not going to look good for any of us, is it? That we thought the money was more important than our kidnap victim.' He resisted adding 'heads will roll', but the point was a valid one. Bolt was appealing to Barry's innate arse-covering instincts, knowing that there lay his greatest chance of success.

And it seemed to be working. 'I'll talk to them upstairs, but I can't see them going for it.' Barry sighed. 'Look, this whole operation needs to be well planned, so I want you back here so we can discuss the details. As soon as poss. Keep Turner and the liaison there with Mrs Devern, just in case they make contact again.'

Bolt hung up, and looked at his watch. It was ten past one. His stomach was growling and he realized that he hadn't eaten a thing all day. He'd grab some lunch on the way back. He took a deep breath. One way or another, he was going to get these bastards. And get Emma back for Andrea as well. The hunt was on now, and on the ground at least, he was the one in charge. This was the part of the job he loved, when the battle lines were drawn and it was all about you and them. Pushing the images of the video aside, he felt a renewed sense of determination.

He became aware of a presence behind him. It was Turner, looking vaguely sheepish.

'Everything all right, Matt?'

'Mrs Devern wants a word with you upstairs. Alone. She doesn't want to talk to Marie.' There was a vague disapproval in his tone.

'OK, thanks.'

Bolt walked back into the house through the French windows. Marie was standing at the bottom of the stairs, looking concerned.

'She's in the first room on the left,' she said wearily.

Bolt smiled, feeling sorry for her. 'Thanks. I don't see there's much I'm going to be able to do either, but I'll give it a try.'

Andrea was in the master bedroom, sitting in a white leather armchair and staring out of the bay window, a cigarette in her hand. She turned as he came inside and shut the door behind him. Her face was set hard, the tears wiped away now.

'You've got to get her back, Mike.' She spoke the words firmly.

'And we're doing absolutely everything we can to bring that about. I know how hard it must be, but you've got to try to sit tight and be patient.'

'Did you never want children, Mike?'

She watched him closely, waiting for an answer, the cigarette burning, forgotten, in her hand. He sighed, wondering how he was going to extricate himself from this conversation.

'The opportunity never arose. Maybe one day.'

'Have you ever been married?'

'I was. Once.'

'What happened?'

'She died. In a car crash. Five years ago.'

Five years. It felt like such a long time, yet in truth it had gone fast. He could still picture Mikaela perfectly, could still hear her voice. But she was someone he didn't like to be reminded of by other people. He liked to keep his thoughts and memories of her to himself.

'I'm sorry,' she said, sounding like she meant it.

'It's OK.'

Silence. He sensed there was something she wanted to add, so he waited for it.

And it came.

'Listen, Mike, I don't know how to say this, but . . .'

She noticed the cigarette then, and flicked the ash into an ashtray on the windowsill before it spilled into her lap.

'What is it, Andrea?'

'I told you about Jimmy Galante, didn't I? About the reason I involved him.'

'Because you needed his help.'

'Yes, and because he was her father as well.'

'That's right.'

'The thing is, I was lying.'

Bolt tensed. 'What do you mean?'

'I mean I was lying when I told Jimmy he was the father. He wasn't.'

She looked him squarely in the eye. 'You are.'

Seventeen

One of Mike Bolt's problems in his younger days
was an inability to say no. He should never have
carried on the affair with Andrea Devern after that
first night of passion in the Bloomsbury hotel. She
was a married woman, with a wealthy husband
who looked after her, and he was an impetuous
twenty-four-year-old cop, so it was always going
to end in tears. But Bolt had somehow convinced
himself that this didn't really matter. He was just
going to see how things went and not get too
involved.

But he had got involved, and in the eight weeks
the affair had lasted he'd found himself driven
ever deeper into Andrea's web. In the beginning
he'd been in control, but that control had evaporated rapidly as he'd become more and more
obsessed with her. He was driven to distraction by
the difficulties in getting hold of her, and in

meeting up for their illicit liaisons. In those eight weeks they slept together on only six occasions, and then suddenly it was all over. Just like that. Not with a whimper either, but with a bang he'd never forget.

But could he really have fathered her child? The thought nagged at him ferociously as he drove back to HQ. But the dates fit. Andrea had convinced him of that back at the house. 'Our daughter's birthday's the second of April,' she'd said. 'We were seeing each other in June and July.'

Our daughter. His daughter. She could be wrong, of course. As he'd found out afterwards, she was also seeing Jimmy Galante at the time. And she was married too, although she'd always claimed that her husband, Billy Devern, was impotent, which was why he'd allowed her to take lovers. Whether that was true or not was still largely immaterial, because the dates fitted. Check them, Andrea had said, and he had, going back in his head to those giddy days, and the truth shouted at him so loudly he could barely hear anything else. It was possible Emma Devern wasn't his child, but there was a damn good chance that she was.

On the seat next to him were photographs of Emma and Pat Phelan which he was taking back to the incident room. Phelan's was face up, but Emma's was face down. He couldn't bear to look at her. Couldn't bear to think that she might be his flesh and blood, and the first he'd known about it was when he'd been put in charge of investigating her kidnapping.

He thought of Mikaela, the woman he'd met a couple of years after Andrea, who'd gone on to be his wife. Mikaela had always wanted children. A boy and a girl, she'd always said. Children, and the big, rambling house with a nice garden. It was Bolt who'd always held back. He'd feared the immense commitment required; with the long hours he worked, he didn't think he could provide the necessary support. But eventually, after seven years together, he'd reluctantly agreed to Mikaela's increasingly persistent requests that they should start trying for a baby.

She was two months pregnant when the car he was driving left the road and smashed into an oak tree, crunching it into a shape that made it unrecognizable. He'd spent six weeks in hospital and now carried three small scars on his face as a permanent reminder of that night. Mikaela's life support system was turned off three days later, without her ever regaining consciousness. Bolt had been too ill to leave his bed to say goodbye. He hadn't even been told of the decision, made by her parents, until almost two days later because it was thought the news would be so traumatic it would worsen his condition.

And all that time – all the time he'd ever been with Mikaela, and through those long hard years since – he might already have had a child. A child growing up whom he'd never seen, and knew absolutely nothing about.

His fingers tightened on the steering wheel and he clenched his jaw, feeling a sudden burst of furious resentment towards Andrea. If he was the father, why had she said nothing to him all these years? And if he wasn't, how could she manipulate him like this?

He pulled over to the side of the road before the fury got the better of him, and took some long, deep breaths, trying to calm himself down. But it was hard. Incredibly hard. That morning he'd been a reasonably happy man with a new girl-friend, coasting towards his fortieth birthday – now only a few months away – having got used to the idea that he was probably never going to have children. And now he'd been told not only that he might have one, but that her life was in terrible danger, and he was the one responsible for getting her back safely.

He sat there for a full minute, his heart thumping so loudly it felt like the only thing he could hear. Then he picked up the photo of Emma – blonde, smiling, fourteen years old, in her school uniform – and stared at it, searching for resem-blances. Was she his? There were similarities, there were differences. He thought of the man – the men – holding her. The men who might not want to return her alive. The men they were now going to try to set up. For the first time, he truly imagined what could happen if their plan went wrong, and his stomach lurched violently. The girl who could be his only child would die.

He put down Emma's photo, but he kept it face up so that he could see the girl he had to rescue. It was time to take responsibility and think straight. Technically, the position hadn't changed; it was just that the stakes had now become infinitely higher.

He took a final deep breath, flicked on the indicator, and pulled out into the traffic.

Part Three

Part Three

Eighteen

It was half past two on Friday afternoon when SG4 Tina Boyd stopped outside the Lively Lounge Club and Casino, a turd-coloured slab of a building straight out of the 1960s school of bland architecture, which sat at the Colindale end of the Edgware Road, about three miles and a thousand years as the crow flies from the leafy Hampstead suburb where Pat Phelan now lived. Looking at it made her feel mildly pleased that gambling wasn't one of her vices. It wasn't that she wasn't interested. She just didn't dare place a bet, even on something like the Grand National, because she knew if she got a bit of beginner's luck and started winning, she'd probably never stop. Tina had an addictive personality. It was part of her genetic make-up. All through her early and mid-teens she'd resisted the peer pressure to start smoking, then at seventeen she'd tried her first cigarette at a party and she'd been putting away twenty a day ever since, with every attempt to stop ending in rapid failure.

She wondered if Phelan was the same. Because he definitely had a gambling problem, and the Lively Lounge Club and Casino was where he sank the lion's share of the money he spent on his betting. And he spent a lot. Tina's team had got hold of copies of the previous year's statements for the five credit cards and one debit card held in his name, and during that period his outgoings amounted to a grand total of £87,288.36 – and this from a man with no actual income that they could find, other than a £1,500-a-month standing order paid into his personal bank account from Andrea's own account, which was held at a separate bank. There'd been a number of further payments into his account over the course of the year, more than twenty-five grand's worth in all, but they were sporadic which meant they almost certainly represented winnings. Even with his wife's £160,000-a-year salary it was an unsustainable amount, and already Phelan's credit limit was maxed out on every one of the credit cards, while he was currently overdrawn at the bank by more than six thousand.

It wasn't that someone getting himself into this situation was all that uncommon. As Big Barry had pointed out earlier that morning, people got themselves into serious debt the whole time. What was interesting about Pat Phelan's finances from a SOCA point of view was that his spending had tailed off dramatically in the last two months, by more than 90 per cent, and in the same period there'd been no deposits of winnings in his bank account. Either he'd turned over a new leaf or, in Tina's opinion far more likely, he was funding his habit from a different source. Since the financial statements all pointed to the Lively Lounge as the venue of choice for his gambling, Tina had decided that it was as good a place as any to start digging into Phelan's background. She could have left it to one of the more junior members of the team but, like a lot of detectives, she liked to get out and about; and if she was entirely honest with herself, she wasn't much of a delegator, preferring to rely on her own ability to get things done.

The needs of the compulsive gambler tend to be of the twenty-four-hour variety, and the club was open. Tina went through the tinted double doors and into the darkened lobby. A blonde girl was at the reception desk talking to an older woman with hair extensions and far too much make-up. The girl smiled politely as Tina approached, wishing her a good afternoon in a Polish accent. Her colleague, meanwhile, said nothing but gave her a more suspicious look, clocking immediately that she was police, even though Tina wasn't wearing a uniform and always made a conscious effort never to give off that aura. Some people simply have a nose for spotting coppers, and they're usually the ones who have the most to fear from them.

Tina smiled at the girl. 'Good afternoon, my name's Tina Boyd from the Serious and Organized Crime Agency.' She held up her warrant card. 'I'd like to speak to the owner, please.'

'I'll deal with this, Barbara,' said the older woman in a deep voice that was midway between a bear and Demi Moore. 'The owners aren't here. They're not based in this country.' Her expression seemed to add, so what the hell are you going to do about that? 'Is there anything I can help with?'

'That depends. Are you the most senior person in the building at the moment?'

There was a moment's hesitation that told Tina the answer was no.

'Well, Mr McMahon's here, but—'

'And what's his position?'

'He's the manager, but I think he's—'

'Well, I'll see him then, thank you.'

'He's busy, Miss whatever-your-name-was,' the woman growled.

Tina wasn't deterred. 'That makes two of us. Can you take me to him, please?'

'I'll call up and see if he's available.'

She picked up a phone behind the desk,

scowling at Tina, who stared back at her impassively, amazed why some people always had to put up a token resistance to the police before they acquiesced, even though the end result was inevitable.

The woman hung up. 'OK, he can see you now.'

Tina followed her through the main gambling area, a big, windowless place with all the charm of an aircraft hangar. Only a handful of the gaming tables were in use, the clientele mainly quiet Chinese men wearing inscrutable expressions as they placed their bets. None of them looked up as Tina and her guide passed by in silence.

Mr McMahon's office was at the far end of the building, up a flight of stairs and along a short corridor. The woman knocked on his door and moved out of the way for Tina to go in, giving her a last glare of defiance as she did so.

'The Serious and Organized Crime Agency,' said the man standing behind the desk as Tina shut the door behind her. 'I've not had any dealings with them. Malcolm McMahon,' he said, putting out a hand. 'Pleased to meet you, Miss . . .'

'Boyd. Tina Boyd.'

They shook hands, and Tina took the seat on her side of the desk.

Malcolm McMahon was a big man who looked like he enjoyed a drink. He was good-looking in a brutish sort of way, with slicked-back grey hair fashioned into a widow's peak as sharp as an arrowhead, and a straight one-inch scar edging away from his top lip. He was dressed in a badly ironed shirt and unfashionable striped tie, while his casino clothes – black suit and dress shirt – were hanging up on one wall, next to a bank of eight small screens that showed the gaming area from various angles.

'I hear you SOCA people aren't even police any more,' he said with a smile. 'You're special agents or something. So, what do I call you?'

'Miss Boyd'll do fine.'

He nodded slowly, accepting this. 'Well, Miss Boyd, we run a tight ship here, and we don't tolerate anything illegal, so I don't know how we came to the attention of SOCA. Do you mind if I check your ID again? Just to make sure you are who you say you are. It's amazing how many charlatans there are these days.'

'Sure.'

Tina produced the warrant card from the back pocket of her jeans and handed it to him, noticing the nicotine stains on his thick, stubby fingers as he took it. He examined it carefully before thanking her and handing it back.

'It's about one of your customers.'

'I don't like talking about our customers, Miss Boyd. They value their privacy, and so do we.'

'This is a very serious case, Mr McMahon. If

you want me to get official and bring officers down here to interview all your staff, I can. But I'm also prepared to talk off the record, and I can guarantee that anything you tell me will be treated in the strictest confidence.'

'So, you want me to grass up one of my paying punters?' he asked evenly.

Now it was her turn to smile. 'No, I want you to help him. His name's Patrick Phelan, and I know he spends a lot of money in your establishment, and has done so for a long time.' McMahon didn't say anything, so she continued. 'Mr Phelan's gone missing, and we're extremely concerned about his welfare.'

'I don't see how I can help.'

'But you know him?'

McMahon sighed and sat back in his seat. 'Yeah, I know him. He's been coming here for a while. Nice bloke, friendly enough. Not the sort to piss people off.'

'When was the last time you saw him?'

He drummed his fingers on the desk. 'Last week some time. I can't remember for sure, but I definitely haven't seen him this week, and I don't think he's been in. I could check for you.'

'No, it's fine. Who does he usually come in with?'

'Various people. The occasional girl, sometimes with a couple of mates. Sometimes alone.' He shrugged. 'I didn't really know any of them.'

Tina reached into her jeans pocket and pulled out a pack of Silk Cut. 'Do you mind if I smoke?' She knew from the way McMahon wasn't settling that he was itching for a cigarette, and from the stale smell in the room it was obvious he usually puffed away in here.

He grinned, and leaned down behind the desk. When his hand re-emerged, it was holding a huge half-full ashtray.

'Didn't realize you were a smoker,' he said. 'Now that it's against the law to have a fag in your own office, I thought I'd best be careful when you came in.'

'That's one law I'm happy to break,' she said, offering him a cigarette.

He took it, and she lit for both of them. A rapport had been struck based on their shared identity as social outcasts, just as Tina had hoped. It was amazing what you could do with a rapport.

'According to his bank statements, Mr Phelan was a big spender, and it didn't look like he was very successful.'

'He wasn't. He'd have a few drinks and he'd start getting reckless. Sometimes it worked – you know, who dares wins and all that – but most of the time it didn't.'

Tina took a drag on her cigarette. 'The thing is, the statements also show that his spending plummeted in the last couple of months, but it sounds like he was still coming here.' She paused. 'Any idea where he might have been getting his money from?'

'We've got credit lines we can extend to valued customers. Pat's a valued customer.'

'But you weren't extending credit to him for two months solid, were you?'

He shook his head. 'No, we weren't. We stopped a few weeks back. He still owes us more than three grand. He asked the other week for more time to pay. He told me he had what he called an alternative means of income. I wasn't happy. I like Pat, but this is business.'

Tina kept her interest in check. 'Did he give you any idea what this alternative means of income was?'

'Nah. He just promised me it was kosher.'

'Was he borrowing money from any other sources, as far as you know?'

This time, McMahon's silence didn't sit naturally. He looked evasive.

'Remember, Mr McMahon, this talk's purely off the record. If you know anything, I can guarantee it won't get back to you.'

McMahon continued to sit there smoking. Tina didn't push things. She waited.

'Look,' he said at last, 'I like Pat. He's a nice bloke. I wouldn't want to think anything bad's happened to him. But if it has, I'd want whoever's involved to suffer. You know what I mean?'

'Sure.'

'This is definitely, definitely off the record, right?'

Tina nodded, realizing something significant was coming.

'Pat doesn't just owe us. He also owes someone you really don't want to be in hock to. Man by the name of Leon Daroyce.'

'I don't know him,' she said, making no attempt to write the name down. Producing a notebook might give this talk an official air and spook him, and she didn't want that. She'd remember the name easy enough.

'He's a loan shark, and a big player round these parts,' McMahon continued. 'I think a few of our punters have used his services, but you've got to be pretty desperate. The rates he charges are high and, like I said, he really ain't a nice bloke.'

'Have you got any idea how much Phelan owes him?'

He shook his head. 'Pat never told me about Daroyce. I just heard rumours. It was one of the reasons I cut the credit lines to him. I was worried we wouldn't get paid.'

Tina was going to have to find out as much as she could about Leon Daroyce and how much Phelan was in the can to him. If Daroyce was such a brutal operator – and with a man like McMahon, clearly no stranger to violence himself, saying it then she was inclined to believe he must be – it was also possible that Pat Phelan had gone to extraordinary lengths to get the money to pay him. Maybe even resorting to the kidnap of his stepdaughter.

'I think that's everything, Mr McMahon,' she said, standing up. 'Thanks for your time, and for being so candid with me.'

He stubbed out his cigarette. 'I'm trusting you, Miss Boyd. If word gets out that I pointed you in Leon Daroyce's direction, things ain't going to look good for me.'

'I keep my word.'

'Yeah,' he said, watching her carefully. 'You look like you do.' He lit another cigarette, blew out some smoke. 'A word of advice. Be careful. Leon Daroyce tends to take things personal.'

Tina opened the door, gave him a cool smile. 'Don't worry about me, Mr McMahon, I'm always careful.'

Nineteen

There was one reason above any other why Tina Boyd was always careful. She attracted trouble. It hadn't always been like that. She'd had a happy middle-class upbringing in the country, the product of two parents who appeared to love each other, and certainly loved her. She'd gone to private school, then to university, studied English and Psychology, did her time on the well-worn backpacking trail. And then, while all her friends took up their office jobs, she'd joined the police. It hadn't been on a whim – well, not entirely anyway. She'd never fancied office work, and she'd always had an inquisitive mind. She was interested in what made people tick. Maybe she should have been a psychiatrist, but somehow she thought she'd learn more about the human condition as a cop. And she had, too, although she wasn't at all sure that it had been a positive development.

For the first few years of her police career things had been remarkably trouble-free. She'd spent two years in uniform – and was one of the few officers in her station who was never assaulted once – before joining Islington CID as a detective constable. As a graduate, she was on the fast track. A senior position looked inevitable, and sooner rather than later.

But then things had started to go wrong. First, she was taken hostage by a suspect she'd been investigating and was hit in the crossfire when he was shot dead by armed CO19 officers. The wound she suffered was comparatively light, and she was back at work within six weeks, to much fanfare and an immediate promotion to detective sergeant. They'd even put her on the cover of one of the issues of *Police Review* shortly afterwards. It should have made her happy, but she knew she didn't deserve the praise. She'd made a mistake which had got her into the position of being shot in the first place, and it looked like she was being rewarded for that. If she was honest with herself – something that she was constantly – then this was the part of the whole incident that had scarred her the most. Tina was a perfectionist, and when it came down to it she'd been found wanting.

Barely six months later, trouble came calling again, except this time it was with a vengeance. A detective she'd been working with closely was murdered while on a case they were both involved in, followed only weeks later by the apparent suicide of her long-term lover, also a police officer, which turned out to be a murder indirectly related to the same case. Suddenly, from being the next big thing, she'd become tainted by association, the kind of cop everyone wants to avoid in case something should happen to them. Someone had even nicknamed her the Black Widow, and the name had stuck.

She never saw the people who'd killed the two men so close to her brought to justice. It was possible that not all of them had been. This knowledge had scarred her too, and she'd resigned from the force, hit the rails, and become very depressed. She might never have recovered – at one point, things had genuinely felt that bad – but then she'd met Mike Bolt, who was then working for the National Crime Squad, and he must have seen something in her because he persuaded her to join his team, and to move across with them when the NCS became SOCA.

She appreciated what he'd done for her, and she worked hard at her job to demonstrate this. Sometimes she thought Bolt was attracted to her, occasionally even that this was the reason he'd hired her in the first place, and consequently she tended to keep her distance from him in the workplace. He was a good-looking guy, there was no question about that. Tall, broad-shouldered, with blond hair only just beginning to fleck with grey, and piercing blue eyes that were so striking she'd thought at first (wrongly) that he wore contact lenses. She almost certainly would have gone for him at one time, but things were different for her now. She'd had her fingers burned far too badly, and the experience had made her more cautious. She'd become a loner, someone who kept herself to herself both inside and outside a work environment, and she knew that some of the team resented her for it, putting her manner down to a brusqueness that wasn't there.

She'd been a fun girl once. Had got drunk, got laid, travelled the world. Smoked dope so strong in northern Thailand she'd hallucinated. Swum, awestruck, with dolphins on the Great Barrier Reef. Had a real life. She didn't really have one any more, and there were times – more often than she'd like – when she was filled with an angry regret over the path she'd chosen, and its bitter consequences, wondering how things might have turned out if she'd taken the office job.

But today wasn't one of those times. She was actually feeling good as she walked along Colindale Avenue in the direction of the Underground, the autumn sun warming the back of her neck. She was on her way back to the Glasshouse and had already called ahead and told

Bolt about Pat Phelan's alleged debt problems, as well as asking him to check out anything they had on Leon Daroyce.

Bolt had seemed pleased with the lead – which he should have been, because it provided them with a motive for the kidnap – but he'd also sounded under strain, which wasn't like him. Mike Bolt was generally calm and level-headed, the type of guy who was able to withstand pressure. It was one of the reasons she enjoyed working with him. She felt she could trust his leadership.

'Hey lady, how you doin'?'

The words, delivered in a deep baritone with a faux American twang, snapped her straight out of her thoughts. She turned to see a silver Merc pull up beside her. The man addressing her through the open window was a well-built, smooth-headed black man in his thirties, wearing shades and an expensive-looking suit.

'I'm not buying, I'm not available, and I'm not interested. So piss off.' She looked away and kept walking, but the car kept pace with her.

Tina didn't take kindly to being accosted in the street by strangers. It happened now and again. This was London, after all. She tended to ignore them, and usually they went away, but it didn't look like this guy was going to. She was a hundred metres from the Tube station now, the irony of the fact that she was only spitting distance from Hendon Police College not lost on her. God knows why this guy was picking on her, but if he decided to jump out of the car and cut up rough, then he'd get a lot more than he bargained for.

She heard the guy chuckle. 'You got some spirit, lady. I like that. A friend of mine would like to speak to you. I hear you might want to speak to him too.'

She stopped, turned his way, saw a white guy with a tight T-shirt and big biceps beyond him in the driver's seat.

'Is that right?' she said. 'And who's your friend?'

'His name's Leon, but to you he's Mr Daroyce.'

Tina cursed to herself. How the hell had he found out about her this fast? Then she thought of that brassy bitch who'd taken her up to McMahon's office, and it came to her. She must have been listening at the door. And there she'd been, saying how careful she always was. *Not careful enough, darling*.

'Thanks for the offer, but I have a rule never to get into cars with strangers.'

'Does it still count if we know you, Tina Boyd?' The man gave her a predatory smile as he made a great show of emphasizing the pronunciation of those last two words.

The use of her name made Tina feel naked and exposed. 'No, it doesn't,' she answered, beginning to turn away.

'If you don't come now, we might have to come and find you, Tina Boyd.' His voice had hardened now, laced with threat.

She turned back. 'What does your friend want?'

'He just wants to talk.' He shrugged his powerful shoulders. 'That's it. Nothing more. I think he might have some information for you.'

He leaned behind him and opened the back door of the Mercedes for her.

Tina made a quick calculation. If they knew her name, they knew she was a SOCA agent. That meant it was unlikely they were going to risk hurting her. Especially when their car, and possibly even their faces, would already have been picked up somewhere on CCTV. And when it came down to it, there was no reason for them to hurt her anyway. She didn't owe Daroyce money, had in fact never met him, which meant the guy in front of her was almost certainly telling the truth.

Those were the pros. There was only one con, but it was a big one. What if she was wrong?

It was a big decision, but in the end – although she'd never admit it to herself – part of the reason Tina Boyd attracted trouble was that she was always prepared to put herself in situations where encountering it was inevitable. And this was one of them. Taking a long look round so that the people walking up and down the street might remember her face if it came to it, she got inside the Merc and shut the door.

'Let's go then,' she said, lighting a cigarette.

Twenty

They drove through back streets heading west in the direction of Queensbury. Tina tried to make conversation, knowing how important it was to create a rapport with the black guy, who was clearly the senior of the two. But now she was in the car, both men were worryingly reticent. The white guy said nothing at all, his friend either answering her questions with an uninterested yes and no or ignoring them altogether.

The journey didn't last long, ten minutes at most, before they pulled into a dingy dead-end road lined with brand-new low-rise council flats on one side and a pair of grim-looking tower blocks on the other. The car pulled into a parking space in front of the first of the blocks, next to an overflowing bright orange wheelie bin that seemed to be attracting the flies. A gang of half a dozen kids on mountain bikes were messing about by a rusty climbing frame over to one side.

'Nice place,' said Tina, wrinkling her nose against the smell from the bin as she got out of the car.

'Mr Daroyce likes to stay close to his roots,' answered the black guy as they walked over to the front entrance.

Tina noticed the kids give him respectful looks as he passed, before passing more hostile eyes over her. *Jesus*, she thought. *What is it about me? I might as well be wearing a flashing blue light on my head.*

They went up to the tenth floor in a graffiti-strewn lift with black smoke stains running down two sides as if someone had tried to set it alight, travelling in silence with only the creaking of the cables for company. Tina was getting more and more nervous. She didn't much like going alone to isolated places with the kind of men your mother warned you about, particularly when she was unarmed and out of contact with her colleagues. She thought about trying to leave but had a strong feeling that they wouldn't let her.

As they emerged from the lift into a dingy corridor only partly illuminated by noisy over-head strip lighting, dark shadows flickering at the edges, she was reminded of something that had happened during her backpacking days. She'd been caught in a sudden storm while travelling by fishing boat between islands in southern Indonesia. Huge dark waves had reared up and crashed over the deck, sending the tiny boat spinning and lurching. The fishermen had looked terrified, their expressions terrifying Tina even more as she clung desperately to her seat, genuinely believing she was going to die. Then the friend she was travelling with leaned over and, with a grim smile on his face, had shouted above the noise, 'It's not much consolation now, but you're going to love telling this story one day!' And she had, too. They'd made it across, the storm had passed, and life had moved on. The moral being, things are never as bad as they seem.

She told herself she'd be out of there soon enough, life would move on, and she'd have a good laugh about it over a long gin and tonic, curled up on her sofa.

The flat they wanted was at the end of the corridor. She knew which one it was going to be straight away, because it looked like Fort Knox. The doorway was covered with an iron security grille, the door behind it reinforced with a series of home-cut steel plates. No fewer than five separate locks ran up one side, and attached to the doorframe was a tiny CCTV camera, its lens pointing out at head height through one of the gaps in the grille.

The black guy produced a set of keys and let

them in, a process that took the best part of a minute. The interior was cloyingly warm and smelled of dope as they made their way through a narrow hallway and into a dimly lit backroom which was furnished with just a table and two chairs facing each other on either side.

Sitting in one of the chairs, with his legs crossed and his back to them, was a short, well-built black man in a peach-coloured suit and fedora of the same colour. The fedora was set at a jaunty angle and had two small peacock feathers jutting from the rim, giving the man the overall appearance of a 1970s New York pimp. He didn't turn round as the black guy moved out of the way and Tina stepped inside, just motioned with a casual wave of a hand for her to take the vacant seat.

'I hear you been asking questions about Patrick Phelan,' said the man from beneath the fedora as she sat down opposite him. 'You a cop, yeah?'

His voice was softer than she'd been expecting, the accent local but with just a hint of something more exotic. As he lifted his head she could see that he was young, probably no more than late twenties, with a round boyish face and dark intelligent eyes. He was definitely not what she'd been expecting, and now that the two men who'd brought her here had disappeared into another room, she felt herself relax a little.

'Yes,' she answered, 'I'm a cop.' She wasn't

technically, she was an agent, but it was never worth explaining it like that since no one ever seemed to understand the difference. 'I work for the Serious and Organized Crime Agency. You must be Leon Daroyce.'

He touched a finger to his hat and half-smiled. 'That's me.'

'And yes, I have been asking questions about Patrick Phelan,' Tina continued. 'We're looking for him.'

Daroyce nodded slowly. 'So am I,' he said softly, hardly moving his lips as he spoke, so that his words came out almost as a hiss.

He leaned forward in his seat and crossed his hands on the table. They were small and surprisingly dainty considering his build, dwarfed by the gold sovereign rings on most of his fingers. He exhaled slowly through pursed lips and fixed her with a gaze that was almost hypnotic.

'Let me tell you something, Miss Boyd,' he hissed. 'I'm an entrepreneur, a small businessman. I lend money like a bank, except unlike a bank I don't ask hundreds of questions. I don't make my customers fill out a pile of forms. You know what someone once said? A banker's a man who lends you his umbrella when the sun's shining, then asks for it back as soon as it starts raining.'

'Mark Twain.'

He shrugged, uninterested. 'Well, I'm not like

that. I don't turn people away. All I ask is you pay me back the money you've borrowed, and the interest on it. That's it. I'm providing a service. And I provided a service to Pat Phelan. Except he seems to have welshed on the deal. He owes me thirty-five thousand pounds, Miss Boyd. And I need to get that money back.'

'I don't see how I can help.'

'Because you're looking for him. What is it that you people want to speak to him about?'

'We think he's involved in a fraud case,' she lied. If Daroyce and his friends were involved in the kidnapping then they'd know she wasn't telling the truth, but she was beginning to think that they couldn't be. Otherwise, why on earth would they have brought her here?

'That sounds like Phelan. The guy's a snake. Is he likely to get bail?'

'I don't know.'

'Listen, Miss Boyd, perhaps you and me can help each other. I need to get my money back from Pat Phelan, because if I let something like this go, then it's going to look very bad on me and my business. Do you understand what I'm saying?'

'I think so, yes.'

'Now, if you hear where he is, all you need to do is give me a call, let me and my people get there first, and I'll pay you ten grand in cash.' He reached inside his peach suit and produced a huge wad of used notes, putting it down on the table in front of her. 'Not bad for five minutes' work, is it?'

She looked at the money, wondered who'd suffered for him to get it, then back at Daroyce. 'I'll see what I can do.'

'No,' he said quietly, 'that's not good enough. I want you to say you'll do it.'

His tone was cold now.

Tina made another quick calculation. She had no intention of helping Daroyce, and she certainly couldn't take his money. However, it seemed prudent to say yes, just so she could get out of there.

'OK, I'll do it. If we locate him, of course. Have you got a number I can get you on?'

His half-smile returned. 'Sure.' He took a card from his pocket and handed it to her. It was blank except for a handwritten mobile number.

She put it in her pocket.

'I still don't understand why you need me, though. It looks like you've got eyes and ears all over the place. You certainly found out about me easily enough.'

'I've looked everywhere for Phelan, but he seems to have done a better job at disappearing than he ever did at gambling. He was supposed to give me a fifteen grand down payment last Sunday. He didn't turn up; neither did it. He asked for a few more days. I told him he had twenty-four hours. But he didn't come through again. So, I've been hunting for him. I know where he lives, but his car hasn't been there, and from what I hear, neither has he. But,' he added, regarding her almost playfully, 'I've got a little clue that you might be able to use.'

'What's that?' Tina sat forward, interested.

'The thing is, Miss Boyd, can I trust you?'

Tina met his gaze, held it firmly. 'Yes, you can trust me. If we find him, I'll let you know. What you do after that is your concern.'

Daroyce nodded, seeming to accept this. 'Phelan's got a girlfriend. Good-looking chick. A little bit old for my tastes, but she carries it well.'

'Are you sure it's not his wife?'

He shook his head. 'No, I know what his wife looks like. It's not her. She's been here, too. The girlfriend. She came with him to deliver a five grand down payment on the debt a couple of weeks ago. I don't know who she is, or where she lives, but they were definitely close, and I had the feeling that, you know, the five grand was her money.'

'Can you describe her?'

'I can do better than that. I can show you a picture.'

He leaned down behind the table and picked up an envelope which he handed her. There was a single photograph inside, a still from the security camera outside Daroyce's door. It showed the faces of a man and a woman, both of whom looked nervous. The man's face was in the foreground, and Tina recognized him as Pat Phelan. The picture quality wasn't fantastic and the woman's face appeared slightly grainy, but even so there was no mistaking who it was, since Tina had seen her picture on the website of Feminine Touch Health and Beauty Spas only hours before.

It was Isobel Wheeler. Andrea Devern's business partner.

Twenty-one

'Do you know her?'

'No, but I should be able to find out.'

Tina was a good liar. She knew how to wear a poker face.

'Good.'

Leon Daroyce smiled properly now, and Tina had to fight to maintain her poker face as she saw his teeth for the first time. There was enough gold in there to stock a small jewellery shop, but it wasn't that which grabbed her attention. It was the fact that every single one of them was filed to a razor-sharp point. Daroyce's mouth was a lethal weapon, those jaws easily capable of murder.

Seeing her reaction, he chuckled – a strange, high-pitched little sound that made her skin crawl. 'You like them, baby? The girls always get a little frightened at first, but when they see what I can do with them, they always come back for more.' He waggled his tongue at her, running it along the points of his fangs.

Tina needed to get out of there. The room suddenly felt hot and claustrophobic. She picked up the envelope, slipped the photo back inside, and stood up.

'Let me get on with things, then.'

'Haven't you forgotten something?' He motioned towards the wad of money.

'I can't take it now. I haven't done anything yet.'

'But you're going to, though. Aren't you?'

'If we find him, yes.'

'You look thirsty,' he said, changing the subject. 'Do you want a drink?'

Tina took a sharp breath. 'Thanks, but I need to get going.'

'Sit down there for a couple of seconds. I want to show you something. Go on,' he said, waving towards the seat, 'it won't take long.'

Reluctantly, she did as requested.

'What is it?'

'Power,' he whispered.

'Sorry?'

He mouthed the word again, then turned towards the door. 'Woman, bring me water!' he called out, and a few seconds later a skinny mixed-race girl, no more than eighteen, with unkempt hair, hurried into the room. She was dressed in a dirty white T-shirt and a black thong, and Tina noticed that there were bruises on her bare legs. Avoiding their eyes, the girl put a small bottle of Evian on the table in front of Daroyce and quickly turned to go, but his hand whipped out like a flailing cord and grabbed her wrist in a tight, visibly painful grip. The girl looked scared, but didn't say anything.

'You know what power is, Miss Boyd?' asked Daroyce, tightening his grip on the girl's wrist, making her wince. 'Power is when you're respected; when you're feared; when people will do anything you tell them. Let me show you what I mean.' He looked up at the girl with gleaming eyes. 'You're mine, aren't you, woman?'

'Yes,' she whispered.

'You're hurting her, Mr Daroyce. Why don't you let go of her arm?'

He ignored her, pulling the girl towards him.

'Now, get on your knees.'

The girl knelt down.

'You don't have to do this,' said Tina firmly, horrified by what might be about to take place. 'I believe you.'

Daroyce backhanded the girl across the face. Hard. The slap rebounded around the room. Tina flinched as the girl's head snapped sideways under the blow before quickly righting itself. She didn't cry out or make a sound. Instead, she remained kneeling, staring straight ahead, her jaw quivering as it tightened against the pain. The fear had gone from her eyes now, replaced by the submissiveness of the defeated.

Tina stood up and addressed the girl. 'I'm a police officer,' she said, pulling out her warrant card and showing it to her. 'You can leave with me now. You don't have to stay here.' She didn't add that the girl could also press charges if she wanted to; they could talk about that later, when they were in a safer location.

The girl said nothing, continued to stare straight ahead.

'Come on,' said Tina, putting out a hand. 'You can come with me now.'

Daroyce chuckled. 'Tell her to fuck off, woman.'

This time the girl looked at Tina. There was a red mark covering the entire left side of her face, several small cuts on the cheek where Daroyce's rings had made contact.

'Fuck off,' she said, without feeling or passion.

'Please. I can take you home.'

But Tina knew it was no use. Even the girl's eyes were blank.

Daroyce's smile grew wider, the teeth showing, as he saw Tina's frustration. Then it disappeared altogether. 'Get out, woman!' he snapped, and immediately the girl got to her feet and hurried out of the door.

Tina shoved the warrant card back in her

pocket. 'I'm leaving, and I want to take her with me.'

'You don't get it, do you, Miss Boyd? She won't go with you. Not in a thousand years. Because she's mine.'

'Slavery was outlawed in this country two hundred years ago, Daroyce. Maybe you missed the bicentennial celebrations.'

'She can leave if she wants to, Boyd. But she won't. Because she owes me, and she's paying her debt.'

'I don't care about—'

'Enough!' His hand slammed down on the table, silencing her. 'The reason I showed you that is so you know I don't fuck about.'

'You're a bully.'

He wagged a finger at her. 'No, I'm no bully. Bullies only pick on the weak. I'm prepared to take on everyone. And I'm also a man of my word, so when people break theirs, I take great offence. And I make them suffer. That little whore fucked me about once, and now she's paying for her stupidity. Just like Pat Phelan will pay for it when I get hold of him.' He stood up, and even though at full height he was still shorter than Tina, he radiated the kind of cruel, low menace that would have intimidated men twice his height. 'Now you've made me a promise as well,' he said quietly, making a point of showing his teeth as he spoke. 'So, if you find the whereabouts of Phelan, I want to hear about it. Otherwise, Miss Boyd, my people will come for you too. Do you understand?'

Again, Tina held his gaze, but she was finding it hard to keep her nerve. She was scared, and he knew it.

'I understand,' she answered.

'Good. Would you like my men to drop you off where they picked you up?'

She shook her head. 'No, it's OK. I'll walk.'

He moved aside to let her pass, and she caught a subtle waft of expensive and very nice cologne that almost made her pause to take in more of it, until she thought about what he'd just done.

'Watch yourself out there,' he whispered. 'The streets round here can be very, very dangerous.'

She ignored him and kept walking, out into the narrow hallway. The big black guy in the shades materialized from a room ahead of her, unlocking the front door for her in silence. She couldn't see the girl anywhere, but if she was honest with herself, she wasn't looking too hard, so eager was she just to get out of there.

There were all kinds of things Tina could have taken from the conversation she'd just had: the large amount of cash Pat Phelan owed Daroyce; the way he'd recently asked Daroyce for just a few more days to pay the money; the fact that he was having an affair with his wife's business partner ... But she couldn't seem to concentrate on any of them as she walked rapidly through the back streets, going in no particular direction, haunted by the face of an anonymous girl who got down on her knees and waited to be beaten by a thug – a man who'd just threatened to turn on Tina as well if she didn't do what she was told.

She felt the pressure building inside her head. She was a tough person. She'd had to be to put up with what life had thrown at her these past few years, but occasionally her strength wavered, and it was wavering now.

She needed a drink. Badly.

There was a pub up ahead, a spit-and-sawdust type of place with a chalkboard outside advertising football games on Sky, and a couple of potbellied builders standing by the door smoking. The door was open. It seemed to welcome her.

She knew she shouldn't do it. Knew what one drink meant. But it was hard. So damn hard. She felt a desperate need to put a glass to her lips, to soften the blows that had rained down on her this afternoon – no, shit, that had rained down on her over the last four years.

You never drink on duty, she told herself. *Never. You work hard, you do well. They might not all like you, but they respect you. If you weaken now, you're finished.*

A picture of her dead lover walked uninvited into her mind's eye. John Gallan. He'd been a good man, a nicer, better person than she could ever be. He'd loved her; he'd said so many times and she'd believed him. John wasn't the sort to lie. Part of her had loved him back, too. Thought that maybe it could come to something. And then he died.

And then he fucking died.

She walked inside the pub, ignoring the slimy look she got from the jaundiced old codger sitting at the bar, and ordered a double gin, no ice, ignoring the voice inside her head that screamed for her not to do it. The decision had been made.

She drank it down in one.

'Bad day?' asked the barman, a gangly teenager with a haystack's worth of red hair.

'Fucking fantastic,' she said, and ordered another.

She put a tenner on the bar and drank the gin slower this time, savouring the fiery taste as the alcohol slipped down her throat. The kick was instantaneous, and she felt the familiar lightheadedness come on, knowing that if she had another, that would be it. There'd be no going back. The work day would be written off. The leads she'd gained, leads that could help save a teenage girl from death, wouldn't emerge until she'd sobered up. Tina wasn't the sort who could work drunk.

She became clumsy and lethargic. Her colleagues would notice it straight away, and her guilty little secret, the one she'd carried for so long, would suddenly be out there for all to see. And she couldn't have that. Tina had her pride. She suffered, but she suffered alone. She didn't want pity, she didn't want help, and right now, she really didn't want to be off this case.

Fuck Leon Daroyce. He wasn't going to beat her. She finished the drink and banged the glass on the bar harder than she'd planned before picking up her change and heading back out into the sunlight.

It was time to get back to work.

Part Four

Part Four

Twenty-two

'I've got authorization for the money,' said Big Barry grimly, looking across his desk at Bolt. 'It wasn't easy. One or two of the top people favoured calling in the negotiators. It took some persuading that not letting on about our involvement was the best course of action. And as you can imagine, no one wanted the responsibility of signing off half a million pounds.'

Bolt nodded. It had just turned four o'clock and he was back in Big Barry's office. Despite the sunny day, the heating was on full blast and the room felt hot and airless. Bolt had an empty feeling in his stomach. He'd tried to eat on the way back to HQ, stopping off at a Pret a Manger to buy a sandwich and a bottle of juice, but two bites and the juice was all he'd managed. The tension running through him made it hard to sit still, let alone concentrate on what Barry was saying.

'If we lose this money,' Barry continued, 'both you and I are going to be in serious trouble. We really can't afford to screw this one up, old mate.'

Bolt nodded again, didn't say anything.

'We'll be providing the bag containing the ransom, and I'm going to have two separate tracking devices sewn into the material where there's absolutely no chance they'll be found. We'll also have two more trackers buried right in among the money, just in case they change bags. Obviously, though, these things aren't foolproof. They can lose their signal. We all know that. So we're going to need major surveillance back-up. I suggest two ground teams. One will follow Mrs Devern, the other will be sent to stake out the rendezvous as soon as the kidnappers confirm where it's going to be, so we have complete coverage of the area and the ransom itself. Then, as a final layer of surveillance, I want a helicopter on standby to take over the pursuit of the money so we make absolutely sure it doesn't disappear on us. Then it's simply a matter of following it to its destination, and that's the moment we bring in the negotiators and try to end things peacefully. The girl gets released, the perpetrators get nicked, and the money lands safely back in our hands.'

He paused, looking pleased with himself.

'What do you think?'

'I think,' said Bolt, trying desperately to be objective, 'that it's very risky.'

Barry looked mildly irritated. He didn't quite roll his eyes but the movement wasn't far off. 'Of course it's risky. This is a professional kidnapping we're dealing with, Mike. It's the type of op that's always risky. It was risky this morning, and you were arguing for it then.'

But this morning there hadn't been the possibility that 'the girl', as Barry had described her so dispassionately, was his daughter. On the way over, Bolt had thought about laying things on the line. Admitting everything. But he'd quickly dismissed this as a bad move. With such a huge personal involvement, Barry would have had no choice but to remove him from the case and there was no way he was going to allow that to happen.

'I've had time to think,' Bolt said. 'These people haven't put a foot wrong so far. If we don't get this exactly right, then they're likely to kill her.'

'Then we get it right,' said Barry firmly.

'You don't think we might be better off bringing in the negotiators? It's possible that if they realize we're on to them, they might cut their losses and let Emma go.'

'And it's also possible that they might not. You said that yourself.'

Bolt exhaled. 'I guess that's true.'

Barry frowned. 'Are you all right, old mate?'

Bolt nodded. 'Yeah, I'm fine.' But he was sweating, and his shirt felt clammy against his skin.

'We've made the decision now,' Barry continued. 'There's no point going back on it. SOCA needs a nice high-profile success. If we get this right – and, make no mistake about it, we will, because we're going to plan it properly – then it's going to look extremely good on the organization, and on us in particular. We don't often get much in the way of praise. Let's make sure we get some this time.'

'OK, but I don't like the idea of the helicopter. The kidnappers get so much as a sniff of it, they're going to panic.'

'We'll keep it well away from whatever rendezvous they choose, don't worry. And it'll only be used as a back-up.'

Bolt wasn't convinced, but he didn't argue. There was no point. Barry had made up his mind about how they were going to play it. In fact, he'd made up his mind before the meeting had even started, which made Bolt feel that his presence was largely irrelevant.

'How's Mrs Devern?' asked Barry.

'She's holding up.'

'Hertfordshire CID still aren't entirely happy with her story.'

Bolt wiped sweat from his forehead with the back of his hand. 'Why not?'

'Well, their officers did find her covered in blood having just left the scene of the violent murder of her former lover.' Barry allowed himself a thin smile. 'You have to admit it's more than a little suspicious.'

Bolt felt like slapping that smile off his boss's face. For the first time in his life he suddenly had an insight into what it must be like to be a victim of crime – the lonely frustration of dealing with officials who were never going to care enough to deal with your plight.

'I'm sure they don't like her story,' he said, trying to keep his voice as calm as possible, 'but her child's definitely been kidnapped. I saw her on the video the kidnappers sent just three hours ago. And the people holding her are definitely after a ransom. So, unless Mrs Devern somehow set this all up herself, and is deliberately putting her daughter through a huge trauma, then we've got to accept that her story's true.'

Barry waited for Bolt to finish. 'I agree with you,' he said eventually, 'but I do get the idea with Mrs Devern that all is not what it seems. I think we need to watch her.'

Bolt nodded. 'Fair point.'

His boss was right. Andrea was a frighteningly enigmatic woman. She was also a manipulator, as Jimmy Galante had found to his cost, and Bolt himself was finding now.

There was a knock on the door, and one of the newer team members, Kris Obanje, a tall, good-looking black man with a fondness for amateur dramatics, appeared.

'There's been a development,' he said with a typical flourish.

Bolt felt his heart race and he clenched his teeth. What the hell kind of development?

'We've just heard back from the phone provider who runs the network Emma Devern and Pat Phelan both use,' he continued, his voice a rich baritone that seemed to resound around the room. 'Phelan's phone was switched off at 4.47 p.m. on Tuesday afternoon in the car park of the dental practice. According to the receptionist, this would have been while Emma was in with the dentist. Emma's own mobile was turned off twelve minutes later at 4.59, a few hundred metres from the surgery, and on the same street. It would have been just after she'd left.'

'That solves the mystery of where they snatched her from, then,' said Barry. 'It must have been in the car park. Shows our kidnappers are willing to take risks.'

'It also shows how technology savvy they are,' said Bolt, 'getting rid of the mobiles straight away.'

'That's the media for you,' snorted Barry. 'They publicize all the ways we can track people. It's no wonder the criminals catch on. We're going to have to interview everyone who was at the surgery that afternoon, see if anyone saw anything.'

'We've also managed to trace the route the car took away from the surgery,' Obanje told them. He unfolded a sheet of A3 paper and laid it on the desk between the two men. It was a photocopied large-scale map of north London, with a curving line of red crosses drawn on it in marker pen running from Hampstead in the south to Barnet and the M25 in the north. 'Here's the surgery,' he said, pointing at the bottom-most cross. 'Here's where Emma's phone was turned off. And here's where they went afterwards.' He traced a finger along the line of crosses, stopping at one in the middle. 'We got a good CCTV shot of Phelan's car here at 5.14.' He unfolded a second piece of paper, this time showing an overhead black and white camera shot of a Range Rover. 'It looks like it might be Phelan driving, and it looks like it might be an adolescent in the seat next to him. We've sent the image over for enhancement. We should have the results back by tomorrow.'

'We're going to have to,' said Bolt, 'because after tomorrow they'll be irrelevant.'

He looked more carefully at the photo as Obanje moved his finger away. The figure in the passenger seat – the girl who might be Bolt's daughter – was a lot smaller than the man next to her, and she had her head turned to one side, making a positive ID impossible. But it was Emma. There was no doubt about that, and he felt a twinge of emotion as he stared at her image.

'If this is Phelan driving, and he's involved in the kidnap, why on earth did he bother taking her to the dentist's first?' demanded Barry.

'Look at this,' said Obanje, producing a third piece of paper. It was another overhead camera shot but this time it was a close-up taken of the rear of the Range Rover. 'This is from another camera on the same street, two minutes later at 5.16. You have to look closely.'

Bolt and Barry both leaned forward so their heads were almost touching. It wasn't difficult to see what Obanje was referring to. There was no mistaking the figure in the back seat, directly behind the driver.

'So there was someone else involved in the initial snatch,' said Barry. 'He gets in the car, presumably at the dental surgery, and either forces Phelan to drive, or it's possible that Phelan's involved, and this gentleman's just helping him.' He turned to Obanje. 'Have we got any better shots than this?'

Obanje shook his head. 'No, this is the best we've got at the moment. And after the car crosses the M25 on the A1 at 5.49, we lose it altogether.

232

Hendon haven't got a single sighting of it after that.'

'So, Phelan's Range Rover could have been abandoned round here somewhere,' said Bolt, prodding the map near to the final cross.

'Could have been, but it's also possible that if they turned off the A1 and took back roads, they could have driven miles without being picked up by cameras. I'll keep on to Hendon, see if we can come up with any more sightings, but I wouldn't hold out much hope.'

'We'll also have a word with the local police, see if they've got any reports of the car being abandoned on their manor,' Barry said. He turned to Obanje. 'Thanks, Kris. Keep up with the good work.'

'It's coming along,' he said. 'She's a sweet-looking kid. We all want to get her back.' He picked up the papers and left the room, the other two watching him go.

The tightness in Bolt's stomach had eased just a little. If the man in the back of the Range Rover had got in the car in the dentist's car park, then it was possible he might have been seen by a passer-by. It wasn't much, but it represented a chink of hope.

He stood up. He needed to get out of Barry's stifling office. 'I'll get a couple of the team to go down to the surgery,' he said, and went outside.

But he didn't go back to the incident room straight away. Instead, he walked down the empty corridor and into the toilet. He splashed water on his face and stared at himself in the mirror.

He wasn't a bad-looking guy. His hair was still more blond than grey, although turning faster than he'd have liked, and he had a long, lean face with well-defined features and the kind of strong jaw that would stand up in a fight. Even the scars – an S-shaped slash on his chin, two small ragged lumps on his left cheek – added to rather than detracted from his appearance, and their effect was softened by his eyes. 'Laughing eyes' Mikaela used to call them. They were a bright, lively blue, and shone with a friendly and disarming interest.

But today they were duller, more brooding, and Bolt could see that he looked haggard and stressed. All his adult life he'd had to cope with pressure. The pressure of being a young man in uniform policing the streets of modern-day London had given way to the pressure of chasing some of the capital's most dangerous armed robbers during the ten years he'd spent with the Flying Squad. He'd been involved in some extremely dangerous operations, but the difference was that in those days he'd been part of a team, sharing the tension with a group of men and women who knew exactly how he was feeling, their support always providing a measure of comfort. Today he was completely on his own as the investigation into the kidnapping of the girl who could be his daughter went on around him.

He'd been operating pretty much on autopilot all afternoon, constantly turning over the various scenarios in his head, thinking back to those long-ago days when he and Andrea had had their brief and passionate affair, trying to work out whether he really was the father of someone he'd never met, and whose first fourteen years he'd completely missed. Wondering now whether he was ever going to meet her, or whether he'd be the man staring down at her dead, broken body. Every time this last thought took hold, he felt himself wince and his heart pound faster.

He forced himself to concentrate on the task at hand. They desperately needed a break, a single mistake by the kidnappers that would provide them with a clue to their identity, and hopefully their whereabouts. But if no one had seen the kidnapper get into Pat Phelan's Range Rover in the surgery car park, it was looking less and less likely that they were going to get one.

For a long moment, Bolt stood there watching the water drip down his face, listening to the constant drumbeat of his heart, knowing that whatever happened today, his life would never be the same again. 'Pull yourself together,' he whispered. 'She needs you.' And he vowed then and there that if he got Emma out of this, he was going to introduce himself to her, and if he was her father – and Christ knows he might never know for sure – he was going to make her part of his life whether Andrea liked it or not.

But in the meantime, he had to force her out of his mind.

His mobile started to ring. He looked at his watch. Twenty past four. He pulled it from his pocket.

It was Tina calling.

Twenty-three

From the moment the cruel one had run the blade of the knife across her face, smiling behind the balaclava at her fear, Emma knew there was no way he was ever going to let her go.

Afterwards, when he'd turned off the camera, he'd stared at her for a long time with his dead fish eyes. 'I think you're lying, you little bitch. You saw my face, didn't you?' He leaned forward so his face was almost touching hers, and sniffed loudly. 'I can smell the bullshit on you,' he whispered.

She promised him again that she wasn't lying, even sworn on her mum's life. Because it was true, she hadn't really seen anything – only that he had dark hair. But he didn't believe her, and just kept staring until finally she shut her eyes because she couldn't bear to see him looking at her like that any more.

'If you are lying, you little bitch, then you're going to fucking die,' he said as he headed towards the steps.

She shouted again that she wasn't, honestly, that he had to believe her, but he didn't reply and a few seconds later he was gone, locking the basement door behind him.

For a long time afterwards she sat hunched up on the bed, her knees pressed against her chest, too shocked and terrified to move, wondering why he wanted to kill her when it must have been obvious that she was telling the truth. Why did he have to be so cruel? She'd never done anything bad to him. She'd never done anything bad to anyone. Her mum called her a carer, and she was. She looked after people. There was a girl at school, Natalie, who was getting picked on by some of the Year 12 girls, and Emma had stepped in, even squared up to one of them to get them to stop (and they had: they'd backed off, even though they were bigger), because she didn't like people being bullied.

But now none of this counted for anything.

When she realized that this was it, that the cruel one really might kill her, the fear was like nothing she'd ever experienced before, far worse than the previous days when she'd at least had some kind of hope that the nightmare might end with her being reunited with her mum. Now she was sure this wasn't going to be the case. As soon as she was no longer needed, that'd be it. The cruel one would get rid of her, and there'd be nothing she could do about it, because she was totally helpless down here.

She wondered how they were going to do it. With a gun, or a pillow over her head? Or maybe with that knife of his? She couldn't bear that. To be stabbed to death. It would be slow, horrible, and there'd be blood everywhere. She couldn't bear the idea of her mum having to identify her in some morgue somewhere when they finally discovered her body. If they ever did find it, of course. She might end up missing for ever, like one of those kids who disappear and are never heard from again. If they had to do it, she hoped they'd give her pills so she could just go to sleep, and that would be the end of everything. It would be awful, and she'd miss her mum and her friends, and even her teachers – well, a couple of them – but at least it would be painless.

But she didn't want to die. God, she didn't. And just thinking about it made her cry again.

And then, as she sat there all alone, something within her changed. She realized that she couldn't just lie there weeping. She had to do something, anything. There was a topic they'd covered in history when she was in Year 9. It was about British prisoners in Germany during the Second

World War and how they were always trying to escape. How often they weren't successful, and got punished for it, but how they kept on trying, and some – quite a few – even managed it.

It was hard, but once the thought of escape was in her head, she got this weird burst of hope. She stood up and tugged frantically at her handcuffs. In the days since they were first put on she'd lost weight, and with a lot of effort she was able to pull the cuff a half inch or so up over her left hand. It wasn't nearly enough to release her, but at least it was a start. Another half inch and she'd be in with a chance. She decided not to eat again. It would make her feel sick and weak, but it had to be worth a try.

Then she pulled at the chain attached to her ankle, trying to yank it free from the wall. It didn't budge the first few times, but then she gave it a huge tug, leaning back and putting all her weight into it as if she was doing a tug of war, and she was sure she heard something give. The metal plate attaching the chain to the wall was brand new and had obviously been put there just for her, but it felt very slightly loose in her hands, and because the wall itself was so old, she felt sure she could get it out somehow. It would still leave her handcuffed, and trailing a chain, but at least she'd be mobile.

She started scraping at the brickwork round the

plate with her fingernails, breaking most of them in the process. Some flakes came away, but the plate didn't get any looser. She needed a tool of some kind, so she scoured the floor all over, hunting in every nook and cranny, until she found an old rusty nail in the corner just beneath the bed frame. Slowly, carefully, she began cutting away at the brickwork with the nail, methodically chipping away at it. It was a slow, painful job, but every time more brick dust fell to the floor she knew she was getting that little bit closer.

She just had to keep praying she had enough time.

Twenty-four

'So, Pat Phelan might be in the frame after all?' said Mo Khan as he and Bolt drove to Andrea's house.

'Well, he's certainly got a motive. He owes a lot of money to a very dangerous man who's likely to use some pretty extreme violence to get it back. He also called that man two days before the kidnapping to ask him for a few more days to get the money he owed him. That's a pretty big co-incidence if he wasn't involved, isn't it?'

Mo nodded. 'And he's not exactly the most upstanding citizen. A layabout and petty criminal who's sleeping with his wife's business partner. The problem is, it doesn't lead us to Emma, and if Phelan is involved, and she knows he's involved, he's not going to want to let her go.'

'I don't know,' said Bolt slowly. 'I would hope that it would mean he's less likely to hurt her because of the personal relationship they have.'

'That's assuming he's got a conscience. Anyone who can kidnap their own stepdaughter and put her through a living hell that's going to scar her for life just to pay off a gambling debt is capable of most things in my book.'

Bolt's fingers tightened on the steering wheel. 'But what I still can't work out is that if he is involved, why did he disappear too? Why not set everything up, make sure he's got an alibi for the time Emma's snatched, and simply stay behind and act innocent, advise Andrea not to go to the police, and wait for his money? Why implicate yourself?'

Mo shrugged. 'Maybe he's stupid.'

Bolt shook his head. 'No, one thing we do know for sure is the people behind this aren't stupid.'

The reason they were going to Andrea's house was to talk to her about these latest developments. Bolt had spoken on the phone to Tina Boyd for more than fifteen minutes and had been impressed by her detective work in uncovering the leads, but also concerned that she'd been abducted from the street and threatened by Leon Daroyce. Bolt was unfamiliar with the name, but a quick check on the PNC had revealed Daroyce as an unpleasant thug with several convictions for violence. He'd also been charged with a number of offences over the years, including extortion and, more ominously, attempted murder, all of which had ended up being dropped as witnesses retracted their statements, refused to testify, or in one case simply disappeared. Clearly he was a dangerous man.

But Tina hadn't sounded unduly distressed. If anything, she'd sounded excited, which wasn't like her. The thing with Tina was that she tended to keep her emotions in check, and usually exhibited a businesslike calm that her colleagues occasionally found disconcerting. He'd offered her the rest of the day off, knowing that however brave a face she put on it she was still going to be shocked by what had happened, but knowing too that she'd refuse the offer, which of course she had. Tina Boyd wasn't the type who liked being treated with kid gloves, something that Bolt had always admired about her, and he'd told her to return to the Glasshouse and help out there.

Bolt was finding it increasingly hard to concentrate on anything but Emma's whereabouts and he knew he looked under stress. His fingers were glued to the steering wheel, and twice Mo had asked him whether everything was OK. He'd replied that he was fine, just tired, which wasn't an uncommon occurrence on his team. They regularly did sixty-, even seventy-hour weeks when they were on a job, but he'd felt bad not saying something to Mo about his plight. They were good friends who knew each other well. But Bolt was well aware that the moment he opened his mouth he'd put his colleague in an impossible situation. He'd done that once before, and had sworn then that he wouldn't risk their friendship a second time.

It had just turned twenty to six when they pulled up outside Andrea's house, having called through to the surveillance team to announce their arrival. Not surprisingly, the team leader reported that there'd been no suspicious activity in the street all day. The kidnappers, it seemed, were continuing to keep a low profile.

Bolt pressed the buzzer on the security gate, and they were let through without preamble. The garden looked even prettier in the dappled late-afternoon sunshine as he and Mo walked towards the front door. It opened and Andrea appeared, dressed in a white LA Fitness T-shirt and ill-fitting trackpants. She'd removed her make-up, and looked older. Her eyes were red, and there'd been recent tears.

'Any news?' she asked.

'I'm afraid not,' answered Bolt as she moved aside to let them in, 'but we've got a few questions we need to ask you.'

Matt Turner and Marie Cohen, the liaison officer, were in the hallway and Bolt nodded to them both as Andrea led them through to her living room. She took a seat on a long leather sofa while Bolt and Mo sat down in armchairs opposite her.

Marie leaned round the door and asked if anyone fancied a cup of tea. Bolt declined. Mo and Andrea both asked for coffee.

'What do you want to know?' she asked, lighting a cigarette with shaking hands and blowing out a line of pale blue smoke.

Bolt wasn't looking forward to this. It felt akin to kicking her when she was already down.

'We've heard from very reliable sources that Mr Phelan has a very large gambling debt. Did you know anything about that?'

She looked genuinely shocked. 'Are you sure? How big?'

'We believe it's tens of thousands of pounds.'

'Oh God, no. He's been staying out late quite a bit, but I had no idea he was gambling. What's he been betting on?'

'He's been losing it in a casino, but the point is, he owes a lot of money to some very nasty people.'

'Have you ever heard the name Leon Daroyce, Mrs Devern?' asked Mo, speaking for the first time.

She shook her head. 'Is he the person Pat owes the money to? Do you think he's the one who snatched Emma?'

'It's possible,' Bolt conceded. 'We don't know for certain. We think it might be that Mr Daroyce is currently looking for your husband to get the money he's owed.'

Andrea took another urgent drag on the cigarette. 'But surely he's the one with the motive. Are you not going to arrest him? Do something?'

'Mr Daroyce and his people are currently under surveillance, so if they are involved, we'll know about it very quickly.' Bolt paused. 'But our source tells us that your husband phoned Daroyce last Sunday night, saying he was going to get him his money in the next few days. That was only two days before the kidnapping.'

'So you're saying he is involved?' she asked, her voice cracking.

'We have to face up to the possibility that he is, yes.'

'He wouldn't do this, you know. He really cares for her.'

The room fell silent. Bolt leaned forward in his seat.

'What we keep coming back to, Andrea, is that if your husband wasn't a part of this conspiracy, how did the kidnappers know his and Emma's movements? We think the abduction happened in the car park of the dental surgery where Emma had her appointment.'

Andrea's eyes filled with tears. 'Don't use that

word, abduction. It makes it seem, I don't know, like some paedophile snatched her and she's not coming back.'

'I'm sorry. Snatched. But the point is, the kidnappers knew she was going to be there. And we need to know how.'

Marie came back into the room with the coffee for Mo and Andrea. Andrea waved hers away.

'Who's got access to this house, Mrs Devern?' asked Mo, taking his coffee and thanking Marie. 'And who knows the code to your burglar alarm, aside from you, Mr Phelan and your daughter?'

'No one except the cleaner, and she's been doing the house for years.'

As Mo took down the cleaner's details, Bolt's mobile rang. It was the surveillance team leader. Bolt excused himself and walked to the other side of the room out of earshot.

'We've got an IC1 female stopping at Mrs Devern's security gate. Black hair, early forties. She'll be ringing the bell any moment now.'

The buzzer sounded in the hallway, and Matt Turner poked his head round the living-room door.

'Are we expecting anyone?' Bolt asked him.

'Not that I'm aware of.'

'OK, ignore it, then. Let's hope they go away.'

A few seconds later the buzzer sounded again, longer this time.

'Oh shit,' said the surveillance team leader down the phone.

'What is it?'

'She's unlocking the gate, and now she's coming through.'

Bolt cursed. This was the problem with operating out of a private address. He hung up as the key turned in the lock and the front door opened.

'Andrea?' came a woman's voice, followed immediately by an accusatory 'Who are you?' as she saw Turner.

'It's all right, Isobel, I'm in here,' Andrea called out, getting to her feet quickly. 'It's my business partner,' she added by way of explanation.

Bolt and Mo exchanged glances as Isobel Wheeler, the other half of Feminine Touch Health and Beauty Spas, came into view. She was a striking woman in her mid-forties whose shoulder-length black hair and olive skin suggested eastern Mediterranean parentage. She was wearing a short black dress that finished halfway down her thigh, and which Bolt thought would have suited a slightly younger woman, and black high-heeled court shoes. She didn't do a lot for Bolt, but he could see why some men might go for her.

Isobel and Andrea greeted each other with a kiss on both cheeks.

'I came to see whether you were feeling any better,' Isobel said, breaking away and surveying the room with a cool confidence that was only a hair's breadth short of arrogance. 'What's going on? Who are all these people?'

Bolt opened his mouth to reply but Andrea beat him to it. 'Pat's gone missing,' she said worriedly. 'I haven't seen him for days.'

Isobel looked shocked. 'Is that why you haven't been in this week? You weren't ill, then?'

Andrea shook her head. 'No. I've been waiting for him to come home, and he hasn't. The police are looking for him.'

'What do you think's happened? Did you have an argument or something?' There was something accusatory in Isobel's tone.

'No, it wasn't like that. He just didn't come home one night. I don't know what's happened.'

Isobel turned to Bolt. 'Why aren't you out there looking for him?'

'I don't believe we've been introduced,' he said coolly. 'You are?'

'Isobel Wheeler,' she snapped. 'Why aren't you looking for him?'

Bolt didn't like this woman at all, but knew better than to react to her rudeness.

'We are looking for him,' he explained calmly, 'but unfortunately there's no law against a man leaving his house, even for an extended period of time, and at the moment there's no suggestion of foul play.'

'Pat wouldn't just walk out,' she said firmly.

'You know him well, do you?'

'I know him well enough,' she said curtly before turning back to Andrea. 'And you can't think where he might be, Andi?'

Once again, Andrea shook her head. 'I've tried everywhere. I've got no idea where he is, or why he went.'

Bolt was impressed by the way she was holding up, but he also found the smooth and natural manner in which she lied unnerving.

Isobel stared at Andrea for a couple of seconds, then leaned forward and gave her a hug.

'Do you want me to stay here with you?' she asked.

'I'll be all right, I promise.'

'Keep me posted of progress, OK?'

'Of course I will.'

'And don't worry about anything at work; it's all being sorted.'

Andrea managed a weak smile. 'Thanks, Iz. I appreciate it.'

'Now, if you'll excuse us, Miss Wheeler,' said Bolt, 'there are details we need to take down from Mrs Devern.'

Isobel nodded brusquely. 'Call me,' she told

Andrea, then pushed past Turner and walked back out into the hallway.

Bolt followed her out and opened the front door for her.

'Have you any idea what's happened to him?' Isobel whispered as she stepped past him on to the steps. 'I mean, really? Because four police officers seems an awful lot to come round to take a missing person's details.'

Bolt shook his head. 'No, we haven't, I'm afraid.'

She gestured in the direction of the living room. 'Watch her,' she said, but before Bolt could ask her to elaborate she'd turned and walked away down the garden path.

Bolt watched her go, wondering what she meant. And wondering too why at no point had she asked where Emma was.

Twenty-five

'I thought you said only the cleaner had access to the house, Mrs Devern,' said Mo as Bolt re-entered the living room.

Andrea was back on the sofa, looking flustered. 'Sorry, I forgot that I'd given a key to Isobel. It was last year. I asked her to check the place while we were on holiday.'

'And there's definitely no one else we should know about?'

She shook her head firmly. 'Definitely not.'

Bolt thought of what Isobel had said on the doorstep.

'Do the two of you get on well?' he asked.

Andrea nodded. 'Well enough. She's my business partner. I've known her for years.' Then her expression changed. 'You're not saying she's got something to do with this as well, are you? First you accuse Pat—'

'No, no,' he said hastily, 'of course not. But we don't think this is a random act. If your husband wasn't involved, we still need to know how the people targeting you knew your movements, and one of the ways would be by bugging your house.'

'But you said you found no bugs.'

'There were none when we looked this morning, but if someone other than you had access, they could have removed any listening devices.'

'Jesus, this is ridiculous. Isobel's a lawyer, not something out of MI5. What would she gain by any of this?'

'We're just trying to cover every angle, that's all,' he said, knowing that if he told her about Isobel's affair with her husband it would probably prove the last straw.

Andrea reached over to the coffee table and picked up her cigarettes again, taking one out of the pack and lighting it.

'Mike,' she said, looking him squarely in the eye, 'is there something you're not telling me?'

The question caught him off guard, as did the fact that she'd called him by his first name again in Mo's presence. Bolt had to consciously resist looking at him.

'No,' he said, shaking his head. 'As I say, these are just routine enquiries.'

As he spoke, he caught sight of an old framed photo of Emma on top of an antique chest of drawers in the corner next to the French windows – a smiling child's face staring at him from an odd angle. For a second he couldn't drag his gaze away, and he felt a bead of sweat run down his temple.

Andrea stood up. 'Well, if you haven't got any other questions, I'd like to lie down for a while.'

He nodded. 'Of course. Matt and Marie will stay here with you.'

She left the room, and Bolt wiped the bead of sweat from his brow. It had been a long day, and he knew that tomorrow was going to be an even longer one. There wasn't much more they could do, so, having instructed Turner and Marie to keep a close eye on Andrea, and promising Turner that he'd be relieved later, he and Mo said their goodbyes and went outside.

Bolt felt a surge of relief to be away from the pictures of Emma. It was torture looking at them.

'I still get the feeling Mrs Devern's not telling us everything,' said Mo as they walked back to the car.

'Shit, Mo,' Bolt snapped, 'her daughter's missing. She's going to tell us everything she can to get her back, isn't she?'

He stopped by the car and took a deep breath, surprised by the anger in his tone. Mo looked taken aback.

Bolt sighed. 'Sorry, I shouldn't have said it like that. It's just, you know ... I don't think she's going to be holding anything back.'

They got into the car in silence. Bolt took another deep breath. The pressure was getting to him. The knowledge that he might lose the only child he'd ever had, and before he'd even met her, was affecting every step he took, and he was beginning to doubt his ability to handle it.

'What is it, boss? What's wrong with you?'

Bolt avoided Mo's concerned gaze. 'Nothing. I'm fine.' It was his stock response, and it sounded utterly hollow. He couldn't even bring himself to instil any meaning into it.

'No, you're not. This isn't like you. I've worked with you, how long now? Four years, five? You never let things get to you. Not like this. You care, but not so much it brings you right down. And you're down now. You haven't been right all day.'

There was a long pause. Bolt sat there with the key in his hand, inches from the ignition, unmoving.

'Come on, tell me,' said Mo eventually, his voice quiet. 'We've shared things in the past.'

'I know.'

'Important things. Things that no one else knows.'

'I know.'

'So, talk to me now.'

In that moment, Bolt knew that the dam had to give, whatever the consequences. He put the key in the ignition but made no move to start the car.

'I had an affair with Andrea Devern fifteen years ago.'

'I thought there was something between the two of you. Back at the house—'

'There's more.'

Mo didn't say anything for a moment, then it seemed to click.

'Oh shit, boss. You're not saying that . . . that Emma's something to do with you?'

'It looks that way.'

He told Mo what Andrea had told him earlier.

'How do you know Mrs Devern, Andrea, isn't bullshitting you?' Mo asked when Bolt had finished. 'Especially as that's exactly what she told Jimmy Galante as well.'

Bolt sighed. 'I don't know, Mo, but the dates fit. I checked them.'

'But she was seeing Galante at the same time, right?'

'That's right. And she was married too.'

'Well, she certainly got around,' Mo said, a hint of disapproval in his voice.

'I don't know what to do. It's ripping me to shreds.'

'Chances are she isn't yours, boss. That's the way you've got to look at it. No offence, but if she was married, seeing another man, and seeing you, it's likely there were others as well.'

'But if it's true . . .'

'If it's true . . .' Mo paused, thinking. Choosing his words carefully. 'Then we've got to make sure we bring her back.'

Bolt ran a hand across his face, the fingers finding the scars on his left cheek. He rubbed hard at the shallow divots in his flesh.

'You saw what those bastards did to Galante. They're not going to let her go, are they?'

'You've got to have faith, boss.'

'Faith in what, Mo? Faith in what?'

'If you haven't got faith in God, and I know that you haven't, then at least have faith in our abilities. We've got out of tight corners before.'

'It's a lot easier said than done, Mo. It really is.'

'I know.'

'Do you?'

'I've got four children, boss. Believe me, I know.'

They were silent again. Bolt felt the tension flowing through his veins, tightening every muscle in his body.

'You know,' said Mo eventually, staring out of the window, 'there's a village in India, somewhere along the Ganges, where they consider cobras sacred. It means they're not allowed to harm them, and because of that, the whole village is teeming with them. In schools; in people's kitchens; in kids' bedrooms; all over the place. But no one takes a blind bit of notice because they're convinced they're not going to get bitten. And, you know, even when one of the villagers is bitten, they think it's a mistake on the cobra's part, and that the poison won't have any long-lasting effect because they worship it. Now, cobra venom can kill if it's not treated. That's a medical fact. But do you know what? In that village there's not one recorded incident of anyone dying of a snake bite. Like I said, boss, you've got to have faith. It'll be OK.'

They looked at each other, and Bolt was impressed by the determination in the other man's expression. It made him feel a little better, glad that he had shared his feelings. He was also surprised by the fact that Mo hadn't suggested he say something to Barry Freud. Mo was his friend, but he was also a professional, and he would know that he was taking a risk by keeping his boss's relationship with both the kidnap victim and her mother silent.

'Not a word about this, OK?' Bolt told him. 'It won't affect how I run this op, I promise.'

Mo nodded. 'OK, boss, but only as long as it doesn't. If it looks like the pressure's getting too much . . .'

'It won't. I promise.'

'But if it does, I'm going to have to say something. You understand that, don't you?'

'Yeah, I understand that.'

Bolt started to turn the key in the ignition, but Mo's next words stopped him dead.

'You were in the Flying Squad when you were seeing Andrea, weren't you?'

Although there was nothing accusatory in the tone, the meaning was clear. The Flying Squad dealt with armed robberies. The woman Bolt had been having an affair with was also sleeping with an armed robber. The potential for corruption was obvious, and it wasn't as if the Flying Squad hadn't had its fair share of corruption problems in the past. Bolt wasn't offended, but it hurt him that his friend had felt the need to ask the question.

'As soon as I found out she was seeing Galante, I finished it,' he said firmly.

'Good. That's all I wanted to know.'

There was another awkward silence. Bolt had crossed the line with Mo once before, two years earlier, and the implicit trust that had always existed between them had come under a lot of strain. It felt like something similar was happening again.

'Come on,' he said, starting the engine, 'let's go.'

Twenty-six

Home for Mike Bolt was a spacious studio apartment on the third floor of a converted warehouse in Clerkenwell, one of the quietest places in central London, and not far from where he'd first been based as a uniformed cop. He'd been there for four years now, having moved in the year after his wife's death, and ordinarily he'd never have been able to afford a place one quarter of the size on his SOCA salary, but the rent he paid was minimal. The reason for this was that it belonged to a wealthy Ukrainian businessman, Ivan Stanevic, whom Bolt had helped out years before in his National Crime Squad days.

The case was remarkably similar to the one he was involved in now. Stanevic's twelve-year-old daughter Olga had been abducted from the street by business rivals of her father's, and Bolt had led the team tasked with getting her back. On that occasion it hadn't taken long to find out who they were dealing with and consequently where Olga was being held. It was Bolt who'd personally negotiated her release with the kidnappers, and she'd been freed unharmed, for which her father had been eternally grateful. It was the only other kidnap case he'd ever been involved with, and the grim irony wasn't lost on him as he stepped inside his apartment and shut the door behind him.

Usually he loved this place. It was hard not to love it since it had been refurbished with absolutely no expense spared. The floors were polished teak; the high, angular ceiling was criss-crossed with mighty timber beams carefully restored to their former glory; but the *pièce de résistance* was the way the old windows had been knocked out and replaced by a huge strip of floor-to-ceiling tinted glass that ran the entire length of one side of the apartment, facing east out on to the bright lights of London, with the high towers of the Barbican rising up behind the buildings opposite. Only the night before he'd sat in his armchair with a glass of 2005 Côtes du Rhône staring out across the city while an old Herbie Hancock CD played on the stereo, feeling quietly satisfied that the money-laundering case had been brought to a successful conclusion, and looking forward to a weekend away with Jenny Byfleet. The world then had seemed a good, decent place, and for the first time in a while he'd actually felt contented. And all the time the clock was counting down to when it would all go suddenly and horribly wrong. Just like it had that night five years ago when he and Mikaela waved goodbye to the friends they'd spent the evening with, got into his car and driven off to their doom.

It had just turned eight o'clock as Bolt kicked off his shoes and poured the remainder of the previous night's Côtes du Rhône into an over-sized wine glass, taking a big slug and trying hard to relax. He'd phoned Jenny on the way home and, trying to sound as casual as possible, had apologized for the fact that he was going to have to postpone. She'd asked if he wanted to rearrange, and he'd said he'd get back to her, hearing her disappointment down the other end of the line as he'd hung up. That was probably it for the two of them, but he was past caring about that. All he could think about was the case, about how Andrea had come back into his life and, even after all these years, managed once again to turn everything upside down for him.

He sat down in his armchair, but almost immediately stood up again. It didn't feel right resting his legs. Not with his mind going like the clappers. Instead he paced the room, thinking about what Mo had said about Andrea not being entirely truthful, and holding something back. He remembered Isobel Wheeler's words: *Watch her*. And most of all he thought back to his own experience with Andrea, and of how one night fifteen years ago, a mere eight weeks into their relationship, she'd dropped such a bombshell that it had ended everything between them with a bang that echoed even now.

He recalled the night perfectly. It was in the days when mobile phones were still the size of house bricks, and long before Bolt had taken to carrying one as a matter of course. He'd arrived home after a few drinks with a couple of Flying Squad buddies to find that he had a message from Andrea on his answerphone, asking him to call her urgently if he received the message before 10.30, giving him a number he didn't recognize, and adding that under no circumstances was he to call the number after that time. If she didn't hear from him before then, she'd call back later when she got a chance. The message had been left at twenty to ten, just fifteen minutes earlier, and Andrea had sounded uncharacteristically scared. He'd called her back immediately, and she'd picked up on the first ring, obviously waiting for the call.

'Mike, thank God you've called. I don't know how to tell you this.'

'Whatever it is, you can talk to me about it, OK? I can help.'

She took a deep breath and spoke quietly. 'There's going to be an armed robbery. Tomorrow morning, between ten and ten thirty. A police van carrying a load of cocaine for incineration from Lewisham Nick to Orpington.'

The shock of her announcement left Bolt cold.

'How do you know about this, Andrea?' he asked.

'I just do,' she said unconvincingly.

'You're going to have to do better than that. I need details. Like where you got the information.'

There was a silence at the other end of the line.

'Andrea, I can't go to my bosses and get authorization to do anything about this until I know more.'

This wasn't entirely true. He could have done if he really wanted to, but the most important thing was to find out how the woman he, a Flying Squad officer, had been seeing for the past two months had details of exactly the kind of major crime he specialized in investigating.

'I've been seeing a guy,' she said. 'His name's Jimmy Galante.'

'While you've been seeing me?' he asked, knowing the answer already.

'Yes.' Pause. 'I'm sorry, Mike. I've been seeing him a while. Since before you.'

He resisted the urge to shout at her, even though he wanted to. Instead, he listened while she continued, telling him how she'd always known that Jimmy was a bit dodgy and operated on the wrong side of the law, but hadn't ever realized the extent of his misdemeanours. Until that evening, when she'd been at his place and overheard a conversation he'd had on the phone in which he'd discussed the robbery with a fellow conspirator. 'He was in the other room, and thought I couldn't hear him, but he's been jumpy all day so when the phone rang I listened at the wall and heard everything he said. When he came back in the bedroom, I was in bed, so he didn't suspect a thing. Then he said he had to go out, and he'd be back about half ten.'

To this day, Bolt remembered how gutted he felt when she told him about getting back into another man's bed, how he'd got that wrenching feeling in his stomach as if someone was tying it in knots. He hadn't seen Andrea for close to a week because she'd said she'd been so busy, and all the time she was fucking some lowlife robber.

'So, you're at his place now?' he said.

'Yeah. I'm meant to be staying tonight. Billy's away on business.'

Bolt sighed. 'And you're absolutely sure about this?'

'Positive. I'd bet my life on it.'

'So why are you telling me this now?'

'Isn't it obvious?'

'Not really, no. I'm surprised you're so keen to shop your . . . your boyfriend.'

'I'm scared of him, Mike. I've been wanting to finish it for a while, but he's not the sort to take no for an answer. He even threatened to hurt Billy if I left him.'

'Tell me something. When you met me, was it a coincidence, or did you plan it?'

'Course I didn't plan it. How could I have done that?'

Bolt was silent. He wanted to believe her, but even though he was a lot younger then, he wasn't entirely naive. Something didn't feel right with her story. But she was giving him a tip, and he felt duty bound to act.

'Do you know where they're meeting up to do this robbery?'

'No. I've given you all the details I know.'

'If we try to stop them, and they're armed, you know what might happen, don't you? Your boyfriend, the guys he's with . . . They might end up getting shot.'

Andrea said that she understood. 'He's the one going out there with a gun,' were her exact words.

And that had been that. The next day the Flying Squad had hastily set up an ambush, following the police van and its cargo of more than a hundred kilos of cocaine, which was being driven by their officers, on its journey from Lewisham police station to an incinerator in Orpington. Sure enough, the robbers made their move, boxing the van in on a busy dual carriageway and forcing it to a halt before appearing, balaclava-clad, weapons in hand. Such was their speed and brazenness that they caught the Flying Squad team off guard, but only for a couple of seconds.

The Flying Squad ambush ethos is surprise, aggression and overwhelming force. As their own cars roared on to the scene, forming a loose cordon around the van and the robbers' vehicles, and disgorged their screaming officers, the back of the security van flew open and more gun-wielding cops leapt out. The shouts of 'Armed police, drop your weapons!' filled the air and Bolt felt an adrenalin kick like he'd never felt before as he stood, legs apart, Colt revolver held two-handed in front of him.

Which was the moment it all went wrong.

There were four robbers with guns outside the car, two more – the drivers – inside. One of them opened fire and a Flying Squad guy called Hammond, who was thirty-one and just celebrating the birth of his child, got hit in the shoulder. Passers-by dived for cover as another of the robbers raised his shotgun, but this time he never got the chance to pull the trigger. Bolt and the guy standing next to him both opened fire, hitting the robber a grand total of four times. Dean Hayes was twenty-five, only months older than Bolt, with a criminal record stretching back into his mid-teens. He died three hours later on the operating table. Only one of the bullets was fatal. It had pierced his heart. A later PCC investigation revealed that it was Bolt who'd fired it.

The cops from the back of the security van grabbed another of the robbers and slammed him to the tarmac with guns in his back, while the fourth robber got off a wild shot before taking a bullet in the shoulder that sent him sprawling. But the first robber, the one who'd shot Hammond, had managed to scramble into the back of one of the getaway cars, a powerful Sierra Cosworth, whose driver then reversed suddenly, knocking down one of the advancing cops and breaking his hipbone. It then smashed into the Flying Squad car that was blocking it in, pushing it into the central reservation and narrowly missing Bolt in the process, before accelerating through the narrow gap it had created.

Several of Bolt's team had been carrying pickaxe handles, and one of them managed to smash the driver's side window as the getaway car passed, showering the driver with glass, and another threw his into the windscreen; but, faced with no direct threat to their lives, they were unable to shoot at the occupants. Bolt remembered being cool-headed enough, even after shooting a person for the first time, to take aim at the Cosworth's tyres, but the car had taken off at such a speed that it was thirty metres away before he had a chance to fire, and with civilians everywhere he knew it would be too dangerous to pull the trigger again.

Police patrol cars from Lewisham station had descended rapidly on the scene and there was a high-speed chase which ended only minutes later when the Cosworth crashed into a parked van. The driver, a well-known face in the criminal fraternity, was captured, but the gunman was nowhere to be seen, having fled the vehicle on foot, still wearing his balaclava.

With the other five gang members accounted for, it soon became clear that none of them was the mysterious Jimmy Galante, a man who at that time had never shown up on the Flying Squad radar. An arrest warrant was hastily put together, and at four a.m. the following morning a Flying Squad team that included Bolt had raided his flat, finding him apparently asleep. Bolt had half expected to find Andrea there still, having not heard from her the previous day, but it turned out Galante was alone, and remarkably unfazed at being prematurely woken from his slumber by half a dozen men in black, all shouting and pointing guns at him.

Galante was a cocky bastard from the start. Even if he hadn't been sleeping with the woman Bolt had fallen in love with, he would have hated him anyway. It just made it worse that he was a criminal, and a good-looking one at that. But his cockiness was justified. Although he had several cuts to his head and bruised ribs, strongly suggesting that he'd been involved in the Cosworth's crash, he'd denied involvement in any robbery and produced a cast-iron alibi for his whereabouts at the time (a café in Islington where he'd apparently been seen by at least half a dozen witnesses, including the owner). Worse, there was no sign of the clothes he'd been wearing, or any firearms residue on his hands. Everyone knew that he could have removed this simply by washing them thoroughly, but there was nothing they could do about it, and because none of the surviving robbers fingered him, Galante wasn't even charged with, let alone convicted of, any offence.

Bolt burned with the intense frustration any police officer feels when a criminal he or she knows is guilty gets off through lack of evidence; the fact that he'd shot one of Bolt's colleagues made it almost unbearable. But bear it he had to, and shortly afterwards Galante disappeared off the scene, moving to Spain, away from the watchful eyes of a vengeful Flying Squad.

Bolt had never heard from Andrea again after that. He'd tried to make contact with her several times but she hadn't returned his calls, and he'd been forced to accept that their relationship was over. But for him, personally, it had been a coup. His information had led to a huge result for the Flying Squad, marred only by wounding and injury to two of their own, and the fact that he'd shot dead one of the gang only increased his kudos among his colleagues. There'd been no repercussions from the PCC – his shooting of Hayes was considered totally justified – and although he'd been asked on several occasions to name the source who'd told him about the robbery, he'd always claimed that it was an informant, and gave no further details. Because the op had been a success, no one had ever pushed him on it.

He continued to pace the room. Continued to think. Always about Andrea. How her information had foiled a major robbery and put a lot of very nasty people out of business, at least one permanently. How she seemed to have turned her life around so formidably in the years since. And how she could have made some serious enemies along the way.

He stopped pacing and put down his wine on

the marble kitchen top. He had an idea, and for the first time in the last few hours he felt a twinge of hope, coupled with something approaching excitement.

Pulling the mobile from his pocket, he dialled a number he hadn't called in far too long.

Twenty-seven

Emma dug away in the gloom with the rusty nail, trying to shut the constant fear out of her mind, forcing herself to concentrate totally on what she was doing. It had been dark for over an hour now but still she kept going, even though every part of her body seemed to ache with the effort. It was a slow, painful job, but she was getting somewhere. She'd created a gap of almost a quarter of an inch between the wall and the plate on the left-hand side, enough almost to get a finger underneath, and when she tugged at the chain it definitely felt looser. If she could just keep at it, eventually it was going to come free. She was sure of it. But God, it was hard.

She heard a noise upstairs – footsteps. She froze. If they saw what she was doing, they'd punish her. The cruel one might even decide that keeping her alive was now too risky, that it was time to get rid of her altogether.

She jumped up, lifted the bed, straining with the effort, and pushed it back against the wall, trying to be as quiet as possible but unable to stop it from scraping loudly on the stone floor.

Please don't let them hear it.

Gritting her teeth, she lay back on the bed, put the nail under her pillow, and reached for the hood.

The footsteps stopped. Was one of them outside the door?

She put on the hood and closed her eyes, hardly daring to breathe, terrified that this might be it. The last few seconds of her life. Had all her efforts of the last few hours been wasted?

But the door didn't open.

Five minutes passed. Then ten.

She lay there in the darkness, her heart going faster and faster, cold beads of sweat running down her forehead as she listened as hard as she could for any sound in the room, knowing that the cruel one always liked to creep up on her.

But she could hear nothing. Only silence. And eventually she plucked up the courage to remove the hood and look around. But the room was empty.

So, he wasn't coming for her tonight.

But she couldn't help thinking it was just a stay of execution.

Twenty-eight

In the old days, everyone in the Flying Squad had had a nickname. Bolt's, not altogether surprisingly, was Nuts, while Jack Doyle, the man he was going to meet, had been known as Dodger. Although he was five years older, Doyle had probably been Bolt's best mate in the squad. He was also the most accident-prone guy Bolt had ever known.

Doyle's long litany of injuries was legendary: three months in traction after falling off a ladder trying to retrieve a football from his roof; a rare and potentially deadly blood infection when he'd stepped on a fishbone on the first day of his honeymoon; and in the most bizarre instance of all, a month off sick with concussion after a pool tournament during which a wildly mishit cueball flew off the table, hit him in the temple and knocked him spark out. Somehow his injuries always coincided with times when the squad were in action, hence the nickname, and it irritated him hugely because he'd always been one of its hardest members, and as a highly successful former amateur boxer was not afraid of a fight. He simply considered himself unlucky.

Jack (Bolt had never called him Dodger) was one of the few of the old team still left at Finchley. He'd moved up the ranks and was now a DI. His experience, coupled with a near photographic memory, meant that if there was ever anyone who could provide Bolt with the information he needed, it was him. Although they'd kept in touch over the years, and still did the occasional fishing weekend away, it had been months since they'd last spoken. Even so, as soon as Bolt explained that he needed to meet up with him urgently, Doyle hadn't hesitated, and told him to name the time and place.

And so it was that barely an hour after arriving home Bolt walked in through the door of the King's Arms, a busy, old-fashioned drinkers' pub just off the King's Cross end of the Gray's Inn Road. He had to look around for a few seconds, pushing his way through the buzzing crowd of drinkers, before he saw Doyle sitting in a booth in the corner, two pints of lager set out on the table in front of him.

Doyle stood up as Bolt approached and they shook hands. As always, the other man's grip was vice-like. With his jutting, granite jaw and square-shaped head, topped with thick black hair, Jack Doyle bore a strong resemblance to a *Thunderbirds* puppet – not that it was advisable to tell him that. He wasn't a particularly big man – no more than five nine, and of slim build – but the look was deceptive. He was all sinewy muscle, and even now, in his mid-forties, there wasn't an ounce of fat on him.

'How are you, Mike?' he asked in a thick Glasgow accent that hadn't mellowed, even after more than a quarter of a century down south. He gestured at one of the pints. 'I got you one in.'

Bolt smiled as they sat down opposite each other.

'Thanks, Jack, I'm all right,' he said, determined not to show the turmoil he was going through. 'You?'

'Not bad,' said the other man wearily. 'Counting the days until retirement.'

They clinked glasses.

'What is it you've got left now? Five years?'

'Four. And I tell you, pal, I can't bloody wait. How's life at SOCA?'

Bolt took a gulp of his beer. It tasted good.

'Busy,' he answered. 'That's why I need your

278

help. You remember the Lewisham robbery, back in ninety-two? The police van carrying the coke for incineration?'

'How could I forget? It's the one where you made your spurs. Took out that toe rag Dean Hayes.'

Bolt nodded. 'That's the one.' He'd never been proud of the fact that he'd killed Hayes. He might have been, as Doyle put it, a toe rag, but that didn't make ending his life any easier, and Bolt felt mildly uncomfortable at it being mentioned now. 'Do you remember what happened to the people who got put away for it?'

'Is this to do with a case you're working on?'

He knew there was no point denying it. 'Yeah, it is.'

'It must be a pretty big case if you wanted to see me this urgently. Can you give me any details?'

'It's an ongoing op, so I can't say too much at the moment.'

'Not even to an old mate?'

'You know I'd tell you if I could, Jack.'

'Fair enough. And you think some of the guys we put away might be involved in it?'

'We don't know yet. But at the moment, I'd like to know their current status, and any intelligence you've got on any of them.'

'Well, you tagged one, and we put away four,

didn't we? Vernon Mackman – he was one of the drivers. One of the best there was, I always thought. He died of cancer five years back while he was still in the Scrubs. As for Barry Tadcaster, he's back inside. He was out six months, then teamed up with a couple of old-style blaggers and got done for conspiracy to rob when one of them turned grass. I don't think he's expected out until after I retire.'

'And the others? Marcus Richardson, and who was the other? Scott somebody?'

'Scott Ridgers. They've been in and out since they got released for the Lewisham job. You know what it's like with blokes like that, professional robbers – they never change. Ridgers carried on blagging; Richardson branched out into smuggling coke into the country. But as far as I know they're both on parole and keeping their noses clean. I haven't heard anything about either of them for a while now.'

'How long did they go down for?'

Doyle thought for a moment. 'Ridgers got fourteen years, I think, and served seven. Richardson got longer – seventeen, eighteen, something like that – because he fired a shot before he got hit himself, so he did time on an attempted murder charge as well, even though he always claimed the gun went off by accident. He served eight or nine.'

'You got an address for either of them?'

Doyle's face broke into a craggy smile. 'My memory's good, Mike, but it's not that bloody good. They'll be on the PNC, though. I'm sure they're both still on licence.'

'I'll check them out.'

'You haven't asked about the one who got away. Jimmy Galante.'

'Oh yeah, I remember him. He ended up in Spain, didn't he?'

Doyle nodded. 'He did, but I heard from one of my snouts that he was back in the country. Someone saw him the other day in a pub in Islington.'

Bolt feigned interest. 'Really? I must look into that.'

Doyle took a slug of his own beer and at least a quarter of it disappeared. For a small guy, he'd always had a prodigious capacity for the booze.

'Whatever you think our boys Richardson and Ridgers might be involved in, you've got to remember they weren't the brightest of sparks. Galante was always the brains of the outfit.'

Bolt tried to picture the two men, to remember anything about them, but they were a blank. It was all too long ago. He wondered whether he was wrong to think that there might be a connection. The Lewisham robbery was ancient history, and as far as he was aware no one, either inside or outside the Flying Squad, knew that it was Andrea who'd helped to foil it. And even if someone had found out, there was still no reason to wait until now, fifteen years later, to do something about it. When he thought about it like that, the whole thing didn't make much sense. But it was all he had, and the fact that Jimmy Galante had been involved in both cases meant that it was better to be here asking questions than sitting around at home.

They sat in silence for a few moments, finishing their drinks, oblivious to the noise around them.

'How well do you remember Richardson and Ridgers?' asked Bolt.

'Not very. There wasn't much to say about either of them. They were just two robbers prepared to get nasty to get what they wanted. I doubt many people'll have fond memories of them when they're gone.'

'Do you think either of them could be capable of the kidnap of a young girl? A fourteen-year-old?'

Doyle frowned. 'Is that what this is about?'

'Between you and me, yes.' Bolt knew he was treading on shaky ground here, talking about the investigation to someone outside it, but he also knew it was the only way he was going to get answers.

'A kidnap for ransom?'

'Yeah. But I can't tell you any more than that, and you've got to keep what I do tell you under wraps, OK?'

'You know me, Mike. I don't blab. What makes you think those two are anything to do with it?'

'Just a hunch.'

'Shit, pal, you sound just like Columbo.' Doyle fingered his empty glass. 'I wouldn't put it past either of them to be involved in something like that. They're criminals, and they're greedy bastards, so if there's money to be had, there's a good chance they'll be there.'

'Do you think they'd hurt her? The girl?'

'Christ, Mike, I don't know. The one thing about armed blaggers is they're pros. They don't add years on to their sentences unless they absolutely have to.'

Bolt felt relieved, even though he knew this was irrational. Jack Doyle was no criminal psychologist.

'You look shattered,' Doyle told him.

'I am. It's been a long day.'

'Maybe you should get home.'

But Bolt didn't want to go back yet. He picked up the empty glasses. 'No, let me get you a drink.'

'Cheers. I'll have a pint of Stella.'

When he returned with the drinks they made small talk for a while, but Bolt found it hard to concentrate on anything other than Emma, and he was conscious that he wasn't good company. It angered him that he couldn't relax with an old friend over a few beers at the end of a long, hard day, and the anger was aimed at Andrea, because it was her doing. If she'd just kept her mouth shut, he might have been able to do his job properly instead of flailing round from place to place, tearing himself apart.

He finished his second pint and got to his feet. 'I'd better go, Jack. Early start tomorrow.'

Doyle stood up as well and they shook hands.

'Good luck with the case, Mike.'

'Thanks. I hope we don't need it.'

'Don't worry, she'll be all right. Blokes like that, they just want the money. They won't risk going down an extra twenty years by killing her.'

Easy for you to say, thought Bolt as he said his goodbyes and walked outside into the cool night air. It was a two-minute taxi ride home or a fifteen-minute walk. He decided to walk, hoping it might calm him down a little, but he'd only got a few hundred yards when his mobile started ringing.

It was Mo. Bolt had left him back at the Glasshouse a few hours earlier. He'd said he was just finishing up and was about to go home, but maybe he'd decided to stay later. He flicked open the phone and put it to his ear.

'Mo?'

'There's been a development.'

His tone was grim, and Bolt felt his stomach constrict at the prospect of bad news.

'What is it?'

'I'm at a house in Tufnell Park. I think you'd better get over here.'

Twenty-nine

It had just turned twenty past ten when Bolt arrived at the address Mo had given him – a bedsit on a residential road of rundown white-brick Georgian townhouses on a hill a few hundred yards north of Tufnell Park Tube station. There were a dozen or so police vehicles as well as an ambulance double-parked on both sides of the street, blocking it off entirely, and small clusters of onlookers, some of them in dressing gowns, standing at the edges of the cordon talking quietly among themselves, clearly both appalled and fascinated by the crime that had taken place in their midst.

Bolt's taxi stopped a few yards short of the bright yellow lines of scene-of-crime tape.

'Christ, what's going on here?' asked the driver as he took the fare.

'Murder,' Bolt told him, and got out of the car.

He showed his ID to one of the uniforms ringing the cordon and was directed to a van where he put on the plastic coveralls all officers are obliged to wear when entering crime scenes. He was exhausted, the remnants of the two pints of Stella he'd had with Jack tasting sour and dry in his mouth.

Mo met him in front of number 42. He looked a little queasy. 'It's pretty bad in there, boss. You might want some of this.' He produced a tube of Vicks and Bolt dabbed some under his nostrils.

Bolt sighed. The last thing on earth he wanted to see right now was a body, and it wasn't essential to the inquiry that he did so since he could easily get the details of what happened from other people, but he wasn't the sort to shirk the unpleasant aspects of the job. 'Let's get it over with,' he said, following Mo through the open front door and into a dusty foyer with plastic sheeting over the bare stone floor. Long threads of cobweb hung from the corners of the ceiling and there was a stale, airless smell, mixed with something else. Something much more pungent.

'She's down here,' said Mo, walking past a threadbare-looking staircase and down a dark, very narrow hallway to an open door at the end, the smell of decay getting stronger with each step.

By the time they reached it, it was pretty much unbearable, and Bolt had to stop himself from gagging.

'Jesus,' he whispered.

'It looks like she's been dead for days,' said Mo, moving aside to allow him access.

The room was small and cramped, dominated by an unmade double bed which took up well over half the floor space. Flies were everywhere, their buzzing irritatingly loud as they vied for space with the four white-overalled SOCOs inside, who were testing the various surfaces for DNA, and taking samples from the body. Bolt could get no further than the doorway, which suited him fine.

A woman lay on her side in an approximate fetal position, her feet and ankles wedged under the bed. She was wearing a pink T-shirt with writing on it that Bolt couldn't make out, and a lacy black thong. Her body was bloated and discoloured where the first stages of decomposition were beginning to take effect, but the maggots that were eating her up on the inside had yet to burst out. From his basic knowledge of forensics, Bolt knew this meant that although death had definitely not been recent, it was also unlikely to be more than four days ago, particularly in comparatively warm weather such as they'd been having.

He stood still for several seconds, staring at her dead, ruined body. The abject humiliation of death depressed and horrified Bolt. It always brought home his own mortality, and the sure knowledge that one day he too would end up like this. Nothing more than rotting flesh, all thoughts and memories of a lifetime gone.

'Have we ID'd her yet?'

Mo nodded. 'That's why I called you. Her name's Marie Aniewicz. She's Mrs Devern's cleaner.'

'Jesus Christ,' he whispered, tensing. 'How old was she?'

'Twenty-five,' answered Mo. 'She'd worked at Mrs Devern's place for just under three years.'

He thought of Emma, only eleven years younger, and was unable to stop himself from picturing her here in the same position.

'It's no age, is it?'

'No, it's not.'

Bolt took a deep breath, temporarily forgetting the thick stench of rancid meat.

'What a waste.'

No one said anything for a while. The SOCOs continued to work methodically, as if this was just a routine task for them, which of course to a large extent it was.

'Do we know how she died yet?'

The SOCO nearest to Bolt, who was kneeling

289

down beside the body taking photographs, heard the question and looked up.

'Looks like a single stab wound to the heart,' he said, his voice muffled by his face mask. 'No other obvious injuries on her.'

He gently lifted her right arm with his free hand and touched a thin tear in her T-shirt at roughly the level of her third and fourth ribs. A small dark patch on the T-shirt, not much bigger than two fifty-pence pieces, marked the spot. The fact that there was so little blood, either on the body or anywhere else in the room, suggested to Bolt that she'd died quickly.

'How was she found?' he asked.

'Like this,' answered the SOCO, 'but with the duvet covering her.'

'It's an unusual position to be in for someone who's just been stabbed. I'd have thought she'd be more sprawled out.'

'It looks like she was stabbed, then placed in this position almost immediately. You can see from the lividity that this is where she's been lying most of the time since death.' He pointed to her underside which was darker than the rest of the body where the blood had slowly collected there.

Bolt nodded, and looked around the room. There were no signs of a struggle. The two lamps on either side of the bed were still upright, as were the handful of framed photos and the pot plant on the chest of drawers against one wall. Bolt didn't look at the photos. He didn't want to see what Marie Aniewicz had been like in life.

'Looks like a professional job,' he said when he and Mo were back outside on the pavement, breathing in the comparatively fresh air, glad to be out of the stifling tomb that was the young cleaner's bedroom.

'No one heard a thing, and there's no sign of forced entry, either to the house itself or her bedsit. And it's been difficult to get hold of witnesses. The other ground-floor bedsit's empty, and the rest of the people in the house are apparently illegals, so they've made themselves scarce. The local cops got an anonymous call reporting a nasty smell coming from her room about six o'clock this evening.'

'Does Barry know? And Tina?'

'I got hold of Barry, and he told me to get you down here. He's at some charity function tonight. He wants a full update in the meeting tomorrow morning. I couldn't get hold of Tina. She left before I found out about this, and now she's not answering her phone.'

Bolt exhaled air through his nostrils. 'This puts a whole new perspective on things, doesn't it?'

'Well, there's no way it's unconnected. We haven't got an exact time of death yet, but according to the doctor who examined the body she's been dead somewhere between three and five days. About the time of the kidnapping.'

'There's only one motive for killing the cleaner, then: they found out the alarm code from her and got access to Andrea's house. Which is how they would have placed the trip switch on the front door and found out what Emma was planning on Tuesday. So it's not an inside job.'

'And Phelan's probably not involved.'

'Almost certainly not. Killing the cleaner was a risk. You'd only do that if you had to.'

'So, either they've got Phelan as well as Emma . . .'

'Or he's dead.' Bolt thought of Andrea, wondered how much more bad news she could take. 'They've already killed two people that we know about. There's no reason why they won't have made it three.' Or four, whispered an uninvited voice at the back of Bolt's mind. The fact that the kidnappers could plan to murder a cleaner just to get access to a house meant that it was highly unlikely they'd lose too much sleep over the prospect of killing Emma.

Bolt wiped a hand across his brow. The night was unseasonably warm for September, and he was conscious that he was sweating again.

'These guys really mean business, Mo.'

Mo nodded slowly, his dark eyes full of

sympathy. 'I know. But as you've said, they took a risk killing the cleaner. Someone somewhere might have seen something. Sooner or later they're going to make a mistake. Remember that, boss. No one's luck lasts for ever.'

Thirty

It was close to midnight by the time Bolt walked through his apartment door for the second time that day. He and Mo had stayed at the crime scene for a further half an hour to talk to the senior investigating officer from Tufnell Park CID. They shared what information they could, but were deliberately vague about most of it because of the secrecy of their own op. Bolt had been apologetic about this but it hadn't prevented the senior investigating officer from getting seriously pissed off and threatening to talk to the head of SOCA to get further details if he had to.

After saying his goodbyes to Mo, he'd found a taxi on Junction Road to take him home. On the way back he'd tried Tina's number to bring her up to date with developments but again she wasn't answering, and he decided to leave speaking to her until the morning. He hoped she hadn't suffered any ill effects from her earlier ordeal, and it struck him that maybe he should have done more to check she was OK. At the Glasshouse earlier she'd been quieter than usual, and they'd hardly had a chance to speak. But Tina was a tough cookie. She'd be all right. And at the moment he had enough on his plate without worrying about her.

The first thing he did when he got back inside the apartment was gulp down a large glass of water in an effort to rehydrate himself and get the taste of stale beer off his breath. The remainder of his glass of red wine was on the kitchen top and he was tempted to finish it off, but quickly dismissed the idea. Instead, he threw off his clothes and jumped in the shower, trying hard to relax himself. He was still tense but less so than he had been, even given what he'd just seen. Perhaps he was simply getting more used to it.

It occurred to him as he towelled himself dry that this had possibly been the worst day of his life, and there'd certainly been a fair share of contenders for that accolade over the years. Mainly because it had been so totally and utterly unexpected, and he'd had so little time to react to the speed and ferocity of events as they'd buffeted him again and again.

He was also aware that tomorrow could turn out to be even worse.

Part Five

Part Five

Thirty-one

Bolt tossed and turned all night, his sleep a series of fitful dozes. In those rare times when he did go under, the dreams came, unwelcome and unnerving. In one of them he and Mikaela were living in Andrea's house with two young children of their own. But the children were nameless, face-less wraiths. He wasn't even sure if they were boys or girls, only that he loved them with an intensity he didn't realize he was capable of. Yet every time he went to hold one of them, they would float out of his grip, leaving him feeling progressively more angry and frustrated. He tried to talk about this to Mikaela but she didn't seem to understand. 'They're our children,' was all she said, and she was smiling as she spoke, because Mikaela had always wanted children. It was he who hadn't . . .

Some time later, in the grey time before dawn,

he'd found himself slipping into another dream, this one far clearer and more violent. He was back at the Lewisham robbery – the gunfight that in reality had lasted a matter of seconds, but which had remained etched on his mind for ever. Only this time the robbers were unarmed. They were standing in a line and trying to surrender, hands in the air, their balaclavas removed, all but one of their faces blurred. The one Bolt could see properly was Dean Hayes, a scraggy-faced youth with a hook nose that had been broken more than once, and dyed blond hair. His eyes were wide with fear and he was trying to say something. But in the dream, Bolt was filled with a ferocious rage. These were the bastards responsible for kidnapping his daughter – all of them. The rage made the gun quiver and twitch in his hands, but that didn't stop him from opening fire, the shock of the retorts echoing in his head. Dean Hayes bucked crazily as he was hit repeatedly, until finally he fell sprawling to the pavement. Then Bolt moved the gun in a slow, careful arc, pulling the trigger again and again, experiencing a burst of elation as one after another they went down, hardly hearing the shouts of his colleagues as they tried to get him to stop shooting.

The last thing he remembered was seeing Andrea standing beside him, dressed in the lacy black negligee she was wearing when he'd first met her all those years ago, the gun in her hand kicking as she too opened fire on the men in front of her, her expression a picture of controlled calm.

And then suddenly the dream ended with the shriek of the alarm, and it was back to a reality he'd rather not have had to face.

He was shattered by the time he got into the office that morning. There was a 7.30 meeting for everyone involved in the operation, except those who were on surveillance duty, either watching the area around Andrea's house or keeping tabs on the movements of Leon Daroyce and his close associates. It was led by Big Barry Freud, and was at least partly overshadowed by the discovery of Marie Aniewicz's body the previous evening. There were no further details on her death, although the initial results of her autopsy were expected by mid-afternoon. One thing, though, was clear: she'd been deliberately targeted, and her murder was linked to the kidnap inquiry. Barry seemed unduly hopeful that the results of the house-to-house enquiries in the area, and a search of the murder scene itself, might elicit clues as to the identity of the kidnappers, conveniently glossing over the fact that they had only a matter of hours left before any such clues became irrelevant. There'd been no breaks in the case anywhere else, and the Daroyce surveillance team had nothing to report to suggest that either he or his people were directly implicated, so, once again, everything hinged on the success of the sting operation they were setting up to catch the kidnappers during the ransom drop.

The bulk of the meeting was spent going over the details of the sting itself and everyone's part in it, and Bolt sensed the growing excitement among those present in the incident room as it became clear they were going to get a chance to bring some truly brutal individuals to justice.

Bolt shared none of this excitement. The tension was building in him again, rising to almost intolerable levels as he heard his colleagues discuss the proposed arrest of the kidnappers and the rescue of his daughter, noting grimly that there seemed to be more emphasis on the first objective than on the second, and that Emma was rarely mentioned by name. Once during the meeting he caught Tina's eye. She was looking tired, but she mouthed the words 'You OK?' at him. He managed a small smile and a nod in return, wondering if his stress was that obvious, and she turned away. He watched her for a second, feeling a sudden urge to unburden himself – somehow he knew she'd understand – but he dismissed it immediately, telling himself not to weaken. There were things he needed to do.

When the meeting was over, Bolt asked to see Barry alone.

'You look bloody awful, old mate,' said his boss when they were in his office.

Bolt was already on his fourth coffee of the day. He hadn't eaten anything more substantial than half a sandwich for more than twenty-four hours now, and the lack of food was making him nauseous.

'I feel it.'

'I'd say take a holiday, but we're far too busy for that.'

'I've got a possible lead,' Bolt told him.

Barry frowned. 'Why didn't you mention it in the meeting?'

'I didn't want to muddy the waters. Everyone's got enough to think about without me complicating matters.'

'If it's a lead, it's a lead. What is it?'

Bolt told him about the armed robbery fifteen years ago, how Galante was strongly suspected of being involved, and how Andrea's information had scuppered it, leaving the other robbers dead or behind bars.

Barry looked incredulous. 'So what you're telling me is that you knew Andrea Devern from the past? Why the hell haven't you said anything before now?'

'I only knew her vaguely. She was a friend of a snout.' He could see that Barry didn't entirely believe him. 'Anyway, two of the gang – Marcus

303

Richardson and Scott Ridgers – are out now, and I think we should view them as potential suspects.'

'Why? Were either of them aware that it was Mrs Devern who shopped them?'

Bolt shook his head. 'No, not that I know of. I was deliberately vague about who'd given me the information so that I could protect Mrs Devern. You know what it was like back then. You didn't have to give too many details.'

'So why do you think they'd be targeting her if they didn't know about her part in putting them away?'

It was a good question, and one Bolt had been thinking about a lot.

'They were probably aware that Jimmy Galante was seeing Andrea – Mrs Devern – at the time, so they may well have known her too. Then, when they come out of prison years later, looking for a way to make money and see how well she's doing, they think, well, why not hit on her?'

'Was any reward money paid to Mrs Devern for the information she gave?'

'No.'

'So they couldn't have found out that way.'

Bolt shook his head.

Barry leaned forward in his seat, adopting one of his thoughtful poses, which consisted of steepling his hands together as if in prayer, his index fingers touching his nostrils.

'It's not much, is it?' he said finally.

It wasn't. But for Bolt it was still something.

'These guys are villains, sir. Hardened criminals. Richardson fired at us when we tried to arrest him. He didn't hesitate. There aren't many people around like that. People willing to kill for financial gain like our kidnappers. They've got to be worth looking into.'

Barry sighed loudly. 'I haven't got the resources, Mike. We've got two surveillance teams out already, and everyone else is concentrating on the ransom drop.'

Bolt knew he wasn't going to win, but when he was back in his own office the first thing he did was access the PNC and check the details of Marcus Richardson and Scott Ridgers.

Richardson was the more brutal of the two, having amassed a total of twenty-three convictions in his forty-two years, including one for stabbing a teacher in the eye with a screwdriver when he was only fifteen years old. He'd been released from his sentence for armed robbery and attempted murder in the summer of 2001 and since then had been back inside twice: once for possession of cocaine with intent to supply, the other time for assault, after he'd beaten his girlfriend so badly she'd been in hospital for three days. He'd been out for just over two years now and it looked like he'd kept his nose clean, although someone with a criminal record as long as his was unlikely to have turned over a new leaf. He was currently living in his native Kilburn, and remained on parole, as he would do until his original eighteen-year sentence ran out some time in 2010.

Ridgers had a similar, if slightly less violent, record. Since he hadn't discharged the handgun he was carrying during the robbery, his sentence had been only fourteen years, which Bolt noted wryly didn't say much for how the courts treated the attempted murder of police officers. He'd been released in 1999 but had gone back in three years later, once again for armed robbery, after he'd held up a betting shop at gunpoint, firing several shots into the ceiling. He was caught minutes later by the occupants of an armed response vehicle that had been passing. It seemed that Ridgers wasn't the luckiest armed robber around, and he'd spent a further four years inside before being released back into an unsuspecting community late in 2006.

Bolt stared at their pictures and tried to remember the initial police interviews with them, but after fifteen years and several hundred other suspects his memory of them both was sketchy. Jack Doyle had said neither man was a budding Einstein, so it was unlikely they had organized something like this, but even so, he couldn't get the feeling out of his head that they were worth pursuing.

Throughout the morning the sense of anticipation in the incident room grew. Although most of those present were still involved in the mundane tasks of sifting through camera footage, everyone knew that later on they were going to be in action. That sense became heightened when it was reported that the ransom money, half a million pounds in cash, had arrived in the building and was under armed guard in the basement.

Bolt was on his sixth cup of coffee, feeling wired and knowing he was going to have to eat soon, when Andrea phoned, asking for him. He refused to take the call, making an excuse. For the moment, he had nothing to say to her. He still had doubts that she was telling the truth about his relationship with Emma. The more he thought about her actions, both in the present and in the distant past, the more manipulative he found her.

Yet, as she'd told him, the dates fitted. There was no way round that. Within minutes he was feeling guilty about not taking her call, so he phoned Matt Turner – who was back on babysitting duties, along with Marie Cohen the liaison officer – and asked him what she wanted.

'She just wants to speak to you, sir,' Turner told him when he came back on the line. 'She wouldn't say what it's about.'

'Tell her I'm very busy at the moment. I'll talk to her later. How's she bearing up?'

'Same as she was yesterday. Tired, emotional . . . like you'd expect.'

'OK. Keep an eye on her, can you?'

'Sure – but, boss?'

'Yes.'

'When exactly am I going to get relieved? I'd like to get where the action is. You know, there's not a lot happening here.'

Bolt sympathized with him. He'd have felt the same way too, but he didn't have the time or the inclination to start shuffling resources.

'Soon,' he said. 'I'll sort something.'

He hung up and stared out of the window at the street below. The sun was shining, a few puffy clouds trailed in an otherwise blue sky, and it looked like it was going to be another warm day, the sixth or seventh in a row after the wet summer. When Bolt craned his neck, as he was doing now, he could see one half of a small park, little more than a thin strip of land with a climbing frame and a couple of trees, set between two office buildings. There was a man sitting on one of the benches, a pushbike propped up beside him, and he was looking up at the sky. Bolt was too far away to see his expression, but he knew from the man's casual demeanour that it was one of satisfaction.

Bolt watched him enviously. He'd always been a level-headed man. You needed to be in his line of business, where part of the job involved stalking your target for weeks, sometimes months, at a time. He was finding this sudden change in him just too much to bear.

He turned away and stood up. He could stand it no more. He had to do something other than sit and wait to react to events that might well shatter his life for ever. He had to get out and start influencing them.

Grabbing his jacket, he walked out of the office, telling Kris Obanje, who was the nearest person to him, that he was off for an early lunch.

It was time to renew some old acquaintances.

Thirty-two

Marcus Richardson's bail address was the third floor of a five-storey block of 1960s flats, one of about a dozen identical buildings built in a loose square, which made up an isolated estate just off London's North Circular Road. Even on a sunny, warm day like this one it seemed a bleak place to live, and the streets were near enough deserted as Bolt parked on the opposite side of the road to Richardson's block.

Because all the flats were reached via an open-air walkway running along each floor, Bolt could see directly to his front door. As he stared up at it, he wondered what he was going to do now that he was here. The need for action had been so great that it had driven him out of the office, but he hadn't thought much beyond that. A recent mugshot of Richardson staring moodily at the camera was on the seat beside him. Balding and unshaven, with a double chin and narrow eyes as cold as flint, he looked like the kind of guy who didn't turn down many things for moral reasons, which was the reason Bolt had focused on him first.

He stared at the photo for several seconds, concentrating on the eyes, imagining the man behind them running a knife across Emma's neck, then turned it over and grabbed the ham and cheese baguette he'd bought at a corner shop on the way over, unwrapping it furiously. The idea of eating made him nauseous but he had to have something to keep him going; he couldn't make it through the day on adrenalin alone. He forced down a mouthful while he pondered his next move. Almost immediately he felt his hunger pangs returning, and he demolished the baguette in the space of a minute, washing the bread down with a half-litre bottle of mineral water.

A couple of kids, one carrying a football, walked past chatting, paying him no heed. He was used to waiting around. It was what a surveillance cop did. But this time things were different and it wasn't long before he was fidgeting. He looked at his watch. It was half past twelve. As one of the senior guys on this case, it wasn't going to be long before he was missed. If he was going to do anything, he had to do it now.

He decided on the simple option. Knock on the

door, identify himself, and if Richardson exhibited absolutely no signs of fear or panic he could probably be eliminated from their enquiries. Hardly scientific, but at the moment Bolt was operating on the hoof.

There was only one problem. When he got up there, there was no answer. He knocked a second time, hard and decisive, so that Richardson would know he meant business. But nothing happened. Either he wasn't there, or he wasn't opening up.

Bolt peered through the letterbox, ignoring the stale smell of socks and old food that came back his way. He was looking straight into a small lounge with a cheap sofa and matching chairs. It was empty. A door directly opposite was partly ajar. There didn't seem to be any activity beyond it.

He stood up and looked around. The walkway was empty, the only sound a crying baby beyond one of the doors further up. He knew the risk he was about to take, but it was all about priorities and right now keeping his job wasn't that high on the list. He didn't like breaking the laws he was paid to uphold, but he'd always been a pragmatic man, and like a lot of surveillance cops he was also a highly competent burglar. It took him less than a minute to open the door using the set of picks he always carried with him. Richardson hadn't even bothered to double lock it, which told

Bolt that even if he was involved in the kidnapping he was coming back to the flat regularly. He was also probably not intending to be out for that long, which meant Bolt was going to have to be quick.

He stepped inside, shut the door behind him and gave the room a quick scan, putting on a pair of evidence gloves as he did so. The furnishings were cheap and old; the only thing of any value was a brand-new LCD TV on a stand. There were a couple of lads' magazines and old copies of the *Sun* spread about, and a pile of DVDs stacked up in front of the TV, but it wasn't as messy as many of the bachelor pads Bolt had seen in his time. He noticed that one of the papers was this Thursday's, and by the look of it had been read from cover to cover.

Bolt knew that most armed robbers tended to be big spenders; it was the nature of their business. They lived life fast and hard because they knew their profession could be ended at any time. They snorted coke, they gambled, they bought women. Bolt had always understood why that sort of life held an appeal for certain people. When times were good, the life of an outlaw must have been a lot of fun, and he wondered how well someone like Richardson coped now, living in a poky little place like this. Not very, was his guess. Like all these guys, he'd want to take a shortcut to easy money, and kidnap could be an attractive option.

It was obvious that Richardson lived alone. There were no photos or pictures on the walls, nothing to give it the appearance of a home, and no self-respecting woman would put up with the stale smell, which got worse as he went through the lounge and into the kitchen. Washing up was piled high in the sink, which was half full of rusty-coloured water, and there were plastic fast food containers everywhere, some still with the remnants of earlier meals.

He gave the bathroom a cursory glance, then carried on through into a bedroom with an unmade double bed and a view straight out on to the next block of identical flats. There was no landline in the flat, and it was definitely empty. There was also no evidence that someone had been held there against their will, or even that anyone female had been there at all recently. Bolt felt a surge of disappointment. He'd been positive he was on to something with Richardson; now unwelcome realization began to break over him.

There was a small cabinet beside the bed with a lamp on it. He checked through the drawers, moving quickly, but found nothing other than underwear and socks. Sighing, he stood back up.

Which was when he heard the movement behind him and the menacing, aggression-laced growl, 'Who the fuck are you?'

Thirty-three

Bolt swung round fast, adrenalin surging through him as he came face to face with Marcus Richardson. The first thing that crossed his mind was that Richardson was a lot stockier than he remembered him. The second thing that crossed it was that the former armed robber wasn't going to be waiting for an answer to his question. Instead he came forward fast, his face set hard, and Bolt saw that he had a small wooden cosh in his hand.

'Thought you could fucking rob me, did ya?' he demanded, raising up the cosh for Bolt to see, his biceps rippling beneath his sweat-stained Lonsdale T-shirt, the eyes just as cold and unpitying as they were in the mugshot.

Bolt had to make a decision, fast. He was trapped, with his back to the wall. He could identify himself, say he just wanted to talk, but he knew it would make little difference. In fact, it might make things worse. Richardson had already worked himself up for violence and Bolt knew that if he got the shit kicked out of him now he'd be out of action for days, and with Emma needing him as much as she did he couldn't have that. Not because of the actions of a low-life bottom-feeder like Marcus Richardson.

He experienced a sudden and ferocious sense of injustice, and in that single moment something inside him just snapped. All the tension that had been building up over the past twenty-four hours – the constant frustration, the crushing feeling of impotence – finally found the kind of outlet it had been waiting for. But he knew better than to go in guns blazing.

'Listen, I'm sorry,' he stammered, raising his hands, palms outwards, in a non-confrontational pose.

Richardson grinned, still coming forward, raising his free hand to grab Bolt by the collar.

'You will be, mate.'

Without a sound, or even a change in his contrite expression, Bolt lunged at Richardson, moving so fast that he took the other man completely by surprise. He grabbed both wrists and yanked them apart to create a gap, and before Richardson had time to react Bolt slammed his forehead into the bridge of his opponent's nose.

It was a good hit, but Richardson was no pushover, and though he stumbled, he didn't lose his footing. With an angry, pained grunt, he pulled his weapon hand free of Bolt's grip. But Bolt still had the advantage, and he used it, butting him a second and third time in rapid succession, creating a deep cut just above Richardson's eye.

This time Richardson did fall backwards, landing on the bed, Bolt going down on top of him with as much force as he could muster. The blood was running into his eyes but Richardson still managed to drive the cosh into Bolt's ribs. Bolt grunted in pain but knew he had to keep up the momentum before the other man got his act together, so he rolled over on to Richardson's weapon arm, effectively limiting the cosh's swing to only a few inches. In such a close-quarters position his head remained his best weapon, and he smashed it down into Richardson's face again and again, feeling a blind, furious elation. He heard bones crack under his blows and felt blood slick against his forehead.

Richardson struggled under him. He finally managed to get his other hand free, and used it to grab Bolt by the collar of his shirt and push his face away, but on this day of all days Bolt wasn't stopping for anyone. Spotting an opportunity, and with his usual inhibitions temporarily absent, he rammed two fingers first into Richardson's left eye, then into his right, digging them in as far as he could, ignoring the high-pitched shrieks of pain coming from the other man.

Of all his tactics, this was by far the most effective. Temporarily blinded, Richardson howled and waved his arms about uselessly. Bolt jumped up from the bed, twisting the cosh out of his hand and throwing it against the far wall.

'Jesus, stop it! Take what you want!' wailed the ex-con, writhing about on the bed, pawing at a face that had become a mask of blood.

Bolt stared down at him, panting. His head hurt where he'd been using it as a battering ram, and the baguette was lurching around his stomach. But he was still in the zone, his anger not yet sated, the realization of what he was doing still way off in the distance.

'Have you been keeping your nose clean, Richardson?' he demanded.

'What?'

'You heard me. What have you been doing the last few days?'

'What the fuck are you talking about?'

Bolt lunged forward and pulled him up by his T-shirt, slapping him hard across the face.

'I said, what the fuck have you been doing the last few days?' He stuck his face so close to Richardson's he could smell his blood, confident he was beyond fighting back. 'Tell me where you've been. Now!'

Bolt threw him roughly to the floor. Richardson lay there, squinting up at him. He used his T-shirt to wipe the blood from his eyes, leaving behind a thick stain. His nose looked broken and he was bleeding from several cuts.

'Nowhere,' he answered. 'Just doing my job.'

'What's your job?'

'I'm a labourer. On a site near Wembley. Why do you want to know? And anyway, who the fuck are you?'

'I'm the person who's asking the questions,' Bolt answered, speaking loudly, knowing that the best way of getting answers was to continue the quickfire questions, taking advantage of his dominant position. 'So unless you want more of the same, you answer them.' He stamped a foot down hard on Richardson's chest as he tried to sit up, knocking him back down. 'Now, where have you just been?'

Richardson looked as if he might make a grab for Bolt's leg, then evidently thought better of it.

'Out,' he said. 'Getting lunch.' He motioned towards the kitchen. 'Check if you don't fucking believe me. It's KFC. Three pieces with fries and coleslaw.'

Bolt had stopped panting now. Above the general stench that pervaded the flat was the unmistakable odour of freshly fried chicken. Realizing he might have made a big mistake, he turned back to Richardson, who was a picture of righteous indignation. In no way whatsoever did he look guilty, and in Bolt's experience people who didn't look guilty generally weren't.

'Are you a copper or something?' demanded Richardson, more confident now as he sensed the doubt in Bolt. 'Because I'm going to fucking sue you if you are, you bastard.' He touched a hand to his face, wiped off more blood. 'Look what you've done to me. That's serious assault, that is.'

But Bolt wasn't going to let things go just yet.

'Scott Ridgers. When was the last time you saw him?'

'You are a fucking copper, aren't you?' Richardson said, sitting back up again.

Bolt took a step back and kicked him hard in the chest, knocking him backwards a second time. 'Answer the question!'

'I ain't seen him in years,' Richardson hissed through gritted teeth. 'I don't socialize with perverts.'

Bolt's jaw tightened. 'What do you mean?'

Richardson saw his reaction, and managed a small, mean grin. 'Oh, didn't you know, copper? Scottie Ridgers is a kiddy fiddler. He likes 'em nice and young. Why? He hasn't been after one of your kids, has he?'

Bolt drove the heel of his shoe into Richardson's face, stamping down hard, then kicked him savagely in the ribs, the force of the blow shunting him across the carpet. The anger roared through him. He spat out curses and kicked him again, even though a voice inside his head was screaming at him to stop, stop, stop! But he couldn't. When the red mist came down, as it did so rarely in his life, he had no control over it.

Richardson wailed in pain, but Bolt kept kicking, conscious enough of what he was doing to concentrate on the body and not the head, but still too lost in the rage and emotion of the past twenty-four hours to cease until his victim was curled up in a ball, silent, unmoving and beaten.

Then the full extent of what he was doing hit Bolt like an express train, and he stepped backwards, retreating into the wall, wondering what the hell he'd become. He had to get out of there.

Turning away quickly, he strode through the stinking flat, past the greasy box of KFC and out the front door. And all the time he was thinking, *What the hell is happening to me?* Acting on nothing more than a general hunch, he'd deliberately disobeyed orders, broken into a suspect's flat and beaten the living shit out of him. And now it looked like his victim was almost certainly innocent.

But he'd got some answers. Not the ones he

wanted maybe, but he'd been doing something to get Emma back, and it had felt good. He'd crossed the line before, and had sworn then he wouldn't cross it again. Yet he just had. And the terrifying thing was, part of him had enjoyed it.

Thirty-four

Upstairs they were arguing again. It was the second time she'd heard them today. Emma couldn't hear what they were saying – the voices were too muffled for that – but she knew it was about her, and was pretty sure what the subject would be: whether she lived or died. She wondered which of the two of them was in charge. She prayed it was the smelly one, but something told her he wouldn't be.

Neither man had been down to see her today. This was unusual. It had been light for hours now, and the bucket she was going to the toilet in needed changing. She was also hungry, and though she'd vowed not to eat anything until she could slip off her handcuffs, she thought she might have to relent on that one. She was using up plenty of energy, scraping away at the wall – a task that had become something of a full-time activity. The chain was definitely getting looser, but it still wasn't budging, and she knew she was beginning to run out of time. The nail had worn down by about a third, and her fingers were stiff and aching. If she stopped eating altogether, she ran the risk of being too weak to escape if an opportunity did somehow arise, although she was still unsure exactly how she'd get out anyway, even if she got the chain free from the wall.

Take it one step at a time, she told herself.

Upstairs the voices stopped, and she broke off what she was doing too, replacing the nail under her pillow and pushing the bed back against the wall so that the metal plate wasn't showing.

For a few minutes she sat there in silence, the butterflies racing around her stomach as she wondered if they'd come to a decision about what to do with her. Maybe they had; maybe they'd agreed it was best simply to kill her. 'Calm down,' she whispered out loud. 'Calm down. Remember what Mum always says. It's the tough ones who rise to the top.'

But when the cellar door opened she had to stop herself from crying out as she pushed herself back against the wall, praying that this wasn't the end, reaching for the hood she had to wear and thrusting it over her head, not wanting to give them any more of an excuse for getting rid of her.

It was the smelly one. She could hear his heavier footfalls as he came down the steps, that wheezing of his. She felt a surge of relief, even enjoyed the familiar odour of his BO, which was stronger than usual today. She heard him stop at the bed, put some food down on the floor, and change the waste bucket.

'Hello,' she said uncertainly.

'All right, love?' he answered, in his gruff voice. 'Did you sleep all right?'

She nodded. 'OK, I guess.'

She could smell his breath as he crouched down in front of her.

'I just need you to do another little message for your mum. I want you to let her know what day it is, so she knows you're OK.'

'OK.'

'So, I'm going to lift your hood up, all right? Just a little bit so you can see the date on the paper.'

She nodded again, waiting patiently while he lifted up the hood and placed the newspaper in front of her face, obscuring her view of anything else. He held it there, giving her plenty of time to see it, and she stared straight ahead obediently, confirmed that it was indeed Saturday, and the hood was replaced. He then recorded a very short message from her before switching off the tape player.

'Well done, love,' he said, trying to sound all cheery, but not quite making it. 'Not long now and you'll be home in front of the telly.'

'What are you arguing about up there?'

'Can you hear us?' He seemed surprised.

'I can't hear what you're saying, but I know you're arguing, because your voices are very loud. Is it about me?'

'Course not.'

She didn't believe him. 'He wants to kill me, doesn't he?'

'No, no, it's not like that,' he said quickly, but he sounded flustered, like one of her friends who'd been caught out telling a lie.

'Please don't let your friend kill me. Please. I never saw his face, I promise, whatever he says.'

'I won't, love, it's all right.'

'Because I know how cruel he is. When he came down here yesterday, he really scared me.'

Beneath the hood, she pretended to cry (she'd vowed not to cry for real any more), hoping this would make him feel sorry for her. And it seemed to work. He put an arm around her and pulled her into his shoulder. The smell of BO coming from his armpit made her want to gag but she forced herself to ignore it. She had to keep him on her side.

'I promise you, darling, no one's going to hurt you while I'm here. I wouldn't let anyone hurt defenceless kids.' His hand stroked her head. 'Tonight it's all going to be over and you'll be going home. I'm sorry my friend had to come down yesterday. I didn't want him to, but it was important your mum took things seriously, you know.'

'He put a knife to my face.'

His arm tensed, almost crushing her. She realized then how strong he was.

'Bastard,' he hissed angrily. 'Did he?'

'Yes.'

'Don't worry, he won't be coming down here again. And he won't touch you, I promise. No one hurts kids on my watch.'

His hand continued to stroke her hair, his gloved fingers slowly massaging her head. It was a horrible, creepy sensation, like spiders running across it, and she really wanted to move away, but she couldn't. He had her pinned.

'Who's in charge?' she whispered, trying to ignore what he was doing. 'You or him?'

'Neither,' he answered, but she heard him hesitate. And that told her everything.

It was the cruel one.

She desperately wanted to feel better, had hoped that his words might soothe her, but as he got up and left, telling her to enjoy her meal, the waste bucket sloshing and slapping against the banister as he mounted the steps, she felt instead a growing sense that something dark and terrible was about to happen.

And it was going to happen soon.

Thirty-five

Scott Ridgers' place was no palace either. He lived in the basement flat of a dilapidated post-war townhouse situated on a back street near Finsbury Park, the paintwork so faded that the people who'd last given it a lick probably owned ration books. The stone steps that led down to Ridgers' front door were caked in an unpleasant combination of dried and fresh pigeon shit, and Bolt had to tread carefully to avoid taking away any unwanted souvenirs from his visit.

The curtains were pulled, and when Bolt knocked on the door, it quickly became clear that Ridgers wasn't in either, although unlike Richardson, he was far less blasé about personal security. The single window, not much bigger than a porthole, was barred, and there were no fewer than three locks on the front door, including two five-levers. They were all in use as well. Bolt wasn't put off.

He could get past almost any locks. The problem was he'd had his fingers burned once already today. Richardson had had no idea who he was, but if he made a fuss and reported what had happened to the local cops, there might be ramifications.

Bolt was in no mood for a further confrontation. His head still hurt from the last one, as did his ribs, where Richardson had dug his cosh into them. But he also knew that having driven over here, he needed to do something. It was ten to two now. He'd turned his mobile off but knew he couldn't keep it off for much longer, and when he did switch it back on he knew he was going to have to come up with a decent reason why he'd gone AWOL on arguably the most important day for his team since it had first been formed eighteen months earlier. It was now or never.

But as he took out the picks, he heard a noise above him.

'He's been gone for days,' said a female voice. 'Your lot probably frightened him off.'

Bolt looked up and saw a short, grey-haired woman in her late sixties dressed in a black trouser suit more suited to a Khmer Rouge guerrilla than a London senior citizen.

'What do you mean, your lot?' he asked with a puzzled smile, wondering how on earth she'd recognized him as a copper. He was dressed casually in jeans and trainers, and that, coupled with the flecks of blood on his shirt, made him sure he didn't look like one at all.

'Are you working for him?' she continued, her tone suspicious. 'The dad?'

'I don't know who you're talking about, I'm afraid.'

'Who are you, then?'

Bolt saw no point in denying his official role. 'I'm a police officer.'

Her expression didn't lighten. It seemed even the nation's senior citizens were against the police these days.

'Haven't you got anything better to do than harass a poor man who's just trying to get on with his life? Scott's a lovely lad. Who sent you? The dad? Can't he let it go?'

'I think you've got me wrong, madam. I'm here to let Scott know that a friend of his has been badly hurt in an accident.'

'Oh, I'm sorry, I didn't realize. Who's that, then? Scott doesn't have many friends.'

'It's someone from the past,' he answered with suitable vagueness, coming back up the steps so he no longer had to crane his neck to talk to her, stepping in pigeon shit on the way. 'You don't happen to know where he is, do you?'

She shook her head. 'I haven't seen him for a few days now. He's probably run off somewhere to escape her dad.'

'Whose dad?'

'Lisa's. That's Scott's girlfriend. I haven't seen her yet, but Scott thinks the world of her. He says she's beautiful.'

Bolt looked puzzled. 'So why's her dad after him?'

'Because he says she's too young,' she answered in a tone that suggested he was being entirely unreasonable. It was clear this lady had a lot of time for Scott.

'And how old is she?'

'It's hard to tell these days, but Scott says she's quite old enough to make her own decisions.'

'I know what you mean,' Bolt agreed. 'Can you remember the last time you saw Scott?'

She thought about it for a moment. 'It was at the beginning of the week, I think. Monday or Tuesday. To be honest, I've been a bit worried. It's not like him not to be around. I usually see him most days when I'm passing. He likes to sit out the front here on his deckchair, watching the world go by. Do you think he's all right?'

'It might be worth checking. Do you have keys to his flat?'

She shook her head. 'Sorry, no.'

The timing of Ridgers' absence was certainly interesting. However, it didn't bring Bolt any closer to finding him now.

'Do you know where Scott's girlfriend lives?' he asked.

She shrugged. 'Over in Paddington somewhere.'

'That's a long way from here.'

'They met on the internet,' she said with a conspiratorial whisper, as if this was some kind of magic.

'That doesn't really help me much.'

'I know her last name, though. Scott told me because it's so pretty.' She pronounced it Boo-sha-ra, with something of a flourish, but then had the good sense to spell it for him. 'Lisa B-o-u-c-h-e-r-a. It's French, apparently,' she explained as Bolt memorized it.

He felt a glimmer of hope. London was a big city, but there weren't going to be many people of that name floating around Paddington. It wasn't much, but he was beginning to grow used to getting by on slim pickings. He thanked the old lady and walked back to his car, without looking back.

When he was inside, he switched on his mobile, dialled 118 118 and asked for the number of a Bouchera in the W2 postcode area. He could have got the information faster by phoning the Glasshouse, but he wanted to avoid speaking to anyone there for the moment.

There was one number listed under that name,

and he called it straight away. A man answered after three rings.

'Hello, is that Mr Bouchera?' asked Bolt.

'Who's asking?' came the gruff reply.

Bolt identified himself, and asked if he was the same man whose daughter Lisa was seeing a Mr Scott Ridgers.

'That bloody pervert. Yes, my daughter has been seeing him. I'm glad you lot are finally taking it seriously now. I want him arrested.'

'I'm sorry, sir, but we can't arrest him if your daughter's over the legal age of consent.'

'What do you mean, the legal age of consent? She's fifteen, for God's sake!'

Bolt's mouth went dry. 'What?'

'She's fifteen years old, mate,' he snapped, disgust in his voice. 'Only just turned as well. Why on earth do you think I called the police about it? They've been getting up to all sorts as well. She even filmed some of it on her mobile phone. He should be locked up.'

Bolt thought of Emma at the mercy of a murdering thug with a predilection for young girls.

'Didn't you know any of this? What the hell are you phoning for?'

'Listen to me,' Bolt snapped. 'Is your daughter still seeing him?'

'Course not. What do you take me for? I

grounded her as soon as I found out about it. And confiscated her mobile. But she's been sneaking out to see him. I got the police round here to talk to her but she wouldn't tell them anything. Denies everything. He even gave her this software that wiped all their conversations off her computer. I've been at my wits' end trying to sort it out. I've threatened her, locked her in her room, even found out where he lived and went round. But the bastard wasn't there.'

'Is Lisa at home now?'

'Yeah. She hasn't been out for the last few days, except for school. She's just moping about, not speaking. I'm hoping she's over him.'

'Have you still got her mobile phone?'

'I gave it back to her yesterday if she promised not to call him. So far, I don't think she has. She's a good girl, you know. That bastard corrupted her. If I could get my hands on him . . .'

'I know exactly how you feel,' Bolt told him, 'but in the meantime you can help us locate him, because we're very interested in talking to him about a number of matters.'

'What kind of matters?'

'The kind that'll put him away for a very long time.'

Bouchera grunted. 'Good.'

'But I need to know straight away if Lisa hears from him, or if you hear him speaking to her.

Understand? And if you can get the number he's speaking to her from, even better.' Bolt gave Bouchera his mobile number, then wrote down the daughter's number and the name of her service provider. 'It doesn't matter what time of day or night it is, call immediately. It's extremely urgent.'

'Course I will,' replied Bouchera. 'I want to see that bastard suffer.'

Bolt thanked him and ended the call. There was still no proof Ridgers was involved, but Bolt's gut instinct was telling him he was definitely on to something here.

Ordinarily, the excitement at getting a lead like this would have been surging through him, but instead he felt a growing sense of dread. Time was running out and Scott Ridgers could be anywhere. If he didn't find him, and the ransom op failed, then he was convinced now that Emma was as good as dead. But he wasn't going to give up. Not while there was still an ounce of fight in him.

Thirty-six

The phone rang as he pulled out into the road. It was a message from Mo, wondering where he was. There was obvious concern in his colleague's voice. The time of the message was 1.27 – just over half an hour ago.

But Bolt didn't call him back. Instead he called Tina. 'I need you to check on whether there are any mobile numbers registered to a Mr Scott Ridgers of Hanbury Gardens, N19,' he told her. It was a long shot that someone like Ridgers would have registered anything in his name, particularly a mobile phone. Criminals don't like giving the authorities a means of tracing them. And even if he'd done so, Bolt doubted whether he would have taken it with him on a job as important and risky as a kidnap. But it was still worth a try.

Tina asked who Scott Ridgers was.

'I'll explain later, I promise.'

'You sound excited. Where are you? People have been asking. I mean, it's a big day, and you've been gone a long time.'

There was a trace of criticism in her voice, something Bolt hadn't heard from Tina before, and he wondered if his team were beginning to lose respect for him. If so, it was something he was going to have to counter. Just not now.

'I've been following something up, and I'm on the way back. I won't be long.'

He hung up and called Mo, telling him a briefer version of the same story – that he'd been following up on a lead – deliberately keeping details scarce. He didn't want to tell his friend too much about Ridgers, still less ask him a favour, because Bolt had the distinct feeling he would refuse.

Mo told him to hold on while he went somewhere private.

'Why are you working on a lead that no one knows anything about?' he asked. 'On a day as important as this one.'

'It's just something that's come up, OK? From the past.'

'Do you want to share it?'

'I'll tell you about it later.'

There was a pause.

'I think this is getting too personal for you, boss,' he said eventually.

It was the first time Bolt could remember Mo questioning his abilities, and it galled him. He felt like telling his old friend to butt out.

'I'm not going to mess this up, Mo.'

'Don't, please. I respect you, boss. Don't make me lose that respect.'

There was a genuine pain in his voice that cut into Bolt, and neither man spoke for a few seconds, both unsure what to say. It was Bolt who finally broke the silence.

'This time, Mo, I'm going to have to ask you to be the one to have faith. I promise you I know what I'm doing.'

'OK. That's good enough for me. But don't try to do everything on your own. It won't work.'

Bolt said he wouldn't, and it was with an element of genuine relief that he ended the call.

There was a traffic snarl-up around Millbank and it wasn't until twenty to three that he finally reached the office, having already found out from Tina that there was no mobile anywhere in the UK registered in the name of a Scott Ridgers of Hanbury Gardens, N19. He hadn't even made the incident room before Barry collared him. He didn't look very happy at all.

'Where the hell have you been?' he demanded.

Bolt knew immediately that he was going to have to tell him, but as soon as he started talking, Barry's expression darkened.

'Let's get to my office,' he snapped, looking round to make sure that no one was witnessing his wrath.

'What's going on, Mike?' he asked, his voice laden with exasperation, when they were behind closed doors. 'I thought I told you not to go running off on a wild goose chase.'

'With all due respect, sir, I don't think it is a wild goose chase.'

Bolt explained about Scott Ridgers' absence over the past few days, though he didn't mention his taste for underage girls, since he wasn't sure what relevance this had.

'So, what the hell does that prove? Maybe he's gone on holiday.'

'He's been gone since Monday. You've got to admit, it's coincidental.'

Barry nodded furiously. 'Yes, it is coincidental, isn't it? But that's all it is. A coincidence. It doesn't help us one fucking iota.'

Bolt couldn't remember the last time his boss had sworn. It was a measure of his anger and the pressure he and they were all under.

'I thought it was better than just waiting around. I'm convinced I'm on to something.'

'Did Tina say there was a mobile registered in his name?'

Bolt admitted there wasn't.

'So you're not on to something, are you? Listen,

340

Mike, you're going to have to pull yourself together. I don't know what the hell's got into you over this, but whatever it is, it's got to stop. And what's happened to your face? You've got a bloody great bruise coming up.'

'I had an accident. Banged my head against the car door.'

Barry's gaze then dropped to the bloodstains on his shirt.

'Are you all right to go through with this tonight? Because if you're not . . . if you're not well or something . . .'

'I'm fine, I promise.'

But even as Bolt spoke, he wondered for the first time whether he really was capable of operating effectively. He thought of Marcus Richardson, his face smeared with blood as he lay curled up in a defenceless ball against his flailing kicks; of Emma, a girl he might never know, chained to a rusty iron bed, a black hood over her head, while an unseen man ran a knife across her neck. Then he forced out the thoughts and focused on his boss.

'I won't mess this up,' he said firmly.

Barry nodded once, accepting the answer. 'Good. I need you fine. In fact, I need you more than fine. You were the one who initiated this op, and it's got to work.' He looked at his watch. 'We've got a final briefing at three thirty for everyone taking part. After that, I want you and Mo to get down to Mrs Devern's place and brief her. It's essential she doesn't mess things up either. There's going to be a lot riding on her.'

'She knows that.'

'Make sure she knows it again.'

'What about the ransom money?'

'You're taking it with you, so don't suddenly go AWOL again.' He smiled to show he was joking, but Bolt wasn't entirely sure he was. 'The rest of the team are going to be following you,' he continued, 'so we'll be ready to move as soon as they call. You'll be in charge on the ground. I'll be overseeing things from here.'

'No problem.'

Bolt nodded decisively because he had a feeling this was the kind of encouraging gesture Barry wanted to see. His boss looked more stressed than Bolt had seen him for a while, and he knew that his own actions weren't exactly helping.

'If this goes well, it'll be a huge boost for SOCA, and for us,' said Barry, watching Bolt closely, looking, it seemed, for answers. 'But if things go wrong . . .' He let the words hang in the air for several seconds. 'If they go wrong, then you and me, we're going to be in a lot of shit, old mate.'

More than you'll ever know, thought Bolt. *More than you'll ever know.*

Thirty-seven

The briefing was short and to the point. It focused purely on how the operation to follow the money, apprehend the kidnapper and rescue Emma was going to work. It seemed like a good plan with an extremely high chance of success to most people. To Bolt it was full of holes.

Afterwards, when he and Mo were in the Jaguar driving to Andrea's place in a convoy of cars containing the rest of the team, the canvas holdall with the half a million pounds locked safely in the boot, Mo asked him about the lead he'd been working on all day. Bolt knew he had to tell his friend the truth now, so he told him about his visits to Richardson's and Ridgers' addresses, leaving out the part where he beat the shit out of Richardson.

'Why didn't you tell me any of this earlier?' Mo asked.

'I didn't want you thinking that I'd lost control – you know, after what I told you yesterday.'

'But you spoke to Tina. Do you trust her more than me?'

'No, I don't. Of course not. I just wasn't sure what you'd say if I asked you to look up Ridgers' number. Also, Tina's got good contacts at the phone companies.'

'And you really think I wouldn't have helped you?' Mo looked deflated.

'Look, I'm sorry.'

Bolt wished he wasn't having this conversation. He wished too that he hadn't opened his mouth the previous day and put himself in such a vulnerable position with one of his most trusted colleagues.

'How did you get that bruise on your head? And the blood on your shirt?'

'I had an accident. Banged my head on the car doorframe.'

'I'm a detective, boss, not a ten-year-old.'

Bolt sighed. 'I broke into Richardson's place. He attacked me. We had a fight. That's how I got it.'

'What the hell is happening to you?' demanded Mo.

'What's happening to me is that it could be my daughter who's imprisoned by the kind of scum who've already killed at least twice, and so won't hesitate a single minute to kill again. That's what's happening. OK?'

'But you can't go round breaking into people's houses and having fights with them. It's just not the way to get things done.'

'What is the way, then? Tell me!'

'To focus,' snapped Mo. 'To focus on making sure this operation's a success. Not on running round on a wild goose chase.'

'It's not a wild goose chase.'

'It is, boss. What proof have you got that either of them has any involvement whatsoever? Absolutely none.' Mo shook his head angrily. 'If it wasn't so bloody late in the day, I'd be talking to Barry about it right now.'

They continued the rest of the journey in brooding silence. They'd never argued before, not like this. They'd had the occasional niggling disagreement and cross words, but it had never got anywhere near the position they were in now. Mo was openly questioning his ability to do the job, and, though Bolt desperately didn't want to admit it, he had some justification too. Another line had been crossed, one from which it was going to be a hard journey back, and he knew exactly whose fault it was.

Thirty-eight

It was after five when he and Mo left the convoy and turned into Andrea's street, having been given the all-clear by the surveillance team watching the house. It was the third time in a little over twenty-four hours that he'd been here, and each time Bolt arrived he felt worse than the time before. He couldn't help wondering how he was going to be feeling the next time he came – if there was a next time.

Heaving the bag containing the money out of the boot, he walked to the gate in silence, Mo following behind. Marie the liaison officer buzzed them through. She was wearing a more concerned expression than usual as she opened the door to him.

'Still no word from the kidnappers,' she told him.

'How's Andrea?'

'She's bearing up, but her nerves are shot with all this waiting. I think all of ours are.'

It was the first sign from Marie that she was getting personally involved in the case. Bolt wasn't surprised. Liaison officers might be highly trained but they were still human, and, he noted wryly, someone like Andrea had always been good at tugging on other people's heartstrings.

'They'll be in contact soon enough,' he said, nodding to Matt Turner who'd poked his head round the door of the study. 'Is she upstairs?' he asked Marie.

'She's in the lounge,' she answered quietly. 'She's been there most of the afternoon. She said she wanted to be left alone.'

Andrea was on the same sofa she'd been on yesterday afternoon. Apart from the change of clothes – she was smarter today, in a white blouse and black knee-length skirt – she might as well not have moved. Her haunted, almost hypnotized expression remained the same, and she only gave him the barest of glances as he and Mo entered the room.

Bolt felt a sudden, almost overwhelming urge to take her in his arms, but he fought it back down. He put the holdall on the floor between them and took a seat opposite her. Mo remained standing near the door.

'They haven't called, Mike.'

'I know. But they will. They want the money, Andrea. That's their sole motivation for this.'

She stared into space. 'I can't lose her. I . . . I just don't know what I'd do.'

Bolt leaned forward in the seat, willing her to look at him. 'You've got to be strong, Andrea. Do you understand?'

'OK,' she said quietly in a voice that didn't fill Bolt with confidence. For the first time he wondered if she'd be able to do what they needed her to do.

'For Emma's sake.'

She nodded, a little more decisively this time, and looked down at the holdall.

'Is that the money?'

'Yes. There's a tracking device attached to the lining on the inside. It's so small it'll be almost impossible to find. There are also two further devices, also very tiny, attached to the notes inside.'

'But surely the kidnappers'll find them?'

'Eventually they will, yes, if they know what they're looking for.'

'Which they do, Mike. You know they do.'

'But we're not going to let them run with this money for long. We'll be following you the whole way as you deliver it. There'll be surveillance teams travelling in front of you and behind. There'll also be helicopter back-up. There's no way you're going to be in any danger.'

'I'm not worried about me, Mike, I'm worried about Emma. We're putting her life in danger here, and I can't stop thinking about it.'

'Look, we'll keep back so we're not noticeable, and you'll be wearing a mike so we can monitor any conversation you have, and a tracking device so we don't lose you either. Mo, can you put them on for Andrea?'

Mo nodded curtly, and attached the devices to Andrea's blouse while Bolt continued.

'When you've delivered the money and with-drawn from the scene, we'll track the money to its destination. The kidnappers may put the money in a different bag but they won't have a chance to check half a million pounds in cash for trackers. We'll then follow them and the money to that destination and arrest them there.'

'But what if Emma isn't there? What if they're hiding her somewhere else?'

It was the big question, one that Bolt really didn't want to think about, because it represented the biggest flaw in their plan.

'The chances are she will be, Andrea. If all the kidnappers are involved in the drop – and given that there are only two of them, three at the most, they probably will be – then they won't want to leave her alone for long, I promise you.'

'It's all chances and likelys though, isn't it, Mike?' she said as Mo moved aside. 'That's the problem. There are no guarantees. They've already killed Jimmy. What if they kill Emma too?'

Bolt could have added that they'd also killed her cleaner, but he didn't. Back at the Glasshouse it had been decided not to tell Andrea about this latest development until after the ransom drop, because of how it might affect her mental state.

'There are no guarantees, Andrea. Not in something like this. But you've got to trust us. We know what we're doing.' He decided to change the subject. 'Have you ever heard of anyone by the name of Scott Ridgers?'

She lit a cigarette with shaking hands, and blew out a thin plume of smoke. 'No. Should I have? Who is he?'

Bolt told her about the possible connection. When he'd finished, she looked shocked.

'You're not saying this has got anything to do with what happened all those years ago, are you?'

'It's possible. We can't find him at the moment.'

'Was it common knowledge that I told you about the robbery, then?' She glanced at Mo as she spoke. 'I swore you to secrecy.'

'And I kept it secret, I promise. It's just a possibility that he's involved.'

'I only ever met a couple of Jimmy's friends, and I don't remember a Scott Ridgers,' she mused.

'Fair enough,' he said, not entirely able to mask the disappointment in his voice. He wasn't totally surprised. Ridgers was a vague lead at best, and now he was beginning to get vaguer.

It was a long shot, but he pulled out of a pocket an A4-sized copy of Scott Ridgers' latest mugshot and unfolded it.

'This is a photo of him.'

The moment she took it, her eyes widened.

'I know him,' she said simply.

Thirty-nine

'He's done work in the garden here before,' said Andrea, still staring at the photo. 'For the firm I use. I've seen him here a couple of times.'

Bolt looked at Mo. His colleague's face was impassive.

'What's the name of the firm?'

'Brandon Landscapes. I've got a business card with all their details round here somewhere.'

She got up and rummaged round in the top drawer of the pine cabinet next to the sofa until she found what she was looking for.

'And when did you see the man in the photo here?'

'He's only been here recently,' she said, handing Bolt the card. 'In the last few weeks. I hadn't seen him before that.'

'Did he act suspiciously at all?' asked Mo, speaking for the first time.

Andrea shook her head, sitting back down. 'No. Just did his job.'

'Did he ever come inside the house?'

'No. I never let any of the gardeners inside the house. There was never any need. And also, quite a few of the people who work for Mike Brandon have criminal records.'

Bolt raised his eyebrows. 'Really?'

'The idea's to help them get back on their feet. I've always thought it was a good idea but, you know, I'm not entirely stupid. I'm not going to give them the run of the place. Not with their backgrounds.' She picked up the photo again. 'God, do you really think he might be involved?'

Bolt suddenly wished he wasn't, after what Bouchera and Richardson had both said about him, but he nodded. 'Yes, I do. And it shows we're on the right track.' He glanced at Mo as he said this.

Bolt looked at the card Andrea had given him and saw that Brandon was a local Hampstead firm.

'Well, we're going to need to get on to them straight away and see if they've got any other contact details for Mr Ridgers.'

He stood up and excused himself and Mo.

As soon as they were out in the hall, Bolt let out a deep breath. He turned to his colleague, hoping for some form of acknowledgement that he'd been right to follow up the lead.

'I still don't agree with how you went about it,' he said grudgingly.

'This is my daughter we're talking about,' Bolt hissed, leaning close to Mo. 'I had no choice. And now we're getting somewhere, aren't we? Because this is way too coincidental. Ridgers is involved. No question.'

'OK, but we still don't know where he is and we haven't got a lot of time to find him.'

Bolt nodded. 'But I was right to do what I did.'

He turned away before Mo could say anything else and dialled the number for Brandon Landscapes. The call went straight to message and he left one, asking Mike Brandon to get back to him urgently. Then he called Big Barry and gave him the news.

Barry seemed to forget his earlier irritation with Bolt, and praised him for his good work. 'We don't want to put out an alert in case any local copper tries to nick him before he's picked up the money. But it's good to be able to put a name to one of them, Mike. Well done.'

Matt Turner emerged from the study as Bolt came off the phone.

'Any chance of getting relieved here, boss?' he asked. 'I'm going stir crazy.'

'Don't worry,' Bolt told him wearily, 'this is all going to be over soon.'

He wasn't sure what else to say so he left Turner

and Mo there and went and stood out in the garden. He had a strong need to get away from everyone. It was a beautiful early autumn afternoon, with only a few wispy strands of cloud and aircraft trails crossing an otherwise perfect azure sky, but he was unable to enjoy the solitude. Like Andrea, he couldn't stand the waiting. It gave him far too much time to think, and the fact that his hunch had paid off was proving to be a double-edged sword. As Barry had said, it was good to be able to ID one of the kidnappers, but the fact remained that he'd also been accused of being a paedophile, and he was quite possibly holding Bolt's daughter. That thought made relaxation of any kind impossible.

He paced the garden for quite a while, then went back inside. He could hear Mo, Turner and Marie talking quietly in the study but couldn't make out what they were saying. Not wanting to interrupt them, he knocked on the living-room door and was unsurprised to see Andrea still in her seat, smoking.

'You know what?' she said through the smoke, without looking at him. 'The contents of that bag . . .' She motioned with a flick of her head towards the holdall on the floor. 'It's just a load of fucking paper, isn't it? I've spent my whole life trying to earn as much as I can of those little bits of paper, and all for what? A nice big house.

A big car. A daughter I might never see again . . .'

'You can't think like that, Andrea. You've got to be positive.'

She managed a weak smile. 'We'll get through it. Won't we?'

'If we're strong, we'll get through it. And tonight we both need to be very strong, and very focused.'

She stubbed the cigarette out in the ashtray and stood up, taking a step towards him. 'Will you hold me?' she asked him. 'Just for a moment?'

She looked so vulnerable that Bolt knew there was no way he could resist, and he went to take her in his arms.

And then stopped, startled by a sound that inspired hope and fear in equal measure.

The ringing of the phone.

Forty

Emma's voice came over the line on loudspeaker. Like the previous day, it was a recording. Unlike the previous day, Bolt's relationship with her had changed, and he experienced a wrenching in his stomach as she spoke, her words nervous and halting.

'Hi Mum, it's me. I'm OK. It's Saturday. I've seen the paper.' A short pause. 'They say that they'll let me go tonight if you give them the money. But you can't involve the police. Please. Otherwise . . .' Another pause, longer this time.

They were in the study. All five of them. Turner, Marie, Mo, Bolt and Andrea. Turner clicked frantically on his laptop, trying to secure a trace. The others stood silent, waiting. Bolt couldn't look at Andrea, even though he knew she was looking at him. The receiver was shaking in her hand. He caught Mo's eyes and saw sympathy there. He didn't acknowledge it. Instead, he stared at a fixed point high on the ceiling, his jaw set hard.

There was a click at the other end of the phone, and then the familiar disguised voice came on the line.

'Do you have the money yet, Mrs Devern?'

'Yes.' Delivered firmly.

'Good. And have you spoken to the police?'

'No.' Delivered just as firmly.

'We have someone with your daughter. He has instructions to kill her at ten p.m. exactly if he hasn't heard from us, so I would advise you strongly to do the right thing this time.'

Bolt flinched at his words, and for a moment Andrea appeared unsteady on her feet; then she began to speak confidently into the phone.

'I told you, I haven't,' she said. 'I just want to get this thing over with.'

'Good. You have sat-nav in your car, don't you?'

'Yes.'

'Munroe Drive in N7 is a six-minute drive away from you in normal traffic. You've got four minutes to get there or the deal's off. Drive to the end and await my call.'

'But—'

The line went dead. Andrea let the receiver drop to the floor.

'Jesus, where are my keys? I've only got four minutes.'

'Don't panic, Andrea,' Bolt told her sharply. 'He's bluffing. Remember, he wants the money. Just stay calm and get to Munroe Drive as soon as you can.' He looked at Turner. 'Trace?'

'Mobile, north London. That's all I've got. If he's following the same MO as yesterday, he'll have switched the phone off by now.'

But Bolt was no longer listening. Pressing his mobile to his ear, he put a call in to Barry in the control room. 'It's on,' was all he said. Then, as he followed Andrea out of the room, he called the surveillance team leader outside.

'It's clear,' came the reply.

'We're on the move,' Bolt told him.

'Good luck.'

I'm going to need more than that, Bolt thought as he hung up. But for the first time in over twenty-four hours he felt better. He was taking charge of a well-rehearsed operation. The stakes were higher than he'd ever known, but at least it was now up to him.

'The mobile he called on was a different one from yesterday,' said Turner, coming out of the study, 'and it is already switched off. Somewhere in N17, not far from yesterday's.'

'Good work, Matt.'

'I want to come with you.'

Bolt looked at him.

'Please, boss. I don't want to stay here.'

There was no time to argue.

'All right, you can come with me and Mo.'

Bolt grabbed the holdall containing the money, and once Andrea had retrieved her keys from the kitchen, they left the house together. The money was heavy and he struggled to keep up with her as she ran down the street to her car. He pulled open the door and dropped it into the passenger seat as Andrea switched on the engine and hurriedly fed Munroe Drive N7 into her sat-nav. She looked terrified, but focused. He wished her luck but she didn't even glance his way. Instead she leaned over, shut his door and pulled away from the kerb.

One minute had passed.

'I'll drive,' Bolt announced, jumping in the Jag with Mo and Turner.

He shoved in his earpiece, switched on the loop mike he was wearing round his neck, and then they were away, doing a rapid three-point turn in the middle of the street. A middle-aged couple walking arm in arm stopped and watched them curiously. *Lucky sods*, Bolt thought. *Not a care in the world*.

There were five surveillance cars and two motorbikes involved in the convoy. As with all surveillance ops, they would switch position constantly so that no one vehicle stood out, just in case the kidnappers had decided to tail Andrea themselves. All communication would now be done by radio, using call signs, so that every person involved could hear what was being said and be able to act accordingly.

Bolt got into position behind a Toyota Auris with Tina Boyd and Kris Obanje inside.

'I think our targets are getting paranoid,' said Mo. 'Munroe Drive's a dead end.'

'Shit. They're obviously checking for tails. We're going to have to be very, very careful here.'

He turned right out of Andrea's road, pulled over while another of the surveillance cars overtook him, then accelerated, his fingers drumming on the wheel as the tension coursed through him. He looked at his watch.

Two minutes.

They turned again, this time on to the Finchley Road, heading north in the direction of the North Circular. Traffic was steady rather than heavy and one of the surveillance bikes roared past them, disappearing into the distance and tucking in behind Andrea's Mercedes, which was fifty yards ahead and weaving in and out of the lanes, moving fast. The surveillance vehicles would be travelling both behind and in front of her, so she could be kept under the eyeball at all times, but her speed and the erratic nature of her driving were making it difficult for them.

Bolt leaned against the window looking

skywards, hoping that Barry was being true to his word and keeping the helicopter back and out of sight. Even in a sprawling city like London, where helicopters are a common sight, it would stick out a mile to the kidnappers. But today the sky was clear.

Three minutes.

Up ahead, the lights went amber. Andrea accelerated through them, just as they went red, the surveillance bike going through just behind her. The two cars in front of Bolt stopped, giving him no choice but to do the same. He cursed, and his finger-tapping on the seat intensified as he counted the seconds in his head as Andrea's car disappeared from sight.

One, two, three ... thirteen, fourteen, fifteen ... twenty-two, twenty-three ...

'Come on, come on,' he hissed.

As the lights turned green again, there was a crackle of static in Bolt's earpiece and a voice came on the line amid a lot of background noise.

'Bike two to all cars, target has just turned into Clearland Road, leading to Munroe Drive. Am taking the next road along, Boothby Avenue. Have lost eyeball.'

Tina's voice broke in. 'Car two to bike two, we're thirty seconds behind. Will turn into Clearland and take the eyeball.'

Four minutes.

Bolt accelerated, cutting inside to overtake the two cars in front before pulling back into the outside lane. He was making up ground fast but they were still way behind.

And then from inside their car they heard the sound of Andrea's mobile ringing, the mike on her blouse picking it up. They heard her say 'hello' and then the kidnapper's voice came on the line, faint but audible.

'Where are you?' he demanded, the voice warped by the suppressor.

'I'm just turning into Munroe Drive now.'

'Drive to the end. Stop outside number twenty on the left. There's a green Renault Scenic parked directly outside. In the driver's-side wheel arch, on top of the tyre, is a package. Pick it up and leave this phone in its place, making sure you switch it off. Then get back in your car and open the package. There'll be two items inside, one of which is another mobile phone. Turn it on, and you'll be called on it with further instructions. In the meantime, drive up to the North Circular and turn right, heading east.'

The line went dead.

'Christ, these guys aren't taking any chances, are they?' said Turner in the back.

Bolt shook his head angrily. 'The bastards know something. They must do.'

'How?' asked Mo. 'We've kept everything under wraps.'

'God knows. But they know. I'm sure of it.'

Tina's voice came over the airwaves, interrupting them. 'Car two to all cars. Target has stopped near bottom of Munroe Drive. She's picked up the package, and she's getting back in. She's turning round and coming back up Munroe Drive. Now turning left and heading back towards Finchley Road.'

'We'll take the eyeball,' said Bolt as he pulled over just before the entrance to Clearland Road, waiting for Andrea's Mercedes to emerge.

Seconds later, she pulled out of the junction, heading north, her driving even more erratic than it had been earlier.

'Car one to all cars,' announced Bolt, 'we're following the target north on Finchley Road, three cars back. She's driving fast. I can't get a good view, but it looks like she's on the phone. Her mike's not picking anything up so she can't be speaking.'

'Shit,' cursed Mo. 'What the hell's she doing?'

'Oh no,' said Bolt.

Barry's voice came over the radio, urgent. 'What's going on?'

'Target is opening the window and throwing something out.'

'That's her mike,' yelled Barry. 'And the tracker she's wearing.'

'She's just chucked something else out,' said Mo.

'I know!' Barry yelled. He sounded almost apoplectic now. 'It's the bloody trackers in the bag lining. How's she finding these things, and what on earth does she think she's doing?'

It was Bolt who answered the question. 'That package she just picked up. It doesn't just contain a phone, there's a bug finder in there as well. The bastards know we're on to them. That's what's happening.'

He couldn't believe it. The kidnappers had been tipped off. But by whom?

Forty-one

Andrea hit the North Circular at exactly 6.26 p.m. and proceeded east, driving fast. No longer able to hear what she was saying, the surveillance cars simply had to do their best to keep up, throwing all hopes of remaining inconspicuous out of the window. Not that that was such a priority now that it was obvious the kidnappers were assuming the police were involved.

In the control room, Big Barry Freud sounded as if he was fighting a losing battle to stay calm. As he sat grim-faced at the wheel of his car, conscious for the first time of the helicopter over-head, Bolt knew how he was feeling. This was no longer a surveillance job, it was a chase, and once again he cursed Andrea. He knew the kidnappers were telling her to get rid of anything which made it possible to trace the money, and knew too that they'd be lacing their instructions with murderous threats to ensure her obedience. Alone in the car with only her thoughts and fears for company, it would have been incredibly difficult for her to say no, but the fact remained, cold and hard, that her actions could also be costing her any chance of seeing Emma alive again. These guys were frighteningly ahead of the game. They were doing everything to make sure they got this money while at the same time minimizing their risk of getting caught. It would be a simple matter to put a knife through Emma's heart when they'd finished with her, just like they'd done to Andrea's cleaner. Bolt cursed himself, too, for going through with this charade. They should have gone the negotiation route from the start, laid their cards on the table, used trained people to get her back, instead of trying to come up with a sexy, headline-grabbing success story that was in danger of falling apart only minutes after it had started.

For twenty-four minutes Andrea drove along the North Circular. Traffic was busy but moving both ways, and though she continued to weave between lanes, there was never any danger that they were going to lose her. At 6.50, she turned on to the A10 going south, taking advantage of the lighter traffic to speed up.

'I can't understand why she's not trying to get rid of the trackers in the ransom money,' said Mo as they accelerated after her. 'They've obviously told her to remove anything that could trace them, and she seems to be cooperating.'

'Maybe she hasn't had a chance to look for them while she's driving,' answered Bolt.

'Or maybe she's only pretending to cooperate,' suggested Turner.

Bolt shook his head. 'No, she's definitely doing what they're telling her.' He took a deep breath. 'They're planning something,' he added quietly. 'God knows what. But they're planning something.'

Ten minutes later, Andrea turned again, this time into Lordship Lane, heading east into Tottenham. Then a strange thing happened. She slowed right down, managing barely fifteen miles per hour in the nearside lane. By this time Bolt and Mo were only twenty yards behind her.

'Car one to control,' said Bolt as he stared straight ahead.

Barry came back in the earpiece. 'Control receiving. What is it, car one?'

'Target driving very slowly. Now down to approximately fifteen miles an hour. Still looks to be on the phone. What do you want us to do? Over.'

'Stay behind her, car one. Just stay behind her. Important thing is not to lose her. Over.'

'Don't worry, there's no chance of that. We're

more likely to crash into the back of her. Over.'

They were coming up to the junction with Tottenham High Road. Andrea slowed down still further and the lights went red.

Bolt stared out of the windscreen. To his right were Tina and Kris Obanje in the Toyota, while one of the motorbike outriders was flanking them. He couldn't see the helicopter any more but knew it wouldn't be far away. There was no way Andrea was going to get out of their sight, so he couldn't see how the kidnappers would be able to pull off getting hold of the money without being spotted. Yet these guys were pros. So far they hadn't made a single slip-up. They had something up their sleeves. He was sure of it.

The lights seemed to stay red for a long time. Bolt desperately wanted to get out of the car, walk up to Andrea's Mercedes and ask her what the hell she thought she was doing, but he knew it would do no good. If they aborted the ransom drop now, their hopes of getting Emma back alive would diminish still further. They simply had to follow her.

He tried to second-guess the kidnappers. Clearly they suspected something was up. They'd originally tried to get Andrea to outrun the police, but had now changed tack, getting her to slow right down. Why? They were waiting for something. But what?

And then it hit him. 'Shit.'

Mo turned to him. 'What?'

'Are Tottenham playing today?'

The lights ahead went green, and the cars started pulling away.

'I'm not sure. I haven't had the time to check. You don't think—'

'Christ, they are,' said Turner, leaning forward between the front seats. 'Five fifteen kick-off.'

Bolt smacked the steering wheel. 'So they'll be finishing up about now. I bet the final whistle's just gone. It makes perfect sense.'

Before he had a chance to say another word, Barry's voice came over the airwaves, his tone frantic, his words immediately confirming Bolt's suspicions.

'Control to all cars, we have a situation. Football fans beginning to exit White Hart Lane on to Tottenham High Road in large numbers due north of target. This could be possible location for ransom exchange.'

Bolt felt a shot of adrenalin go through him. Possible location? It was damn near inevitable.

'Give me current target location.'

'Car one to control, she's turning left into Tottenham High Road, and she's accelerating fast.'

'Keep her in sight!' Barry howled. 'All cars, keep her and the money in sight! Over.'

But Andrea wasn't stopping for anyone. She weaved between the two lanes, driving like crazy, even though the traffic was slowing in front of her as, up ahead, a wave of close to forty thousand white-shirted football fans poured on to the street.

Bolt cursed loudly as they tried to keep pace, squeezing between two cars in a manoeuvre that smacked both wing mirrors out of position, and accelerating through the gap. Andrea's initial burst of pace had put thirty yards between them. No more than a hundred and sixty yards in front of them mounted police were in the road, stopping the traffic as the road became a sea of white. Already fans were crowding the pavements, coming towards them on both sides of the road, their raucous shouts filling the air.

Andrea suddenly pulled up on the kerb and stopped. A second later she was out of the car, the phone no longer to her ear. She ran round to the passenger door, pulled out the holdall, heaved it over her shoulder and started walking as fast as she could manage under its weight.

Bolt's earpiece was suddenly filled with every surveillance car and bike trying to talk.

'Car three to all cars, she's on the move. What do you want us to do? Over.'

'Bike one to control, I'm ten yards behind her vehicle. I have the eyeball. Do you want me to intercept? Over.'

'Control to bike one, does she have the bag? Over.'

'Yes, she has it. Over.'

'Shit. The money trackers say the damn thing's still in the car. The stupid bitch has removed them too. Control to all vehicles, follow on foot. Now. Do not lose her. Or the bag. Go! Go! Go!'

Bolt, Mo and Turner were out of the car like a shot, leaving it in the middle of the road as they ran to where Andrea was already being swallowed up by the advancing crowd. Bike one was ahead of them, pulling off his helmet as he ran, but Bolt was faster, overtaking him and dodging through the fans, his gaze fixed firmly on the back of Andrea's head.

Only fifteen yards and closing.

The explosion came out of nowhere, followed by a flash of very bright light somewhere in the crowd up ahead. Bolt shut his eyes and covered his head instinctively, but the moment he opened them again there was a second blast, coming from roughly the same direction. Panicked shouts broke out and there was a sudden surge of people barging and shoving into him as they attempted to get away from the explosion's source. He was knocked backwards and had to fight to keep his balance as he struggled through them, looking round frantically for Andrea but unable to see her among the mass of humanity blocking his view.

And then he was choking and his eyes began to water. It felt like someone had squirted ammonia in his face before dumping a load more down his throat. Tear gas. The bastards had let off tear gas grenades. The panic suddenly grew vastly worse as people began to experience its noxious effects, most of them doubtless fearing that this was some kind of terrorist attack. Bolt was battered like a ship in a storm as he tried to hold his ground amid the choking stampede, eyes squinting against the pain, his shirt pulled up to cover the lower half of his face.

Then a large empty space opened up in front of him. A handful of members of the public were on the ground, one with a cut on his head. Right in the middle, barely ten yards away, was Andrea. She was kneeling on the pavement, hands clutching her face. There was no sign of the holdall. Sirens were starting up now, and mounted police were galloping towards the scene, but they were still too far away to be of any immediate help.

Eyes still streaming, Bolt tried to focus on the backs of the fleeing people, his eyes scanning wildly in all directions. He saw Mo and Turner only a few yards away, standing close together. Mo's face was in his hands, while Turner had a handkerchief to his and was also looking around desperately.

And then he caught a glimpse of the holdall, slung over the shoulder of a guy in a black baseball cap. He was rounding the corner into an adjacent street, moving fast as he was carried along by the fleeing crowd, already disappearing from sight.

Still choking, Bolt leaned into the mike and spoke rapidly. 'Suspect fleeing with bag into . . .' He looked for a street sign, couldn't see one. 'Into one of the streets off the high road, heading due west.'

'Control to all units,' shouted Barry through the earpiece. 'Do not lose that bag! We are trying to get CCTV up and running.'

'There he is,' spluttered Bolt, still swallowing acrid-tasting gas as he pointed.

Turner had already spotted him and was pushing through the crowds of supporters in his direction, followed by Kris Obanje and Tina Boyd. It was Turner who was moving the fastest, as if being cooped up in Andrea's place had given him a huge new reservoir of energy, as well as a point to prove. He wasn't the biggest or strongest of guys but he ploughed through the mob, shoving people aside as he ate up the distance between himself and the holdall.

'Mo,' yelled Bolt, 'stay with Andrea!'

Before his colleague could reply, Bolt was past him and joining the chase, his eyes beginning to sting less as the fresher air hit them.

It was fifteen seconds since the first explosion, and already the gas was dissipating, and its effects wearing off on those who'd been affected. Now most of the crowd were coming to a halt as their more voyeuristic tendencies took over, creating a dense wall which acted as a perfect cover for the fleeing suspect. 'Police! Out the way!' Bolt screamed as loudly as he could as he charged into them, no longer seeing the point in trying to keep a low profile. Being football fans, they weren't in a desperate hurry to be cooperative, but Bolt was a big man, and one who knew that if he lost the guy with the holdall then he'd almost certainly lose the daughter he'd never known, so today he wasn't stopping for anyone. If he'd had a gun, he would have waved it, even fired off a couple of shots in the air and risked the sack.

Still yelling, he pushed right through them, ignoring the outraged cries and the insults, catching up with Tina and Obanje and passing them. Turner was ten yards further ahead, at a point in the street where the crowd was beginning to thin. Ten more yards separated him from the man with the holdall. Turner was running, the suspect walking quickly. In a few seconds he'd be on him, and that would be it because Bolt and the rest of them were only seconds behind.

And then there was a blurred movement in the corner of Bolt's eye. It was so quick that it took him a second to register the man in black cap and sunglasses and brand-new Tottenham shirt as he ran headlong into Turner from the side. Bolt caught a glint of metal as the man's hand shot out once, making contact, and then he was dancing past him and running for the other side of the road, in the opposite direction to the man with the holdall. Turner stopped running and seemed to stumble, his hand reaching to where the man had hit him, and then he fell to one knee, while fans milled about him, wearing vaguely curious expressions.

Bolt stopped when he reached him, putting a hand on his shoulder. 'Matt, you all right?'

Through the earpiece, Barry demanded to know what was going on. It was only then that Bolt saw the growing bloodstain on his colleague's shirt.

'Shit!'

Turner looked up, his eyes wide and fearful, his expression almost childlike. 'I think I've been stabbed, boss,' was all he said, and then he put a hand out to steady himself and lay down on his side, almost as if he was about to go to sleep.

'Officer down!' yelled Bolt into the mike. 'Stabbed by second suspect. We need urgent medical help immediately.'

'What the hell happened?' yelled Barry in his ear, his tone close to full-blown panic as the full enormity of what was happening began to hit home. 'Control to all units, secure the scene. Secure the money. Armed back-up is arriving shortly.'

Bolt knew that the important thing was to stay calm and take the lead. In the ten seconds since Turner had got hit, the man with the bag had disappeared. They had to get him. Obanje and Tina had arrived now and Bolt yelled at Obanje to keep up the chase and Tina to stay with her injured colleague.

'What about the one who stabbed him?' she demanded.

'He's mine,' hissed Bolt, jumping to his feet.

The knifeman had run off down Tottenham High Road and he, too, had disappeared from view, but Bolt wasn't going to give up that easily. He didn't give a toss about the money, that was irrelevant, but this bastard, whoever he was, had seriously injured one of his men, as well as put Bolt himself through over a day's worth of personal hell. He hadn't got a good enough look at him to see whether or not it was Ridgers, but he didn't think it was. Guessing that he would keep the black cap on to avoid being ID'd by CCTV cameras, and knowing he wouldn't have got far, Bolt took off after him, ignoring the frantic chatter in the earpiece.

He almost hit a police horse and took no notice

of the shouted command of its rider as he ran down the middle of the road between the lines of stationary cars, his eyes scanning the pavements and the legions of white-shirted fans. There was no black cap anywhere to be seen. Not on either side of the road. It was like looking for a needle in a haystack. Except for one thing. The herd mentality remained in full flow, which meant that almost everybody had turned in the direction of the mêlée behind, and some were actually moving towards it, their movement hesitant. One man, though, stood out, simply because he was walking purposefully away from the scene, his pace far too quick. He was keeping to the inside of the pavement, trying to remain out of view as he weaved between other fans. Bolt had hardly got a look at him earlier, but he was the right height and build, and he was thirty, maybe forty yards ahead.

It was him, Bolt was sure of it. He wiped his eyes, spat on the ground to get the taste of gas out of his mouth and kept running, going flat out in his desperation to get hold of him.

Thirty-five, thirty, twenty-five, twenty yards. His footfalls sounded artificially loud on the tarmac. Two uniformed cops in full riot gear stood in the road surveying the crowd uneasily, their batons drawn. One of them heard Bolt's rapid approach and, as if he was looking for someone to lash out at, lifted his baton menacingly and shouted at him to stop. Bolt didn't even slow down. He just pulled out his warrant card and yelled 'Police!' as loud as he could, and miraculously the cop simply got out of the way.

Unfortunately, the suspect also turned round. The expression on his face was one of pure shock, even behind the black shades, and in that single moment Bolt knew he was looking at the right man.

The suspect took off down the street, knocking over a middle-aged woman in his haste and stumbling before regaining his balance. Her husband shouted something and threw out a hand to grab him but he was nowhere near quick enough. This guy was speedy, and he had one hell of a lot of incentive to get away from his pursuers.

Bolt was less fit than he should have been. These days he only got to the gym once a week at best, and he was beginning to put on a few pounds round the middle. Today, though, he was powered by pure rage, and he kept pace with his target. He screamed at him to stop, loud enough so the whole street could hear it. People turned his way, then towards the fleeing suspect, who reacted by pulling out his knife and waving it wildly in front of him. It was an effective move. The crowds parted, no one wanting to tackle a knifeman.

Bolt sneaked a quick look over his shoulder.

Two of the team, Dan Blakeley and Cliff Yakonos, were running along behind him, but were still a good twenty-five yards back, while the helicopter continued to hover impotently overhead. And Bolt was unarmed. If he caught up with the suspect, he'd be taking a huge risk. He thought about this information, accepted the risk, and kept running, ignoring the pain in his lungs and beginning to gain on his target half-yard by half-yard.

'Suspect two running south on Tottenham High Road,' he shouted into the mike. 'He's armed and dangerous. Request immediate back-up.'

'This is control. Back-up on way. ETA one minute.'

Without warning, a large man in his thirties, with a kid of about ten who must have been his son, jumped at the suspect as he ran past, trying to grab him in a bear hug. It was a brave move. Brave, public-spirited and totally rash. He got a grip, knocked the suspect against the window of a charity shop, but wasn't quick enough to neutralize the knife. The suspect reacted ruthlessly and instinctively, driving it directly into the man's upper body with a single bloody lunge, his face contorted with rage and desperation. The man went down like a falling tree, probably dead before he hit the ground. His kid cried out, 'Dad!' It was a terrified, shocked howl, a sound that would live with Bolt for a long time. It was a savage reminder that death can be so quick. One second you're a living, breathing, smiling human being out with your boy to see your team play football on a glorious evening, the next you're gone. For ever.

'Suspect two has stabbed member of public; urgent medical assistance required,' Bolt yelled into his mike, but it wasn't urgent. The guy was dead. Like Andrea's cleaner and Jimmy Galante. Maybe even Emma. Laid low by a killer without the slightest regard for human life.

A fury filled Bolt. It was stronger than any he'd felt in a long, long time, maybe ever, dwarfing the emotion that had soared through him as he kicked and beat Marcus Richardson, and it seemed to give him a blind, terrible energy.

The man's intervention might have cost him his life but it also cost the suspect five or six yards. He took off again as soon as he could, waving his bloody knife as he ran past the son he'd just deprived of a father, but he now had only a handful of yards on Bolt. A junction was coming up ahead, and when he reached it he turned hard right, his body almost jack-knifing in his bid to keep momentum. Bolt kept coming, not even thinking about hesitating as he too took the corner, even though he knew the suspect could use the blind spot as an ambush point. He was moving beyond logical risk assessment and into the realms of pure revenge. He was going to beat the information he needed out of this bastard, would kill him if he had to, but there was no way he was losing him. No way at all. It was an incredibly liberating thought.

When he rounded the bend, the suspect had gained a few yards and was racing across to the other side of the road through the blocked traffic. There were fewer people milling about on the pavements here, and no sign of any police either. But also less cover for his quarry, and Bolt knew that as long as he kept pace, feeding the suspect's position into the mike, then he wasn't going to get away.

After thirty more yards, the suspect looked round and saw Bolt still right behind him. He turned back and kept running, but Bolt was conscious of the knife in his hand. It was a stiletto, the blade probably eight inches long, still slick with the blood of two men. All Bolt had to fight with was the standard-issue police pepper spray. That and the pure rage that was driving him on. Neither of which was any guarantee of success. He knew that if he'd had a gun on him he'd have used it without a second's hesitation to bring the bastard down. He'd have put a bullet in his leg, and beaten the whereabouts of his daughter out of him while he lay helpless. Because the fact remained – indeed, it was branded right on the front of his brain in flaming white-hot letters – that if he lost this man, Emma was as good as dead.

The suspect turned a hard left. Bolt did the same, shouting the street name into the mike, but he wasn't looking where he was going properly and he slipped and lost his balance, jarring his knee as he hit the deck hard, and rolling on to his side. He ignored the pain, jumped up and kept running, cursing the fact that his clumsiness had lost him five yards and counting.

The street led up to the entrance to a high-rise council estate. It was a dead end for cars. Bolt cursed. He knew that if the suspect got inside the warren of alleys that these characterless sixties estates always featured it would mean he'd almost certainly slip through the net. Jesus, where the hell was the back-up? Even the helicopter was no longer overhead; doubtless it had been sent to chase the money. It disgusted him that the recovery of the half a million pounds was more important to his bosses, and their bosses, than capturing a brutal knife-wielding killer and possibly saving the life of a fourteen-year-old girl, but then in his heart he'd always known it would be. The whole British justice system was built on the protection of property above the protection of lives, which was why armed robbers were always put away for two, three, sometimes even five times as long as child molesters.

Bastards. In those taut, desperate seconds, Bolt was a man entirely on his own, out on a limb and having to do everything himself, knowing that failure was unthinkable.

The armed response vehicle seemed to materialize from nowhere. In fact it had come out of a side road up ahead, just in front of the entrance to the estate. It stopped dead, blocking the way, and the three officers were out in an instant, their MP5s pointed straight at the suspect, who was twenty yards from them.

'Armed police! Drop your weapon!'

Bolt reached into his pocket for the pepper spray, knowing that the suspect was going to turn and run back his way, away from the guns, meaning it would be up to him to make an arrest.

But the suspect didn't. He kept on going. Charging right at them, yelling something that sounded remarkably like a battle cry.

'Don't shoot him!' shouted Bolt. 'Take him alive! For Christ's sake, we need him!'

'Armed police! Drop your weapon now!'

'Don't shoot!'

The suspect was only ten yards away from them. Still running, he pulled back his arm and threw the knife. It hit one of the ARV officers in the arm above the elbow, slicing right through the bicep. The cop dropped his gun and grabbed uselessly at the knife's handle, which was jammed halfway into his arm, stumbling as he did so. For the suspect, it was a suicidal move. Bolt knew it, and knew too what it meant. He saw a dead girl; a funeral; a lifetime of wondering how he could have done things differently.

The bullets sounded like firecrackers in the empty street, their noise reverberating hollowly off the high walls of the surrounding buildings. Two two-round bursts. The suspect flew backwards, arms flailing as he spun round before crashing to the ground, his sunglasses flying off and clattering across the tarmac.

'Police!' screamed Bolt to identify himself, holding up his warrant card as he ran over to where the suspect lay. He knelt down, felt for a pulse, knew it was pointless. There was something there, but it was fading fast, and even as his fingers squeezed the wrist and he shouted at him not to die, his voice full of desperation, it disappeared altogether. He was gone. His eyes were closed, his mouth ever so slightly open, a single drop of blood forming in one corner. It wasn't Scott Ridgers, either. This guy was young – late twenties, maybe thirty – an ordinary, unblemished face, olive skin and thick black hair suggesting a background from somewhere in southern Europe. Bolt had never seen him before, knew nothing about him, would probably never know anything about him, other than the fact that his death might have ramifications for him that lasted for the rest of his days.

And as he knelt there, staring down at the dead man, unable to understand why the ARV cops couldn't have used a non-lethal option like a taser or a baton round to bring him down, his worst fears were confirmed as Barry's frantic voice came over the earpiece.

'Control to all units. What do you mean you've lost suspect one? Find him! I want the whole fucking area locked down! We have to get hold of that money! Over.'

They'd failed. And God alone knew what happened now.

Forty-two

'Why the hell did you remove all the tracking devices, Mrs Devern?' demanded Mo Khan, barely able to contain his anger. 'You must have known it was going to help them get away.'

Andrea, ashen-faced, shocked like all of them, glared at him. 'Because they knew about them, that's why!' she yelled, her voice close to breaking. 'They knew you were there. How the hell did that happen?'

The question hung in the air.

Twenty minutes had passed since the fatal shooting of suspect two. Two police helicopters continued to hover overhead, moving in lazy circles, hunting for a quarry who had long since disappeared, leaving a trail of chaos in his wake. The worst of the crowds were gone too, although there were still large groups of pedestrians hanging around to see the aftermath of the action, and because they were spilling out into the road they were causing serious traffic congestion. The operation to clear the area to allow police forensic teams and ambulances in was being further complicated by an apparently unrelated outbreak of fighting between rival fans further up on White Hart Lane. The competing blare of sirens filled the air as Mo, Bolt and Tina stood beside one of a line of police vehicles clustered round the corner from the street where the body of suspect two still lay where it had fallen. Andrea was in the back of one of the cars, sitting with her legs out, holding a plastic bottle of water.

The mood among everyone at the scene was one of complete shock. The operation had been a complete failure. Half a million pounds of taxpayers' money had walked away from right under their noses; worse than that, a member of the public had been killed, one of the team's own number seriously wounded, and the one suspect they had managed to apprehend had decided to go out in a blaze of glory rather than be taken alive. It couldn't really have gone any more wrong. The only positive was that, unlike the stabbed fan, Turner was still alive, although the seriousness of his condition wasn't yet known. He'd been airlifted to the Homerton Hospital in Hackney whose expertise in dealing with knife injuries, honed through years of practice, was legendary, so he was in the best possible hands. Even so, as they all knew, that might not be enough.

Bolt felt as if he'd done ten rounds boxing a man twice his size and speed whose speciality was headshots. He couldn't seem to think straight, was finding it hard to come to terms with the fact that he and his people were being out-thought and outfought by the men who'd taken Emma. He knew he couldn't give up, but standing there among the wreckage of the op, he was getting perilously close.

'What happened, Andrea?' he asked. 'We lost communication with you after you stopped to pick up the package.'

'I got a call on the phone that was in it. It was Emma screaming.'

Bolt swallowed. Told himself to keep calm.

'Just this one terrified scream. Then it cut out and he came on the line. He said that this time Emma was screaming out of fear, but the next time it would be out of pain, unless I did exactly what I was told. Those were his exact words. He told me to use that thing to start removing all the bugs and trackers' – she pointed at the bug-finding device that was now in an evidence bag in Mo's hands – 'and I tried to tell him I didn't know what he was talking about, but he told me he knew I'd gone to the police, and if I tried to deny it then he'd . . . he'd make Emma scream again.' She stared at them each in turn. 'I had no choice. Don't you see that? I had no choice. I want my daughter back.'

'Well, you went about it the wrong way,' said Tina, her tone exasperated.

'What do you know? Have you got children?'

'No, but—'

'But nothing. You have no idea what you're talking about.'

Tina opened her mouth to reply but Bolt stepped in. This was getting them nowhere.

'OK, Andrea, so you followed their instructions. You removed the tracking devices and threw them out of the car. But not the two that were attached to the money.'

'No, they told me to leave them in the car when I got out.'

It was a logical move from the kidnappers' point of view, lulling the team into a false sense of security by letting them think they'd still be able to follow the ransom. It also showed that at least one of those involved had fairly expert knowledge of tracking devices.

'What was the last instruction you received?'

'To get out of the car and start walking up the road. I was told I'd be met by someone. I started walking and the next thing I knew there were these loud bangs, everyone was running, there was that gas ... I remember shutting my eyes, getting knocked about by all these people running, and then someone punched me in the side of the head and grabbed the bag.' She touched the left side of her face where she'd been struck. The area was red and beginning to swell.

'And did you get a look at your attacker at all, Mrs Devern?' asked Mo.

'No, I didn't see anything. It all happened so fast.'

She took a gulp from the water and hunted round for her cigarettes, but couldn't find them.

'Has anyone got a smoke?'

Tina reached into her jeans, pulled out a battered pack of Silk Cut and a cheap lighter, and lit two cigarettes, one for Andrea and one for her. Andrea gave her a curt nod of acknowledgement.

'So, the person on the phone made you remove all these devices,' said Tina, a hint of scepticism in her voice, 'which you did ...'

'That's right.'

'And did he at any point tell you when you were going to see your daughter again?'

All three of them looked at Andrea.

'He said I'd be seeing her very soon. As soon as he'd verified that the money was all there.'

'When did he say that?'

'During the car journey. Twice. He said it twice.'

'How did he say he was going to make contact to tell you where to find her?'

'He didn't.'

'It seems like you were very trusting,' said Tina. 'You made it impossible for us to track either the suspects or the money, yet you were offered very little in return.'

'All right, Tina,' said Bolt, concerned about the aggressiveness of her questioning, 'there's no point going over all this now.'

Andrea shot Tina a look that was both angry and incredulous.

'What is it? Don't you believe me or something?'

'No,' Tina replied, 'it's just that I can't understand why you did it.'

'Look, don't blame me because someone leaked the fact that I'd brought the police in. This is your fault not mine.' She took an urgent drag on her cigarette and stood up. 'I'm going home.'

'I'm afraid that's not possible for the moment, Andrea,' Bolt informed her.

'Back off, Mike. They've still got my daughter. They could call. So, if you're not arresting me, I'm going, and I'm going to need a lift if you're holding on to my car.'

She pushed past them and started walking in the direction of Tottenham High Road.

'Wait here,' Bolt told the other two and hurried

after her. 'Listen, Andrea,' he said when he was alongside her, 'you've got to let me know the second you hear from the kidnappers, OK?'

'What, so you can fuck it up again?' she snapped, without breaking pace. 'No way. I'll take my own chances from now on.'

Bolt grabbed her by the shoulder and swung her round so that she was facing him.

'That's not fair, Andrea, and you know it. I did everything I could.'

'Let go of my arm. You're hurting me.'

Bolt was conscious of several uniformed cops watching him. He ignored them. 'Please,' he said, 'tell me when they call.'

'Mike, what the hell's going on?'

Bolt looked round into the eyes of Stephen Evans, the former head of the NCS, now the assistant head of SOCA, who was flanked by several other equally grim-faced men in suits. Bolt let go of Andrea's arm and she walked away rapidly, passing Evans and his colleagues before they had a chance to say anything. Evans whispered something to the men with him and they went after Andrea while he approached Bolt.

Bolt knew Evans from the past. A short, compactly built man in his late forties with a neatly clipped moustache and a military bearing courtesy of an earlier career in the army, he'd helped him once before when he'd found himself in trouble, and had a well-deserved reputation for looking after the interests of the men and women in his charge. But this time it was different, and Bolt knew it.

'Hello, sir,' he said with a sigh. 'Long time no see.'

Evans stopped in front of him. 'Yes, it is. And I'm sorry we've got to meet again under these kinds of circumstances.'

Bolt nodded grimly. 'I know.'

'I'm afraid I'm taking over the running of this op from SG2 Freud. Because of the way it's gone, he's been suspended pending an investigation. The same goes for you, Mike. As the team leader of the central team on this, I can't afford to keep you on.'

Bolt took a step back as he absorbed the hit.

'Don't do this, sir. I've got a good lead. There's a guy called Scott Ridgers with a long criminal record who's been doing gardening work for Andrea – Mrs Devern – until very recently. He was part of a gang of robbers she informed on fifteen years back. I think he might be our suspect one.'

'I know all that, Mike,' said Evans coldly. 'We've already got surveillance in place outside his flat in Finsbury Park.'

'But he's not there, is he? And the guy's a paedophile—'

'We're dealing with it.'

'Listen, sir, please—'

'No,' Evans said with a brutal finality. 'You're off the case, Mike, suspended until further notice. The IPCC will be getting in touch with you for a witness statement, so don't go disappearing on holiday. I'm sorry, but that's the way it's going to have to be.'

Bolt knew there was no point arguing. The decision had been made. He watched as Evans walked past him and over to Mo and Tina. He caught their eyes but said nothing. Instead, he simply turned away. He was no longer wanted or needed here.

Forty-three

Emma scratched away at the brickwork with the nail. It was so worn down now that it stuck out barely half an inch from between her thumb and forefinger, the end blunt and splayed. Progress was desperately slow. She was on her hands and knees, the bed pushed out from the wall to give her room, but her back still ached from where she'd been bent over for what felt like hours, and her fingers were almost numb with the pain and stiffness. But she refused to stop because she knew that her life might depend on success. Even more so now, after what had happened earlier.

A couple of hours or so after she'd recorded the message to her mum, telling her it was Saturday and that she was coming home soon, there'd come the familiar sound of the cellar door being unlocked, and she'd wondered if it was the smelly one coming down to collect the plate she'd used for breakfast. She'd had to push the bed as hurriedly and as quietly as possible back against the wall, and slip on her hood.

But his footsteps hadn't come. There'd simply been a cold, dead silence, and she'd known without a shadow of a doubt that it was the cruel one who'd come to visit, the one whose footsteps she could never hear.

An icy sensation had crept slowly up her spine as she sensed his presence in the room with her. Watching. Could he have spotted what she'd been doing to the wall? Had he heard her move the bed? Was this the end? Right now?

'Die, bitch!'

The voice was mocking and close.

She'd felt a sudden rush of air, and his hand had grabbed her shoulder in a tight, vicious grip. She'd screamed, instinctively – a terrified wail – and he'd laughed.

And that had been it. He released his grip, and she thought she heard something click, like a tape recorder. His parting words were delivered in a quiet sing-song voice, just before the cellar door shut again: 'Back later, bitch, back later.'

Ever since then she'd been working frantically, stopping every so often to yank at the chain, ignoring the frustration when still it seemed no looser. The sheer terror she was feeling kept her going, but it was also tiring her out. She wanted to sleep desperately, to lie down and shut her eyes. Forget this awful nightmare. But she refused to stop, knew that if she did she'd probably never start up again.

And then finally she got her break. For the first time, the brickwork really started crumbling. Full of hope, she scratched away even harder, and a load more brick dust poured down so that two of the screws holding the plate in place were almost completely revealed. She grabbed the chain and pulled furiously. Something gave, and one of the screws came out completely. She kept at it, but she simply didn't have the strength to tear it free.

But she was nearly there. A quick rest, and she'd carry on.

She lay back on the bed, her eyes shutting almost immediately. She was so tired, so weak. She felt herself dozing, drifting away . . . tried to come back, but never quite made it . . .

Forty-four

Bolt was sitting in heavy traffic on Tottenham High Road, only a few hundred metres away from where it had all gone so badly wrong. Darkness had fallen, and the sound of the sirens was becoming more sporadic. The helicopters still flew overhead, but their constant circling felt pointless and redundant. Not for the first time in his life he was left on the outside, no longer wanted on an investigation he'd helped to get started.

He didn't want to go home, not with Emma still out there somewhere. The two mobile phone calls the kidnappers had made to Andrea's landline had come from round these streets, and he doubted that the guy with the money had gone far. Much easier to disappear into a nearby house, away from the helicopters, the pursuing cops and the prying eyes of the CCTV. It would take some nerve to organize the ransom drop so near to where they were holding Emma, but nerve had never been in short supply with these people. He was sure that suspect number one was Scott Ridgers, and if necessary he'd drive round and round hoping that at some point Ridgers emerged from his hideout. It was the longest of long shots but it had to be better than doing nothing.

The traffic was moving at a snail's pace, and the worn-out buildings around him – cheap take-aways, charity shops, a few boarded-up wrecks – felt foreboding and claustrophobic. It was on nights like this that he hated London with its noise, its litter and its gridlock, and he felt an almost physical yearning for space. He remembered back to the day he'd bumped into Andrea on the Strand, and how it had been the start of their affair. What if he hadn't been there? What if he'd been doing something different, and their paths had never crossed that second time? How much happier a man would he be now.

Which was when that old nagging thought struck him. What if their meeting hadn't been spontaneous? What if it had all been a set-up? Perhaps Andrea's lover, Jimmy Galante, had wanted inside information on the Flying Squad and had encouraged her to take up with Bolt in order to get it. He thought back, trying to remember if she'd ever pumped him for informa-tion, but nothing came to mind. But then, of course, she might not have been doing it on behalf of Galante. She might have taken up with Bolt of her own accord, using him to bring Galante down, either because she was genuinely desperate to leave him and could think of no other way of doing it, or . . . or what?

God knows. He sighed, wiping sweat from his brow and turning the air con higher.

The sound of his mobile ringing jolted him from his thoughts. He looked at the screen but didn't recognize the number. He flicked it on to hands-free and took the call.

'Mr Bolt?'

Bolt recognized the slightly officious tones of Lisa Bouchera's father and tensed a little.

'Mr Bouchera, how can I help you?'

'He's called my daughter.'

Bolt felt a sudden flash of excitement. 'When?'

'Just now. I was outside in the garden but when I came back inside she was crying. She told him she didn't want to see him any more and he started calling her all these filthy names.'

'I'm very sorry to hear that,' Bolt told him. 'We can make sure he doesn't call her again. Have you got access to your daughter's phone?'

'I can get it. Hold on.'

A few seconds later he was back on the line. Bolt asked him to go into the Calls Received screen.

'OK, let's have a look.' There was a pause. 'All right, I'm in.'

His hands shaking, Bolt pulled out his notebook and pen.

'Read me out the top number.'

The moment of truth.

Bouchera reeled off a mobile number and Bolt wrote it down. By using a mobile to make the call to his girlfriend, Scott Ridgers had effectively given out his location, and, Bolt hoped, Emma's location as well. The excitement he was feeling was so powerful it actually made him nauseous for a few seconds.

'And he was the last person who called her?'

'Yes. It was just now.'

Bolt looked at his watch. Five to eight. Just under an hour since the money had disappeared.

'Thank you, sir,' he said, 'you've been a great help.'

'And you. Let me know when you've got the bastard in custody.'

'Course I will,' Bolt said, ending the call.

He took a deep breath, brutally aware that he was suspended and that unless he played things right this lead counted for nothing. He had to do something, and fast. Mo or Tina – who did he call? Who did he trust?

Mo was the colleague he'd always trusted the most, but things had changed between them these past twenty-four hours, possibly irreversibly. Tina, meanwhile, was the person on the team with the best access to the phone companies, and he remembered the look she'd given him in the meeting that morning. Was it empathy? Some kind of understanding? He was stepping over a line by contacting her, he knew that. Asking her to put her own job in jeopardy as a favour to him. And she was such an enigmatic person, so difficult to read, that he had no idea whether she'd help him or not.

There was only one way to find out. He dialled her number, willing her to answer, concentrating so much on this latest development that he didn't even notice that the traffic ahead of him was moving until he heard the horns blaring. As he touched the accelerator and moved forward, her voice came on the line. Clear and businesslike as always.

'Tina Boyd.'

'Tina, it's Mike.'

He heard her sharp intake of breath.

'I didn't expect to hear from you. There's no more news. Matt's in surgery at the moment.'

His thoughts returned to Turner. Poor sod. If only he'd stayed behind at Andrea's house.

'Listen, sir, we're snowed under here. I'm going to have to go.'

'I need a favour.'

'But you're suspended.'

'I know that, but this is urgent, and it's to do with the case. I've got a mobile number for Scott Ridgers – that suspect I was talking to you about earlier who turned out to be one of Andrea's gardeners. He's just used it, literally minutes ago, to make a call. If we can get a trace on that number, it'll lead us straight to him.'

'How did you find this out?'

Bolt explained as briefly as he could.

'I can speak to Steve Evans, but I'm not sure he'll be able, or willing, to authorize it.'

'No, don't speak to him. I can tell you now, he won't authorize it. Just do it. Please.'

'I can't, sir. You're suspended. It could cost me my job.' She sighed. 'I'm sorry.'

'She's my daughter, Tina.'

'What?'

'Emma Devern. She's my daughter. Check with Mo if you don't believe me. It's why I've been so highly strung since this all began.'

'God, I . . . I don't know what to say.'

'Don't say anything. Just help me, please. If we don't act fast, Emma could die.'

'I can't believe you're putting me in this position, Mike.'

'Do you think I want to? Look, there's no way on God's earth I would ask you to do this unless I absolutely had to.' He could hear the desperation in his voice, hated it.

Tina was silent for two, maybe three seconds.

'OK, let me have the number.'

He reeled it off for her.

'I'll do what I can, but it might take some time.'

'This is my daughter. There is no time.'

'If you're lying to me,' she said evenly, 'I'll kill you.'

Forty-five

Emma awoke with a start, sitting bolt upright. It was dark in the room, and her mouth felt bone dry. She wondered how long she'd been out. Without a watch it was difficult to tell, but it was a while. Half an hour, something like that. She rubbed her eyes, swung her legs off the bed and remembered that she'd been very close to getting the chain free from the wall.

And then she heard a loud bang. It was the sound of the front door shutting.

They were back.

She grabbed the chain with both hands, closed her eyes and pulled as hard as she could. There was a crack – something giving – and more dust showered on to the stone floor. She could hear footfalls on the floor above, but no voices.

Clenching her teeth, ignoring the nauseous feeling flowing through her, she kept pulling, leaning back so her whole body was behind it, knowing this could well be her last chance.

Another crack.

Movement near the cellar door – a shuffling of feet.

They're coming.

She was out of time.

And then suddenly she was falling back off the bed, landing painfully on the floor with the chain uncoiling on top of her.

She'd done it. The metal plate had come free.

Forty-six

Bolt was driving aimlessly down yet another grimy terraced back street when the call came. The clock on his dashboard said 8.07. Only nine minutes since he'd got off the phone to Tina.

So much of a person's life seemed to him to boil down to those single, long, terrifying moments of anticipation when you're given the hugely important news you've been waiting for: the results of medical tests; exam results; a jury's verdict; the location of the man who's holding your daughter.

'Tina,' he said, his voice hoarse, 'what have you got?'

'The phone's still on. The location's been triangulated to an area around a farm called Woodlands in Crews Hill.'

'Where the hell's that?'

'Just north of Enfield, south of the M25.'

She gave him the address and he fed it into the car's sat-nav system. The distance was just over six miles from where he was now. He swung the car round in a rapid three-point turn so that he was heading back towards the main road.

'Thanks, Tina.'

'What are you going to do?'

'I'm going to go and check it out. If it looks like it's a lead, I'll call in straight away.'

'This could put me in huge amounts of trouble, Mike. They're going to know the info's come from me, and you know as well as I do that it's totally illegal to get an unauthorized triangulation.'

'If it comes to nothing, there's no way it'll ever get back to you. You've got my word on that. And if it does lead somewhere, I'll come up with a reason why I found out about Ridgers' location without mentioning your name. I really appreciate this, Tina.'

'I talked to Mo. Christ, I can't believe she could be your daughter.'

There was a silence then, because Bolt didn't really know what to say. Tina ended it by wishing him good luck.

'Call us as soon as you've checked it out,' she added.

'Sure.'

He cut the connection, and accelerated on to the main road, ignoring the blast of the horn from the driver he'd just cut up. All that mattered to him was getting to Scott Ridgers.

Six miles and counting.

Forty-seven

Emma put the bed back in its original position so that it covered the hole in the wall and the brick-dust on the floor, and waited in silence with the hood in her hands. Her elbow ached where she'd smacked it on the floor, and she felt sick and thirsty.

The movement upstairs had stopped a few minutes ago, and now she couldn't hear anything. She wondered what to do. The problem was, she might be mobile, but the fact remained that she was still handcuffed and locked in here, and the chain was still attached to her ankle, which was definitely going to slow her down if she did make a run for it. And the silence scared her, because silence was what she associated with the cruel one.

Back later, bitch.

Maybe he was sharpening his knife right now?

But she couldn't just sit there waiting for him to come and kill her. Otherwise all her efforts would be in vain. No, she had to do something. A plan formed in her mind. She'd hide at the top of the steps behind the door, and when he came inside she'd push him down them before he had a chance to spot her. Then she'd make a break for it. It was pretty lame as plans went, but it was the best she could think up at the moment.

She lifted up the ankle chain and started to get up from the bed. And then stopped as the key turned in the lock and the door opened.

She was too late.

Hurriedly, she got back on the bed and let the chain slip to the floor. Her hands were shaking and she felt fear running up her spine. Was this it? The last seconds of her life, in a dingy, cold basement miles from home?

Silence.

She made no move to put on the hood as she stared towards the staircase.

The light came on, and she squinted against its brightness.

'Emma,' came a voice from the top of the steps, 'it's me.'

She felt a surge of excitement. It was the smelly one. She was going to be OK.

'Hi,' she said quietly. 'I'm here.'

'Put your hood on, honey. OK? It's almost time to go home.'

She did as she was told, hardly able to believe her luck.

'Am I honestly going home?'

'That's right,' he answered in that wheezy voice of his. 'It's over. Your mum paid the money so you don't have to stay here any more.'

She heard him come close. Smelled him, too, the BO so strong now it made her gag beneath the hood. He put something down on the floor by the bed and she thought she heard water sloshing.

'Am I going to go now?'

'Very soon. We'll just get you ready. Then there'll be a little journey, and that'll be it. Back home to your mum. First I'm going to give you a little wash, though. So you're all nice and clean.'

She felt a wet sponge on her left arm. It made her feel cold and itchy. He ran it slowly up and down before starting on the other one.

'Bet that feels good, doesn't it?'

'You don't need to do this. I can wait until I'm home.'

'I want to do it.'

He moved her arms to one side and lifted up her T-shirt, rubbing the sponge on her tummy in small circles. Water dripped down towards the top of her skirt, and she heard him swallow. It was a really horrible sound, like something a frog would make.

'What are you doing?' she whispered.

'Just washing you, darling,' he replied, lifting her T-shirt higher. Swallowing a second time.

That was when she realized with a sickening feeling that the nightmare hadn't ended after all.

Forty-eight

The driveway that led down to Woodlands Farm was situated on a quiet wooded road half a mile south of the M25, a simple wooden sign attached to a beech tree announcing its presence. There were no other houses in the immediate vicinity, making Bolt think that it would be an ideal place to hold someone without arousing suspicion.

The tension coursed through him. Scott Ridgers had motive; he'd worked at Andrea's place and then disappeared at the same time that Emma had gone missing. And as a fully fledged city boy, why else would he be out here in the back of beyond?

Not wishing to announce his presence, Bolt drove thirty yards further along the road before pulling up on the verge and manoeuvring his car as far into the trees as it would go. He killed the lights and got out. Through the darkness created by the thick concentration of trees, he thought he could just make out lights, but it was difficult to tell. According to the sat-nav, Woodlands Farm was set back at least a hundred yards from the road.

Knowing how short time was, he moved swiftly, making for the driveway. His plan was to approach from the front as quietly as possible and recce the place. If there was no sign of Ridgers, he'd break in. He'd taken the law into his own hands enough times today to worry about doing it again, and it was possible that his actions had already cost him his job.

The advantage, however, was that he now had nothing to lose.

Forty-nine

Emma knew what was coming. The dirty, stinking pervert wanted to have sex with her. Was *going* to have sex with her if she didn't do something about it.

A gloved hand touched her knee, and she gagged beneath the hood.

She had an idea. It was her only chance.

'Can you undo the handcuffs?' she asked, trying to make her voice sound as if she might be interested in what he was about to do to her. 'Then maybe we can . . .' She let the words trail off.

'You're not teasing me, are you?' he said, seriously. 'I don't like girls who tease me. I've had too much of that recently.'

'No, course not. I've done it before, you know.'

He chuckled. 'Ooh, you are a naughty girl, aren't you? I think maybe we can make things a bit more comfortable for you.'

He stopped sponging her and she heard him fiddling around for the key. She tensed as he found it and unlocked the cuffs, slipping them off. She heard him stand up, then the sound of a zipper being pulled.

Now! Now! Now! a voice in her head screamed.

She pulled off the hood and jumped up from the bed in one movement, kneeing him in the groin as hard as she could. He gasped in pain and staggered backwards, clutching himself with both hands.

For the first time, she got a look at him. He was dressed in jeans and a dirty white T-shirt, and his face was covered by a balaclava. Tattoos adorned his arms.

Picking up the chain, she ran past him, dodging beneath a flailing arm as he tried to grab her.

'You little cow!' he bellowed, lurching after her, still holding on to his balls.

She took the steps two at a time, the chain still in her hand. Her limbs felt stiff and painful from the sudden burst of exercise, but adrenalin drove her on because she knew that if he caught her, this time he'd kill her for sure. He hadn't locked the door from the inside, and she yanked it open and ran out, slamming it behind her.

She was in a hallway. A door ahead led through to a living room, one to the right looked like it led outside. She turned hard right, ran across the hall and grabbed the handle. It turned, but the door didn't open. Panic flooded through her.

Behind her, the cellar door flew open and banged hard against the wall as he came stumbling out after her.

There was a second handle. Tucking the chain beneath her arm, she turned the two of them simultaneously, and this time the door opened.

A gloved hand snatched at her collar, but she kept going, hearing it rip as he lost his grip, and then she was out into the night, breathing in fresh air for the first time in days. There was a gate and fence ahead, beyond them trees. The gate was shut. She knew he'd catch her if she ran towards it, so she darted left, running along the front of the house, past an outbuilding, making for a field with long grass up ahead.

She could hear his footsteps on the gravel behind her, and the sound of his heavy breathing. He was only feet away now. Pure fear drove her on, the sure knowledge of what he'd do if he caught her making her legs pump far faster than she'd ever thought they were capable of. She'd never been much of a runner, and at school she'd hated athletics, even though her Games teacher, Miss Floyd, always said that she had the perfect build for it, being slim and small-chested. And now, finally, when it really mattered, she was proving Miss Floyd right.

His breathing got fainter as she began to open up some distance between them. She was running into the long grass now, and she felt a surge of elation which lasted no more than a second. As she pumped her arms to speed herself up, the movement tightened the chain and caused her to trip up and lose her footing. She fell forwards, the uneven, stony ground charging up to meet her, and her hands hit it palms first.

Desperately she scrambled to her feet, but it was too late. With a roar of triumph, he came down hard on her back, knocking the wind out of her in an agonizing rush.

'Oh God!'

'He can't help you now, you little tease!'

He laughed as he sat astride her and twisted her round roughly so that she was facing him, his knees digging into her upper arms. She stared into his balaclava-clad face, saw dark eyes glinting excitedly through the slits, and felt terror surge through her as his gloved hands fiddled impatiently with the zipper on his jeans, pulling them open.

He grabbed her wrist and thrust her hand towards his groin, pulling her upright as he did so. 'Feel me,' he hissed, and she cried out as the hand made contact. But he'd moved as well and his knee was no longer pinning her free arm. Taking her chance, with the free hand she scrabbled around in the grass until she found a sharp piece of flint half the size of her palm. It wasn't much of a weapon, but it was all she had. Operating entirely on instinct now, she drove it into the side of his head and dragged the sharp edge down the side of his balaclava.

He yelped in pain and smacked her hand away, letting go of the other one at the same time, but Emma pressed her advantage, ramming the flint into the top of his thigh, only centimetres from his balls. Cursing, he jumped off her, keen to get out of the way before she did any more damage, and she saw her opportunity. Scrambling to her feet, she took off again, the chain trailing loosely behind her as she made for the tree line, not daring to look back.

She hit the trees at a sprint, branches crunching underfoot as she was swallowed up by the darkness, tearing through brambles, ignoring the pain as they scratched and clawed her, just wanting to keep running, to get as far away from him as possible. Faster and faster, almost blind now in her desire to keep going.

She fell headfirst, landing on a bed of leaves. She could still hear him but it sounded as if he was some distance away. He hadn't seen or heard her fall, she was sure of that. Part of her wanted to jump back up and keep going, but a bigger part told her that it was best to stay put, hidden.

Slowly, very slowly, trying to control her breathing, she inched forward on her stomach, pushing herself under a thick holly bush until she'd got her whole body underneath it, the jagged leaves scraping against her head and back.

She could feel his heavy footfalls getting closer. Step by slow step. She'd never been so scared in her whole life and it took all her willpower just to stop herself from crying out. She squeezed her eyes shut and bit her lip.

'You've cut me, you little cow,' he hissed, his voice carrying through the darkness. 'And after all I've done for you as well. I kept you alive, and you do this.'

Another footstep. Almost next to her now. She forced her eyes open, and had to stifle a scream. He was right by the holly bush, his black Caterpillar boot only feet away from her face, a hulking black shadow blocking out the moonlight as he sniffed the air like some kind of predator.

She stayed utterly still, frozen to the spot, not even daring to breathe. Waiting. Hoping. Praying that he wouldn't discover her.

Please. I just want to go home. See my mum. End this nightmare.

He seemed to stand there for ever, and she felt her lungs tightening, crying out for air.

Move. Move, please. I can't hold it in much longer.

And then suddenly he did, the footfalls starting

again as he skirted the holly bush and began to move away.

She shut her eyes and thanked God, exhaling as silently as she could and slowly taking in much-needed air. Kept listening, telling herself that she only had to lie there another few minutes and everything would be all right. He'd give up his search, and she'd make a run for the nearest road. Get help. Go home.

She never heard the movement behind her, just caught a reek of stale sweat. And then the chain that was attached to her ankle was suddenly round her neck, choking her, and a triumphant voice was whispering in her ear, 'Found you.'

Fifty

Bolt walked slowly down the track as it ran in a curve through the woodland and then straightened as the tree line ended and an old two-storey cottage in need of a lick of paint appeared in front of him, nestled between two ramshackle outbuildings. There were lights on downstairs and the double-gates that led to the front of the house were wide open. A dark-coloured Range Rover was parked in the driveway.

He moved off the driveway and on to the long grass lining it so that his movements didn't trigger any lights, and approached the gates quietly using the darkness as cover.

But as he reached them he heard the sound of footsteps on gravel coming from somewhere up ahead. His view of whoever it was was blocked by the Range Rover as he crouched down behind the fence so that he couldn't be seen.

Then he heard it. A strangled sob, definitely female. He felt a ferocious jolt of emotion that almost knocked him off his feet as he realized that it was almost certainly coming from Emma.

This was confirmed in the next few seconds when she came into view, barely a silhouette in the gloom and smaller than he'd imagined, staring straight ahead. But it was definitely Emma, just as Bolt knew that the man dragging her by the length of chain round her neck was Scott Ridgers. He might have been wearing a bala-clava, but that didn't matter. It was him.

Bastard.

Ridgers had a small-bladed knife in his free hand which he kept close to Emma's side to ensure she didn't struggle. Even in the darkness, Bolt could see the terrified expression on her face, and he felt the rage build within him. But there were at least twenty yards between them, which would give Ridgers far too much time to react if Bolt charged him. He was going to have to be patient, look for an opportunity.

Then Ridgers said something to Emma that chilled Bolt's blood: 'We're going to have some fun now, baby.'

Emma managed a strangled sob, and Bolt had to shut his eyes and hold on to the fence for support.

When he opened them again, they'd reached

the front door. He watched as Ridgers pushed it open and shoved Emma inside, following her in without looking round.

And chuckling. The bastard was actually chuckling.

He also made the biggest mistake of his life. He didn't shut the door behind him.

Bolt took a deep breath. Moving as quietly and swiftly as he could, he followed them into the house.

Fifty-one

The chain round her neck was choking Emma so badly she could hardly breathe as he dragged her through the hallway. The cellar door was still open and he pushed her towards it.

Oh God, she couldn't go back in there again, not having come so close to freedom. And she knew that if she went back in, this time she definitely wouldn't be coming back out. Not alive, anyway.

She went limp in his arms, and he cursed.

'Come on, move it,' he snapped, angry now, pressing the blade of a penknife he'd produced earlier against her ribs.

She stayed limp, and started to make horrible choking sounds, as if she was dying.

'If you're fooling me about . . .'

He let her drop to her knees and loosened the chain a little.

'Water,' she gasped.

'All right,' he said, hauling her to her feet and manhandling her through the hallway in the direction of the kitchen. 'You can have some water. Then we'll have some—'

He suddenly stopped as they reached the kitchen door and he switched on the light. She felt him go tense.

'Where is it? Where the fuck is it?'

He shoved her roughly inside, letting go of the chain and sending her sprawling to the floor.

'The bag!' he yelled, his voice filling the room. 'The bag with the fucking money! It was on here!' He pointed a gloved hand at the empty kitchen table. 'Where the hell is it?' He paced about inside the room, rubbing a hand over his face beneath the balaclava, his eyes wide and angry. 'I can't believe this. Someone's taken it. Someone's taken my money.' He stopped and slammed his hand down on the table, hitting it so hard the legs wobbled. 'My fucking money!' he roared at the ceiling.

Emma cowered, terrified, pushing herself into the corner of the room, away from his rage and frustration.

'I'm going to find whoever's done this,' he muttered. 'I'm going to find him now. And when I get hold of him . . .' He shoved the penknife he was holding back into the pocket of his jeans, then yanked open one of the drawers, took out a huge kitchen knife and ran a finger along the blade. 'When I get hold of him, I'm going to fillet the bastard.'

He turned and pointed the knife at Emma. The blade shone in the glare of the overhead lights. 'Stay there, all right? Don't you dare move an inch if you ever want to see your mum again. OK?'

She nodded, trying not to sob. 'OK.'

He swung round and stormed out of the door, knife in hand.

And immediately cried out in surprise.

The next second he was flying back through the door with another man hanging on to him and shouting something that filled her with sudden and delirious relief: 'Armed police! Drop your weapon!'

Fifty-two

But that was the problem. Bolt wasn't armed when he charged Scott Ridgers. He wasn't even carrying standard-issue pepper spray, which had been taken off him earlier. He had nothing but surprise. He grabbed Ridgers' wrists and twisted them away from his body, paying particular attention to the hand holding the kitchen knife, and trying to butt him as he'd done Marcus Richardson earlier that day. But the blow he caught Ridgers with as they both crashed into the kitchen barely glanced the other man, who had the good sense to move his head, and as they hit the kitchen table, disaster struck. Bolt lost his footing and slipped, sliding along the tiled floor on one knee, desperately trying to keep hold of his foe, even though his head was now only level with the other man's groin.

Ridgers was fast, and he took advantage of

Bolt's plight to tug his wrists free and slam a knee into his face. A piercing, hot pain shot through Bolt's nose and he wobbled in his kneeling position, unable to react as Ridgers then lifted a leg and delivered an accurate kung-fu kick to the side of his head. This time he fell backwards, landing against something white and hard. His head throbbed savagely where Ridgers' boot had connected and he could feel the blood pouring out of his nostrils and on to his lips. He tried to focus through the pain, saw the huge knife in Ridgers' hand, and knew that he was helpless.

Jesus. After all this, he'd failed.

Then he saw Emma crouching in the corner of the room, her eyes wide with shock.

'Run, Emma!' he shouted. 'Run!'

Ridgers took a step forward, pointing the knife down at Bolt, ignoring Emma now. 'Where's my money?' he roared. 'Where's my fucking money?'

Bolt rolled on to his side, thinking fast, assessing his options . . . knowing full well that he didn't have any. Emma leapt to her feet, but instead of running for the door, she ran at Ridgers and sank her teeth into his knife arm, just above the elbow. He cried out but didn't relinquish his grip on the knife. Instead, he grabbed her by the hair and yanked her off in one movement, the force of his attack sending her crashing into one of the worktops.

Adrenalin born of pure rage shot through Bolt, briefly substituting the pain and dizziness. He started to get up.

But it was too late. Ridgers was bearing down on him, and there was murder in his eyes as he brought back his knife arm to deliver a blow that Bolt knew would not only end his life, but would mean the end of Emma's too.

And then there was a loud crack, followed a second later by the sound of breaking glass, and suddenly Scott Ridgers pitched forward as his legs went from under him. His head smacked hard against the fridge and he collapsed to the floor, landing on his side on Bolt's legs. A thin stream of blood poured from the smoking hole where his right eye had been.

Emma screamed as he convulsed in his death throes.

'Stay down!' Bolt yelled at her, kicking Ridgers' body off him.

Four more shots exploded through the night air in rapid succession, showering the table and floor with shards of glass. Emma screamed again, and Bolt crawled over to her, moving as fast as he could and ignoring the glass beneath him. Grabbing her in his arms, he pulled her under him so that she was shielded from the gunfire. She was shaking with fear and sobbing, and he held her tight, thinking how small and vulnerable she was.

Even in those dramatic moments he felt a kind of love he'd never experienced before.

'Just stay still,' he whispered. 'I'm here now. You're going to be all right.'

For ten seconds they lay there together in a tight, tangled embrace. There were no more shots. Silence had returned, and Ridgers had stopped moving. But the fact remained that someone had just murdered him, and that person was close by.

'Stay where you are,' Bolt told Emma as he got to his feet.

'Where are you going?'

'Just stay there, help's coming.'

Keeping low, he killed the kitchen light and crept over to the back door. A yard, with outbuildings to the left and right, ran about twenty yards to the beginning of the tree line. It looked empty, but, as Bolt turned the key in the lock and slowly opened the door, he knew he was being foolish. It was one thing risking your neck to save your daughter, it was quite another to chase a gunman while he was unarmed.

But whoever had fired the shot that killed Scott Ridgers was also involved in this, and Bolt was in no mood to let him get away. And if he was carrying half a million in cash, his escape was going to be a slow one.

Bolt slid through the gap in the door on his hands and knees, then made a dash for the nearest outbuilding, where he stopped and peered round at the trees. He could hear nothing. The night was silent with only the lightest of breezes. The gunman was gone.

He was being an idiot. He could never do this alone, and he couldn't leave Emma alone with a corpse either. He wiped the blood from his face, pulled his mobile from his pocket and put in a call to Tina as he jogged back the way he'd come.

'I've got Emma,' he told her once he'd briefly explained what had just happened. 'She's OK, but the guy who shot Ridgers is gone. You're going to have to get people over here quick. We need to get a security cordon in place and seal off the whole area.'

Ignoring the fact that she was being ordered around by someone who was suspended, Tina said she was on it and hung up.

Bolt stepped back inside the kitchen door. Emma was sitting on the floor, staring into space. She turned his way as he entered, and for several seconds they simply looked at each other in silence.

Emma looked utterly exhausted. Her clothes were torn and sweat-stained, and her blonde hair was matted and dishevelled, parts of it stuck to the thin layer of grime that covered her face. But none of that mattered. She was beautiful. And she was safe. He felt a wave of emotion sweep over him and he had to grit his teeth so that he didn't cry.

'Who are you?' she asked uncertainly.

Who am I? Your father, I think. A man you've never met before who's linked to you inextricably and for ever. Someone who's sweated blood these past hours trying to find you, who wants to get to know you, take you places, be a part of your life, and explain why he hasn't been there for so long. Who needs you so badly you can't imagine it.

'I'm the police,' he said.

'Will you take me home?'

He took a deep breath, fought back the tears. 'Of course I will.'

Fifty-three

But he didn't take her home. In fact, he hardly had a chance to talk to her.

Within minutes, the first of a long line of police and ambulance vehicles were on the scene, and she was taken away from him. After checking that she didn't need emergency medical treatment, the paramedics whisked her off to the nearby Chase Farm Hospital where she was to be reunited with her mother before being debriefed, and for Bolt, that was largely that. He was left alone on the periphery, watching as the local police sealed off the murder scene.

Within half an hour, the area around the farmhouse was teeming with activity, and floodlights had been set up to illuminate proceedings. Bolt was introduced briefly to a DI called Baker, who was running the CID nightshift at Enfield Nick, and who had the initial responsibility for investigating Scott Ridgers' death. He looked more like an accountant than a copper and when he spoke it was in a flat estuary accent, but he had sharp, intelligent eyes that didn't look like they missed a lot, and Bolt had a feeling that when he went down to the station later to give his statement he was going to get a serious grilling about how he, a suspended SOCA agent, had ended up at the scene, particularly as the ransom money was missing. But he was ready for it. After everything else that had happened today, he was pretty much prepared for whatever was going to be thrown at him.

He was leaning against the farmhouse's front fence, drinking coffee from a plastic container, when a car pulled up just behind the line of police vans on the driveway, and Steve Evans got out, followed by Tina and Mo. Their expressions were grim and businesslike, but as they got closer Tina nodded at him from behind Evans's shoulder and gave him the barest hint of a smile. Mo just nodded.

Evans, meanwhile, was just plain pissed off. 'I thought I told you you were suspended, Mike,' he said, stopping in front of him.

'You did, sir. I got a lead on Scott Ridgers. I thought I'd check it out. As a concerned private citizen.'

Evans didn't look mollified. 'And you tracked

him down here, only for him to be shot dead by an unknown assailant while you were struggling with him. That's the story I'm getting from DI Baker.'

'Yes, sir. Someone shot Ridgers from outside the kitchen window while I was fighting with him inside. I'm assuming it's the same person who disappeared with the money from the ransom drop. I phoned Tina as soon as I could so that she could alert the local police, and I've been here ever since.'

Evans looked sceptical. 'It always seems to be you who gets in these situations, doesn't it? How did you end up here?'

Avoiding Tina's eyes, he told Evans the story he'd already rehearsed in his head.

'Ridgers told his girlfriend where he was staying in case she needed him. When her father told her that he was wanted for a very serious crime, she gave him this address. The father phoned me because we'd already spoken earlier today. Obviously I was suspended, and I didn't think my word would count for much, so I decided to come up here myself, just to check things out. As soon as I arrived, I saw Ridgers dragging Emma into the house, and decided I was going to have to intervene immediately.' He shrugged. 'The rest you know.'

Evans stared at him for several seconds. He had

a hard, intimidating gaze that carried the heavy weight of authority. Bolt, who was used to such looks and wasn't affected by them, held it firmly.

'Well, you're still suspended, Mike, and I don't want to see you around again until you're back on duty. Understood?'

The rebuke was painful, especially as he'd done so much to break a case that was about to go very high-profile, but not entirely unexpected. Evans was right. He still shouldn't have been there.

'Sure, I understand.'

'Good. Now, I need to go and see DI Baker. If you'll excuse me.'

Evans moved past Bolt, leaving him alone with Mo and Tina. Mo asked how Emma was. His tone was stiff and formal, and Bolt had noticed that he hadn't called him 'boss' for some time now.

'She's good,' he answered. 'As well as can be expected, anyway. But it's going to take her a while to recover.'

'But she will recover. Kids always do. They're resilient like that.' Mo looked towards the house. 'I'd better go inside.'

'OK.'

Mo managed a weak smile that confirmed to Bolt that their relationship had taken a serious beating.

'I hope you're back on duty soon,' he said.

'I will be.'

'Good luck.'

Mo turned and walked towards the gate. Tina made no move to follow him.

'You not going with him?'

She nodded. 'In a minute.'

Bolt smiled at her. He couldn't help but think she looked pretty in the moonlight.

'Thanks for what you did, Tina. It saved Emma's life.'

'Thanks for covering for me.'

'I couldn't really do anything else, could I? Not after you put your job on the line.' He sighed. 'How's Turner?'

'Still critical, but he's off the operating table now. It looks better than it did.'

'Thank God for that. Any other developments in the case?'

It was her turn to smile now. 'You're the one who seems to be creating the developments, Mike.'

'I didn't have anything to do with Ridgers' death, you know.'

'I never thought you would have done.'

He wondered why he'd felt the need to tell her that. Had he really moved so far from his position as law enforcer that he had to justify himself to his colleagues in case they suspected he might be a killer?

'It wouldn't surprise me if Mo thinks I did, though,' he said, rubbing his eyes.

'Mo likes to do things the right way. He's pissed off with you, but he still thinks you're a good cop.'

Tina was wrong. Mo didn't always have to do things the right way. Bolt remembered that at one time Mo had done things for him way above and beyond the call of duty, but that maybe now he'd grown weary of bailing his boss out.

'You look whacked, Mike.'

'I am. It's been a long day. But, you know, I don't like the idea of going home knowing there's still someone out there who's a kidnapper and a killer, and who's now at least half a million pounds richer.'

'The police here have found Phelan's car in one of the outbuildings. But no sign of Phelan.'

Bolt was surprised. He'd almost forgotten about Andrea's husband.

'I don't think it was Phelan who killed Ridgers,' he said slowly. 'I just can't see that he's the one behind this. I mean, the guy's a fly-by-night, a minor criminal, and an inveterate gambler. He's hardly a criminal mastermind.'

'But if his car's here, then why isn't he?' asked Tina. 'If he wasn't involved, I would have thought they'd've disposed of the car and the body together, because there'd be no point doing it separately.'

'I suppose so, but if he is part of this, then why did they bother killing Andrea's cleaner?'

Tina shrugged. 'Good point. God knows.'

They fell silent, and Bolt yawned.

'You'd better go in, Tina. Steve Evans won't be pleased if you're talking to me. You'll keep me posted of how things go though, yeah?'

She nodded. 'Of course I will.'

As she walked past him, she patted his arm reassuringly and he realized it was the first time in their two years working together that she'd ever touched him.

'You did a good job tonight, Mike,' she said. 'You'll be back on duty soon.'

He watched her go, thinking of all the things he'd done today, so many of which could still cost him his career. He'd been in law enforcement for twenty years. It was the only job he'd known, and despite the constraints it imposed and the huge tedium of much of the work, he loved it. If they sacked him, he had no idea what he'd do. But the fact remained, there was no way he'd have changed any of his actions because in the end, illegal or not, they had got him the one thing he wanted most: his daughter back.

He thought about Pat Phelan in the photograph with Emma and Andrea at Andrea's house, all close up together, the happy nuclear family. If he was involved, it would be a betrayal of epic proportions. Fear can make a man do some strange things, and owing big sums of money to a violent thug like Leon Daroyce was going to make someone like Pat Phelan very frightened. But even so, Bolt still didn't buy the fact that he was the man who'd escaped with the money.

The problem now, with the other conspirators dead, was finding out who was.

Part Six

Part Six

Fifty-four

Whatever doubts Bolt had about Pat Phelan's involvement in the kidnap of his stepdaughter, the fact remained that they were largely irrelevant. He was off the case and, for the moment at least, off the team.

It had been a long night. He'd been at Enfield Nick until the early hours, giving his statement to two of the local CID and taking their questions. He'd stuck to the story he'd told Steve Evans about why he'd been on the scene in the first place, but made sure he told the truth about everything else, and it soon became clear that they were treating him as a witness rather than a suspect in the murder of Scott Ridgers. Formalities complete, he'd eventually made it home a little after three a.m. and collapsed, exhausted, into his bed straight away, able to relax for the first time in close to forty-eight hours.

He slept late. It was gone eleven when he finally rose from his bed, cleaned himself up, and put on a fresh pot of coffee. There was a message on his mobile from Mo telling him that Matt Turner was still on the critical list but that the operation had been a success and the doctors were confident he was going to pull through. He also added that Emma had been debriefed and had confirmed Bolt's version of events, then finished by wishing his boss luck and hoping he'd be back on duty soon. He sounded a little contrite, and Bolt guessed that this was his apology for the way he'd been the previous day.

It was good news about Turner. He'd go down the hospital to visit him as soon as he was well enough to be seen.

As he poured the coffee and made himself a couple of slices of toast, his thoughts turned to Emma. It was a strange feeling knowing that he had a daughter who for fourteen years had grown up only a few miles away. But he felt happy about it, and hopeful too. He wanted to become a part of her life now, although he knew that this would have to wait a while, at least until she'd recovered from the worst of her ordeal.

But at the very least he needed to know how she was getting on, and when he'd finished his toast he called Andrea's landline. Marie the liaison officer answered. She sounded tired, but brightened a little when she recognized Bolt's voice.

'It's great news that we've got Emma back,' she said. 'Andrea's ecstatic, as you can imagine.'

'Is Andrea there?' he asked.

'Yes, they're both here. Do you want to speak to her?'

'Please. Just tell her it's a quick courtesy call. I'm sure she's busy.'

'I'll go and find her. Hold on.'

Marie clearly didn't know about his suspension. In fact, it didn't seem that she'd been told much, which under the circumstances was probably no bad thing.

A few seconds later he heard the receiver being picked up. But it wasn't Andrea. It was Marie again.

'She says she's very busy at the moment, Mr Bolt. Can she call you back later?'

He tried to keep the disappointment out of his voice. 'No problem. I'll wait to hear from her. But Emma's fine, yeah?'

'She's asleep at the moment, but yes, she's bearing up well, although the doctors say she's quite dehydrated.'

He wanted to ask something else, to keep the conversation going in the hope that Andrea would change her mind and take the call, but he wasn't sure what, so reluctantly he said his good-byes and hung up.

He turned on the TV and found Sky News. The main report was on the failed ransom drop. The man shot dead by police had not been named, but the young father he'd fatally stabbed had been identified as thirty-five-year-old Anthony Randolph of Waltham Abbey, Essex. A photo of him on his wedding day flashed up on the screen, followed by a photo of Matt Turner looking particularly deadpan, as the reporter described him as fighting for his life in intensive care. A camera panned round a largely empty Tottenham High Road, lined with strips of scene-of-crime tape, as the report continued, but it was clear that information was scarce, and there was no mention of the kidnapping, or of the separate but linked death of Scott Ridgers.

Bolt felt resentful that he was no longer involved in an investigation he'd done so much to break. He wondered whether Phelan had shown up yet, and briefly contemplated phoning Tina, but decided against it. She'd done more than enough for him already, and he didn't want to lose her respect by pushing her further.

Instead, he finished his coffee and got dressed, knowing that he had to do something, anything, to ease his frustration.

Which was when he had an idea. Outside, the

sun was shining and it looked like it was going to be another beautiful day. He grabbed his shoes and looked at his watch. Five minutes to midday.

It was time to catch up with some old friends.

Fifty-five

When Tina Boyd pressed the buzzer on Andrea's security gate at just after 2.30 p.m. she'd already done a seven-hour day and was finally on her way home, albeit in a slightly indirect way. She'd already spent more than two hours there that morning with Mo talking to Emma, listening to her harrowing account of the past few days while her mother sat beside her, holding her hand. Tina had been impressed by how brave and lucid Emma was in the interview, answering all their questions quietly and carefully, and although she'd looked tired, and thinner than she did in the photos that lined the house, her overall demeanour suggested that the damage she'd suffered wasn't irreversible. It was too early to say for sure, and Tina was no psychologist, but she'd come away feeling positive, and also proud of her boss, who according to Emma's testimony had saved her life and almost lost his own in the process. Emma had asked where Bolt was, saying she'd like to thank him properly, and Tina had told her that she was sure they'd get to meet soon, looking at Andrea as she did so.

Andrea had looked away.

Andrea's voice came on the line now, far brighter and chirpier now that she'd got her daughter back, but it immediately lost its lustre when Tina introduced herself.

'Oh, back again?' she said wearily. 'I'm afraid Emma's asleep at the moment, and I don't want her disturbed.'

'That's OK. It's you I've come to see. Can I come in?'

Andrea buzzed her through. She'd changed since Tina had left earlier and was now wearing a long T-shirt and a pair of khaki hotpants that showed off shapely legs and freshly painted, bright red toenails. The haggard, terrified woman of the last couple of days had now almost completely disappeared. It was quite a transformation.

'I've sent the liaison officer away,' she said as Tina stepped into the hallway. 'It's just me and Emma now. Like it's always been. Any word on Pat yet?'

'Nothing at the moment, I'm afraid.'

'God knows what's happened to him. I still

don't think he's involved, but if he is . . .' Her face darkened momentarily but then returned to normal as she pushed thoughts of her husband aside. 'Do you have more questions for me, then? Is that why you're here?'

'Shall we go through to the living room?'

'OK.'

Andrea stretched out the word, trying to gauge from Tina's expression what this might be about. Tina didn't give anything away, so Andrea led her through, taking her usual position on the sofa. Tina shut the door but remained standing.

'I wanted to ask you some questions about Emma's father. Her real one.'

Andrea sighed loudly. 'God, do we have to? I mean, is it important? I could do with a rest myself, you know.'

'We need to discuss it now.'

'Don't take that sort of tone with me.'

'You said in your statement on Friday that Emma's father was James Galante.'

'That's right.'

Tina pulled a folded sheet of paper from the back pocket of her jeans, holding it out in front of her.

'Do you know what it says on here?'

Andrea didn't say anything, but she was looking less sure of herself.

'It says that Emma was adopted.'

454

Andrea swallowed.

'By you and your then husband, Mr William Devern, in September 1994. When she was seventeen months old. I got a copy of the birth certificate from Somerset House this morning.'

'Christ. Keep your voice down. Emma doesn't know.'

'OK. But it makes me wonder, Mrs Devern, how many other things have you been lying about?'

Andrea reached for her cigarettes, which Tina now recognized as a sure sign that she was feeling stressed.

'It was only that I wanted Jimmy to help me and I thought if I convinced him he was Emma's dad then he'd never be able to say no.' She got up and opened the French windows, lighting up and blowing smoke out into the garden, her arms folded in a defensive gesture. 'You'd have done the same in my position, except you don't know that, because you've never had kids. She may not be my flesh and blood, but she's still my daughter. I brought her up. No one else, because Billy was dead within a year. Just me.' She blew out more smoke and glared defiantly at Tina.

'When are you intending to tell Mike Bolt that he's not Emma's father?'

The question made Andrea flinch.

'So, he told you about that, did he?'

'Only when he absolutely had to.'

'I'll tell him soon enough. When I've got my head back together.'

'You almost destroyed him, Mrs Devern. He's suspended from his job because of you, and it's possible he'll lose it over this. The least you can do is put him out of his misery.'

'I told you, I'll tell him soon.'

'No. Either you call him now, or I do. And I really think it would be best if it came from you, don't you?'

'Listen, Miss Boyd, you've got no idea what I've been through in the last week. What I've done, I've done to protect my daughter and help to get her away from those animals and back with me where she belongs, and I'm not going to make any apologies for that.'

'He still needs to know,' Tina insisted. 'Today.'

Andrea unfolded her arms, softening her stance.

'Can you tell him? Please? Say I'm very, very sorry and that I will call him, I promise. It's just . . .' She paused, and Tina could see that her eyes were filling with tears. 'Not today.'

'OK. I'll call him outside.'

As she walked through the French windows, Andrea stopped her with a hand on the arm.

'I do care for him, you know,' she said quietly, a tear running down one cheek. 'A lot more than you think.'

Tina nodded. She didn't believe a word of it.

She walked up to the end of the garden, well out of earshot, and dialled Mike's number, knowing that he was going to take this hard.

When he answered, he sounded in a good mood and there was a buzz of conversation in the background.

'Tina, how's it going?'

'Not bad. Where are you?'

'In a pub in Finchley. Relaxing with some old Flying Squad buddies. I figure, I'm suspended, I may as well enjoy myself. What can I do for you?'

The moment of truth. And straight away she knew she couldn't do it. Not when he was enjoying himself. It would just have to wait.

'I thought you might want a quick update on things, but if you're out with your friends—'

'No, I'd like to hear what you've got.'

She gave him a summary of where the investigation was, but there really wasn't a lot to say as things were running down now. There was still no sign of Pat Phelan. They'd put surveillance on Isobel Wheeler's house in case he turned up there, but that was pretty much it.

'And have you seen Emma?'

Tina stiffened. 'Yes, she's well. Back at home now.'

'And Andrea?'

'She's fine too.'

'Thanks, Tina. I really appreciate you keeping me in touch with things.'

'I'd want to be, if I was in your position. Anyway, you'd better get back to your friends.'

She rang off, cursing herself for being such a coward. Now she'd have to call him again later.

She sat down on the garden's loveseat and lit a cigarette, in no hurry to go back inside. As she basked in the mid-afternoon sunshine, she realized with surprise that she was going to miss Mike Bolt now that he was suspended. Things had changed between them these past few days. She'd seen a vulnerable side to him for the first time, and she was flattered that he'd turned to her when he needed help, seeing something beyond the hard shell she surrounded herself with. She hadn't had romance in a long time. It was over three years since John had died. Since then there'd been a couple of one-night stands and a brief holiday fling in Thailand. But now she felt the first hint of attraction, and it unnerved her.

She stubbed out the cigarette in the grass and stood up slowly. It was time to go home.

But as she reached the French windows, she stopped. Andrea was back on her sofa, but there were two men in suits in the room with her whom Tina recognized as detectives from the farm the previous night. They were obviously trying to keep their expressions as calm and inscrutable as possible as they turned towards her, but there was no escaping the excitement in them.

'We've got a new lead on Scott Ridgers' killer,' said the younger of the two, a fresh-faced youth with thinning hair and a spray of freckles. 'A big one.'

Fifty-six

The Coach and Horses was the pub where Finchley Flying Squad members past and present liked to drink. There were always a few old faces in on a Sunday lunchtime, mainly the local guys, but today was the first time in a long while that Bolt had made it.

The lunchtime crowd was thinning out now as Bolt came off the phone to Tina and returned to the table where he'd been drinking for the last two hours with today's Flying Squad contingent: Ron 'Scissors' Austin, silver-haired, still serving, nearing retirement; Marvin 'Mad Dog' Bennett, a huge black guy now working on the Met's Operation Trident; Big Tim Pritchard, once the squad's Romeo, but now a few stones above his ideal weight courtesy of his desk job at Scotland Yard; and the ever injury-prone Jack 'Dodger' Doyle.

'Who was that, your girlfriend?' grinned Scissors Austin as Bolt sat back down with his drink.

'No such luck. Colleague.'

'You want to get yourself out more, pal,' advised Jack Doyle before resuming his story, which involved a long-ago one-night stand he'd had with a female DCI from Hendon.

Bolt wasn't really listening to the story. His mind was elsewhere. He wanted to talk to Emma and had thought that Tina's call might have been her or Andrea getting in touch. The fact that it wasn't disappointed him. It had been good to catch up and trade war stories from the good old days, but now, as the conversation moved on to sexual conquests, he decided it was probably time to go.

Doyle finished his story of fumbled, drunken lovemaking (which had resulted, somewhat inevitably, in him falling over and twisting his ankle so badly he'd been off work for three days) with a flourish and plenty of illustrative hand movements, amid much laughter. When he went off to the toilet, Big Tim, not to be outdone, started on a story of his own, involving a relationship with a pretty uniformed PC from Finchley Nick.

'Tracey Bonham was her name. Anyone remember her?'

'Yeah, I do,' said Scissors. 'Pretty little thing.

Red hair. Don't tell me she had a fling with an ugly sod like you.'

Big Tim's seat creaked precariously as he leaned back on it. 'Watch it, old man. That girl was in love with me, I tell you. I liked her as well. We almost got engaged at one point.'

'I never knew that,' said Scissors sceptically. 'Are you sure you didn't dream it?'

'I don't remember her at all,' said Mad Dog, shaking his head.

Bolt swallowed the last of his pint. To be honest, he didn't either.

'Well, I didn't bloody dream it, all right? We did nearly get engaged, and I reckon we would have done as well, but then she ends up running off with some scuzzy little bastard who turns out to be one of Dodger Doyle's snouts.'

Scissors looked mortified. 'Christ, she dumped you for a snout?'

'All right, all right. Don't rub it in. He was one of these real charmers, you know. The sort gullible women go for.'

'What, like you, you mean?' chuckled Mad Dog.

'No, not like me. I'm sophisticated and good-hearted, as well as being beautiful. He was just a long-haired toe rag with a nice line in patter. But he had things with a couple of the girls at Finchley Nick. Then he got done for receiving a load of hijacked hi-fis, after he started trying to flood the market with them. He even sold one to Tracey.'

'Serious?'

'Yeah. She ended up leaving the force over it eventually. Christ, what was his name now?' Big Tim looked up and saw Doyle returning from the toilet. 'What was his name, Jack? That snout of yours a few years back. The one who got done for all them hi-fis. Pat somebody or other, wasn't it?'

'I've got it,' said Scissors, banging his empty pint glass on the table. 'It was Pat Phelan. Right long-haired nancy. He was one of yours, wasn't he, Jack?'

'Christ, I can't remember that far back,' said Doyle, re-taking his seat.

But as he spoke the words he glanced across at Bolt and their eyes met. Bolt felt his fingers tighten around his empty glass. Doyle looked away quickly and picked up his pint, trying too hard to appear natural.

Bolt stared at him, feeling adrenalin course through his body. There was a news blackout. Pat Phelan had not been mentioned at all in the media. Yet Jack Doyle clearly knew of his relevance to Bolt, which was why he'd instinctively glanced his way.

Their eyes met again, and it was suddenly as if everyone else in the room had melted away, leaving just the two of them there, at opposite ends of an empty, silent table.

Instincts. They shape so much of human behaviour. And in those single, dark moments, every instinct in Bolt's body told him that he was staring at the man who'd telephoned Andrea at home and in her car, and who one way or another had masterminded the whole thing.

Fifty-seven

Jack Doyle drained his pint and stood up. 'Well, boys, I've got to go. Things to do, people to see, you know the score.'

He shook hands with the boys.

'I've got to go as well,' said Bolt, getting to his feet.

'Don't fancy one more for the road, gents?' asked Big Tim, looking disappointed at the prospect of losing half his potential audience.

'No, sorry, I've had a long few days,' said Bolt, doing his own rounds and having to hurry as he followed Jack out of the pub.

'I'd give you a lift, Mike,' said Doyle, fumbling for his car keys, 'but I'm going in the wrong direction. See you soon, eh?'

He nodded briefly, a smile so tight on his face that it looked like it had been fixed there with botox, and made no attempt to shake hands as he started walking up towards the car park at the back of the pub.

Bolt kept pace alongside him.

'She was my daughter, Jack.'

Doyle looked at him with a puzzled expression. 'Who was?'

'Emma Devern. The girl whose kidnapping you organized.'

'What the hell are you talking about?'

'You know exactly what I'm talking about. Why did you target Andrea? Did Phelan get you in on it?'

'Whoa, Mike. I think the stress of this kidnap case you've been on's got to you. Why don't you go home and get some rest? Because I promise you, you're talking shit.'

He carried on walking, and once again Bolt kept pace, even though he was experiencing the first signs of doubt.

And then it struck him.

'You were off sick for the Lewisham job, weren't you? The one where I shot Dean Hayes.'

'I'm not talking about this, Mike. Now fuck off.'

Doyle clicked off the central locking as they reached his car, a silver Ford Mondeo, parked up against a fence round the back of the pub and out of sight of the front door.

'You were off sick, so you never knew about the ambush until afterwards. That's right, isn't it?

Shit, Jack. I never had you down for corrupt, but you were involved, weren't you? You were in on it.'

Doyle's features hardened as he opened the driver's door. 'You're pissing in the wind, Mike. And you can keep pissing as long as you like, because none of it's going to hit me.'

'There'll be evidence, Jack. You know it. I know it. So, where's the half million? Under your bed? Safe for a rainy day? We'll find it.'

Doyle shook his head. 'Well, *you* won't, will you? You're suspended.'

And with that he got inside the car.

Bolt felt rage bubble up inside him. He looked around. The car park was empty. He had to act. Now.

'You think I'm going to let you drive away after what you've done to my daughter?'

He strode round to the driver's door and yanked it open.

'No, I don't,' said Doyle as Bolt went to grab him. 'That's why I've got this.' There was a snub-nosed revolver with a scotch-taped handle in his left hand, and it was pointing up at Bolt. 'Now, step back from the car, nice and easy.'

'You won't shoot me here.'

'I wouldn't place a bet on that if I were you.'

The cold expression in Doyle's eyes told Bolt that it was best to comply, and he took a step backwards, realizing as he did so that he'd made a serious miscalculation. What the hell was he going to do now?

Doyle got out of the car, keeping the gun down by his side and glancing briefly over Bolt's shoulder to check that the car park was still clear. Then he threw his car keys on the driver's seat.

'OK, Mike, you're driving. Get in or I'll put a bullet in you right now.'

'Don't do this, Jack. It's over, can't you see that?'

'Get in.'

Bolt took a deep breath and complied, while Jack got in the back. He pointed the gun through the gap in the seats.

'All right, let's get moving.'

'Where are we going?'

'Just start driving and turn right out of here.'

Bolt started the car and pulled out, heading slowly through the car park, hoping that one of the Flying Squad boys would come out of the front door and ask for a lift.

'Go on, get moving,' Doyle snapped, shoving the gun in Bolt's ribs.

There was a big gap in the traffic and, knowing he had no choice, he pulled out on to the Finchley Road and started driving north, trying hard to figure out his options. He was certain Doyle wouldn't pull the trigger while he was driving, and pretty sure he wouldn't even if he stopped and jumped out – not in such a public place with pedestrians and other traffic about – but pretty sure wasn't good enough. Jack Doyle was both a killer and a desperate man. It was a bad combination.

It struck Bolt that Doyle was almost certainly trying to work out his own options, and he decided that his best policy was to distract him. He needed to keep Doyle talking.

'Why the hell did you have to do this, Jack?' he asked, his voice laced with disappointment.

'It's not like you think, and I didn't know she was your daughter. I just wanted my money back.'

'What do you mean?'

'That Lewisham job was going to be my retirement fund. Instead, the whole thing went tits up and almost cost me everything. If I hadn't got Galante out of the country he'd have definitely grassed me up. For years I never knew who'd fucked things up for us. You never named your source, remember?'

'Yeah, I remember.'

'Very chivalrous of you. Except the problem was one day you did tell me.'

Bolt frowned. 'When?'

'Remember that fishing trip you and me went on to Ireland a couple of years back, the last time you got yourself suspended? Well, it was then. We got pissed one night in that pub near Kilrush, the one with the big log fire. I asked you about the job then. I wasn't even that bothered about it. I just wanted to know.'

'And I told you?' Bolt vaguely remembered saying something now, but it had been an extremely drunken night.

'Yeah, you told me it was that bitch Andrea Devern. I didn't even know she was Galante's squeeze at the time.' Doyle cleared his throat. 'Anyway, I looked into things and saw she'd done very, very nicely for herself. Unlike me with a divorce, kids I don't see, and a whore of an ex-wife who's nicked all my money and half my pension.'

Bolt didn't bother telling him that this was hardly a reason for committing kidnap and murder. Instead, he kept quiet, letting Doyle talk. All the time pondering his options.

'And then I heard she'd married that piece of dirt Pat Phelan. You know, I met up with him a few months ago? I was going to sound him out about getting involved, but the flash bastard couldn't stop telling me how much money he had now that he was married to a rich girl, really rubbing it in. He laughed at me. You know that, Mike? The bastard laughed at me. Well, he ain't laughing now.'

'Where is he?'

'Not far away. I'm surprised you lot haven't found him yet.'

He pulled a crumpled pack of cigarettes from the sports jacket he was wearing, drew one out and lit it.

'You know what gets me? The whole thing was planned brilliantly. I really put effort into it. I let Ridgers and his prison buddy, a toe rag called Karl Roven, do all the hard work, and the idea was they'd turn up back at the farm last night and I'd take them both out. Bang bang, just like that. Then with Pat Phelan disappeared off the face of the earth, he'd end up getting the blame for organizing it all.'

'What about Emma? What were you going to do with her?'

'She was always going to get released. I'm not that cruel. I don't mind getting rid of scum like Ridgers and his mate, but I don't hurt kids.'

Somehow Bolt doubted it. If Doyle was cruel enough to lock Emma in a cellar and subject her to such a terrifying ordeal, he was definitely cruel enough to dispose of her afterwards.

'What about the cleaner? Was she scum as well?'

'That was a pity,' Doyle answered, sounding genuinely regretful. 'I got Ridgers' prison buddy, Roven, to get to know her. It was the only way we could get the alarm codes to plant the bugs. I tried getting past the alarm a couple of times myself, but it was too sophisticated. And once Roven had the information, he had to get rid of her.'

'But we never found any bugs in the house.'

'We used the simplest ones of all: a couple of mobile phones planted in the house and set up to hands-free kits. All we had to do was put them on silent and auto answer, then dial the numbers, and we could hear everything. The reason you never found them was because they'd both run out of batteries by Friday, so they wouldn't have shown up on all the new-fangled stuff you use these days. I didn't think we'd need them beyond then.'

Bolt knew it was possible to turn standard mobile phones into covert listening devices with only a few standard modifications. They should have thought of that. Not that it would have made any difference in the end.

'You know, I can't believe a friend of mine – someone I've known for, God, how long is it? sixteen, seventeen years? – could do what you've done and sit here trying to justify it.'

Doyle sat up in his seat and glared at Bolt, blowing smoke into the front of the car.

'I saved your life last night, Mikey boy. Remember that. If I hadn't put a bullet in Ridgers, he'd have cut you to pieces, and you know it.' He dragged hard on the cigarette. 'I saved your life, even though you turning up there nearly ruined everything for me. Just like you turning up now has.'

'Forgive me if I don't apologize for wanting to rescue my daughter from the animals you hired.'

'You know I'd never have done it if I'd known she was anything to do with you. Like I say, all I wanted was my money.'

Bolt stared at him in the wing mirror.

'You keep saying that, "my money". Andrea ran a business she'd built up from scratch. What did she owe you?'

'How do you think she started that business? There was other money that Jimmy Galante had stashed away that went missing after he left the country. Money that she had. Don't ever make the mistake of thinking that bitch is whiter than white.'

Doyle opened the window and chucked his cigarette butt out.

'Go straight across at the lights, and don't try anything. There's a turning up here somewhere.'

'Where are we going?'

'Just for a little drive.'

Bolt knew what was coming. He slowed down as the lights went red, and the Mondeo came to a halt.

'So, you're going to kill me then?'

Doyle looked pained. 'Course not, Mike. We go back way too far for that.'

'Sure we do.'

The lights went green and Bolt pulled away. He knew that Doyle couldn't afford to leave him alive, even if he was an old friend. When you were responsible for as many killings as he'd been this past week, you became hardened to it, and Jack Doyle had always been a hard man, unafraid to make tough decisions.

The mobile in Bolt's pocket rang.

'Aren't you going to answer that?'

Bolt pulled it out, but Doyle extended his free hand. 'Give me that,' he said, taking it off him. He examined the screen as it continued to ring. 'Who's Tina Boyd?'

Bolt tensed. What could she want now?

'She's a friend.'

Doyle smiled knowingly. 'Friend, or girlfriend?'

'Friend.'

The mobile stopped ringing and went to voice-mail, before ringing again for a few seconds to announce a message. Doyle put it to his ear, still keeping the gun firmly on Bolt.

But as he listened to Tina's message, something happened. As Bolt watched in the rear-view mirror, Doyle's face, blotchy and lined after years of too much boozing, began to drain of colour, and his breathing rate increased.

'Shit!' he hissed, throwing the phone to the floor. It clattered under one of the seats. 'Shit,

shit, shit! How the hell do they know about me?'

Somehow they were on to him. Bolt wondered whether this was a good or a bad thing. He had a grim feeling it might be the latter.

'It's over, Jack,' he said, trying hard to stay calm, looking for a chance to get out of range of that gun. 'You can give yourself up. None of what you've said in here's admissible in court. You'll get done for kidnapping, but you'll miss the murder charge.'

Behind him, Doyle fidgeted in his seat.

'It ain't going to happen, pal,' he said after a short pause. 'They know. Somehow they know I pulled the trigger on Ridgers. What am I going to do?'

'Give up.'

'Fuck you. No way. Got to think, pal. That's what I've got to do.'

He exhaled deeply, still training the gun on Bolt, his expression distracted as he desperately weighed up his options.

Bolt noticed he wasn't wearing a seatbelt.

Without warning, he slammed his foot down on the accelerator and swung the wheel hard left, cutting up the car in the next lane.

'What the hell are you doing? Stop, or I'll shoot!'

Bolt's whole body stiffened, expecting a bullet any second, but he kept driving, aiming straight at a line of concrete bollards on the edge of the pavement.

'Stop, you bastard, stop!'

There was a tremendous bang as Bolt hit the nearest bollard head-on, his foot still flat on the floor, and the sound of shattering glass and crunching metal. At exactly the same time, a shot rang out in the car, louder than the initial crash and deafening Bolt as he was flung forward in his seat like a stringless puppet. Out of the corner of his eye he saw Doyle smash into the front passenger seat, then fly backwards, his legs flailing wildly, before disappearing altogether.

Then the airbag shot out, driving the wind out of Bolt as it smothered him in its rubbery grip. For a few seconds he was crushed against his seat, unable to move, not even sure whether or not the bullet had hit him. Then, realizing that it hadn't, he managed to yank open the door handle and struggle free, desperate to get out.

He staggered round the front of the Mondeo, conscious that he was outside a parade of shops, some of which were open. Shocked onlookers were gathering fast, the majority of them looking at something round the back of the car.

'He's got a gun!' someone called out, and the small crowd moved backwards quickly.

Doyle was lying on the pavement about ten feet from the back of the car, propped up precariously on one elbow, the revolver hanging loosely from his hand. He must have been flung out of the back window, but somehow had managed to retain his grip on the gun, which was typical of him. He'd always been single-minded. Blood stained his shirt and sports jacket, and a huge gash had opened up one cheek like a second, bleeding mouth. He was in a bad way, but when he saw Bolt, something flashed in his eyes and he tried hard to lift the gun.

For a long moment they simply watched each other, oblivious to everyone around them, each man trying hard to come to terms with this terrible turn of events that had destroyed things between them for ever. Then Bolt began walking towards him, steady, confident strides that ate up the distance fast.

Doyle's eyes narrowed, but he was having difficulty focusing and the gun was shaking in his hand. Several people in the crowd gasped but no one made a move to intervene. It was as if they were watching the last dramatic scene in a TV cop drama.

Blood leaked out of the corner of Doyle's mouth, running down his chin. Bolt saw his finger tighten on the trigger, the end of the barrel pointed towards his belly, and he felt a lurch of adrenalin that almost lifted him off his feet. In that second, he leapt forward, stamped on the wrist of

Doyle's shaking gun hand and drove it into the pavement. Doyle grunted and fell down on his back, losing his grip on the revolver.

Bolt snatched it up and pointed it, two-handed, down at Doyle's chest, holding it steady, his face as hard as stone.

'Don't do it!' someone in the crowd cried out, shrill and fearful.

But he was never going to. There was no point. Emma was safe, Jack Doyle was finished, and finally his rage was fading, to be replaced by a leaden sense of regret that an old friendship he'd once thought so strong could have ended up like this. Tattered, bleeding, and ultimately hollow.

Doyle's eyes closed and his head rolled to one side, more blood trailing out of his mouth and dripping on to the concrete.

Bolt took a step back, then another, until he reached the car. He propped himself up against it and noticed the crowd watching – twenty, thirty strong now – for the first time.

'Someone dial nine-nine-nine,' he said with as much strength as he could muster.

Then tiredness seemed to overwhelm him and, still clutching the revolver, he slid down the car and landed in a sitting position on the tarmac.

It was over.

Fifty-eight

Tina Boyd stood in the shadows thrown by the low-rise council flats and looked through the darkness at the brand-new four-door Lexus GS parked behind the chainlink fence on the other side of the road. It had just turned twenty past ten and she'd been standing there for more than an hour already. She wondered if she was wasting her time. Probably. But Tina wasn't the sort to give up that easily. She'd give it another half an hour before calling it a day.

She stifled a yawn. It had been a manic weekend but at least events had come to a comparatively clean conclusion, which, as most police officers would tell you, is very rarely the case. Pat Phelan had at last turned up, although the manner in which he did so left something to be desired. A thorough search by Enfield SOCO of one of the farm's outbuildings revealed his dismembered remains inside a barrel of sulphuric acid, where they were dissolving steadily; they would probably have been little more than sludge had they been left for another week. His teeth had been forcibly removed, and identification had only been possible because a large 'Ban the Bomb' tattoo on what was left of his upper arm was still just about visible, and was recognized by Andrea Devern.

The other main development that day had been the uncovering of the third person involved in the kidnap, DI Jack Doyle of the Flying Squad. A woman who lived a hundred yards from the farm had heard the gunshots the previous evening and had gone outside to investigate. She'd seen an unfamiliar car parked down the lane from her house, and because of the circumstances she'd written down the registration number. A few minutes later she'd seen a man return to the car and drive away. Because there were a number of farms in the area, and the sound of shotguns being fired wasn't that unusual, the woman hadn't called the police. But when they'd turned up at her door earlier that day as part of their general enquiries, she'd told them about what had happened. The car was quickly traced to DI Doyle, and when the witness was shown his photo she was able to say that it bore a very strong resemblance to the person she'd seen. Not enough for a conviction perhaps, but ample justification for an arrest warrant to be issued, and from that moment on his fate had been sealed. However, before he could be arrested, he'd been involved in a car crash, and was now seriously ill in hospital. A gun recovered from the scene with his finger-prints on it had subsequently been confirmed as the weapon used to murder Scott Ridgers at the farm.

The reason why it was only a comparatively clean conclusion rather than an absolutely perfect result was that Matt Turner was still very ill and Mike Bolt, who more than anyone deserved credit for the op's overall success, was suspended until further notice. It didn't seem fair. And this was the main reason Tina was hanging around in the dark in a bad part of town, waiting. Because sometimes doing the job and upholding the law didn't neces-sarily provide the justice it was meant to. Sometimes you had to dispense that justice your-self, as an individual. Like Mike had done yesterday.

There was movement across the road. A group of men emerged from the entrance to the mono-lithic tower block, three of them in all, moving purposefully, their voices low. They stopped at the Lexus and got inside, pulling out seconds later.

Tina retreated further into the shadows and

took out her mobile as they drove past her. It was an unregistered pay-as-you go she'd bought on Tottenham Court Road earlier that day, and as the Lexus came to the end of the road and turned left, she dialled 999, asking for police.

'Hello, can I help you?'

'I've just seen three men get into a car armed with guns.'

'Are you sure about this, madam?'

'Absolutely,' she said breathlessly. 'They walked right past me.'

She gave her location, the make and model of the car, and the direction it was travelling in, waiting patiently while the operator took all the information down.

'And can I have your name, madam?'

'I don't want to get involved, I'm too scared.'

And with that, she ended the call, switched off the phone, and walked back to her car.

When she'd phoned the number Leon Daroyce had given her an hour earlier she'd disguised her voice and said he could find Pat Phelan at a flat in Colindale, where he was holed up with a lover, hoping he'd take the bait. And now it looked like he had done. She had no idea whether Daroyce and his two associates would be armed or not, but it didn't really matter since when the police stopped the car they'd find the five grams of cocaine she'd planted in the glove compartment.

It had taken all the burglary skills she'd learned at SOCA to bypass the Lexus's sophisticated alarm system, as well as one hell of a lot of nerve, but it would be worth it. Armed with the coke, the police would be able to execute a search warrant on Daroyce's premises, a place she was absolutely sure would be full of illegal contraband.

It might not be enough to put him away for years, or even months, but at least she'd done something to disrupt his business and pay him back for the ordeal he'd put her through two days earlier, and a search of the flat would probably mean freedom for the girl he'd abused as well, which had to be a good thing. He would probably work out who'd been behind it, and might even want to extract some kind of revenge when he was back on the street, but she doubted he'd risk killing a SOCA agent. Whatever he might like to claim, Daroyce was a bully, and bullies tended to be cowards when it came down to it.

She knew what her former lover, John Gallan, would have thought of her actions. He'd have disapproved, not only because what she'd done was potentially so dangerous, but also because he'd always believed in the absolute sanctity of the law he'd been paid to uphold. But as Tina and countless many others had found to their cost down the years, the law didn't always punish the bad, just like it didn't always protect the good.

Sometimes you just had to bend the rules, even if that did mean planting evidence.

Somewhere deep inside, the realization of what she'd done and the huge risk she'd taken worried her. But nowhere near enough to regret it, and there was even something of a spring in her step as she walked down the quiet, litter-strewn street and heard the first of the sirens converging on Leon Daroyce.

Epilogue: Two Days Later

It was a cool, drizzly day, very different to the Indian summer of the past ten days or so, and Mike Bolt and Andrea Devern were standing on Hampstead Heath, looking up in the direction of Kenwood House.

Andrea looked good. She was dressed in a three-quarter-length raincoat, her long auburn hair flowing over the collar. Her eyes were bright and alive in a way Bolt hadn't seen since their affair all those years ago.

'I really didn't want to do it,' she was saying to him now. 'It's no consolation, I know, but I was under huge amounts of pressure. Will you forgive me?'

Bolt looked at her. Andrea Devern had put him through hell, there was no doubt about it, but she'd also had one of the best reasons going for doing so. The safety of her daughter. Not his, unfortunately, he knew that now, but he could still sympathize. Today was the first time the two of them had seen each other since the chaotic aftermath of the ransom drop, but what should perhaps have been an awkward meeting felt anything but.

But then, Bolt thought ruefully, *Andrea has always had a way of making me feel good.*

He smiled. 'Sure, I forgive you. Maybe I'd have done the same in your position.'

'No, you wouldn't. You're not like that. You're a good man, Mike. You've got too much integrity.'

He shrugged. 'Maybe. But we all do desperate things sometimes. I'd like to see Emma at some point, too. I know she's not mine, but it would be nice to see how she's getting on.'

'I'll get her to call you when she's feeling better. She's been sleeping most of the past few days.'

'But she's OK?'

'Yeah, she's doing well. She's a fighter, just like me. She's upset about Pat. She liked him.'

'How do you feel about it?'

'I've shed my tears. He wasn't such a bad bloke, and I'm glad he didn't betray either me or Emma. That's a comfort.'

'Good.'

'And what about your colleague, Turner? The one who was at my place. How's he getting on?'

'He's out of intensive care and they say he should make a full recovery, but he's going to be in hospital for a while yet.'

'I hope he's all right. He seemed a nice guy.'

Neither of them mentioned Jack Doyle. He was still in a bad way in hospital but Bolt had little doubt he'd survive. Jack wasn't the kind to give up. He'd always been too bloody-minded for that, although he had little to look forward to when and if he did finally make it.

'And how about you, Mike?' asked Andrea. 'How are you managing? What's going to happen about your suspension?'

'I don't know yet. I'm still waiting to hear what action they're planning to take against me.'

'They shouldn't take any. You were a bloody hero. If it wasn't for you . . .'

There was no need for her to finish the sentence. They both knew what she meant.

He wasn't sure that he had been a hero, though. More likely he'd been a fool, and it was foolishness that still might cost him his job. But he didn't regret his actions, had even stopped worrying about the whole thing these past couple of days. What would happen would happen anyway, so it was easier just to think about something else.

They were silent for a moment, each watching the other. Conscious that there was still something there. Finally, Bolt spoke again.

'The reason I wanted to meet you today was because I had a question.'

Andrea looked wary. 'OK . . .'

'That day we met in the West End all those years ago, when we went back to your hotel. That wasn't, you know . . .'

'What?'

He suddenly felt embarrassed to bring it up.

'It was genuine coincidence, right? You didn't know I was going to be there?'

'You asked me that before. A long time ago.'

'And now I'm asking it again.'

Andrea smiled a little sadly. 'Have I been that bad to you that you could believe it wasn't?'

'I just wanted to hear it from your own lips again. Now that this is all over.'

'It was genuine coincidence, Mike. I promise.'

She'd lied to him before, but he chose to believe her this time. Perhaps it was easier that way.

'So, what now?' she asked, and there was an element of invitation in her hazel eyes.

He'd thought a lot about this these past couple of days, and hadn't known the answer until he'd arrived here today and seen Andrea as she should have been – happy, attractive and spirited.

'Well?'

'We do the same thing we did fifteen years ago, Andrea.' He looked her in the eyes and smiled. 'We part company.'

Her expression didn't change. 'Are you sure? I thought maybe there was still something there between us. Something that might be worth exploring.'

He leaned forward and kissed her on the cheek, lingering just a second over her scent, wanting to hold her but not knowing where it would end if he did, before moving away.

'Good luck, Andrea,' he said.

The invitation remained in her eyes for another second, then faded as she accepted the inevitable.

'And to you, Mike, and to you.'

He turned and left her there, striding away purposefully, wishing perhaps that things could have been different – that Emma was his daughter, that Andrea genuinely loved him, that they could end up as the kind of happy family he and Mikaela had never had the chance to create. But knowing too that he'd made the right decision. It was time to make a clean break with the past, start looking towards the future.

And where better to start than with a twenty-eight-year-old artist from St Ives with raven hair and a dirty laugh.

As he walked out on to Spaniards Road, he took out his mobile and called Jenny Byfleet, hoping that she was in a forgiving mood.

THE END

SEVERED

ne night stand.
ne dead girl.
ne bad day.

wake up in a strange room
a bed covered in blood. And
have no idea how you got
re.

side you is a dead girl. Your
friend.

phone rings, and a voice tells
to press play on the room's DVD machine.

film shows you killing your girlfriend. Then you're told to go
an address in East London where you're to deliver a briefcase
await further instructions.

re's no way out. If you're to survive the next 24 hours, you
st find out who killed your girlfriend, and why.

ore they come for you too...

'Great plots, great characters, great action'
Lee Child

r those who like their thrillers breathless, as well
as bloody, this will be just the ticket' *The Times*

THE BUSINESS OF DYING

...aturing DS Dennis Milne: ...-time cop, part-time ...sassin.

...a cold November night and Dennis Milne is waiting to kill ...e unarmed men.

...ical and jaded, Milne earns ...ney on the side by doing what ...does best: punishing the bad ...s.

...he's been set up. This time, ...ead of shooting drug dealers, ...kills two customs officers and ...accountant.

...hunter has become the hunted. With his colleagues and his ...mies closing in on him, Milne must use all his skills just to ...alive.

...explosive first novel by the bestselling author of *Relentless*.

...ght me with its gut-wrenching reality. A compelling début'
Gerald Seymour

'A remarkable début...Pace, twists and a savage sense of place make this a guilty pleasure' *Guardian*